SOMEONE'S UPSET

The creature came out of nowhere, even as the image of wreckage and fiery death faded from the screen hovering over the jungle path. Tek had been enthusiastically approving the use of technology to overcome numerical inferiority. He was still smiling when it hit.

It had the body and head of a small, wingless, oriental dragon and the legs and tail of a tiger. Over ten feet long, it dwarfed the current form of the young god as it tried to drag him into its massive jaws.

Tek changed one hand into a powerful waldo and forced the creature's head away. It breathed flame, but before the gouts of orange reached the bleeding war god a sheet of the latest ablative tiles interposed itself. Then Tek struck back, summoning a forty-five auto and pressing the gun into the scaled chest as he fired. Bullets ricocheted off the scales on the dragon's chest, but the force of the weapon's blast threw the two combatants apart.

The Dragon-Tiger circled, looking for a chance to jump the young god. Twice it lashed out, but Tek avoided the blows. Then, almost as an after thought, the god summoned his own dragon. The *whop* of the helicopter's blades met the half dragon's roar when it perceived this new foe. The roar ended with the deceptively soothing tone of the gunship's twin gatlings firing six hundred rounds per minute into the creature. Within seconds nothing remai~~~~ ~~~scraps.

Tek dissolved the ~~~~~~~~~~~~~~~~~~~
toward Mentor and m~~~~~~~~

"Someone's upset, ~~~~~~~~~~
lapsing at the teacher~~~~~~~~
but especially on th~~~~~~~~~
can hurt one.

THE GODS OF WAR

Created by

CHRISTOPHER STASHEFF

BAEN
FANTASY

THE GODS OF WAR

This is a work of fiction. All the characters and events portrayed in this book are fictional, and any resemblance to real people or incidents is purely coincidental.

A Baen Books Original

Baen Publishing Enterprises
P.O. Box 1403
Riverdale, N.Y. 10471

ISBN: 0-671-72146-1

Cover art by Stephen Hickman

First printing, December 1992

Distributed by
SIMON & SCHUSTER
1230 Avenue of the Americas
New York, N.Y. 10020

Printed in the United States of America

TABLE OF CONTENTS

BIRTH

Tek arose out of the sand of the nearly endless desert that is the furthest boundary of form for Valhalla and Olympus. The exact location, paradoxically, was near one edge of the infinite ethereal plane. Such concerns of physics and geography were barely of concern to the gods. In a way he was created by the transistor and conceived in a million targeting computers. That made the silica and metals from which he was born ironically appropriate.

Mankind's newest war god would later speak of how he rose majestically from a virgin bed of silica and rare earths. Actually the young god staggered for a few paces, knelt with one pale hand pressed to the ground for a long time, then instinctively shaped some of the ethereal matter into a low wall and leaned against it as he rose on unsteady feet. Even as he stood, his shape flowed and ebbed. Like all new gods, Tek was weak, devoid of any real measure of strength or even self-awareness.

It is the faith of their believers that powers men's gods. Tek's faithful were few and unaware that they had given rise to yet another war god. In this case it was their blind faith in the technology of armaments

1

that had summoned him forth. But few believed in the power of technology to win a war. He received a surge of strength when the U.S. Congress funded the development of an Atomic Weapon. But this was barely enough to make the godling aware of his own existence. Years may have passed, perhaps decades, but Tek was not yet capable of sensing clearly the passage of time.

For a long time it was just enough for Tek to exist. The novelty of it all, the sensations, the flow of mana across this ethereal plane into which he had been summoned, were new and exciting. His form reflected the new god's confusion and wonder. It flowed from that of one type of humankind to another, now tank commander, now an engineer designing a better fighter plane, now a marine equipped to land on a hostile shore. Sometimes the form wasn't human at all. Such things didn't matter to a god. He spent a quite pleasant period as a tank clattering about the shapelessness encountering only those obstacles he himself imagined into existence.

Then there was a war.

"Damn," radarman third class Elliott Bromley muttered as he detected the blips that represented a flight of Japanese dive bombers approaching from northwest of Midway Island. "Sir, hostiles at bearing 295, forty miles and closing. Maybe Kates."

"Alert the CAP and scramble another flight," he heard the captain of the Hornet order before the intercom closed.

Not a single one of the unescorted dive bombers made it through the reinforced fighter cover. Every one of the five thousand men on the two carriers knew what had brought them to safety. The pilots had been brave, but the technology that gave them the warning had made the difference. The new god gained a lot of believers that day—though they didn't know who they now worshipped.

Driven by a war fought around the world, his priests labored under a stadium to build a truly worthy sacrifice to the newly born god of war, a god that was born of the technology of war, not of the heroism it still occasionally inspired, nor by the myth of the glory of victory. Believers in the government filled the coffers of the universities and laboratories that were this god's temples. But the demands of a new god are great and the people's faith was weak. Somewhere Tek recalled fanatics called Wobblies smashing his machines in a fitful time before he had even been aware. The pain, when he had been so weak, had nearly destroyed him.

Unsure and nearly powerless the godling moved to defend himself and his faithful and then watched as his technology and the power of those who served it, and him, spread. But such growth is slow, for people change their gods slowly. The papers spoke of heroism and courage, not competence and calculation. The generals stood oblivious to enemy fire or wore pearl-handled revolvers in a vain attempt to bring back the ways of the old gods. The sergeants fought him too, and were more effective, teaching the men to be brave, not dependent on the miracles the new god offered. But the new god got his revenge there, inspiring a man who knew no better to create new sergeants, technical experts who were beyond the sway of the soldiers who had made war their own until now.

It is a funny thing, being a god, at least the kind that man summons from places he doesn't know exist. You have the potential for immense power, but know nothing until your followers believe in it. It was a year before Tek could leave the ethereal plane covered in a dusty blanket of of sand and germanium where he had been born. By this time Mars and Thor had noticed something disturbing the ether, but Tek's weakness and insubstantiality protected him. Still, the gods are notoriously jealous. But all of the old gods men had summoned were too involved in this new war to pay more than an instant's attention to the distantly discordant note in the music of the spheres his new presence caused. Thor did react by inspiring his Teutonic faithful to greater frenzies of ceremony and to swear yet more resounding oaths. Mars, hard pressed to defend the island that sheltered the last of his forces, was too concerned to react at all. Tek sensed their challenge, carefully calculated his minimal chances of success in a direct confrontation, and remained silent.

By the end of the second year Tek could take on the form of his most ardent followers. He even adopted the "glasses" they all seemed to wear as part of his war god's regalia. The lab coat and pocket full of pencils would hardly have impressed his sword-wielding predecessors. After inspiring the greatest minds of humanity to listen unconsciously to him, Tek was able to give them guidance. Their efforts moved quickly. Though the new god was not really sure what he was inspiring, he was sure it would bring the faithful victory and make him the predominant god of war from then on.

By the time the coven of science worshippers and technicians had completed the device, Tek had learned how to travel in any form. Sensing that his glory was near, the godling became the crewman of the bomber that would test the device. Using what stength he could, and the distraction of the death throes of Thor's followers in Berlin, he ensured that any of the seven and half million glitches possible did not interfere with the test.

When the device was released from the B-29 high over the desert, Tek wanted to see first hand the results of his follower's labors. He transferred his awareness to a coyote who had been living well off the construction crew's garbage. It was resting in the shade only a few miles from the point of impact.

When the atom bomb landed, Tek discovered another new sensation, pain. Followed quickly by death. The experienced horrified him, and he exulted in it. In that instant he became a true god of war, and realized how powerful the other, earlier gods must be. In the next few millionths of a second Tek calculated that someday he would need to become the only god of war and opened four files to study the problem. In the meantime, Tek knew he had to be cautious. His faithful were few and the fate of those who spread a radical new belief was most often martyrdom. His followers were not the type to whom this would appeal to and so the god of scientific, calculating war concentrated on giving them the tools to gain control of the generals, and especially the sergeants.

Elsewhere the old gods felt the shudder, but were unable to pull away from the worldwide drama long enough to react. It was almost fifteen years before Tek would again attempt to act, and despite his careful calculations he allowed himself to be swayed by the faith, rather than the skill, of those who invoked him to aid them in their war.

THE WINGMAN

by Diane Duane

He was squinting through the eyeslit of the tank, trying to make out whether that was a boulder five hundred yards in front of him, or just another swirl of dirt lingering in the still air, left by the Mark Ten Centurion in front of him, when the voice spoke to him.

New week, it said.

He sighed. That much effect being human had had on him: all the emotions that came with bodies, that used breath and blood to express themselves, were becoming a habit. But not so much of a habit, yet, that they interfered with his work.

He counted briefly in his head while he steered around the boulder—it was one—and over a dune. Then, silently, so that his tank commander wouldn't hear him, he said, *June 5th?*

That's right.

He started to sigh again, and stopped it. *I was just getting used to this,* he said. *You have to have known earlier.*

Now, the voice said, *I did know earlier. Now I always have. This is the problem with free will, of course. You let them have it, and then the Universe itself has to sit around on hold until they make up their minds what they're going to do. But now they know. And so do I . . . and now, you.*

He agreed inwardly, and wrinkled his forehead a couple of times to get rid of the drop of sweat that was trying to trickle into his eyes. It was about a hundred and five outside the tank: what it might be inside, he hated to think. *I'm going to need a transfer,* he said.

The resigned and weary sound of him must have caused the source of the voice some amusement. *You could have a miracle instead.*

He thought about that for a moment. He hated transfers, the usual kind anyway: they hurt. *All right,* he said, *if that's all right with you.*

Is there anything that isn't? the voice said. *But nothing's free . . . you know that. Miracles cost, sooner or later.*

He raised his eyebrows. *So what else is new? . . . What did you have in mind?*

Well, how about this—

Rain is the most occasional kind of event in the Negev in May: at least, rain that makes it all the way down to the ground. Usually it evaporates hundreds of feet up, doing the barren, thirsty ground beneath no good. But what these brief showers *do* produce is rainbows; sudden, splendid, suspended unfounded up in the middle of the hot blue air, like a sign.

He saw the rainbow form, and smiled wryly for just a second before doing what any good Israeli tank driver would do in such circumstances, what his tank commander was doing too, having also seen the sign in the sky. Head already decently covered by his tanker's helmet, he started to bow himself back and forth, and began to recite the blessing one says on seeing a rainbow, giving thanks for the repetition of the promise that the world would never again be destroyed by water. He began to do this, as custom required, before doing anything else whatever. Like stopping the tank.

The huge old cedar loomed up out of the dust, and he saw it coming, and couldn't do a thing. The tank crashed into it, leaned up against it, knocked it over, then bounced on over the top of it—and on top of the officer's jeep that had been parked in its shade, while the officer was out in the sun overseeing the tanks participating in this exercise. He finished saying the berukha, and breathed out a little, not needing omniscience to know exactly what was going to happen. Destruction of one of the oldest trees in a place where trees were scarce, at best—and of a very annoyed officer's jeep: transfer, in a hurry. Not a prejudicial one, for his tank commander would be able to testify at the hearing that his driver had only been following religious tradition exactly. He would be out of the tank corps in a hurry.

The sound of swearing from behind him, though, made Micha'el wonder whether he should just have taken the usual mode of transfer, annoying as it was, and been done with it.

He could swear he heard the voice chuckling quietly as Ari started screaming at him to stop the tank.

Three days later, he was transferred to the airfield near Ha'ar Azuz. It would have been two days later, except that the third day he spent out in the dust, in fatigues, with a shovel and a hundred cedar saplings, paid for out of his own salary. He took his time about it; since it was him planting them, they would prosper, and he was careful about how they were positioned. He was annoyed, though, about having his salary docked to pay for them. He would have done it anyway.

The airfield was hardly distinguishable from the rocky waste all around it. The Heyl ha'Avir, the air force, had gone to some trouble to keep it that way. All buildings, even the hangars, were partially buried, surrounded with rock rubble right up to their walls: their roofs were covered with sand and more rock. The runways could not be hidden so easily, but the concrete was the same pale color as the local sand, having been made of it. In most of the day's sunlight the whole place was an eye-burning pale beige, except for the dark caves of the open hangar doors. In those darknesses could be glimpsed the occasional glint of silver, being hastily painted over.

Micha'el knew what those glints were, and wanted to get a look at them right away; but he behaved correctly, as always, and went to see the base commander first. The man's office was in one more sand-mortared Nissen hut, next to the biggest of the hangar buildings. Micha'el knocked at the door, and waited there in the burning wind for a good while before the voice told him to enter.

The commander didn't look up for a while. He was writing furiously, in a fat neat cursive, filling out a report, probably. After a few minutes he said, "Your paperwork came in this morning, Captain bar-David. Sort of a last-minute thing, don't you think? Where were you six months ago?"

Micha'el blinked. His paperwork always sorted itself out, no matter what he had been doing on his last assignment—it would be a poor sort of organization he was working for if mere bureaucracy couldn't be handled effectively. His records would now show him to have been air force from the start of things. "I'm not sure what you mean, sir."

"No, I'm sure you're not," said the commander, with heavy irony somewhat ruined by his having to stop in the middle of his writing and fumble around

his desk for a bottle of liquid paper. "A sudden attack
of heroism by—yourself? Or one of your relatives up
in the thin hot air by the top of the organization? To
just have you added to a team that took enough
training to get used to each other and work smoothly
as it was—never mind that, just throw you in there
without any thought of a new man's effect on the rest
of a group. It'll make you look good when what could
start happening, any day now, finally happens. A dangerous assignment, some nice showy flying, off you go
with some good career experience, into a promotion.
Huh?" All this while the commander had been painting delicately at his error: now he put the bottle aside
and looked up. The commander's eyes were cruel-
looking and angry: the mind behind them reeked with
fear, but not for himself. "Whereas it won't go that
way, not really: it never does. More like this: one of
my men gets himself killed getting you out of some
tight spot you get into, you go away after it's all over
with a medal and a promotion, is that it—?"

Micha'el blinked, and said: "No, sir. I don't think
so."

The commander stared at him for a good few seconds. Micha'el returned the gaze, as calmly as he
could. The human body he wore, no more than twenty-
two and running mostly on hormones, kept shouting
things at him that mostly translated as Fight! Kill! Hit!
Yell! He busied himself with ignoring it, though not
without a moment's longing for his usual body, non-
physical, created before entropy and hence endlessly
obedient: not like this poor deathridden shell, this
seething mess of mud, chemicals and electricity, with
ideas of its own, almost all of them mistaken and needing constant overriding.

Finally the commander looked away and picked up
his pen again. "For your sake, it had better not be
that way, that's all I can say. There's too much riding
on what we're out here to do to let someone's personal
ambitions put so much as one screw loose on what's

out in those hangars. I catch you being stupid or careless around my people or with my planes, I even get wind of it, and I'll ground you. Six feet deep, if necessary. Do I make myself clear?"

"Perfectly, sir," Micha'el said.

The commander stared at him in thinly veiled disgust, as if expecting something else: some flare of anger, some protestation of innocence. But Micha'el had served under too many commanders in his career to waste his time that way. He just stood quiet.

"Go on, get out of here," he said. "Pilot quarters are down at the back of hangar three. Second one to your left."

Micha'el saluted and left, closing the door carefully behind him. Through it he could hear a soft mutter of swearing.

Hangar three was one of those with its doors open. He paused in the doorway for a moment, smelling the air. Paint—cans of it, over on one side, and sprayers: and over there on the left, half painted, the Mirage IIIC.

He walked over to it slowly. The Dassault Mirage was not much to look at compared to some of the planes he had flown; not as graceful as the Spitfire II, not as hi-tech as the F-117a. But in its time, in this time, it was the fastest fighter aircraft in this theater, and (he thought) the best. No matter that it turned like a bullet: it went like a bullet, at Mach 2 and better. It had its weaknesses, but its strengths—that speed, and an indomitable ability to lift a lot of weaponry and deliver it accurately—more than made up for problems like its too-noticeable radar signature—

"What do you think?" said the voice from off to one side. He turned to see the young man in the paint-stained coveralls come from around the back of the Mirage. Dark hair, dark eyes: nothing unusual in this part of the world. But the grin caught him by surprise, after the cool reception in the commander's office.

He looked at the plane again. "The sand over

there," he said, "is pretty much the same color as over here. Should be a good match."

The young man laughed as he came over. "Should be," he said. "You're the new guy? Duvid ben-Akiah." He held out his hand.

"Micha ben-David."

They grinned at one another conspiratorially as they shook hands. In the armed forces, Duvid and David were not just names: they were a pejorative—a "desk-duvid," someone holding down a backlines position out of cowardice or ineptness, was about one of the worst things you could be called. It was no help that it was a common name: you worked twice as hard to avoid being thought of as a duvid by anyone.

"How many of these do you have?" Micha'el said. It was a temptation to say we, but that would be premature.

"Fourteen here. Sixteen over at Zenifim, another twenty up by Karkom. You've flown them?" Here there was just a moment's suspicious look; Duvid was wondering whether this was some displaced Mystre-jockey or other lowlife.

Micha'el just nodded. "These," he said. "And I was testing the Five."

Duvid sucked in breath, and his eyes gleamed in anticipation. "How is it? How many do we get?"

He smiled. "It hums. The force has ordered fifty. But the French haven't delivered them yet."

Duvid frowned. "What's keeping them?"

Free will, Micha'el was tempted to say. But he shook his head. "Could be money. I don't know."

Duvid shrugged. "Never mind that—come meet the others. They're still having lunch. Right now we don't have anything to do but paint the birds and do mainte-nance on them, and take a briefing every couple days." He led the way off across the hangar.

Four days, said the voice, *and they'll have more to do.*

So I gather, Micha'el said, *or I wouldn't be here. When do I get* my briefing?

Soon enough. Not everything's in place yet. There was a thoughtful silence. *But it's a new manifestation named Tek this time, if you were wondering. Operating in isolation and anxious to test itself. I'll brief you when all the decisions have been fated.*

Micha'el smiled at that. *I can wait,* he said silently.

There were thirteen other pilots, which pleased him; it meant there was no one he would have to displace, either by temporary physical mishap or some method more permanent. They were a crazed crowd, much of a piece with other young flyers he had worked with in various wars; intelligent, quickwitted, rude-mouthed, endlessly energetic, aggressive, and somewhat politically hotheaded. *Running mostly on hormones,* he thought, as his own body fell into chemical-ridden camaraderie with others of its own kind, and began smoking what they smoked—some of the foulest cigarettes he had ever tried not to inhale—and drinking what they drank, mostly Coke. If they had had any alcohol, they would have refused to drink it—they knew how tense the situation was becoming in their part of the world, and they knew their job was to be ready. They were ready. Meanwhile they grilled Micha'el about his politics and his flying, and when they were initially satisfied that he might fit in, they jumped him, the second night in, hog-tied him, and painted him in sand camouflage to match his plane, the fourteenth one, Nesheh. After that, they considered him one of them.

"I would have thought you'd wanted to wait to see how I fly," he said, trying not to breathe while he poured paint thinner over his head to get the last of the beige out of it.

Duvid shrugged at that, leaning on the shower-room wall with his arms folded. "*Nu,* we'll find out in a day or so. But you couldn't be too bad, if you were testing

Fives. Maybe you were, maybe they sent us a hamburger—well, too bad, you're our hamburger now. If you turn out to be too much of one, you'll probably have an accident before we have to go into combat. Probably break a leg or something if you don't struggle too hard. We wouldn't want to hurt the aircraft."

And that was that. He helped them with their painting—dreadful work, in the heat—and began speaking as they spoke, a dreadful amalgam of Sabra slang and fighter-pilot talk, much contaminated by the passage through their training of various American and RAF advisors. He smoked their awful cigarettes, and drank Coke until he thought he could become airborne merely from belching, and bided his time.

He flew with them the same day they took their first briefing together: June 4th, the day before it would happen. The commander was as angry as he had been when Micha'el had first seen him, but for different reasons this time: he was terrified for his young pilots, the chicks who had been under his wing for all this while. The uproar Egypt had made in the UN the day before had been dreadful, and though no word had come from Jerusalem, the commander had his suspicions. The pilots did too, and were buzzing with excitement. It pleased the commander, and horrified him at the same time, and the turmoil of his soul got under Micha'el's skin and made him itch all through the briefing.

"There is no change in the situation," the commander said. "If trouble starts suddenly, it is an air war we'll be concerned with—for the first good while, the tanks will not be our problem. Syria and Lebanon are not as much of a problem as them." He jerked his head westward, and all the young heads nodded thoughtfully: that way was Egypt. "They have five aircraft to every one of ours, various MiGs in various configurations. The more modern versions, the nineteens and twenty-ones, are more versatile craft than ours—at least, when they're flown by better pilots."

Micha'el's buddies snickered at the unlikeliness of this. "Your advantage, your *only* advantage, gentlemen, is that all their pilots are Soviet-trained, and ninety-nine percent of Soviet pilots don't have the initiative God gave a clam, because their bosses have noticed that any one of them who does, flies his MiG straight off to where the money is. Their pilots are trained to do exactly what they're told, and they wouldn't push their own eject button if ground control didn't tell them it was all right. So hotheaded idiots with a little initiative, like you, can make a mess of them, if you only watch your six, and watch out for that one percent of their pilots who have the brains to use their aircraft correctly. They may never fly again after that engagement, when their GCIs have blown the whistle on them, but you'll be dead and you won't care."

There was a bit of silence at this. The reminder of the six o'clock position as seen from a Mirage was always a little sobering: the narrow cockpit and its high-backed ejector seat were so positioned that there was no rearward view worthy of the name, despite the fact that in this age of heat-seeking missiles, the lethal cone that lay straight behind was any warplane's most vulnerable spot.

"It's never safe to second-guess orders ahead of time," the commander said, "but it's a safe guess what ours will look like when war breaks out." Not *if*, Micha'el thought. "With an advantage of numbers like theirs, and the further advantage of their radar system—also a little present from the Soviets, and a lot more sensitive than anybody else's, including ours as far as I can tell—there is only one possible plan. Don't let their aircraft up. Get there at top speed, get there before you can possibly be there, and kill them on the ground. Crater their runways first and then smoke anything that has managed to scramble to meet you. Runways first. I'll say it as many times as I have to, until you snore it in your sleep. Runways first. After that, you can take them at your leisure, and they'll never get up to go bother our tanks and our people. It won't matter then whether their pilots are half bird, or whether they belong inside a bun. Runways first. Here—" He pointed at the map, indicating one spot, and another, and a third. "No telling which one we'll be sent to. It doesn't matter. Know them all, know the way there in your sleep, get there and crater it. And then have all the fun you like, but whatever you do, bring your planes home. We've only got seventy of them."

And yourselves, Micha'el heard his heart cry. But he would not say it to any of them: he was a soldier too.

The pilots nodded, but not out of any great concern. They had heard it all before. They waited until the commander dismissed them, and then they went out and got ready for the day's exercise.

Duvid was already in his cockpit, going through pre-flights, by the time Micha'el was climbing into Nesher, next on the flightline. "Gotta be quicker than that," Duvid shouted at him over the scream of the warming engines. His voice was harsh, almost angry.

Micha'el was surprised to see that the eternal good humor had slipped. He scrambled a bit getting up into the cockpit, shook his shoulders—there was always an itch there when he was in confined quarters, his deep self's memory of his usual shape, fretting against the present physical one. He subdued the itch and pulled the canopy down, locked it. Duvid's mechanic signaled him forward, and Duvid bounced instantly forward and rolled, the Mirage doing that little nose-nod it always did when you popped the brakes. Micha'el went straight after him. Protocol allowed double launch from the runway: he caught up with Duvid, and they went straight up together, third and fourth of four.

There he laid to rest the pilots' concerns about whether he belonged in a bun or not. Better now than tomorrow morning, he thought. There was little to it.

Half his gift, half his reason for being, was the ability to sense others' reactions and react to them first; mortal or immortal, it had never mattered. Now he locked his deeper self into theirs, knew every turn and bank and matched it, anticipated their evasive moves while they were still nothing but fire running down a pilot's nerves. The commander came at him, under his six, to see if he had been listening; Micha'el arched up and over and back in the new Immelman, did the 180-degree flip as half a hesitation roll, and trottled up: with gravity helping, the skin leaning back from his face, he was on the commander's tail barely a second later. They were working at altitude, where the Mirage's engine was happiest and the flight characteristics of the big delta wings enabled it to turn much more quickly than down in thick air. All of them would have a harder time of it, down low, where they would be trying to evade the radar; but for now, Micha'el smiled and let them know that he had the art handled, and didn't need any coaching, or concern.

They were an hour in the air. He came down as sweat-soaked as any of them—the cold of thirty-thousand wasn't enough to temper the heat of that relentless sun glaring into the cockpit—and as his wheels came down, the thirst hit him all at once. He taxied down to in front of Three, where the crew chiefs were waiting: waited till his wheels were chocked, then popped the cockpit and almost fell out, onto Jesh, who was holding out an empty Coke bottle full of cold water.

He drank and drank. As he finished, Duvid poked him in the side, so he choked, and said, "Don't believe in G, do you?" He sounded impressed.

Micha'el raised his eyebrows and traded his bottle for another full one. "Didn't want you to think I was slow."

"Yeah," Duvid said. "Okay." He took a bottle for himself, and walked away.

That horrible sense of resonance hit him again. It

felt no better than it had the first time, however long ago—there had been no time, just then, so trying to date it was meaningless. Back then it had been the certain knowledge that the bright power with which he had been intimate, his peer, created with him, would shortly burn dark, and rebel. He would triumph—he had known that too—but the knowledge was not even slightly satisfying. It's not fair, he thought now, the human version of the thought. He was my brother—And he sighed and withdrew from the memory, and said, *Not him*.

Yes, the voice said. It almost sounded weary. *It's in your briefing. Later, when it's dark.*

He handed the bottle back to the crew chief, and followed the other pilots into the relative cool of the hangar.

The sun went down in its usual peach-colored splendor. There was a lot of dust in the sky that evening, so that those who were interested in such things could look at it with binoculars, or even the naked eye, and count the sunspots. Lounging there in the hangar door with some of the others, he remembered the arguments about it that other time, when he had been with a group of Crusaders: some of them had become very upset, insisting that the sunspots were some kind of evil sorcery, because the Church said the Sun was perfect and couldn't have marks on it. All a long time ago, but he remembered those sunsets, the same color as this one, and the smells of spices on the air, the tents flapping in the evening wind, the spears stuck in the ground, the idle sharpening of swords. Nothing had changed: the warriors still didn't want to be far from their weapons. The pilots lounged around, drank Coke, smoked the awful cigarettes, and their eyes lingered on the Mirages, all fueled, the engines quiet, but otherwise ready.

They were quiet. *They feel it coming*, Micha'el thought. That had not changed either. He had been perhaps the first creature made specifically to be a

soldier: all of them since partook in some small way
of his nature, and part of it involved that sense of
what was about to happen, and when. Other parts of
his nature . . . were no one's problem but his own.

He's on the radars, the voice said.

Predictable, if nothing else, said Micha'el. Tek
always would prefer the shiny new toys to the really
important part of the battle, the warriors themselves.

*Unfortunately he's selected the toy that could make
the difference,* the voice said. *With warning, all these
lads' valor will come to nothing. That warning must
be prevented.*

After that— Micha'el said.

The images became real inside him. The flights of
Mirages, Mystres, Ouragans, even Magisters, streaking
across into Egypt, just as the first limb of the sun
reached up over the horizon; the Egyptian MiGs
scrambling to meet them. The glitter of combat in the
early morning, swift movement, smoke trailing down.
Very little loss on the side to which he had been
assigned. But what loss there was, inevitable. Duvid,
for one.

I told you there might be a price, the voice said.

Micha'el nodded. *I keep paying this one, though,*
he said. *How many battles, now? I know I have to
defend them. I promised I would defend the helpless,
be the Champion. Yours, and theirs. But they keep
dying. Aren't we supposed to be doing something
about that? Aren't we trying to have them not have
to die any more?*

A long while before that happens, the voice said,
dispassionate. *And something else is required for that.
Their agreements to stop.*

Micha'el sighed, nodded. *A while yet,* he said.

"Pretty quiet tonight," Duvid said.

Micha'el looked at him in mild surprise, took the
Coke he held out. "This stuff," he said, "is rotting my
teeth by the day. I want to go on leave and have a
nice clean beer."

"Me too," Duvid said, "but no hope of that for a while." He took back the bottle, took a swig himself.

"You scared?" he said.

Micha'el smiled, not easily. "Not since the first time," he said softly. "Then—I wasn't sure. It could have gone either way, I thought. Afterwards . . . it had always been OK, since the very beginning." He laughed, not a happy sound. "You?"

Duvid swigged from the bottle, handed it back. Very quietly, but with no change in his face, he said, "I'm going to die."

Michael just looked at him. "I tried telling Jesh," Duvid said. "He just looked at me as if I was nuts. The thing is, it's okay. It really is." He looked at Micha'el's face. "You believe me," he said, rather surprised.

"Hard not to," Micha'el said. "How do you know?"

"Just a feeling. No," Duvid said. "A knowing. It was a suspicion, earlier. I'm sure now, though."

"You approve?" Micha'el said. It was the harshness of his own voice, now, that surprised him.

Duvid grinned. "Do I get a vote?"

"I'm not sure," Micha'el said. This was true enough: his level of creation didn't always understand the rules as they applied to human beings. "But I think maybe it helps if you can accept it."

There was silence for a while. "I don't know if I can do that," Duvid said. "But I can go out shooting."

The Coke bottle was empty. Duvid looked at it for a moment, then walked away.

"I think," Micha'el said softly, "it may come to the same thing."

He didn't sleep that night. He didn't always have to, even when in a human body; and tonight, he would have found it particularly difficult. He was being tempted. About an hour before dawn, he was still standing there, looking east now. The morning star was hanging there like a particularly bright landing light.

Is it possible, he thought, leaning against that hangar door—alone, now; the rest of them had long since gone to bed—*it it possible to go against one's nature?*

No answer.

Typical. *Free will,* he thought ironically. Even we have it. That was what started the whole problem, wasn't it? But that was a long time ago. Here and now he was faced with the problem: could he disobey? Certainly he could. Would it be wise?

That was not the point. Wouldn't it be *right*?

And what would make it so? The chance of saving one innocent life? This was a war, or was going to be. Many of the innocent would die in it. That was one of the tragedies and injustices of war: that was one of the reasons why, at one end of time or another, he looked desperately to see himself out of a job. Why should this one innocent be spared, just because he had taken a liking to him? Doubtless there was reason in his dyng; it would hardly be happening, otherwise. It had to be allowed to occur. Meanwhile, he, like all the soldiers ever since, could do nothing but take his orders, whether he understood them or not, and execute them. And the same again, tomorrow, and tomorrow. . . .

I could say no, he thought. Others had. But not for reasons like this: it had been pride, all that while ago, not pity, that had caused his brother to say no, and had caused him to take up his spear for the first time. He thought for a little while of that combat, of all the levels on which it had taken place. The mortal body ached and twinged at the images, memories which it was incapable of harboring, or handling. This was part of the danger for him of being in-body—he was incomplete, and vulnerable to the dangers of mortality: fear, uncertainty, delusion.

Micha'el shook his head. *No advice, for once,* he said to the night.

Silence.

For a long time he stood there, unmoving.

If he can bear it, he thought at last, *and him a mortal, without even any certainty about the levels of life above and below his—then I, who know better, can hardly do worse. 'Go down shooting,' as he says. At least I know what I'm shooting at.*

He looked up at the stars.

But oh, this is hard!

No answer now, either. His own commander, like other good ones, once the order was given to an experienced officer, had the sense to stand back and let him execute it.

Never mind, he thought at last. Some habits were too old to break . . . he hoped. He leaned back, and closed his eyes to start work.

Forgetting the body itself was always the hardest part. You didn't dare dissolve your connection to it entirely—it might not be possible to re-establish it. But at the same time, it got in the way: its perceptions were geared only to this level of being . . . and Micha'el had business higher up.

He let the body fall away, and very cautiously felt around him in the dark, the way someone might who had dropped something valuable on a floor that was also covered with broken glass. He didn't want to give an alarm. This by itself was so counter to his usual way of operating—the obvious entry, the straightforward challenge, directly given—that he had astounded himself, earlier, by even thinking of it. The idea had come to him after they had jumped him in the dark, preparatory to his being spraypainted. It had been (he had noted to himself, ruefully, about the third can of paint thinner) extremely effective.

Gently, gently he felt around him. Gods left a sort of signature in the "field" of physicality, a result of the casual way their natures overrode the physical around them. The signature was not a hard profile, but a locus of nexi, a sparkling fuzziness that looked to those who could see such things much the way chaff looked on radar. When a god was embodied, the signature was more muted still. But Micha'el felt sure he knew within three guesses where Tek would be. A radar installation: the best-equipped, shiniest, newest one of all of them; and, if embodied, in the person of the greatest potential power there. Tek was unsubtle, and liked to throw his weight around on every available plane.

Micha'el smiled, a still small effusion of power in the dark void through which he moved. Carefully he laid the "hand" of his mind, testing, over the radar installation at al'Arish, on the coast. Nothing there but a general, muted sense of unease, disturbance. He removed it, slowly, waited for any signs that he had been noticed. Nothing: he was alone in the dark and the silence.

Carefully he reached out to the radars at al-Qusaymah. At first he almost jerked back, thinking he felt something sharp and hot; but it was plain old human emotion, this, someone's fear or hatred, or both, piercing through into the higher levels in dream. *I suppose* someone *there might be asleep*, he thought, though it seemed a little odd. Surely if this was the day—and it was—the whole place would be roused and on alert. But no matter.

He withdrew his probe of thought and turned his attention to his third guess. Very slowly, very delicately indeed, he reached out toward Jabal al-Misheiti. He felt, as he had felt in the other two installations, the hard sharp crackle of the radars combing the fabric of things as they looked sideways at the world. But there was something extra, a faint taste or smell, of something *in* the radar beams—the same way bioelectricity can be felt to have a little something extra about it when it carries thought.

Micha'el smiled again. He knew what that something was. He took a deep breath—and laughed at himself: how the body began to change one's idiom after a while, even when you were out of it—and concentrated on making himself seem as little there as possible. In the void, he was void as well; the faint radiance that had been about him now went out. His darkness moved over the face of things, low, following the radar, pretending to be returning radiation, the familiar bounce. Packets of radiation passing him carried that signature, the one he was after, more and more strongly. A cold scent, a taste of metal, the nerveless buzz and whine of captive electrons being scourged along gouged-out pathways by a pitiless taskmaster. Tek was there, all right, and not totally embodied, or not in one place. Some of him was in the radars themselves. *That's Tek for you. He's the type that can never resist becoming his tools.* He controlled his elation. It was the best possible advantage for him . . . as long as he could keep Tek from noticing him, and changing the status quo.

Closer and closer he crept with the strengthening signal. Shortly he was seeing what he had desperately wanted to see; that bloom of light in the void which meant a significant part of a god's being was in one spot, embodied. The bloom of light beat steadily, inturned, concerned with itself, and paid him no attention at all. The timing of the beat reassured him; it cycled in seconds rather than milliseconds—a human body, not a mechanical one. *A good thing this era's computers are still too stupid to be any good to inhabit,* Micha'el thought: Tek could have made dreadful use of anything much smarter than a PC.

He paused just long enough to be sure of his target, for when he struck, the body-shell might die: he had no wish to kill any more innocents than necessary. There was indeed the pale, weak glimmer of the body's original soul, unconscious, crushed down and helpless against what overrode it. It couldn't be helped now. Micha'el gathered himself and his power, and flung himself down out of the void onto the chilly, shiny bloom of light, smothering it.

The other fought him, of course. They clutched one another, and he was almost stifled by the cold grip of metal around throat and heart, half blinded by the icy glint off the mirror-glazed eyes. What the other saw, he had no idea; his whole business now was to hang on, to hold Tek helpless for a good while. Past dawn, anyway. It would not be easy, for Tek was a god, and he was rather less than one, by choice.

What the people in the radar installation thought of it all, he could only imagine: they doubtless saw their Soviet advisor crumple to the floor and lie there helpless, barely breathing. Micha'el felt sorry for the poor invaded body, but had less time to worry about it than about the radars. They were paralyzed: there was enough of Tek in them to make sure they weren't controllable by the humans in the installation—but not enough of Tek for him to activate them. Tek thrashed and pushed and tried to pry enough of himself out of Micha'el's grasp to free the radars up; but Micha'el held on grimly and would not let him go. He was burnt by Tek's cold, scorched by his fire: but he would not let go. He had had cold before, in the outer darknesses, and fire like no one had experienced since, and survived them both. He might not be divine, but it was going to take more than this tinkertoy god to make him give up.

The morning star was setting: even here, outside the physical world, he could feel the light changing, the dawn coming up. Humans were moving about, concerned, in the three radar centers; things didn't seem to be working, and they couldn't understand why. Shortly they would be running about like ants in an overturned anthill, as the alert came through from Cairo, as the tanks started to roll north over the border. The alert came, and the panic began. And still Micha'el held onto Tek, scorched and blinded, and would not let him go.

The sun was about to come up. Across the desert, faintly, with the ears of a body leaning almost unconscious against a wall, Micha'el heard the klaxons at the base, heard the frantic scrambling of pilots heading for their planes. He let go, reeled away. Tek reared up and reached out for him, and seeing the weak point, Micha'el whispered sorry! and swept a knife-edge hand at the faintly silver-shining connection winding from the bloom of power that was the god, to the radars. It snapped. Tek fell fully back into the poor human body: it would live, all right, and it would take him some time to re-establish his connection with the radars. If he bothered—

Gasping, Micha'el flung himself back to his own body. It was a terrible feeling, as always, this cramming of one's essence back into a container too small, too simple, crumbling at the edges every time you moved. Someone was shaking him. "Wake up! Dammit, we've got to—"

"Leave him—"

"It's all right," he mumbled, and managed to get his eyes open. Duvid was shaking him; Micha'el reached out, grabbed his arms, stopped him. "I was asleep on my feet."

Duvid shoved Micha'el's helmet into his hands and ran for the flightline.

They flew, all of them. It was ten minutes to Jabal al-Misheiti, riding the flaring thrust of full reheat. They met no resistance as they crossed the border: their own radars registered the presence of no others. It was bizarre. The tanks had started moving into the Gaza less than an hour ago. The air should have been full of planes.

It was not. They dove down out of the bright morning into a valley empty of anything but lovely runways. Each of the Mirages had nearly five thousand pounds of bombs slung under it; they used them there, lavishly, the commander making helpful suggestions as to

placement, and sounding happy for the first time
Micha'el had ever heard. Before the Cyrano air-to-air
radars noticed even the first MiG approaching, the
runways looked like the surface of the Moon, and the
hangars were rubble, with at least thirty planes inside
them.

"They got at least one flight up from down south,"
the commander said calmly. "I see twenty. No more
runways, gentlemen."

"Gotcha, Boss," said one pilot after another. And
Duvid sang out: "Eyeballs!"

They were streaking along low; the MiGs knew
where their best maneuverability lay. Almost as one
the Mirage pilots yanked on their sticks and went for
altitude. Not too much—

The MiGs closed. It got busy in the air. The commander had specified a weapons mix for the group
that would leave them something to do with after the
bombs were all gone: everyone had at least two air-
to-air under the wings, and everyone had full loads in
the twin 30 mm DEFA cannon-packs. The morning
became full of tracer as the MiGs tried to keep heading north. The flight had no intention of letting them
do so. One tried to go under the group; Micha'el saw
a Sidewinder head for the 21's tailpipe, and hatch, like
a phoenix's egg, in fire, bursting the silver shell—

There was no way to keep an eye on Duvid,
although Micha'el desperately wanted to do so; wanted to
see him go, and bid him farewell, if he could not stop
it. But the air was too full of bogies, twisting and
spiraling. The Cyrano radar shouted for his attention.
Someone streaked across his twelve, right in front of
him, he could hardly believe it—the vertically-split
maw of a MiG-19's nose intake, almost straight on,
running away from one of the other pilots: he pulled
back hard on the stick, 4 G turn at least, followed
almost side by side, popped his airbrakes for just the
merest instant to let the MiG overshoot, and let the

cannons speak. A bloom of fire in front of him, he veered away, his shoulders itching as they always did—

"Eight left," the commander said. "They're trying to break. Don't let them!"

The whole fight was indeed drifting northward. Micha'el broke right, saw a tailpipe so close even the radar didn't see it first, and sent a Sidewinder after it: broke hard left and up, felt the shudder against his tailplane and wings as the MiG blew. Seven. The fight was drifting upwards as well, the MiGs trying to prevent it, unsuccessfully: they had no guidance from their radars, their GCI was silent, and the Mirages pushed them up and up into their optimum operation area, where they no longer turned like bullets, where their engines worked better than the MiG's—

And Duvid went down past him. No more warning than that, just the one-winged shape spinning downward, the canopy a charred crater, blasted away; a silver glint, spiralling, then a smoke and a pillar of fire, fire in the sand. Micha'el didn't swear; it was not in his job description. But he went up to kill what had killed his friend.

Another Mirage came down past him as he arrowed up. Someone good was up there; or someone who knew how to do without GCI. Or someone who had never needed it, he thought, seeing the topmost MiG as it dropped toward him, closing nose-on. Micha'el angled in towards the MiG, making for a close pass so that it couldn't turn onto his six. He blinked then at his own mistake; the triple 23mm cannons on the MiG lit up, sending tracer looping out in lazy, incandescent blobs that accelerated insanely as they whipped over the cockpit canopy. An Atoll AAM flared out from under its left wing and went scything past him. It was a pointless thing to do, because the missile was unable to make a lock at point-blank range, but lock or not it still came so close that Micha'el flinched, seeming almost to feel the heat of its rocket exhaust as it roared by. He could feel another heat as well,

one he recognized. Angry, he thought, don't fly angry!
He pulled the stick back and pushed the Mirage into
a 6-G climb, straight up.

He can't follow that, Micha'el thought. He'll turn
off horizontal, or bug out, if he's got brains. Cannons
for him, when I level out—He looked back over his
seat, and was horrified to see the 19 only a hundred
yards away, climbing with him cockpit to cockpit. Mirrored goggles flashed at him in the sun.

Tek, he thought, horrified. Whatever pilot had been
in that plane before, he wasn't there now. Micha'el
throttled forward, but not fast enough to elude the
other's fire, with his own six exposed while he climbed
vertical. Desperately Micha'el rolled off the top and
spiraled downward, Tek following and firing. They
dropped into a classic rolling scissors, each trying for
an angle on the other. The tight turns were losing
Micha'el his speed, pulling him down into the range
where the MiG could turn and handle better—

He saw a break, found it, ran nearly miles downhill,
getting some separation, getting his momentum back.
Two miles—but barely six seconds at the rate he was
going. Time to suck in a couple of breaths, blink, fight
the G. He turned, went after his pursuer, fired the
cannon: clean misses—then angled up at sixty degrees
again. Again the MiG came up after him. *He shouldn't
be able to do that in that plane—Micha'el thought,
annoyed. But then maybe the plane had a little help—*

He could do it himself. But the thought went across
the grain. When you fought in-body, you fought with
the weapons you came with. Usually. But Tek was not
playing by the rules. Up he came, hot on Micha'el's
tail, in a machine that shouldn't know how to climb
like this—

Cheaters never prosper, Micha'el thought. *One
more try.* He would not lose his speed again the way
he had last time. He turned, dived to get his momentum back, let Tek play with the 6 G's again, as he
was. Two more miles, six more seconds—

He came about hard and came at Tek head on again, but this time with a little offset, just enough so that Tek couldn't fire his cannons. They passed again and both went vertical. There was no mistaking the sense of air being interfered with, something dark changing its density, making it behave differently. Micha'el frowned, played his card. The VIFF wouldn't be invented for a while yet, and it was at best the mark of a lazy pilot who shouldn't have allowed his enemy on his six in the first place. But he pulled in closer to Tek's line, let his throttle lean back to idle, and popped airbrakes and flaps together, dropping 50 knots of airspeed in a matter of a second. Tek viffed too, but not with his plane: the darkness about him heated the air, changed its viscosity; he dropped back.

Damn! Micha'el thought then, seeing what his adversary would do, and finding no way to do his job, and fulfill his mission, but to match him. He would not need a miracle this time. *But you told me there would be a price, didn't you?*

No answer. He had expected none; nor would there be one until the debriefing. Micha'el smiled grimly, resigned himself to an argument with his Boss, and had a word with the air himself.

The other pilots, most particularly the commander, would never quite be able to describe what they saw. In clear air, the MiG seemed somehow to be in shadow: and in clear air, the Mirage going after him suddenly was wider than it was; a silver glitter, like ice in the sun, like great bright-feathered wings suddenly extended, shone all around it, and the Mirage dropped behind the MiG again. A tail of fire burst forward from it, the Sidewinder leaping away like a lance of fire. It seemed to miss. For a moment the commander thought he saw another Sidewinder—but that was impossible, the new man had already fired two. A burning line of light, like a lance of fire, or a sword, caught the MiG halfway down the fuselage. Straight into the ground it flew, seemingly under control, and the blackness that had followed it dissipated.

One other thing followed it; the Mirage, spiraling in. It was not out of control, either. There was a clear hesitation on each quarter of the roll; the commander thought of the insouciant maneuver of the man, the day before—and on the fourth quarter-roll, aircraft and ground met and became one. The commander blinked. Impossible to have seen what he thought he saw; thumbs up, the smile under the helmet. And now nothing but fire.

Above them, the air was clear.

Three hours later, there was no Egyptian air force. Three hundred of three hundred sixty planes were caught on the ground and destroyed after their runways were made useless. Of a total of thirty that managed to make it into the air from bases in the south, all were destroyed or crash-landed for lack of runways.

Elsewhere, an archangel was reassigned, and an annoyed god, betrayed by technology not quite far enough along to be of use to him, sulked mightily, then curled up for a good long sleep. One that would last until another desert conflict woke him. In that regard, everything went exactly as planned. Tek would have had much too much fun with the proliferating and occasionally erratic atomic technologies of the '70s and '80s.

As it was, the corridors of upper existence rang with a cheerful taunt:

Cheaters never prosper.

HEROES

In the desert the Leader waited. He followed the laws of Allah, but he had seen the power of the desert spirits. Once more he was there to ask their aid. This made him very uncomfortable, but he had no choice. His nation was destitute. Worse than their over-whelming debt to the Americans and Japanese was the disgrace of being unable to pay back the monies borrowed from his fellow followers of Islam. The recent, unsuccessful war with their eastern neighbor had been costly. He controlled what was still unques-tionably the greatest military power in their part of the world, but this would soon mean nothing. His creditors, other nations, also were meeting secretly on plans to impound the oil that was his nation's only wealth. With his people starving and no replacement parts, his magnificent military machine would collapse.

If the cost of war had caused his dilemma, then he would use another war to solve it. There was another nation, small but rich. His well-trained forces could overrun it within hours. No one would care about such a tiny land and the loot would sustain his government for a decade.

But to attack, he wanted the aid of the desert

demons. They had saved his army once when the waves of fanatics had almost broken his lines. Even before they had promised him glory, rule over all of the Desert lands. He wanted their reassurance before attacking. With their support he would reign supreme.

The first impression was what the Leader expected. A wall of blowing sand drifted toward him. As it neared, a small part of the wall detached itself and flew to where the uniformed Leader waited. Bits of grit blew painfully against his face and fouled his moustache, but the Leader stood patiently. Seconds later a giant whirlwind appeared and a face formed within.

"You seek our aid?" the voice sounded of distant thunder.

"If I do not make war on a neighbor, my rule will end," the Leader explained quickly. He had learned before that there was no benefit from bluster when dealing with the Djinn.

"If the new god does not destroy you, the desert will give you victory," was the ambiguous answer.

"Then I should attack?"

"The cunning one has a plan. Act quickly, before your real enemy is prepared."

The Leader bowed his agreement. The real enemy was obviously the Americans. If the Djinn were aiding him, their desert would swallow up their armor and helicopters. This would be his most glorious victory. All history would remember him as the man who ended the Capitalists' reign. Fired with visions of eternal fame, he hurried to order the attack.

Tek woke slowly, reluctant to give up the security that more than a decade of oblivion had provided. He rose, aching, from the sand and glanced at the bunker which he had formed. Instinctively he knew it was obsolete. His bombs would be greater now and his ingenious followers would have found new ways to hide from the holocaust they threatened.

His shoulder ached where the safety straps had bitten into them just before the crash. As he moved his shoulders to free sore muscles, both hands tightened into painful claws. Those hands had been clutching the controls when his fighter had slammed into the sands of the Gaza. It was only by using a bolt of his precious mana that Tek was able to move them freely again. "You can't kill a god," which he instinctively knew, "but you can make him wish you had."

With a gesture the bunker became a mile deep shelter, appropriately mimicking the mass of concrete and thick steel doors that now formed the core of Cheyenne Mountain for the sole purpose of protecting the SAC computer. The ethereal matter was almost effortless to manipulate. Just for esthetic purposes he added the entire antennae array from the USS Anzio. The garage-door-sized radar dishes began instantly emitting a microwave chorus soothing to Tek. On the horizon were the blurry images of the guards walking the perimeter and SAM 9 sights. These guardians were more for show than effect, but they were becoming more effective as Tek's power grew.

Next, the still sleep-muddled young god summoned a mirror, changed it to a closed circuit HDTV set-up and viewed himself. Somehow the image fell short of representing his full nature. He wondered how the other gods did it. In his short bursts of activity Tek had never even spoken with another god. He could sense their presence, from powerful beings and whimpering, forgotten images near to fading away. But caution learned from two traumatic defeats had imbued in Tek a high degree of prudence.

A few moments of scanning his memory banks and Tek decided that his form was also outdated. He searched some more, unsatisfied with any of the images and impatient to discover what had summoned him from his sleep. The form itself was acceptable and Tek was quite pleased with the feel of it. There was just the right mix of logic and very little contaminating emotion, the pointed ears and rising eyebrows were a bit unusual. But then, he was a god and could look any way he wanted.

"Hokey," the voice said, "and not really effective."

The voice came from just behind Tek, a dangerous thing to do to a god of war. Tek spun. Lightning blazed from one hand and an Uzi chattered from the other.

"Hey, take it easy!" The voice came from overhead this time.

Kneeling, Tek aimed upwards, but did not fire. Overhead floated the figure of an unarmed man, his arms spread and hands empty. The man was dressed in the uniform of a field grade officer, and his badges labelled him an instructor from Sandhurst.

"I'm on your side," the figure assured floating down to land a few feet in front of the young god. "I'm just the Mentor. It's my job to help you."

There was a pause as the Mentor studied Tek's reaction. The barrel of the Israeli submachine gun never wavered. The smile became a bit more forced.

"It's not like you've done so well so far," the Mentor added showing more bravado in his words than in his eyes.

"Help, how?" Tek demanded, but let his aim waver.

Mentor's smile grew wider and more sincere. "Why, so far you are trying very hard to be a god, but obviously have no idea how to do it."

"And you do?" Tek tried to not sound belligerent. So what if he had made a few miscalculations. He hadn't had time to create a complete probability curb on most actions.

"Actually, yes," the Mentor explained apologetically. "But as a Muse I have the power to bring you the images that can teach you how to use your powers to the fullest."

"At what price?"

"Oh, I'm not in it for profit. I'm a Muse and we have no need for more than our art." With this the man's robes changed to a more comfortable shirt and slacks. He was also suddenly gangly, wore glasses, and was smoking a pipe. He now looked very much like a university professor.

"How is your art going to help me? Not to say that I need help," Tek demanded. "And how did you know to come here?"

"Well." Mentor spread his hands and then clasped them in what was obviously a familiar pose. "Some of the old war gods are not too happy about your appearance. On the other hand, there are a lot of other gods that would be happy to see those blowhards shown up a bit."

At the mention of the other war gods Tek scanned the horizon. His system was nearly impossible to pass through without setting off the alarms. Every inch of the sky was scanned and the results analyzed every half-second.

"Since some of them sensed you had reawakened, the word went out to assist you. Now most of the gods are busy with their own causes. They haven't any time for a newcomer until he proves himself. This means that someone else has to take on the role of welcomer and teacher. As a Muse the duty is mine. That is all we muses do any more, but we do it well . . . despite TV. Hence my appearance here."

"So what do I need to learn?" Tek was less belligerent this time. Something of an accomplishment since he was, after all, a war god.

"Well, to begin, let's look at your form." The Mentor's voice had taken on the slightly distracted tones of an artist at work. "I don't think that image is for you. Most humans get nervous when their gods appear in the form of aliens."

"Aliens?" Tek questioned. Had his followers progressed so quickly that they now travelled the stars?

"Yes, as in beings from another planet," the Mentor explained. "There really aren't any on the Earth. At least none I'm aware of. You have taken the likeness of a non-human, fictional character."

"And if I am a god of the humans, I should use a human form?"

"It is more traditional, though some of the oriental gods would dispute that," the Mentor agreed.

"So what do YOU suggest?" Tek's tone implied he was going to be very critical. He studied the Mentor, his Muse. Forms are mutable in the ethereal plane, but just for this reason, he calculated that the form chosen would tell him much of those he would meet.

"Here, if you want to do an alien," the Mentor continued smoothly, "let's use one that looks human. Not only that, but one that conjures up images of great power . . . more godlike and all that."

In the air above the two gods a series of clips from the last three Superman movies scrolled past. At first Tek was critical, but the form was pleasing. When he caught himself smiling, the young god was forced to admit the Mentor was probably right. Humans who saw him in this form would be impressed. His desire to maintain control of the situation meant Tek also had to add his own changes.

"The countenance is pleasing and the sense of power appealing, but that red suit with a big "S" on it has to go," he insisted. "I'll stick to my flight suit for a while yet."

"You're the war god," the Mentor agreed with a shrug. "This may take a while, and I must have your attention. For that, you will know what it is to be a god. Some of the old gods will come. Now that you are powerful enough to be noticed, the curious or the jealous will come here."

Tek scanned his defenses. Watching the gesture, the Mentor shrugged. "Those can protect you from the lesser beings of this plane. The full-powered gods such as yourself, once you understand your place and power, will pass through them as they will."

"So what should I learn first?" It was half question and half challenge.

"Heroes?"

"Heroes?" Tek questioned. "What need have I of those?"

"You want to learn about war? They are the heart of war."

"Or were," Tek observed with a satisfied smile.

"Someone has to plug in the computer," the Mentor commented without inflection. "I am here to bring you the tales that teach you to use the power that will soon be yours. Do we begin?"

Tek nodded, wondering for just an instant what had awakened him.

GORDON'S QUEST

by Christopher Stasheff

Shang-Ti rested in his great golden throne. His eyes were closed, his breath came and went like the ocean's tide, but he did not sleep. In his trance, the strife and joy and sufferings of his people, the Northern Chinese, came dimly, filtered through his concentration, but he was able to dismiss most of those who called on him. The people who had invented him, the ancient Chinese of the Shang Dynasty, were three millennia dead. While they lived, he had been a very busy god indeed, managing a legion of subordinate gods and nature-spirits, lending his might to prevent the worst of disasters to the Shang kings and their people, and striving to inculcate some trace of the strong moral sense that was the very core of his being, to the

41

people from which he had sprung. But inevitably the dynasty, and the people, had grown corrupt, had begun to think more of their own pleasures and gain than of others, and in their self-preoccupation, had begun to think less frequently of their gods, to believe in them less strongly. As their faith weakened, so did Shang-Ti, until at last, he was unable to aid them in their constant battles against the barbarians who sought to steal the riches of their civilization. Finally, the barbarians had ridden in, as they had again and again, slain the king, looted, raped, pillaged, and burned, and left only smoking rubble behind them. For a few centuries, villages here and there tried to maintain some vestige of civilization; their faith had strengthened, giving Shang-Ti some power to assist them; but there had not been enough of them, and there had been far more of the barbarians. They did believe in their bloodthirsty gods, believed most strongly, and there were very many of them. Shang-Ti had led his own diminished band against them, but his vitality was sorely depleted, as was that of his subordinate gods, and finally, the last of his believers perished. He persisted as a memory, a folk-tale, an historical note; but when the Chou Dynasty arose from the ashes of the Shang and extended its reach far beyond the Yangtze Valley, they worshipped other gods, and there was little to disturb Shang-Ti from his slumbers—which was fortunate, for he was very tired.

So he rested, rarely disturbed. Oh, an historian here and there occasionally impinged upon his awareness, but only with interest, not with a demand; the Taoists occasionally roused him, but more often with blessings than with petitions, so he had some strength with which to answer those requests that did come. But they were rare, and his peace was deep.

Then suddenly, some force yanked him rudely from his contemplation. With indignation, he focused his perceptions to see what mite dared intrude upon him. It was a country school teacher, he saw, who had come to Canton to take his civil service examinations, failed them, and fallen ill, with fever and deliriums—and with shock, Shang-Ti discovered that he was caught up in that delirium, borne into a role quite alien to him, by the force of that simple school teacher's belief, unleashed from his subconscious by the fever. Bits of pieces of some Christian tracts that the man had glanced at, whirled together with his Taoist upbringing, and Shang-Ti was startled and dismayed to find himself wrapped up in a role he would never have chosen, repellant to him because of the deception, the impersonation, of a god who was far more than a god, and through the fevered imagination of the hallucinating scholar, he had been burdened with a son who had never been one of his own, made purely of that scholar's imagination, goaded by the scraps of tract and scripture, and fueled by hatred of the Manchus who had conquered China two hundred years before. In disgust, Shang-Ti found himself goaded to actions he would never have performed, found himself smiling upon the naive school teacher within his own dream, found himself speaking words he had never thought.

Then it was over, for the school teacher had wakened from his fever-dream. The imagined son was gone, the alien role was cast away, and Shang-Ti sat limp and dazed in his great golden throne, shaken by the force of human hatred and desire needing to justify itself in fanatical belief. For a timeless moment, he sat, recuperating. . . .

Then he stiffened, galvanized, as that same force took hold of him again, only doubled now, then tripled, then magnified tenfold. The school teacher had remembered his dream, had read more Christian scriptures, and had gone forth to convert his fellow men to a faith that Christians in the West would scarcely have recognized. To Shang-Ti, it seemed a bizarre and twisted faith, as it did to those Westerners who finally learned its full set of beliefs—though to them, it was strange, even blasphemous, because it incorporated so many elements of Chinese religion.

To Shang-Ti, it was alien, even sacriligious, because of the Western ideas that wrapped it about.

But at its core—ah, at its core, it was purely the strivings and yearnings of Hung Hsiu-Chuan, the school teacher from whose fevered brain it had sprung, and who had gone out, wielding his patchwork Christianity like a sword with which to smite the demons—and the Manchus, to drive them out of China. He sought to destroy the Ching Dynasty, and return the rule of China to the Chinese. . . .

Led by himself, Hung Hsiu-Chuan, Great King, who had declared the rule of the Tai-Ping Tien Kuo, the Great Kingdom of Heavenly Peace; Hung Hsiu-Chuan, visionary, prophet—and the Younger Son of God, and Younger Brother of Christ.

Tseng Kuo-Fan was Chinese, but he did not much mind the Manchus—after all, they had become almost completely Chinese, even though they still refused to accept a few civilized customs, such as binding the feet of their women. He did not even mind the fact that the Manchus made all Chinese men shave their heads and wear a pigtail down the back; he did not mind it, for he had grown up with it, as had his father and his grandfather and grandfather's grandfather before him.

It did irritate him that no Chinese could ever rise to the highest posts in the land, that the equivalent of dukes and earls, the mightiest of mandarins, must always be Manchus—but thus had it been even with Chinese dynasties; the highest posts were always held by blood relatives of the royal family; and since Tseng Kuo-Fan had passed the highest of the civil service examinations, he could ascend by sheer ability to the second level of the bureaucracy.

He had already made great progress; he was now a general in the Imperial Army. He had far more to lose than to gain.

But these ignorant upstarts, these hill-country rebels, Hung Hsiu-Chuan and his "princes," could very easily upset all that, and deprive him of a lifetime of striving. More deeply, though, they disturbed Tseng Kuo-Fan in a far more profound way.

The Manchus did not, for if they had conquered China, China had then conquered them; they had been concerned only to gain the luxuries and riches of the oldest continuing civilization in the world, and guarantee that wealth and privilege for their progeny. They did not truly wish to change it.

But the Taipings did. They had broken the statues of Buddha and the Bodhisatvas; they had smashed the images of the Taoist gods, and the soul-tablets of Confusius. If they conquered China, they would eradicate all rival religions, and with them, half the culture and thought of China. Perhaps even worse, they would expunge the Confucian civil service system that had given China continuity through periods of anarchy and barbarian conquests; they would alter the very soul of China. Already they had brought in Western guns and Western organization; they had dreamed up new ways to use those weapons far more extensively than even the Manchus had, improvised ways of using them that even the English and the French had not; they ran their conquered provinces like Army units, with strict segregation of the sexes and virtual slave labor for all but the soldiers; and they looked to the West for their inspirations, not to Confucius or Lao-Tze or any of the sages. Given their heads, they would no doubt remodel China to resemble one of the nations of those upstart barbarians, those foreign round-eyed devils, the Europeans.

Yes, all in all, the Taipings were a greater threat to China than the Manchus . . .

And to Tseng Kuo-Fan and his family. Though it galled him a little to fight for the conquering Manchus, they were quite the lesser of the two evils.

Hugi came to Tyr, where he stood watching the einherjar battle. The raven spoke with the cawing voice of his kind: "Heimdall has heard a commotion at the far end of the world."

Tyr's blood ran cold, as it always did when news came of Heimdall's hearings. He knew that the voice might be that of a raven, but the words were those of Odin. "Is it the Time?"

"Nay," said Odin's messenger, "for these are not giants, nor do they approach. Come to my master."

Relieved, Tyr came.

"Nay, 'tis not the Ragnorak come upon us," Odin confirmed, when Tyr stood before him by the ash tree.

"Who are they, then?" the one-handed god asked.

"They are the yellow people of the Jade Emperor and Kung Fu-Tze."

Now, Confucius was not called a god, and Tyr knew it well—but he knew also that the sheer power of belief of billions of souls had elevated the sage's ghost till he had become just as much a god as Odin himself . . .

. . . and no more.

"What quarrel brews among them?" Tyr demanded.

"They contend with one another in civil war."

Tyr relaxed. "What business is it of ours?"

"They have made themselves a new god—or rather, wrapped an old one in Christian clothes. They have set him against the gods of the Manchus, and strive to conquer China away from those northern invaders. They seek to drag the Emperor off his throne and expel all Manchus from the Middle Kingdom."

Tyr shook his head. "There is still nothing in here to concern the gods of Northern Europe."

"But there is—for the descendents of our people seek to trade with these Chinese, and will be sorely oppressed if the school teacher's god triumphs. Moreover, if his followers conquer China, the sleeping dragon shall waken, and may threaten even the island fortress of the Angles, the Saxons, and the Danes."

"And the Normans, though they had forgotten us by the time they conquered." Tyr's face had set into grim lines. "Can these silly slant-eyes truly threaten the West?"

"There are very many of them," Odin pointed out, "and they are valiant warriors, if they are given decent leadership. The school teacher has chosen good generals, and his followers have begun to triumph over the forces of the Emperor. Already he holds a third of China in his sway, and has declared that he is the rightful Emperor, that the Mandate of Heaven has been withdrawn from the Manchus and has come to him. He calls his reign the Tai-Ping Tien Kwoh—The Heavenly Kingdom of Great Peace."

"Is that why he sheds so much blood?" Tyr scowled, gazing off toward the East. "I had thought the Englishman to be right when he said that China was a sleeping dragon."

"Then the schoolteacher Hung Hsiu-Chuan may waken that dragon—and if he does, let the West beware."

Tyr locked gazes with Odin again. "There are many dragon-slayers among our brood."

"Go find one, then," Odin commanded. "Find me a hero who can bind the will of England against these upstarts who would make a god of bits and pieces. There are many in Britain who think these Taipings are good, for they seem to be Christians. Make me a hero who shall see the school teacher for the blasphemer he is, and unite the English to see it, too."

Tyr shook his head. "Heroes are made as much as they are born. I shall seek a man who is the raw stuff, and make a hero of him."

And the god of the single hand was soon to be seen, here and there, walking through England again. Those who saw him turned away their eyes, and tried to pretend they had not seen—and certainly spoke of him to no one, for they knew that when Tyr was seen about the land, war would come for England.

But one man did not turn away.

* * *

Charles George Gordon was off duty, walking the seashore near Pembroke Dock, gazing at the roaring surf that mirrored the tumult in his own soul, but gazing beyond it at the deep rolling swell that showed him the tranquility to which he aspired. He had been wandering for perhaps an hour when he met the one-handed man.

Gordon had only been graduated from the Royal Military Academy for a year and a half; he was twenty, and waiting for orders to his first assignment, eager for the excitement of the fray. He knew, in a way that was neither remote nor academic, that he might be killed, might even be maimed, might undergo horrible pain—but the thought did not deter him. He was sure that he could endure any pain God saw fit to allot to him—had he not already undergone self-imposed hardships, fasting and long marches? If God saw fit to call him home to heaven before his alloted threescore years and ten—why, he was ready.

But he was not ready for the encounter with the old mendicant, whose gaze fixed him with an intensity that stabbed through to his very soul.

He saw the old man sitting on his heels by a small fire, and pity moved his heart, though he was careful not to let it show in his face. Surely the man was in desperate need—all he wore were the skins of animals, and a pair of sandals. Gordon came up to the fire, reaching in his pocket for a shilling, reflecting that he must not seem patronizing—he knew what pride was; who should know better? "Good day to you, my man."

"Good day to you." The old beggar looked up, raising an arm in greeting—and Gordon thrilled with shock to see that his wrist ended in a metal cup; the hand was gone. He forced himself to look away, to look at the old man's eyes—a mistake, for that glittering gaze held Gordon transfixed; for a moment, he could not have moved if he had found himself staring down the muzzle of a musket.

Then the old man looked down at the partridge that was roasting over his little fire, and Gordon could move again. A delusion, no doubt—but he thought twice about offering the alms he had intended. He stared at the man, at a loss for words—and the more so because he realized that the furs the old man wore, were clean, almost new, as clean as the man himself. He wore nothing but a jerkin and a kilt, only skins with the fur left on. His long grizzled hair was held back by a headband that shone like burnished gold— or, no, surely it was brass, but darker than brass.

He did not look like a man in need.

Oh yes, he was lean, and the bones were prominent in his cheeks—but except for the long moustaches that hung down below his chin, his face was cleanly shaved, and his arms and legs were thick with muscle. He did not look to be a man in need—rather a man in his element, whose life gave him all he needed.

But that could not be! He had no house, or he would not have been cooking by an open fire; he had no proper clothes. There were no wild men left in England, in Victoria's reign; what could he be?

"You are wondering where my hand is."

Gordon could only nod; had he been so obvious?

"I left it in the mouth of a wolf. Seat yourself." It was a command as much as an invitation. "Partake of my meal."

Gordon was revolted, but also strangely attracted. He found himself sitting slowly, and murmuring, "Thank you."

"It is as you will." The accent was not West Country—nor any other dialect that Gordon recognized. Perhaps a touch of the Prince Consort, perhaps an echo of the German . . .

"Where are you bound?"

There was a time when Gordon would have said, "I don't know;" but on his first posting, he had met Captain Drew, the closest thing to a friend he had had in that grim and dingy place—and Drew had taught him a strange thing: Christianity without a church. It had come as a revelation to Gordon, with his New England Puritan mother and three generations of Army Gordons gone before him. Discipline he knew, and always rebelled against it, though he had already begun to insist on it from his subordinates—if there were such a thing as a subordinate to a subaltern. Church he knew, and resented its boredom intensely. But Drew prayed quietly, by himself, and made no great show of his faith; it had been only a chance comment at first, a reference here and there, but long explanations when Gordon asked for them. For Gordon, religion had ceased to be an inconvenience, had become an obsession.

So now, when the old man asked him where he was bound, he replied, "Where God wills." The words came automatically, as easily as one might say "To Aberdeen" or "To London."

The uncanny gaze fixed him again, and the odd guttural voice said, "Are you not bound for glory, young soldier? Do you not yearn for it?"

"No," Gordon said.

The old man nodded as though it were no surprise. "There is one thing you do yearn for, though."

"Yes." Gordon met his gaze. "Heaven."

The old man nodded. "Do you not mean—death?"

"Of course," Gordon said impatiently. "Death is the gateway to Heaven."

The old man's smile was almost lost in his moustaches. "You shall have it—some day. For you must earn it, must seek it as Galahad sought the Grail. But you may begin your quest in the Crimea. Request your posting."

"I have," Gordon said, feeling irritation begin. "The Army ignores me."

"Then ask Sir John Burgoyne."

Gordon could only stare, again feeling the thrill, the chill, of that single-minded gaze. How could the old man have known that the War Office's Inspector-

General of Fortifications was an old friend of the Gordon family? "What are you, then?"

"Your genius, perhaps." The old man rose—perhaps not so old after all, perhaps only in his fifties . . . "Perhaps a messenger, come to tell you that you shall find what you seek in the East."

But he was going away! "Wait!" Gordon cried. "Your bird!"

"Take it," the one-handed man told him. "It is not the last of my suppers you shall eat."

Gordon stared after him, feeling the chill rise up his spine like mercury in a thermometer. Then he shook it off, and looked down at the grouse. When he looked up again, the old man was gone. Disappeared.

Gordon stared at the place where he had been for several minutes, then looked slowly down at the grouse. Carefully, he took it from the fire, tore loose a leg, and began to eat.

The Bear roared, its little eyes blazing, huge claws reaching out to rake at Tyr—but the one-handed god batted the huge paw aside with contempt. "I am fated to fight the Fenris Wolf, beast! How pathetic are you compared to that great Foe!"

"You are all of you only very little men!" the Bear growled. "You could not stand against me, if there were not so many of you!"

"Then call your own army," Thor rumbled, hefting his hammer. "These men are the grandsons of grandsons' grandsons of those who worshipped me, and I shall strengthen their arms!"

"I shall craft them wondrous weapons," Wayland the Smith added.

"Only the three?" The Bear roared in mockery. "Where is the fourth? Where is the trickster, where is Loki?"

"Loki has his own business," Thor said grimly. He was angry at the Flame-god, but was quite willing to turn that anger on the Bear. "We shall not need him."

But they did.

The guns thundered, the horse under him screamed and stumbled. Gordon shouted and leaped clear, proud that even in such extremity he had not cursed nor sworn. But he did call upon his God. "Lord help me now!" he cried, as he sheathed his saber and drew his revolver. He walked straight toward the belching Russian cannon, staring at the Slavic faces behind its breech. Terror surged within him, fought to tear loose and overwhelm him, but he fought it down sternly and went step by step toward the cannon, thinking, *If it be thy will, O Lord, then I shall die; if it be thy will!* For he knew the Russians were almost as bad as the Papists, with their drinking and treacheries, ignoring the clear, shining doctrines of true Christianity.

Bullets whistled about him, shells burst to right and left—but not a scrap of lead touched him, not a shard of shrapnel. He came through the smoke unto the breech of the gun, and the gunners looked up, staring in horror out of their broad Slavic faces, as though they were seeing a ghost.

Gordon raised his pistol, and fired.

"He is blooded," Tyr told Odin. "The war is done; for fifteen months he has toiled at mapping the borders laid down by the treaty."

Odin frowned. "How will that aid in making a hero of him?"

"Because," said Tyr, "it has given him a love for wild, open lands, simple living, and rough people with ways that are new and exciting to him. Never again he will never be content to remain in England for very long."

Odin nodded thoughtfully. "It is well done. But how shall you confront the Chinese gods? What force of immortals can you assemble, to support your champion?"

"I will begin with the oldest," said Tyr, "with the war-god whose people are so long gone that we have forgotten their name. Then I will come to the Celts."

Lugh looked up from the spear he was sharpening and saw the One-Handed stalking toward him out of the mist between their realms. He leaped to his feet, brandishing his spear and shouting, "Can I never be done with you? Begone, invader! Away, or I will slay you again!"

"Then I would slay you," Tyr returned, irritated by the Celt's bravura, "and we would both be alive again in a second, to continue it all again. Have you not learned, oh Chalk-Hair, that we can only die if humans cease to believe in us?"

"Then how is it you still live?" Lugh taunted. "The White Christ chased you all out of Britain years ago!"

"No more than yourself," Tyr returned. "Have the Britons ceased to light fires on Samhain? Have they ceased to dance about the Maypole? Come, you know these things of old, and know that the Island People today are as much your children as mine!"

"They are that," Lugh growled, "more's the pity."

Tyr heaved a sigh. "You were ever poor losers, you braggart Celts. Is it of no matter to you that our island people are at war again?"

"When are they not at war?" Lugh returned. "When they extended their sway around the world, they took up the challenge of constant warfare, somewhere in the world."

"But now they contend against the Dragon," Tyr said, "or will, soon—and millions of souls shall fuel the power of the god they worship. Come, it will take all of us to defend our folk this time—even the Ancient Ones, in whom the Britons have only shreds of belief. We must bind together now, as surely as we are bound in the blood and bone of these descendants of our worshippers."

Lugh scowled. "We are so bound, aye. But who

shall you find to bind them all to one mind for this war? They are a contentious lot, and are forever arguing as to what course of action to take. Why, they could not even agree to forge an empire—it fell to them almost by accident, and by the commerce of their merchants more than their lust for power!"

"That is true," Tyr said, "but the army always followed to protect the merchants—and I have found us a soldier who can bind their determination together, whether he will or no."

"What paragon is this?" Lugh demanded. "Cymri or Celt, Briton or Dane?"

"Come and see for yourself." Tyr turned on his heel and stalked away.

Lugh glowered after him, then hefted his spear and followed.

The campaign was done, its echoes were dying inside his head. He walked by the waters of the Black Sea, already restless again. Orders had come to go to Bessarabia and survey the border with Russia, to be sure it conformed to the Paris treaty—but it was only dull routine, and there was no chance there for fighting, for death.

So he walked by the sea, its tranquility soothing his soul; the gibbering terrors were laid to rest, and the sight of the sea and the tranquility of its endless beating were healing his soul.

He saw the one-handed man.

He stared at the figure sitting by the fire ring—but the coals were dark, there was no meat, and no flame. Then, slowly, Gordon came up to the ashes. But he did not sit; he had not been invited.

The old man looked up. "Sit."

Gordon sat.

"You have won glory." The old man did not ask; he knew.

Gordon shrugged impatiently. "It means nothing." Nonetheless, he touched the medal on his breast. "I have not found death."

"Not for yourself, no. But it shall come, it shall come."

Gordon's eyes glowed. "Soon?"

The old man shrugged. "How quickly is 'soon'? In three years' time, you shall have another chance."

Gordon was sorely disappointed. "Three years? For three years I must rot in peace?"

"There will be work," the old man assured him. "You will discover new delights; you will not decay." The old man looked down at the roast, then looked up again. "There is much glory to be won for your God, much fame to be gained for His name."

Gordon felt the cold chill again, the thrill; his heart leaped. "Will there be war?"

"For England, yes," the one-handed man said. "For you, there will be more hunting."

The terror screamed to be let out, but Gordon kept it locked in. His eyes shone with gratification. "What quarry?"

"The Dragon," the old man said.

Then he rose and turned away. "Eat of my supper."

"I shall." Gordon lowered his gaze to see that the meat was done; he took the spit from the fire. He did not bother to look up; he knew the one-handed man would be gone.

"Bow down, and do not even seek to raise your hands against me!" the shining figure proclaimed. "Am I not the God your Englishmen worship? Am I not God the Father?"

"You are not." Loki gestured, and the flames of glory died, showing only a venerable Chinese sage. "You are Shang-Ti, the ancient father-god of China, and have deluded that poor dreamer Hung Hsiu-Chuan into mistaking you for the Father of Christ, and your son of Jesu."

"*I* deluded *him*?" The sage's mouth tightened. "Say rather that he has trapped me in his delusion—he, and a hundred thousand of his followers!"

Thor laughed, and the clouds shook with his mirth. "Oh, well done, Loki! Well have you seen through his imposture!"

"To no purpose, barbarians!" Shang-Ti snapped. "Can your soldiers fight against one who believes he fights for the son of their God? What will the real Son say? What will the Father? What of the God your foreign devils claim to worship? What of Jehovah?"

"Hush! Do not speak His Name!" Tyr glanced about uneasily. "He is above and beyond this conflict, Ancient One—above and beyond all things. For we are but fabrications of the minds and hearts of human beings, given life by their deepest, most secret yearnings—even as they are of His."

"Their belief will give me strength to stand against you and all your kind!"

"All?" Tyr looked back over his shoulder at the Celtic gods and, beyond them, the dim and distant elder gods of Britain. He turned back to Shang-Ti. "There are many of us, Old One. But there are many of yours, too. Call up your vast array of deities."

"I cannot!" Shang-Ti said bitterly. "This dunce of a school teacher has bound me into a religion in which there is only one God. I am bereft of my entourage."

Tyr raised an eyebrow. "Then you stand alone against us?"

"Let your puny Englishmen come!" Shang-Ti blustered. "My people shall swallow them, chew them up, and spit them out, as they have done to so many before!"

"They have not chewed *me*, Ancient One." The Manchu war-god stepped up beside Tyr and Odin. "And my lance is still in your heart."

But Shang-Ti wrenched out the lance and threw it back with contempt. "They have swallowed you, they have chewed you—and even now prepare to eject you. You, and all who are yours!"

"Indeed?" The Manchu's eyes glittered dangerously.

"Then I must rip out their bellies while I am still within them!"

England had forced a new treaty on the Chinese and withdrawn her gunboats, but the Emperor refused to sign it. Well, not refused, exactly, but there was one delay after another, cavil after cavil, excuse after excuse. Finally, in exasperation, England had sent Lord Elgin to make sure the treaty was signed—and Sir Hope Grant, with 15,000 soldiers, to clear his way.

It was late, very late, when Gordon received his orders. He strode the decks with impatience; he barely restrained himself from blowing into the sail, to try to hurry the ship faster. When they were becalmed and the great paddlewheels alone drove them, he stood calm and chill on the outside, but was almost feverish with anxiety inside.

And sure enough, by the time he came to the China coast, the first few battles had been won; the Union Jack flew over the Taku Forts. But Lord Elgin and the army had advanced only as far as Tientsin, and Gordon joined them there.

Elgin gave the signal, and Sir Grant moved his troops northward. An Imperial army blocked his way, with Manchu bannermen at its center, tall and burly in bright half-armor, banners fluttering overhead. Almost as intimidating were the troops of Mongol cavalry on the wings, sturdy men with pointed, fur-trimmed caps who rode tough little ponies. Gordon looked upon them and felt an echo of the dread that Europe had felt when Genghis Khan's horde had ridden in from the steppe.

But the Europeans had fast-moving cavalry of their own now, and cannon and grape-shot, as well as a musket for every infantryman—and they blasted by the numbers, laying down a continuous field of fire while they advanced, row upon row, volley upon volley. The Mongol cavalry rode as a mob, and broke upon the wave of bullets; the proud Manchu bannermen charged and stumbled as the grapeshot hit them. The Manchu cannons boomed in reply, but the stone balls fell short, or flew wide.

To Gordon, in the thick of it, the battle seemed interminable, as all battles did; time stopped as he urged his troop on, seeming to ignoring the hail of musket balls about him—though secretly hoping one would strike him. But none did, and suddenly it was all over; the bannermen and the Chinese infantry were in full retreat, the Mongols were galloping away. Sir Grant would not let his men follow; their mission was to bring Elgin to Peking, not to conquer China.

But his strategy seemed odd; they swung north of Peking, and came down through the Summer Palace. Gordon stared in awe at mile after mile of perfectly manicured garden, of dainty dells and miniature pagodas next to ponds that were expanded to lakes by the scale of the models. There was not one palace, but two hundred, some with scores of rooms, some of merely a dozen—pavillions and summerhouses and arbors, made of precious woods and decorated with jewels.

But there was litter on the grass, and cups and plates left on the tables, for the Emperor and his household had fled in frenzy, farther north to Jehol, only days before the French and English came.

So the guns rained cannon balls and grapeshot on Peking, and Prince Kung graciously agreed to discuss terms. An agreement was signed—by the Prince, not the Emperor, but Kung was his brother and regent, and the Emperor was reputed to be ill. Elgin declared amity, and demanded that the prisoners the Manchus had taken be returned.

They came in bullock carts—carts carrying wooden boxes. The English and French looked upon the remains of their countrymen and their loyal Sikh troops, and paled, and trembled.

The Army screamed for blood to answer the blood that had been shed, the tortures that had been visited on their men. A few were still alive, and told of the pains inflicted by the Board of Punishments. But the treaty had been signed anew; Britain and France had pledged amity again; they could not strike through to conquer Peking and punish Prince Kung and his torturers, nor march north to capture the ailing Emperor himself. Lord Elgin strode through the Summer Palace, sunk in brooding thought, then emerged to announce the punishment to be visited on the Manchus—a punishment that would smite only the Emperor and his nobles, by destroying a treasure that had been reserved to them alone:

The Summer Palace.

The French diplomat protested at the destruction of such beauty, that had taken centuries in the building, but Elgin stood firm. His own officers warned that by destroying the Emperor's private pleasure-park, he would undermine Chinese respect for the Manchu regime; he would strike at its foundations, and the government of China might crumble. Elgin stood firm.

"Begone, you barbarian monkeys!" the Manchu gods were drawn up in a wedge. "If your hairy devil-people dare to seek to strike at our Emperor, you shall die on our spears!"

But Tyr stood between Thor and Lugh, his own spear poised in his palm, a shield fastened to his handless arm. Behind him, in array, stood the gods of the Danes and the Angles and Saxons; beyond them stood the gods of the Celts. Even farther back stood the shadowed gods of the Elder Britons, and in the distance, dim but menacing, hulked the gods to whom Stonehenge had been erected.

"We are far more in number than you," Tyr informed the Manchu gods, "but that matters far less than our strength; for your people have begun to turn away from you, to forget you—and the Chinese gods have never stood with you. Give way, or perish."

The old gods of Great Britain began to march.

* * *

"You are an engineer," the major told him, for he was an officer in the Engineers, truly enough. "You shall destroy the Birthday Garden—the Wang-shaw-ewen, as they call it—destroy it, and all its buildings."

Gordon had little use for art and sculpture, but even he could appreciate the beauty he had been sent to destroy. An order was an order, though, especially when he could see the sense of it—and he had seen the bodies of the tortured British. He led his men out on an overcast morning, the air heavy and oppressive. They broke into a palace, and Gordon stopped, amazed at the wealth of china and porcelain and gold and jade—the statues, the tea sets, the chess sets, the accumulated bric-a-brac of two hundred years, but all made of precious metals or stones, or of fragrant woods inlaid with gems.

He could not stand to see it all go up in flames. "Take what you can," he told his men—then, as though the words were dragged out of him: "and break the rest."

Hundred-year-old vases of eggshell porcelain shivered into a thousand slivers; delicate cups and teapots shattered. Finally the soldiers went through the palace with their torches . . .

And through the groves of fruit trees, and the sculptured bushes.

In other gardens, other English and Indian troops were doing the same; in still others, French troops looted what they could and broke what they could not carry. The accumulated loot was divided up, and the smoke of the fairyland-made-real ascended into the sky, a pillar of darkness that proclaimed the Emperor's weakness. The citizens of Peking looked up, and took note; in the months that followed, merchants brought the tale outside the city, and it spread through all of China. The Chinese learned of the Manchu Emperor's humiliation . . .

And the sheer brute power of those uncultured

barbarians, the Foreign Devils who could break price-less beauties beneath their heavy boots, and scarcely notice.

But Gordon was restless. He had come to China to find death, not to destroy a beautiful garden. The English and French troops had withdrawn, but 3000 British soldiers stayed behind at Tientsin, to make sure the Chinese paid the indemnity specified in the treaty. The force was commanded by General Stavely, whose sister had married Gordon's eldest brother Henry. Impatient, Gordon filled his time by surveying the country around Tientsin when on duty, and riding long distances to keep fit, when off-duty—seventy miles at a stretch. He explored the region of the Great Wall, seeking passes by which Russia might attack China. Restless or not, he found himself almost at peace, almost happy, for the scenery and the strangeness of it all held him entranced, and he thrived on the work.

After a year and a half, though, the Taiping rebels in the Yangtze valley began to move again toward the treaty port of Shanghai, and the international trading community settled there became nervous. Stavely decided to reinforce the garrison, sending two regiments and a group of Engineers—commanded by Gordon.

Gordon arrived on the scene, his appetite keen for action, only to find that the British were cleaving to a policy of strict neutrality—the international army of Indian, British, and French troops would fight if Shanghai were attacked, or if the Taipings came within thirty miles of the city, but they could not go farther afield; they were to be defensive only. Gordon was put to work constructing new defenses, wondering why his superiors could not see that the best defense was a good offense. He learned something of the Taiping religion, and was fascinated by its strangeness at the same time as he was incensed at its distortions of sound Protestant Christianity. He learned more when he was sent to survey their outpost, Tsingpo, at the very edge of the thirty-mile region that the Western powers regarded as sacrosanct.

The Chinese merchants, however, were in no mood to wait until the fearsome Taipings should come to them. They had hired an American adventurer, Frederick Townsend Ward, who had put together a small army of a few thousand mercenaries, and had not been too concerned about the honor or legal background of his men. He had lost as many battles as he had won, but was at least doing something to hold the Taipings at bay.

Then the British took Tsingpo, thanks in no small measure to Gordon's excellent information—and Ward was killed chasing the Taipings as they retreated. His second-in-command, Burgevine, took over—but Burgevine had little respect for law, and less for morality; he was a former gun-runner, and a flagrant opportunist looking for the best deal. He and the polyglot army captured Kahding on the northern edge of the thirty-mile boundary, and he let his men loot their fill—and slaughter the Taiping prisoners.

General Stavely was shocked, and determined to remove Burgevine from the command. He would replace the blackguard with a proper soldier, one who was concerned not for riches, but for Right. He looked about him to see what officer he could spare . . .

And the choice fell on Gordon.

Tseng-Kuo-Fan was Commander-in-Chief of the Imperial forces against the Taiping rebels, but Li Hung-Chang was governor of Kiangsu Province, and Tseng's general in the east. Li held up the pay for Burgevine and his troops, so Burgevine rounded up a few of his roughest men, marched on the bank, beat up the banker, and took the cash. Li promptly fired him, then accepted Gordon's appointment to command the little army (though he insisted on a Chinese co-commander, to make sure Gordon did as Li wanted).

Thus Gordon, the regular-army officer, with a tradition of service stretching back three generations, took command of a mercenary army, determined to teach them discipline and end their excesses. He began by renaming them: the Ever-Victorious Army.

His Chinese soldiers were impressed. His Western bandits were not. They tried to mutiny, twice; Gordon put them down with stern resolve. Half of them deserted; Gordon was just as glad to see them gone. He recruited replacements and trained them, making sure they knew discipline from the beginning. Finally Governor Li gave him his orders, and with 3500 men, two batteries of field artillery, and four batteries of seige artillery, he embarked for the town of Chanzu, which was steadfastly resisting a Taiping siege.

Gordon had not wasted his five months in and around Shanghai. He had surveyed every acre within the thirty-mile perimeter, and knew the location of every village—but more importantly, he also knew the location of every stream and canal, and how they interconnected to form a network of waterways. He collected a small fleet of river boats, equipped them with cannon fore and aft, and put them under the direction of Yankee skippers who knew river navigation from the United States. The time come, he marched his men on board and cast off to work his way through the canals and rivers of Fushan Creek, which connected Chanzu with the Yangtze.

As they steamed up Fushan Creek, a party of Taipings appeared out of the rice paddies to either side. They began to lay down a field of fire around the *Hyson,* Gordon's "flagship." Gordon commanded the gunners to fire; the 32-pounder in the bows boomed, and grape-shot raked the Taiping line. Their fire faltered, but kept up. A second cannon shot silenced their fire, and a third made them retreat—they were an experienced army, and knew the meaning of cannon. However, they had brought none themselves; and as Chanzu came in sight, Gordon saw the Taipings leaving the city.

Li was delighted, and conferred on him the Order of the Yellow Button. His troops grinned and strutted; they had taken the town without a bit of risk, or a musket fired.

On the other hand, they weren't allowed to loot. Many deserted.

Immediately after, Li summoned Gordon. The summons rankled, but Gordon knew better than to refuse a senior officer, which Li was, in effect. The governor's expression was masked, his face impassive. "I have had a communication from Prince Kung. He commands me to reinstate Burgevine as commander of the Ever-Victorious Army."

Gordon stared. "What?" Then he recovered his composure. "Surely, sir, I have proved my worth!"

"Thoroughly," Li agreed, "and it is a hundred times that of Burgevine's. I will not conceal from you, Major Gordon, that I have no use for foreign devils—but you are superior in manner and bearing to any of those with whom I have the ill-fortune to come into contact, and you at least mask that conceit which makes most of them repugnant in my sight. I consider you a direct blessing from Heaven."

Gordon held his face immobile while he adjusted to the shock and delight, then said, "I thank Your Excellency. But why, then . . ."

"Burgevine shall remain where he is," said Li, "far from Shanghai. I have been entrusted with the governance of this province, and Prince Kung has no authority to countermand me unless he finds me totally unworthy of my post, whereupon he may replace me. I have refused his request."

Gordon went back to his tent and wrote to the British Legation in Peking, saying, "I must distinctly decline any further doings with any Chinese forces." Li learned of it, and persuaded him; Gordon changed his mind. Li commanded him to march on Taitsan.

The Taiping commander there had offered to defect to the Imperialists with all his garrison. Li sent a force to take over the town—and the Taipings fell upon Li's troops, killing thirty and taking three hundred prisoner. Gordon was to avenge this treachery.

Gordon packed his three thousand remaining men into small gunboats, shepherded by the *Hyson*. He surrounded the town and blocked all but the Eastern exit, which led towards the sea. Unable to escape and knowing they would be executed for treachery, the Taipings fought with grim desperation. Gordon's cannon pounded their stockade, and in only three hours, had opened a huge breach in the wall. Gordon rushed his infantry forward in their gunboats. The captains brought the vessels as close as they could, then the howling troops poured out to charge the breach. But spears rained from the wall, and musket-fire crackled in an unending series as bullets battered down at them. The charge wavered, then receded.

Gordon rallied them with shouts and gestures with his cane; they understood few of his words, but comprehended his tone. Gordon held them in position while his howitzers raked the walls and cut down the defenders. After a storm of shot, he charged forward, his infantry behind him with muskets, following the madman who threatened the Taipings with nothing but a rattan cane; they could not know that he hoped one of the balls would strike him down as he fought to free the Chinese from a rule more tyannical than that of the Manchus.

But as one rank of Taipings fell from the blasting of Gordon's howitzers, another popped up in its place, firing down at the attackers. Still the Ever-Victorious Army came up to the breach—but it filled with Taiping defenders, stabbing with spears and slashing with swords. Gordon's men blocked and thrust in their turn, the clank and clash of steel riding high over the staccato musketry. Incredibly, the Taipings managed to force Gordon's men back from the walls.

Gordon retreated again and rallied his men while his cannon battered at the defenders atop their wall and by the breach. Then Gordon waved his cane, shouting, and charged out again. Howling, his infantry pelted after him.

The Taipings filled the breath with steel, but Gordon laid about him with his cane, and his men shot their way in with musket and pistol, then chopped at the ranks with swords and stabbed with bayonets. Taipings died left and right; so did Gordon's men. But, somehow, the Taipings gave way; suddenly, there were no more of the long-haired rebels in front of them, and Gordon and his men surged on into the town.

The Taiping casualties were great, very great. For his part, Gordon had lost almost one man out of ten. But he was deeply impressed with the courage and loyalty of the Chinese, both the Taipings and those in his own army. He found them quick to learn, and ready and willing to follow him into battle. They were very courageous—in some instances. They would outdo even his Europeans for bravery.

But again, Gordon prohibited looting, and made it stick. Worse, when the decimated army returned to base, he threw them right into stiff training for the next battle; he'd already been told they were to march on Quinsan. There were rumbles of mutiny when the soldiers found they weren't to have a few weeks of R & R. When he announced the marching orders, every officer resigned. The next morning, when Gordon ordered the army to parade in marching order, no one came, except his own bodyguard.

Gordon already knew who the probable ringleaders were; he arrested them instantly, and clapped them into irons. Then he announced that he and his bodyguards were leaving for Quinsan; they would pause halfway, and anyone who did not answer at afternoon roll-call would be dismissed.

Most of them answered at roll call. The others would not be missed.

A Taiping general named Ching had defected to the Imperialists. Governor Li knew just how formidable he had been as an enemy, and gave him general's rank, and an Imperial army. At Quinsan, General Ching determined to attack the eastern gate. Gordon disagreed—the eastern gate was the most strongly fortified, and the western gate would be the Taiping's escape route to Soochow, where a larger Taiping garrison waited. So Gordon left Ching to attack the eastern gate and took the *Hyson* and his gunboats toward the western gate. Before he arrived, though, the Taipings proved him right—they began to march out through the western gate. Gordon fired a few shots, left half his army to guard the gate and keep the rebels penned, then set off after the retreating Taipings. As darkness fell, he gave up the chase and turned back; but as his gunboats approached the western gate, gunshots battered at his ears. As he came up to the half of his army left on guard, he saw a huge mass boiling out through the western gate—all the rest of the Taiping garrison trying to break through his lines in a body and retreat to Soochow, eight thousand strong.

It sickened him, but Gordon was outnumbered more than two to one. He gave the orders; the *Hyson*'s cannon boomed, and the howitzers echoed her. Shot and ball tore apart the Taiping ranks. They broke and ran every which way—but they did not retreat back into Quinsan.

Gordon fired, and fired again and again, sickened by what he knew he was doing, but seeing no alternative—any other course of action, and the Taipings would have swept his little army away. All through the night his guns pounded; finally, Taipings began to go back into the city.

Dawn showed him a field of corpses.

Gordon knew that his men regarded their base in Sungkiang as their haven for rest and recreation, most of it immoral and all of it damaging to discipline—so he set up a new headquarters in Quinsan. The men didn't like it; the first time he ordered parade, the artillery regiment stayed in their quarters. They did, however, send a message threatening to turn their guns on their European officers, and on any of the Chinese enlisted men who sided with Gordon.

That was flat-out mutiny. Gordon knew better than to try to laugh it off. He ordered the artillery men out and lined them up, his officers around them with their weapons cocked and ready.

"Who dreamed up this treacherous notion of blasting away us officers?" Gordon demanded.

The artillerymen glanced at the Europeans who held their guns at the ready, but no one answered.

Gordon's jaw firmed. "I will have one man in every five shot for mutiny!"

A mournful groan rose from the ranks.

One corporal in the front row was groaning louder and faster than any. Gordon stepped forward, seized the man, and spun him out of ranks toward his own bodyguard. "Shoot him!"

Two of Gordon's men pinned the man's arms and forced him to his knees. A third drew his pistol, pointed it at the man's heart, and fired.

The groaning ceased. The artillerymen stared in shock.

Gordon surveyed them, his face grim. "You are all under arrest! Give me the ringleader's name within the hour, or I shall carry out my threat and execute every fifth man!"

The ringleader was delivered up and executed within the hour. But the next morning, there were many fewer men on parade, and by the end of the week, two thousand of Gordon's troops had deserted.

After all, if there was to be no loot, no rape, and only pay that was late—why stay?

Gordon understood only too well. He wrote to Li, complaining that the Imperial paymasters had fallen behind in paying the troops, and resigned the command of the Ever-Victorious Army. So saying, he bade farewell to his troops and returned to Shanghai.

There, he found out that Burgevine had recruited hundreds of rascals and defected to the Taipings.

Gordon went back to Quinsan immediately, sure that if he were not there to hold them, the remnants of the Ever-Victorious Army would follow Burgevine into the enemy camp.

But the Taipings' doom was clear for all to see now, and the Ever-Victorious Army had no wish to die with them, or with its old commander. Finally, two months later, Gordon's pickets brought in a peasant with a secret message: Burgevine had not been greeted with delight by the Taipings, and had not been appointed to a high post. He asked Gordon's help in escaping.

Gordon provided the men and the cover. Burgevine stepped into his tent with a wide grin to thank him, then went on to say, "Here now, we're the best two commanders in the East, and you know it. Let's make common cause, and leave these Imperials and Taipings to kill each other off! We'll take the Ever-Victorious Army to Peking, seize the Dragon Throne, and be emperors ourselves over the richest nation on earth!"

Gordon could scarcely believe his ears. Had Burgevine's drinking finally caused him to become demented? "I must politely refuse," he said. "I am a British officer, and cannot forsake my position. But I will assist you in as many respects as I can."

What he could do, was to give Burgevine a safe-conduct and an escort back to Shanghai—and to hand the escort a letter for the American Consul, requesting that Burgevine leave China without delay.

Tseng Kuo-Fan's generals had pushed the Taipings back from west, north, and south; Li had pushed them in from the east, and they were crowded into Nanking, surrounded by Imperial troops. Ward's mercenary army could have been a difficult and unpredictable problem for Li, but Gordon had resolved it. Only one other city remained in Taiping hands: Soochow, on the east. Reducing it was Li's job. Gordon was eager to take the Ever-Victorious Army to capture the city, and Li was only too happy to let him.

Gordon replaced his deserters with Taiping prisoners, who were happy to be out of prison with their heads still on their shoulders, and to have an opportunity to earn good money into the bargain. Gordon wasn't completely sure that they wouldn't go over to the enemy, so he had his officers watch them closely. Gordon's riverboats and artillery blasted his way through ranks of Taipings to Soochow, and he soon had every gate blocked.

The Taiping officers commanding the garrison knew they had no chance left. Only one of them refused to surrender; they handled the problem neatly with a knife in his back and a sword through his neck. Then they sent word to General Ching, offering to surrender on terms. He promised to spare their lives, and those of their men. They opened the eastern gate to him, and the Imperial troops marched in. As soon as the garrison was secured, they fell to looting, including the women and girls, and butchering anyone who got in their way.

Gordon would have none of it for the Ever-Victorious Army. He packed them aboard their steamers and went back down the canal to Quinsan, to Li's advance headquarters, where he demanded a bonus of two months' full pay to replace the loot he had not allowed them to take. Li agreed to give them a single month's bonus, and invited Gordon to attend the formal surrender of the Soochow garrison. Indignant, Gordon declined—which was just as well, since Ching beheaded the nine Taiping commanders.

For two months, Gordon wrangled with Li over this treacherous action, but Ching was too valuable to the governor, and he would not censure the former Taiping, but took the blame himself. Finally, having

exonerated Gordon completely, he managed to pacify
him and persuade him to aid in the steady, relentless
advance on Nanking, acre by acre and town by town.

At Kintan, Gordon finally gained part of his wish—
he was hit by a bullet, but only in the leg. Then came
news that a Taiping commander had sallied out of
Nanking and was trying to retake Quinsan. Gordon
ignored his wound and took his army east to cut off
the Taiping advance. He took their flying column
unaware and chased them back toward Nanking. Then
he joined up with Li's troops and moved on
Changchow.

Changchow was a very tough nut to crack. His cannon made the breach well enough—the wall crumbled
under the pounding of ball after cannon ball—but the
Taipings held the gap against two storming charges.
On the other side of the town, Li met with similar
resistance.

Now Gordon showed his engineering skill. Under
cover of night, his men dug trenches with breastworks,
through which soldiers could file, safe from enemy
fire, unobserved, until they spilled out only a few yards
from the breach. At dawn, his artillery began a conti-
nous bombardment which lasted all morning.

The guns blasted from the bows of the river boats
behind them, beating in a heavy rhythm, blasting
Taipings back and away from the breach in the wall
of Changchow. Gordon shouted and waved his cane
for the bombardment to cease, then waved it overhead
as he plunged ahead, limping, but leading the charge.
Two thousand throats echoed his shout, and the Ever-
Victorious Army plunged after him, a motley collection
of Americans, Frenchmen, Germans, Chinese, even a
few British. As the guns fell silent, Gordon's men
poured out of the trenches and through the breach as
musket balls flew all about them, from the long-haired
Taiping defenders on top of the wall. Men fell on each
side of him, and Gordon yearned for a musket ball to
strike him, but none did. Leading the charge with no

weapon but his rattan cane, Gordon leaped up on the heap of rubble, his army behind him . . .

And stopped, galvanized, staring into the muzzle of a 32-pounder cannon.

Time seemed to stop for him; he braced himself, and a gush of relief shot loose within him, for the death he had longed for had certainly come . . .

"We cannot have that!" Wayland the Smith reached out an unseen hand to the firing mechanism. "This son of our kind has much to do for us yet!"

The Taiping pulled the chain, the hammer fell— and the flint broke.

Gordon stood galvanized, the moan of fear behind him transforming into a shout of victory as his men poured through on either side of him and pounced on the gun-crew, bearing them down. Behind them, the rest of his little army streamed through the breach.

Gordon stood like a rock around which the flow parted, going limp inside—with disappointment. He would not be relieved of the burden of life after all.

He disbanded the Ever-Victorious Army soon after; none of them watched the armies of Tseng Kuo-Fan slaughter the tottering, starving remnants of the great Taiping army.

As the English newspapers told it, though, Gordon was not only there—he also defeated the Taipings almost single-handed.

Hung Hsiu-Chuan swallowed wine mixed with gold leaf, and died—but Gordon did not.

"We have our hero made," said Tyr, "and England has followed him in their hearts. The Taipings are no longer."

Odin nodded. "It is well done."

In the distance, Shang-Ti lay limp and exhausted in

his great golden throne—but his subordinate deities were gathering around him again.

The mad heathen nightmare was ended; the eerie slide of sing-song speech still echoed in his head, the flames of burning villages still glared in his mind's eye; so Gordon walked by the sea at Gravesend, where the Army had sent him to build new forts that he knew very well would do nothing to protect London if a sea-borne invader approached. He had told the War office of this, too, but they had ignored his advice, as his superiors always seemed to, so he was going ahead and doing his duty, and trying to get it done with as quickly as possible; but a few days into the new task, the news had come that his father had died.

So he walked by the sea.

In anxiety and depression, he walked through night, even though the sun was shining, looking about him for distraction, for insight. Gordon felt the old terror still lying there, knew it, and disregarded it; already he was restless, yearned for more work . . .

And there he was, the one-handed man, bent over the simple cookfire, and the spitted haunch that revolved over it.

How like to Father he seemed!

Gordon stepped up by the ring of stones, looking down at the furs, at the shoulder-length hair, the bronze circlet that held it—for surely, yes, it must be bronze, and Gordon had begun to suspect who the old man must be, though he could not admit it, admit any such superstition, not he, who was so devoted to God.

But the grizzled head lifted, the clear gaze pierced to his brain, while Gordon realized, amazed, that he did not look so old now, no, not nearly so old as he had ten years before. The old face held itself immobile, but under the long moustaches, the mouth moved and said,

"Welcome home, Chinese Gordon."

"Do not mock me so!" Gordon cried. "You know it was not glory that I sought!"

"I know," the one-handed man agreed, "but your people do not. They need heroes, Gordon. You must serve them in this."

"I must serve none but God! I have no wish to be lionized. You know what I support!"

"Yes—death. Are you so hungry for it, then, with your father so recently gone to it?"

"More than ever!" How could the old man know so much about him? "If he has gone, why should I remain behind?"

"For glory," the old man said simply, "if not for yourself, then for your God."

Gordon met his gaze levelly. "Will He release me from the burdens of this life, then?"

"I have told you that you shall find death in the East," the old man reminded him. "I did not say you would find it soon."

"But how am I . . . !" Gordon bit off the cry of distress, unwilling to show any weakness.

"How can you walk, without your father's hand to uphold you?" The old man's gaze never wavered. "Lean upon your God."

A huge peace flooded Gordon's soul, a well of strength brimmed within him. He stared at the old man, realizing how true his words were, how completely right. "Thank you."

"It is as it should be. Do you still wish death?"

The yearning blazed forth with an intensity that was almost frightening. "Yes!"

"If you are so hot for it, then, kill yourself!" It was challenge, a dare.

Gordon stood rigid, anger in his eyes. "I cannot. Suicide is a sin; I would lose Heaven, I would go to Hell. I must be killed by another, and be killed in a worthy cause, giving my life for the welfare of others, even as Our Lord gave his for us!"

"Then continue the hunt."

Gordon's heart leaped. "There is quarry again?"

"Not for England." The one-handed man glanced down at the empty fire-ring. "But for you . . . ?" He looked up again. "You will always find a way to a war. If there is none, you will make it."

And, gaze unwavering, he faded from sight.

Gordon stood frozen, staring at the cold ashes of the fire, feeling the chill again, but not the thrill.

Then, slowly, he turned away to the sea, numb to the heart, realizing that his soul must have needed a great deal more healing . . .

And sorely disappointed that the hunt was done.

He saw the one-handed man again, fifteen years later, as he walked by the sea, newly returned from Egypt, where he had done such excellent work for the Khedive—excellent, but so well done that he had stirred up his own small war against the slave-traders who toiled their heart-sick goods across the wastes of the Sudean. But though he had found war, he had found few willing to fight him . . .

And he had not found death.

He walked by the water, a man in his middle years, but still hale and hearty with the iron regimen he forced upon himself—careful diet, punishing exercises. He looked up toward the rising land, and noticed a man bent over a fire. With a shock, he recognized the skins, the bronze circlet. Surely this could not be the same man, though, for he no longer seemed old, no older than Gordon himself . . .

But the head lifted, the piercing-eyed gaze stabbed into him, and Gordon saw it was the same man.

"Dine with me, Gordon."

Slowly, Gordon sat by the fire. He wrinkled his nose at the smell of the meat; he knew it too well, now: goat. "What of the hunt?"

"There will be good hunting indeed. Would you be the hunter, or the quarry?"

Gordon felt excitement surge, and an echo of the

old familiar terror—but only an echo, now, and his ancient greed was stronger than ever, almost desperate. "The hunter, by choice," he said slowly.

"Do you truly care?"

"Nay." Gordon almost smiled, discovering with surprise and delight that it was true. "So that it be for the Lord, I wish only the hunt."

"Then you shall have it. The lion stands at bay." The one-handed man rose, and turned away.

Gordon did not watch him go. Slowly, he took the spit from the fire.

"Egyptians?" Sutekh spat. "These weaklings are nothing compared to the Egyptians of old! The Ansar who follow this Mahdi, now—they are worthy successors to the ancients who worshipped me as their war-god! There is so little left of their blood left, in these Turkish and Arab creatures to the north, that I have no love for them. But the Mahdi is their successor in heart, at least—worthy to follow the Pharaohs of the First Dynasty! He shall hurl your pale Northern worms out of the Nile Valley; he shall grind them to paste!"

Tyr stood alone against Sutekh, and laughed. His good hand twitched, but Sutekh did not strike—yet.

Gordon saw the one-handed man for the last time, as he stood on the steps at Khartoum, watching the horses and camels boil up out of the desert, their riders screaming and brandishing their swords.

"The Khedive told you only to withdraw the troops, Gordon."

Gordon looked up in surprise, quickly masked. "Can you walk outside England, then?"

"It is rare that I have any wish to. You should have withdrawn the troops."

Gordon said evenly, "England should never retreat."

"Death is your wish, Gordon, not theirs."

Gordon's gaze faltered. "I know. I should have sent them away, should have stood here alone—but I was sure England would send an army to bear me home, in spite of Gladstone and his Liberals!"

"Even as you said—the people forced his hand," the one-handed man corroborated. "The people, and the newspapers. The army comes—but its vanguard will not arrive for two more days."

Gordon bowed his head. "My soul is heavy with their deaths."

"But light, with your own?"

"England must never retreat!"

"Then England will be hacked to bits."

Gordon gave the one-eyed man a long, level gaze, amazed to realize that the stare of those eyes no longer stabbed into him. "That is acceptable. Bloodied, but indomitable."

The one-handed man held his gaze, and nodded. "The Lion does not retreat where he has made his den. But what good can he do if he is slain? What good is your death?"

"As good as my life," Gordon retorted. "If I am slain, England must send an army to rescue my bones."

"It is even as you have said, Gordon of Khartoum," the one-handed man said, his eye gleaming with pride. "They shall come; in fourteen years, they shall avenge you. So much for England. What shall you achieve for Gordon?"

"Gordon matters not at all."

"Gordon shall find death," he one-handed man corrected. "Yet you have had glory, whether you wished it or not. In glory you have lived, and in glory you shall die."

Gordon did, as the Ansar swooped down upon him. The tribesmen came screaming into the garden, but checked at the sight of the tall, relaxed Englishman, one hand on his saber, the other on his revolver. The battle-lust reasserted itself; the tribesmen screamed, forgetting the Mahdi's orders that Gordon was not to be harmed, and the spear struck into his chest, spinning him around. Even as he fell, more spears found his body. Then a tribesman stepped up, and his sword swung down.

The Mahdi cried out in anguish when they showed him Gordon's head.

"The children of my heart have triumphed!" Sutekh exulted. "Begone, One-Hand—you have no place here!"

"Even so," Tyr said, as imperturbable as ever. "I go—but I shall come again."

And he did.

OLD GODS
AND NEW

"Is that the type of follower I must have?" Tek seemed genuinely shocked.

Mentor smiled slightly, almost seeming to enjoy the godling's discomfort. After a pause that was several seconds longer than needed, he nodded.

"No!" Tek protested. "That is not how a war should be fought. Once perhaps, but no more!"

Again Mentor nodded. Then he spoke slowly, choosing his words carefully. "You are young. We all were once. There is much you do not yet understand. Chinese Gordon was hero of another war god."

Tek stood, uncertain as to how to reply. He knew there were other gods, that he could sense, but virtually nothing about them. Finally the war god spoke.

"Tell me of the other gods." His voice was mild, but edged with urgency.

"Which ones?" Mentor asked. "There are thousands. Men have worshiped trees, or rainbows, or gods so dark I shudder to call their name." The teacher sighed. "I suppose you mean the young gods, the ones who rule today?"

"No," Tek corrected. "I know how to be new. Show me a tale of an old god. One that shows me what the other war gods are like."

MORRIGAN

by Morris G. McGee

Being a goddess isn't what it used to be; being a goddess in the Twentieth Century is almost sad; and being a goddess in Ireland has little future. Oh, I know there are a few who follow my ways: the I.R.A. who bombed the protestant church in Armagh in May 1994 murdering all within and the Orange Lodge who planted mines on the road to the Catholic shrine in August of the same year and killed 45 children. It is not like the old days in Europe when Celts worshipped me as the Badb, as Neman, as Macha, as Morrigan. As Morrigan I was the most awful and bloody of the immortals. I am rage, battle fury, and death.

Things were different in the spring of 1014. I had many servants. The best was Sihtric Silkbeard, the King of Dublin. He was cruel, dishonest, sensual, and vain: everything I liked in a king. I put myself in his body . . .

The King of Dublin stared into his silvered mirror from Byzantium. The face he saw was plump, the lips narrow and hard, his eyes pale blue and his long hair and beard yellow and soft as fine silk—hence his name: Sihtric Silkbeard. Sihtric wore soft silk robes that came via the Viking City of Kiev from the silk roads far to the unknown East. Sihtric liked the feel of silk—it reminded him of the skin of his favorite concubine: soft and comfortable against his skin. "More wine," he ordered. "Where is my spy?"

"Here, King," said a small man near the door, "I just returned from the High King."

"Since I am a Scald I was entertained by the Bard of the High King at Cashel. I was well fed and given gold rings by the High King, himself." The small man pulled himself up proudly, "The High King liked my stories, he speaks our tongue as well as a Dublin man."

"My dear stepfather," the King sneered, "what does the old man have on his mind?"

"Complete submission of all the Irish Sub-Kings and complete submission of all the Kings of the Viking cities."

"What makes Brian Boru think he can accomplish this thing?"

"Men and gold, King, men and gold."

Sihtric nodded, "I know, that is why my ships have gone to Norway, Daneland, The Orkneys, The Hebrides, to Man, and even to Iceland. I have invited warriors to join in smashing the High King of Ireland. The plunder will attract them like flies to dung."

"You forget, King," interrupted Swen Thorson, Dublin Keeper of the Treasury, "You swore fealty to the High King and married his granddaughter."

"I know," said the King, "but all changes if we defeat Brian Boru in battle. He is an old man, at least eighty-five or more. His sons and grandsons will have to lead and they are not the war leaders that the old man is." He fingered the gold cross that hung from his neck; the cross, when reversed, was a perfect Hammer of Thor—Sihtric didn't take chances.

I had heard enough. I journeyed West looking for the High King. I did not find him there. He was camped in his great tent near the River Boyne at Tara of the Kings. I moved into his thoughts.

"Are we ready, son Murchad? Can we cross the river to Dublin, breach the walls and take Dublin?" The High King, Brian Boru, sat on a soft pile of deer hides watching his oldest surviving son. He was wrinkled, his face bearded and mustashed in white, his tall, thin body was wiry and strong in spite of his great age. His right hand rested on his great two handed sword. He was dressed in warm wool robes that were dyed a bright red, bordered in red leather on the sleeves and the bottom hem.

Murchad, a heavy-set man with flowing red beard and hair flecked with grey nodded at once. "We should move as soon as we can, before Dublin is reinforced. We captured a few of the Dublin men trying to sow discord among your people." Murchad wore two great swords, swords bigger than any carried by other Irish and bigger by half than Viking swords. In battle he used both, one in each hand.

Murchad wore fine linked chain mail over a light brown wool tunic with an under coat of soft linen. One of his War-Band carried his mail sleeves and his mail leggings.

"So be it," said the High King, "Send the call to all in Ireland to meet us the Monday before Easter ten miles North of Dublin."

Now I knew when the battle would take place, so I moved on to the Orkneys. At Kirkwall I found Sigurd, Jarl of Orkney. I listened with him as he heard the message from Dublin.

". . . and there will great riches for all who aid in the downfall of the High King."

Sigurd Dirgi—the Stout—sat silently for a few moments, stroking his curly brown beard, his blue eyes darting around the room at his eager men. "We shall go a-Viking into Ireland. What say you?"

The men roared their approval. Sigurd thought to himself 'why not the Jarl of Orkney as High King? Why not rule the Irish? It would be a splendid gift for my son Thorfinn when I die. Thorfinn? He is too young, I'll foster him with the King of Scots—he owes me that much—I married King Malcolm's daughter. I go to Dublin and return with all of Ireland.'

Good! He was greedy. I moved on to the Isle of Man where Sigurd the Stout was overlord and heard the same message delivered to Brodar the Dane who ruled for Sigurd of Orkney.

". . . you will share in the riches of Ireland with your Lord Sigurd and enjoy a fine fight."

This last moved Brodar, a warrior skilled in the sword, the axe, and the spear. He was tall, over six feet, broad of chest, with long muscular arms hardened by years of training and fighting. Riches and lands where he could be Chief Lord filled his mind along with thoughts of blood and killing.

Brodar may have been a Viking but his mother must have been Irish for he thought like one of my own. I followed messengers to Norway, to Iceland, and to the Hebrides. All were coming to Dublin: Snorri the Priest from Iceland—a Christian priest and a priest of Odin, Sigurd from Orkney, Brodar from Man, and Vikings from Norway, Daneland, the Hebrides and troops from Leinster in Ireland.

The army of Brian Boru laid waste to all of Leinster, then at the end of March 1014 moved on Dublin. "They will meet us North of the River Liffey," said Brian, "We can be sure of that. We must keep watch on the beaches to the East for the Vikings will try to land troops from the sea."

Brian's old friend, the priest Maolsuthain, said the Mass and blessed all the warriors. In his homily he recalled the many victories of the High King and the blessings of peace that the High King brought to all Ireland.

In Dublin Sihtric greeted his allies in his great hall. There were Danes from Daneland and Jorvik in the north of England mixing with Icelanders, Orcaddians, Manxmen, and Vikings from the Hebrides. The last to arrive were Jarls from Norway.

"The High King is only a few miles North of the River Liffey. Our army will cross and meet him on the fields of Clontarf. Our horsemen will be able to harry his flank to the West and our men from the Long Ships will surprise him from the sea," Sihtric said with confidence. "We outnumber him two to one."

"What kind of warriors are these Irish?" Sigurd of Orkney wanted to know.

Swen Thorsen the Keeper of the Treasury answered, "They fight hard, but they are lightly armored. They are strong spearmen, they carry three or four long javelins which they throw from their horses at full gallop. They can kill at great distance."

"We have strong chain mail," grunted Brodar of Man, "We need not worry about spearmen from afar. How are they at hand to hand fighting?"

"When the battle fury comes on them, they are the finest in the world; but if they have a set back, they often run."

I listened a while then moved to the High King's camp. I listened inside the mind of Murchad, Brian's eldest.

He was standing next to his father, addressing his troop leaders, his brother Tagd and his brother Donnchad chief among them. Tagd was tall and wiry as his father. He dressed in chain mail over a surcoat of deer hide dyed bright blue-the same color as his eyes. Donnchad was built in the solid way of Murchad, only smaller. His chain mail was on a coat of sheepskins dyed yellow. All of Donnchad's men wore yellow cloaks so he could see where they stood in battle.

"I will lead the center battle; brother Tagd will lead on the right; and brother Donnchad and your son, Toirdelbach, will guard the left—the beaches and the sea. We will strike on the right and center, holding firm on the left. Agreed?"

There were nods of agreement, then the High King asked, "We fight on Good Friday?"

"Aye," said Murchad.

I screamed for joy. They would fight on the day when their god was weakest!

On the North side of Dublin Bay in the early dawn of Good Friday, 23 April, 1014, the forces prepared for battle. The Irish with some Viking allies who hated the King of Dubin moved into position. The Viking army moved slowly North from the banks of the Liffey and across the little River Tolka.

I prepared, too. I caused a drizzling rain, and I called up a high wind. The first to attack was Murchad and his spearmen. They rode full tilt toward the Viking line and hurled their sharp missles. I caught most in the wind and they were wasted. Murchad's flew straight and true. It came down at an angle through the armored chest of one of Sigurd of Orkney's followers. It went through him and into his horse behind him. The horse bolted toward the Irish lines, the man mewing like a tortured kitten. As he passed through the Irish lines, Murchad sliced off his head and the mewing stopped.

The Vikings were stunned for a moment. They roared defiance, then started forward at a slow trot. The horsemen in their mail coats of iron rings, studded with bronze and gold, seemed to glitter when a weak sun came out. The Vikings of Dublin, without their King, and the men of Leinster under Maelmore were in the center; the flanks were led by Sigurd of Orkney on the left and Brodar of Man on the right. In front of all were Vikings from Daneland and Norway. They moved faster toward the Irish.

Murchad had his Munstermen and the men of his tribe, Dal Cais, prepared. They struck together.

Above the battle I set up fearsome screaming, the sound of gigantic birds fighting above their heads. All heard hungry demons cry for blood. They saw terrible shapes moving toward them.

Then Murchad charged, both his swords flashing. He cut down Vikings on the left and right. His War-Band followed, killing dozens, some as they turned in fear to run. Only Sigurd of Orkney did not run; he waited for Murchad; he taunted the Irish prince. Murchad rushed at Sigurd, swung his right hand sword and cut through Sigurd's neck armor and helmet straps. Before Sigurd could move, the left hand sword sheared cleanly through Sigurd's exposed neck. The headless body swung the sword once then fell with great gouts of blood staining the grass.

Murchad moved on still in battle fury. His horse was lathered and winded as he drove on a Warlord from Dublin. The man swung his battle-axe at the horse's chest, cutting deeply. The horse stopped in his tracks and threw Murchad forward over his neck. Murchad landed on the Dubliner and they wrestled for position. Murchad grabbed the bottom of his enemy's coat of mail, pulled it over his head and attacked with his dagger. Murchad had his man weakening with repeated dagger blows to the back. With his last breath, the Dublin man drew a knife from his boot, plunged it into Murchad's groin, pulled it up until he hit Murchad's breastbone, then he died.

Murchad stood up slowly, holding in his guts with both hands. "I do not think I will ever be High King of Ireland," he said as he died.

The Irish Bards and the Viking Sagas sang of the great fight and the feats of princes and Jarls, but they did not tell all. The Irish were finished and the Northmen were also finished.

Murchad's War-Band wrapped his body in cloaks and placed it on a horse and sent it back to his father, the High King. They extracted revenge from all who faced them, pushing them into the River Tolka. The river ran red with blood. They drove the Vikings and the Leinstermen back to the River Liffey where boats helped some escape to the safety of the walls of Dublin.

Donnchad and his son, Toirdelbach, were waiting when the Viking longships scraped ashore. Through the young man's eyes I watched as the Vikings fell into the trap, pinned against the shore.

"We have them," the young man screamed, "Kill them before they escape!" He threw his javelins at the disembarking Vikings. One caught an Icelander full in the face, under his nose and out the back of his head. "Faster," screamed Toirdelbach, waving his arm over his head. Three arrows entered his exposed armpit, puncturing his lungs. He tried to speak, but a stream of blood choked off all sound. He died in silence.

Donnchad looked at his son in sorrow then led his men to the shore where they killed all the Vikings who still lived.

On the Irish right Tadg, the High King's second son, felt the enemy weakening. Above his forces I screamed and the Vikings from Daneland and Iceland wavered.

Tagd shouted, "At them, now!" The Irish pushed them toward the fords on the River Tolka, slaying scores when they were hip deep in the water. Now it was a foot race. One exhausted Icelander, Snorri the Priest, stopped and waited. "Why do you not run?" Tagd asked.

"I am from Iceland and I cannot run that far by nightfall."

Tagd struck him with the flat of his sword, "Live Icelander and go home." Snorri the Priest was one of the few spared. The rest were driven to the Liffey and rescued by the boats from Dublin.

Tagd stopped his men on the river bank. "We have

won a great victory. Send word to Murchad and the High King," he ordered.

One who survived, Swen Thorsen, wet and bleeding climbed the steps inside the North wall where Sihtric watched the battle in safety. "You lost, King Sihtric. The High King's men have the field." Swen pulled off his bloodied mail and sat with his back to the wall. "It is only a matter of time until the walls will be breached by the High King's men. What will you do, King?"

"I will wait."

"We have lost men—six or seven thousand," Swen said sadly. I know Sigurd of Orkney is dead. The Leinstermen are all but destroyed. What are you going to do?"

"I will wait," said King Sihtric.

Out of the field Brodar of Man fought on the right. He charged the troops under Donnchad, cutting through with the loss of all. He was riding alone, circling back South when he caught sight of a great tent.

Brian Boru knelt by the body of his eldest son, Murchad. "Why did you die and I live?" The old man wept and prayed for the soul of his son. He stood as Murchad's men told of the battle feats. They handed him Murchad's great swords. At that moment, they heard a fierce battle-cry from the North. They turned to see Brodar at full gallop, closing on the High King.

Brian Boru acted as the great warrior he was. He swung his son's sword at his attacker, cutting his right leg off at the knee. Brodar screamed in anger and in pain.

Brodar staggered in his saddle but held on. He spun his horse and with his battle axe cut at the High King. The axe cut deep into Brian Boru's skull, killing him instantly.

Ten swords finished Brodar, too late.

A heavy rain came out of the dark afternoon sky soaking the field of Clontarf and the dead.

I laughed and laughed and laughed. I had won

*again. Ireland would be at war forever. The High King
and his son and grandson would be buried at the stone
church in Armagh. The Irish kings would fight one
another for over a century. Then one would invite
Normans from England, Normans who would become
English, giving gifts like Strongbow and Cromwell,
gifts as bloody offerings to me, gifts like Drogheda.*

*King Sihtric Silkbeard? He ruled for over twenty
years, then became a monk of the holy isle of Iona
where the kings of Scots are buried. Sihtric finally died
praying for his worthless soul. I laughed for years.*

SACRIFICE

The image froze on the intertwined bodies of Brodar and the High King. Rather than disappearing, the giant screen television remained floating in front of Tek and Mentor.

Tek was not surprised that he was unaffected by the carnage. He was, after all, a war god. Casualties were simply part of the equation. He was rather amazed at how emotionally, even enthusiastically the humans slaughtered each other.

"Are all humans so bloodthirsty?" he asked.

"Sort of makes you wonder why they need a war god at all, doesn't it?" Mentor agreed while adjusting the color and contrast on the screen.

"It rather makes me wonder how any are left," Tek observed.

"Billions of 'em," Mentor assured. "Plenty for you to work with and lots left over to be slaughtered for the fun of it."

"Ancillary casualties," Tek corrected.

"Whatever you call them," Mentor gestured and the television vanished. "Charlemagne always looked forward to reaping among the other side's peasant levies."

"And yet the peasant came the next time? Still willing to fight?" Tek wondered.

"By the thousands," Mentor assured him.

It was then that Tek realized how little he understood the people he was a god for. It took him a moment to phrase his question, but Mentor waited patiently. Somehow that bothered Tek, who still had a nagging sense of urgency. Finally he knew what he needed.

"Can you show me something that will explain why people are willing to die?" Being unable to actually die, even after sharing the experience with the coyote, Tek found the entire concept alien.

"I have just the thing," Mentor agreed smiling. "A tale written by a modern author that is based upon a story told back when the old gods' place was being usurped."

The figure floated before Tek, then turned to the screen he had conjured. A human appeared on it, a young woman with short, blonde hair. She was typing on a small computer and even though he instinctively knew all about the complicated device, Tek admired its utility.

As they watched, the woman opened an old book and, occasionally glancing at it, began to write.

SIR JAMES THE ROSE

by Katherine Kurtz

1

Fairytales, as part of the folklore of our human race, tend to be an interesting mixture of allegory, historicity, and unabashed imagination. Elements of all three ingredients lie at the root of most fairytales—though historical details tend to slip and transmute in the telling, as stories are handed down, and a good storyteller rarely will let faces get in the way of a good story.

Folksongs tend to have the same kinds of origins as fairytales, though historical details often will lie closer to the surface because of the very way songs evolve, usually in response to topical events or at least a prevailing emotional climate. However, because folk-songs are primarily an oral tradition, and were almost exclusively so until Francis James Child and others began collecting and writing them down in the last century, they may be even more subject to slippage when it comes to nailing down factual backgrounds. In both fairytales and folksongs, however, if we look beyond the surface story, we are apt to find that far more questions are raised then answered.

Such is the case in the Ballad of Sir James the Rose (Child No. 213), sometimes subtitled "The Buchanshire Tragedy." The possible story behind the story has haunted me since the first time I heard the version sung by Steeleye Span, probably fifteen years ago. Other versions provide a few more details, but like most old ballads, James the Rose has gone through many incarnations over the centuries, mutating and incorporating material from many sources.

For our purposes, however, the crux of the storyline is that Sir James the Rose, the young heir of Loch Laggan, has killed "a gallant squire" and is on the run. Furthermore, "four and twenty belted knights" have been sent out to take him. Pretty important squire, to justify sending out a posse of that size. Just who was this squire, anyway?

Then there is the "nurse" at the House of Marr who, James believes, is his friend and will hide him—which she does, only to betray him to his pursuers just a few verses later. Why? Some versions have her as his leman—which, if he had been unfaithful or otherwise betrayed her, might offer a motive for her action—but in the versions where her reaction to the outcome is given, even she doesn't know why she did it—or doesn't say, at least.

Which leads us to some interesting speculations on what *really* may have been going on in this ballad.

11

Sir James the Rose

(or "The Buchanshire Tragedy")
Child No. 213

Traditional words by Michael Bruce,
d. 1767

Oh, have you heard, Sir James the Rose,
The young heir of Loch Laggan,
That he has killed a gallant squire,
And his friends are out to take him.

And he's gone to the House of Marr—
The nurse there did befriend him—
And he has gone upon his knee
And begged for her to hide him.

"Where are you doing, Sir James?" she said.
"Where now are you riding?"
"Oh, I am bound to a foreign land.
For now I'm under hiding."

Refrain: "Where shall I go? Where shall I run?
        "Where shall I go, for to hide me?
        For I have killed a gallant squire.
        And they're seeking for to slay me!"

Then he's turned him right and round about
And rolled him in the brechan,
And he has gone to take a sleep
In the lowlands of Loch Laggan.

He had not well gone out of sight,
Nor was he past Milstrethen,
When four and twenty belted knights
Came riding o'er the Leathen.

"Have you seen Sir James the Rose,
The young heir of Loch Laggan?
For he has killed a gallant squire,
And we're sent out to take him."

Refrain:

"You'll seek the bank above the mill
In the lowlands of Loch Laggan,
And there you'll find Sir James the Rose,
Sleeping in his brechan.

"You must not wake him out of sleep,
Nor yet must you affright him.
Just run a dart right through his heart
And through the body pierce him."

They sought the bank above the mill,
In the lowlands of Loch Laggan,
And there they found Sir James the Rose,
Sleeping in his brechan.

Refrain:

Then on spake Sir John the Graeme,
Who had the charge a keeping.
It'll never be said, dear gentlemen,
We killed him while he's sleeping.

They seized his broadsword and his targe
And closely him surrounded.

And when he woke out of his sleep,
His senses were confounded.

Now, they have taken out his heart
And stuck it on a spear.
They took it to the House of Marr
And gave it to his dear.

Refrain:

III

The pony could not go much farther. James knew
that. The shaggy little garrons of the western Highlands were hardy and sure-footed, but even they had
their limits. This one, his second mount since the pre-
vious noon, had carried him bravely all through the
night, but now, as it picked its way torturously down
the bracken-feathered hillside, it, too, was staggering
with exhaustion, its chestnut coat streaked with lather
even in the cool, pre-dawn stillness.

Not for the first time, the animal missed its footing
on the rocky track and nearly went down, flinging the
young heir of Loch Laggan heavily against the high
pommel of his saddle. He snatched at a handful of
mane and somehow managed to keep his seat, but the
stumble slammed his targe against the back of his
head hard enough to make him gasp. He choked back
a moan as he shrugged the targe back into place and
rubbed at the spot where it had hit, straightening up
only painfully. The weight of a basket-hilted broadsword dragged at his right shoulder, but shifting its
leather baldric did little to ease the ache.

He dared not stop, though. Not yet. He thought he
had gained a little on his pursuers, by skirting Loch
Laggan and heading east toward the Vale of Marr after
dark, but the summer nights were short, and darkness

would not cloak him much longer. Once the sun rose above the purpled hills, anything moving across the heather and bracken would be all too easily spotted. He must find a hiding place, and soon, to wait out the daylight and regain his strength, or he would lose whatever advantage he had gained by his panicked, pell-mell flight. They would find him and they would kill him.

Not for the first time he regretted his hot temper and unruly tongue. He certainly had not been looking for trouble when he left his father's house—had it only been yesterday?—but he most assuredly had found it. He had not even intended to ride in the August heat, else stout trews and leather jerkin and sturdy, knee-high boots would have replaced the simple deerskin gillies and the brechan kilted over his shirt of fine linen. His inner knees were chaffed raw from the unexpected hours barelegged in the saddle, his legs scratched and bloodied from riding through the gorse, and his ankles ached from rattling against unrelenting stirrup steel.

Thank God he had not gone out totally unprotected. No son of a noble house would have thought of venturing out of doors without a dirk and broadsword at his side, even to a simple market, but God alone knew what had prompted James to sling a targe across his back as well. It had saved him, when his ill-considered remark about a village lass elicited what had seemed to him a totally unprovoked attack from one of the squires of Clan Graeme. Whether it could save him again remained an open question. He was under no illusion that he could dodge his Graeme pursuers indefinitely.

The pony stumbled again, nearly going to its knees, and when they had both recovered James reluctantly reined in to let the animal blow while he scanned the horizon. Against the eastern sky ahead, awash with ever more alarming stains of salmon and gold, the bleak outline of heather-covered hills offered little

prospect of shelter for a fugitive. Mountains blocked
the way north, wreathed in mist as the early sun began
to warm the dew. To the south, however, just visible
against the brightening horizon, the jagged, crow-
stepped roof line of a fortified tower house jutted
unexpectedly into the dawn.

James knuckled at his eyes and looked again in dis-
belief, then immediately kneed his tired mount in that
direction without further regard for caution. He had
not thought he was heading so far south, but the mass
of pinkish sandstone starting to glow in the rosy dawn
was unmistakable—and perhaps a refuge, if news of
his folly had not yet reached here, which he thought
not. Six years James had spent as a fosterling at the
House of Marr, serving as page to the lady of the
house and beginning his martial training with the laird
and his levies.

But it was not the Laird and Lady of Marr who
would be James' salvation today, if indeed salvation
was to be his. Lady Marr had cared for him as she
did all her fosterlings, but it was her brother's widow,
the Lady Mathilda, who had taken an immediate fancy
to the young heir of Loch Laggan and brought him
up like her own son—and more than son.

But he must not think about that now. Whatever
ties remained between James and the Lady Mathilda
de Bohun, they would count as naught if she refused
to help him. His pursuers could not be far behind.
He must find a place to hide until the night returned.
He was almost giddy from exhaustion and lack of
sleep.

The promised heat of the day was already in the
air, close and still, as he urged the pony down the
narrow track that served as road. He slicked back his
tangled hair behind his ears and tried to make himself
more presentable as the animal picked its way past
the outlying steadings and neared the village nestled
around the castle's barmkin wall. Ahead, the castle's
gates were swinging open for the day—all normal, so

far as he could tell, but procedures could have changed since his last visit. He could feel the hackles rising on the back of his neck as he rode closer, and he scrubbed a torn and none too clean sleeve across his face in a nervous gesture. The tantalizing aroma of new-baked bread wafted above the more earthy smells of hay and manure, reminding him of his hunger, but he put it out of mind to watch the men manning the gatehouse, alert for any sign that he was expected.

But apparently no word of his transgression had yet reached the House of Marr. Nor did his disheveled appearance seem to elicit any alarm or suspicion—or perhaps the guards remembered him from happier days. No sooner had he passed under the gatehouse and into the forecourt than a boy in shirt and brechan very like his own came running from the stable block to take his pony, offering neither question nor comment as James swung down with a groan of relief, though his appraisal of the pony's condition clearly bespoke disapproval.

"If'n ye want sommat tae eat, ye'll have tae wait 'til after prayers," the boy said neutrally. "An' th' Laird's awa."

"I didna come to see the Laird," James murmured, twitching his baldric and targe into place and scanning the yard for the one he *had* come to see.

Across the yard, hard against the barmkin wall, the door of the little chapel had opened to frame a brown-robed monk who began ringing a hand bell. The other denizens of the castle already were heading in that direction, and James instinctively joined them, skirting the stables and the kitchen lean-to and melting into the shadow of a slype passage until the figure he sought appeared in the doorway of the keep, shepherding a dozen young girls and boys down the wooden forestair that led to ground level, shooing her charges in the general direction of the chapel and following decorously behind. When the children had passed abreast of him, James' hand shot out of the shadows to grasp her wrist and draw her to him, his free hand lifting one finger to his lips to beg her silence.

"Jamie!" she murmured, her expression shifting from alarm through joy to puzzled concern. "Jamie, *mo chridh*, what is't?"

Trembling, James drew her farther into the shadow, out of sight and hearing of the last stragglers filing into the little chapel, pressing his lips to her palm as he sank to one knee before her. Despite the fact that she had been nurse at the House of Marr when first he came there, she had not been that much older than he. Perhaps she was all of thirty now, though her widow's coif hid the glorious red hair and made her look older. A little sob escaped his lips as she bent to kiss him gently on the top of his head, and he cradled her hand against his cheek, not wanting to meet her eyes.

"Och, Jamie, Jamie, what's amiss?" she murmured, gently smoothing his dishevled hair. "Where are ye ridin' at sich an early hour? Compose yerself, my jo. It canna be as bad as all o' that."

"Aye, it *can*," he whispered. "Ye must hide me, my lady. I have killed a man, an' they're seekin' for to slay me!"

"Ye killed a man? Who? Why? How?"

James shook his head. "I dinna know his name. He was wi' some Graemes, but—"

"Was *he* a Graeme?" she interjected.

"I canna say. I dinna think so. Some squire, is all. I—said sommat I oughtn't, about a lass. He came at me wi' a blade. The next thing I knew, he was dead, his blood on my dirk, an' his friends were tryin' to take me prisoner." He dared to steal a glance at her. "But I didna mean to kill him, I swear it! It was an accident. Will ye hide me, my lady? Come night, I'll be off again, to some foreign land, but now I'm after hidin'."

Obviously moved, she bit distractedly at her lip and considered, gently clucking her tongue as he suddenly rose, still holding her hands and staring down at her in silent entreaty.

"Och, Jamie, Jamie, daurlin. What's to be done? Ye swear it was an accident?"

"By'r Lady, I do!" he answered fervently.

She sighed, then seemed to gather her resolution. "Weel, the laird's awa, thanks be, but I still canna hide ye here. Sanctuary's what ye need, but nae here." She cocked her head. "Aye, there might be a way. D'ye ken the bank above the mill, where the stones stand in the field beyond?"

"Aye."

"Then, haste ye there. The summer heather's high an' fine, an' will hide ye for a while. Roll up in yer brechan and take a sleep, while I think what to do. 'Tis safe enough, the Lady's bower. Surely ye canna have forgot *that,* silly lad!"

He grinned at her despite his nervousness, well remembering a warm spring night, not so very long ago, when a callow, inexperienced boy of fifteen, who looked a lot like himself, had gone by ancient custom to stand on that very mound at the full of the moon, there to offer up his young manhood to the gods. Spreading his brechan beneath the starry canopy of night, he had given salute to the moon in blood-red wine, spilling some on the ground from a little wooden quaich before draining it to the dregs and lying back to wait. He had expected some kind of oracular dream, perhaps even an erotic one. He had *not* expected that the Goddess Herself would come to him, mantled in moonlight and a fall of glorious red hair that veiled her almost to her knees. . . .

"Jamie, lad, are ye payin' attention?" Mathilda said softly. "I'll have no arguments from ye now. Go an' rest. I'll do what's needful, if they should come."

*   *   *

Come they did, hardly half an hour later: four and twenty belted knights riding o'er the Leathen two by two on tall, blooded horses, all brisk and impressive in their trews and leather jerkins and the muted green and blue plaids of clan Graeme. Basket-hilted broadswords gleamed at every side, and most of them carried spears as well. Mathilda watched their approach from a window in the laird's solar, hoping against hope that they would bypass Marr and keep on riding, but they clattered through the village and up to the castle gates without hesitation, though only a handful actually entered the yard. When she spotted the bright red hair of her brother John among the blue bonnets sprigged with laurel splurge, she knew there was nothing for it but to go down.

"Have ye seen Sir James the Rose, the young heir of Loch Laggan?" one of the older knights was asking the steward and the yard in general, as Mathilda stepped cautiously into the doorway at the top of the forestair and paused to watch and listen.

The steward flicked just a ghost of a glance up at her, his seamed face expressionless, then folded his arms across his chest and looked the knight up and down. "Th' Laird an' Leddy are nae at hame. Who wants tae know?" he said.

"Sir John Graeme, Summoner of the Clan Graeme," said the man whose presence had drawn Mathilda to the stair. His red hair gleamed in the early morning sun as he kneed his horse past the steward to pause below the stairs and gaze up at his sister. "He's killed a squire, Mathilda, and we're sent out to take him."

Stiff and defiant, Mathilda moved out onto the landing. "Four and twenty knights to take one poor, frightened boy? Why, he's hardly more than a squire himself."

Graeme eyed her shrewdly. "Aye, that may be, but the man he killed was hardly any ordinary squire. Is he here?"

Something in his expression suddenly suggested just *who* the squire might have been, and the realization sent Mathilda hurrying down. Her brother had dismounted as she came, and was waiting for her at the bottom, bonnet in hand. Taking his arm, she led him into the little chapel, instinctively drawing him to the Lady's shrine, over against the north wall. This early, so soon after morning prayers, the chapel was deserted, but it already was far too warm for comfort. Not a breath of air stirred, even the candle flames standing still and unflickering in the altar lamp and before the wooden effigy of Madonna and Child.

"It was Angus, wasn't it?" Mathilda managed to whisper, fixing her gaze on the feet of the carved Lady, standing between the horns of a crescent moon. "Not just *a* squire. It had to be the *carline*."

When he did not answer, she bowed her head, pressing her clasped hands briefly to her lips in silent prayer that somehow it was all some terrible mistake.

"He said it was an accident—that they'd quarreled over some stupid remark he made about a village girl. It wasn't anything to get *killed* over."

"No."

His one word unleashed all her growing despair. Chilled despite the closeness of the room, and blinking back unbidden tears, she lifted her unseeing gaze to the halo of stars above the head of the wooden Madonna, still unable to look at him.

"Must he die, then?" she whispered.

He sighed and glanced at the tiled floor, at the toes of his dusty boots, at the spurs gleaming on his heels, wrists resting on the basket hilt of his broadsword while his gloved hands toyed with his bonnet.

"If it were only the retribution for murder," he said slowly, "I might be persuaded to turn a blind eye for the sake of my little sister—say he'd eluded us, fled to England. It *wasn't* intentional, after all, and I know what the boy means to you. But the gods demand their compensation as well. Your Jamie has cheated them out of their own. He's the only one who can repay that debt in valid coin."

She gave a bleak, despairing nod as he finished speaking, not yet able to look directly at him. "He trusts me," she whispered. "He went upon his knee and begged for me to hide him. He told me what he'd done. How can I betray him?"

"Unless you prefer to betray *them,* I'm afraid you have no choice," the Graeme said softly. "Where is he, Mathilda? Here in the house?"

She shook her head.

"Where, then?"

Raising her eyes to those of the wooden Madonna, Mathilda de Bohun, nee Graeme, crossed her arms on her breast and took a deep breath.

"You'll seek the bank above the mill. You'll find him there, sleeping in his brechan. I—told him it was sanctuary."

Graeme nodded. "Aye, it is that, I suppose. But sanctuaries *are* sanctuaries because of what happens there. Unfortunately, yon Jamie is about to learn far more about a sanctuary's principal function than any of us would have wished."

"Is there no other way?"

"I really wish there were, but—" He glanced at his boots again and sighed. "Look, Mathilda. He's a sensible lad, if you'd chosen him. I'll *try* to explain—"

"Try to explain why I've betrayed him?" she refused. "No! You mustn't frighten him, or even wake him. Just pierce him through the heart and be done with it!"

"I can't do that, lass. You know I can't. But I *will* try to make him understand why he must die. And I'll make it as quick as I can."

She would have argued with a lesser man, but she knew that in this case there was no appeal. At least at the hands of John Graeme, death would be quick. Under the circumstances, she could ask for no more than that. Nor could James. She let her brother give her the ritual kiss of peace, but she could not bear to watch him go. As his steel-shod footsteps retreated from the little chapel, she crumpled to her knees before the wooden Madonna, tears welling in her eyes so that the votive light at the statue's feet swam and shimmered in her sight. After a few seconds, she wiped at her eyes with one hand, then touched her tear-damp fingertips to the statue's bare feet in offering.

"Forgive me my tears, Mother," she whispered, recalling her role as priestess as well as lover to the one she mourned. "He is Yours, as I am, and You may take him when and how You will, but I wish—I wish he might have served You in other ways. Still, let him serve You well in *this*, if such must be. . . ."

Outside, the Graeme's men sat waiting quietly on their blooded horses, half a dozen in the castle yard and the rest outside the barmkin wall. Hugh, the knight who first had made inquiries about Sir James, had dismounted to hold Graeme's mount, and came to attention as Graeme emerged from the chapel doorway. Not looking at any of them, Graeme went to his horse and took a longish, cloth-wrapped bundle out of the near saddlebag, tucking it deep inside the folds of his shirt and brechan.

"We'll leave the horses here," he said briskly. "He's somewhere up on the bank above the mill. Fan out and move very quietly. We must take him alive."

Steel slithered from four and twenty scabbards as the Graeme and his knights started up the hill. They sought the bank above the mill in the lowlands of Loch Laggan, and there they found Sir James the Rose sleeping in his brechan. Hugh was the first to spot him, and silently deployed the men in a double ring of twelve. Slowly and cautiously he and Graeme closed the inner ring of knights until they were hardly a blade-length away from the deeply sleeping James. Their quarry lay with his head pillowed on his targe,

one arm bent across his forehead to shut out the sun
and the other outflung across his broadsword, oblivious to their presence. Carefully Graeme sheathed his
own sword before bending to slowly ease James'
weapon free of its scabbard, one boot ready to pin the
wrist if James should wake before the deed was done.
When he had strightened, he gathered his men's
attention with a glance and then set the blade to the
boy's unprotected breast. At his nodded signal, Sir
Hugh yanked the targe from under the sleeper's head.

James came awake with a start and only just avoided
impaling himself on the blade Graeme held, crying
out as Graeme's boot stayed his wrist from reaching
for a weapon that was no longer there.

"Hold, or you die *now!*" someone shouted.

James froze at the command, for at the same instant
the full import had registered of the glittering sword
ring surrounding him—and the identity of the man at
the other end of the sword pressed to his breast. With
sinking hopes and empty hands outflung, James fell
back on his brechan, still absurdly calculating his
chances.

"Steady, lad," the Graeme said impassively. "This
can be quick and painless or very unpleasant, indeed.
You killed the wrong man. You killed the *very* wrong
man."

Now, what did the Graeme mean by that? New
suspicion made James' throat go dry as dust as his
gaze darted anxiously from face to face, irrational justi-
fications flashing through his mind. How had they
found him? They knew what he had done, and now
they were going to kill him! But he was barely eighteen. Surely they could not *really* mean for him to
die!

"It was an accident, I swear it!" he managed to
croak. "I didna mean to kill him. I dinna even know
who he was."

"Shall I *tell* you who he was?" Graeme replied
softly. "His name was Angus Graeme, which makes

him kinsman of every other man here besides yourself. But more important than that, he was the *carline*, the intended Substitute for the *Ceann*'s next seven-year cycle. His time was not yet come, but you killed him: wrong time, wrong place, wrong way. Do you understand what that means?"

Starting to tremble now, James opened his mouth several times like a beached fish, suddenly understanding all too well.

"It means that you have a choice in how you die," Graeme went on relentlessly. "That you *will* die is a foregone conclusion, since you murdered a man. The blood debt is owed to Clan Graeme. Your life is forfeit.

"But you can redeem your deed, in part. Your life still is forfeit, but you can make it mean something." Graeme glanced up at the sky, at the sun climbing higher in a bright, clear morning, then looked back at James, shifting the point of the broadsword down to rest against the captive's breast.

"What's it to be, then, lad? Do we hang you, like the common murderer you are, or will you choose the nobler way, and pay your blood debt to us and to the gods with your own blood?"

Appalled, James closed his eyes and tried to think— *made* himself think about it slowly and carefully. He knew vaguely what Graeme was talking about, but he had never really thought much about it. Oh, there had been speculation around the hearthfires late at night with other young men who also did not know, especially during the long winters—something about a great sacrifice that marked the seven-years, somehow tied in with the potency of the chiefs and the prosperity of their clans.

He had never been witness to any of it, of course. That was reserved to the clan elders, a mystery only for the initiated. February and August seemed to be the favored months for speculation—Candlemas and Lammastide, when even the Church hailed the

Mother of God in her broader aspect as Queen of Heaven and paid homage to the Sun, the primal god-force behind the first fruits of the harvest, somehow separate and different from Father, Son, and Holy Ghost. Intellectually, James even knew that those were the times when the clan elders were said to make actual sacrifice to the old gods, ensuring the fertility of the land, the fecundity of the sheep and cattle and horses, the potency of the *Ceann* and of the clan itself—though somehow he had always thought of such sacrifices as symbolic, like the Mass. He supposed he realized that animals sometimes were sacrificed, but it had never really registered that human life sometimes was required. Not really. Not literally.

Yet ancient tradition insisted that it did happen, at least in time of great need, or when the chief was growing old. Christian though the highlands might be, everyone knew that the veneer wore thin at the great quarter festivals of the year. All through the year's turning, a variety of ancient practices continued openly in the Highlands, side by side with the rites of the White Christ.

James knew many of the more harmless ones at firstland. Some of his earliest memories were of welcoming in the May, twirling and weaving to the skirl of the pipes and the beat of the drum as he and the other children danced around the Maypole. From the age of seven, he had leaped over the Beltane bonfires with the others. Familiar, too, was the kindling of the needfire at the Winter Solstice, and the gathering of the sacred mistletoe.

And on the night of the first full moon following his fifteenth birthday, a rite far older than any ritual of the White Christ. . . .

The memory conjured an almost overwhelming image of Mathilda—no, a woman who *looked* like Mathilda—red-haired and glorious, but also mantled with a majesty of power he almost could see, as She came to him in the moonlight, but a little way from here, and—

Mathilda! *She* had told them where to find him!

As the realization came, James opened his eyes and started to jerk upright, but the sword in the Graeme's hand still pressed unyielding against his breast. Suddenly the Graeme's red hair and pale eyes connected with *hers,* and James subsided at once, letting out a long, despairing sigh.

"She's yer sister, isn't she?" he said softly, searching the Graeme's eyes.

Puzzled, Graeme nodded. "Mathilda? Aye. I thought you knew. She is a de Bohun by marriage with Lady Marr's brother, but she was born a Graeme."

"An' what else is she?" James insisted. "What was she when she came to me that night? Ye know about that, don't ye?"

With a sigh, Graeme stepped back a pace and stuck James' sword into the earth beside him, signalling his men to back off as he crouched down to look at his captive, one hand resting on the basket hilt. He did not object as James cautiously sat up.

"I think you know what else she is, Jamie," Graeme said in a low voice. "And if you have any understanding of that office at all, then you'll also understand why she told me where to find you. She could do nothing else, given what you'd done."

"Then, she wants me to die?"

Wearily, Graeme shook his head. "Nay, lad. She'd chosen you to be her consort. In time, you might have become for your clan what I am for Clan Graeme— the Summoner, the guardian of the old ways, the keeper of the mysteries."

"And the sacred executioner?" James said.

"When required," Graeme conceded. "But no more often than once every seven years—less often when the *Ceann* is young and vigorous. Your clan's chief is not yet thirty, but mine is fifty-three. Six years ago, when he was forty-nine, a Graeme offered himself as a willing substitute for the *Ceann*. At that time, divination was performed to determine the *carline*, the substitute victim for the next seven-year. Angus Graeme drew the black bannock and accepted his lot, thereby taking on all the destiny—and protection—of his sacred status. For you to kill him as you did was sacrilege as well as murder."

"I didna know who he was," James whispered, dizzily trying to take it all in. "God help me, I didna know. Must—must I take his place, then?"

"Not *must*, but *may*," Graeme replied, "but only in a sense and only if you choose it. Because his blood is on your hands, you owe a life to the clan. But if you choose to offer up that life to the gods, in expiation for your sacrilege as well as for murder, then the debt is paid, the balance restored." He glanced up at the sun, climbing inexorably toward its zenith. "You haven't much time, I'm afraid. Hanging a murderer requires no preparation, but the—other is best done before noon."

Noon! As James squinted up at the sun in horror, he realized he had less than an hour. And Graeme was crouching there, calmly talking about killing him! Nor was there any possibility of escape; that had been clear from the moment he awoke. Graeme really was asking him whether he would rather hang or—

"How—" James' voice broke and he had to start again. "How would—the other happen?" he managed to whisper.

With a deep sigh, whether of relief or regret, James could not tell, Graeme looked him in the eyes. "I'd rather not frighten you with details," he murmured, "but I promise you, it will be quick. Far better than dangling at the end of a rope—for you and for the clan. You will feel very little pain."

"But—"

But there really *was* no choice. He had killed a man of Clan Graeme, and he owed the clan a life. If he could cancel out at least a part of his guilt. . . .

James knew what he must do. Fighting down the queasy fear that was building in his belly, he made himself swallow, somehow managing to keep his voice steady. "I understand. What's next, then?"

Without ceremony, Graeme got to his feet and pulled James' broadsword out of the ground, laying it flat across both palms and presenting it before its owner.

"This is your own blade, Sir James the Rose," the Graeme said formally. "Have I your oath upon it that you will see this endeavor to the end, and that you will not try to escape the destiny you have freely chosen?"

Before he could think about what he was doing, James scrambled to both knees and set his hands flat on the blade between Graeme's. "I swear it."

"No, repeat the entire oath," Graeme insisted. "You must say the words yourself."

Drawing a deep breath, James closed his eyes briefly and then repeated the words he knew Graeme had to hear.

"I swear upon my ane sword that I shall see this endeavor to the end, an' that that—I willna try to escape the destiny I have freely chosen. So help me, God."

"So mote it be," Graeme murmured, as James bent to kiss the blade. Even as James straightened, Graeme was thrusting the blade into the ground again, gesturing for James to stand and offering a hand to help him up. James declined the offer, preferring to get to his feet without any help, but he found he did not resent that the offer had been made. Nor could he even conjure up any animosity toward the man who soon would take his life. He was a little surprised to find that his legs were quite steady under him as he stood up.

"We're going to the mill pond to bathe," Graeme said to Hugh, who had been waiting in the background all the while. "We'll join you very shortly."

Pointedly, but not unkindly, Hugh glanced up at the sun, fast approaching its zenith, then saluted both of them with his sword and turned on his heel. As he started up the hill, the others fell in two by two behind him, the blades of their broadswords gleaming in the sunlight. James watched them go, seeing in his mind's eye the mound atop the hill, with its circle of standing stones, only stirring from his reverie when Graeme touched him lightly on the elbow.

Wordlessly he followed the older man down the heathered bank to the mill, to the still pool just above the mill itself. Beyond the mill, he could see the House of Marr and its skirting village, the pink sandstone glowing like a jewel in the summer sun. He tried not to think about the woman waiting there as, at Graeme's gesture of invitation, he laid aside his brechan and stripped off his shirt and gillies to plunge naked into the water.

The cold cleared his head even as he sluiced away the dirt and sweat of his last day's venturing. He plunged his head underwater repeatedly, and the thought crossed his mind that if he simply let himself sink to the bottom and breathed in water, he *might* be able to end it all himself—Graeme probably could not get him out in time—but James had given his word. Besides that, the enormity of his crime had penetrated fully by now, and he realized that Graeme was right. Only by carrying through with what he had promised could he set the balance right again.

What Graeme had proposed, and what James had agreed to, was the only just resolution of a most unfortunate but inescapable set of circumstances that James had brought upon himself. If he *must* die—and he freely acknowledged the blood debt he owed Clan Graeme by killing one of their own—then far better that it be for a double reason, to carry his remorse to the gods along with his prayers for Their blessings on the clan whose messenger he had slain. It was right. It was proper. He had not *planned* to die so young, but it seemed the gods had other plans for him.

He was smiling as he surfaced in an explosion of

bright, crystal-chill droplets, shaking his hair like a spaniel, grinning at the surprised Graeme, who had knelt at the edge of the pond to wash his hands and face. The look on Graeme's face turned from suspicion to satisfaction as James calmly swam back to that edge of the pond and began to climb out.

"Did ye think I'd drown m'self?" he said lightly, slicking back his hair with both hands before wrapping himself in the brechan Graeme held out to him.

With a slow, faint smile, Graeme shook his head. "I'm sure it crossed your mind," he said quietly, "but I was reasonably certain the thought would keep on going. Ah, Mathilda chose you well, lad. What a grand consort you would have made her."

Shivering a little, even in the noonday sun, James wrapped his brechan more closely around him and shrugged, trying not to see *her* face.

"Does she know? What's goin' to happen, I mean?"

"Aye. Just remember that her duty is no easier than yours, lad."

Nodding, James lifted his gaze beyond Graeme, to the narrow, rocky path edged with gorse that could cut a man to ribbons, then glanced wistfully at the gillies lying atop what was left of his once fine shirt of linen. "Do ye think I could have m'gillies back— just until we get there?"

"Aye, of course."

James tried not to think about Mathilda as Graeme knelt and himself slipped the gillies on James' feet, fastening each with careful attention. As soon as the older man had finished, James lifted his eyes to the upward path and set out, aware that Graeme was following, but forcing himself to put that knowledge to the back of his mind. In just a little while, he would be setting out on another journey for which there was no guiding path. If he truly must die, he hoped he might be granted the grace to die well, at least. He kept telling himself that the way he had chosen was better than death by the noose, but it was death just the same.

His feet did not seem to know that, though. All too quickly, James found himself climbing the bank above the mill, past the place where they had taken him. Once he stumbled, but Graeme was there to catch him, only nodding silent acknowledgement when James tried to stammer his thanks. The sun cast hardly any shadows as they climbed, and the standing stones on the plateau beyond the hilltop looked smaller than they had by moonlight, the last time James paid them any mind.

No heather or bracken or even gorse grew within the circle of the stones—only tawny, lion-colored moss studding the rock here and there like velvet patchwork, interspersed with tattered bits of peeling grey and white lichen. (He thought it had been green, that long-ago May night.) The larger stones stood as tall as a man, twelve of them, the grey and black speckled granite glittering with flecks of mica in the sunlight. Graeme clansmen stood in the spaces between each pair, facing the center, each with his basket-hilted broadsword at rest before him. More waited inside.

Smaller stones marked three of the quarters inside the circle, each nearly the height of a man, each with a man beside it. A smooth earth mound occupied the western quarter, where a fourth stone would have stood, and the man waiting there cradled a set of pipes in the crook of his left arm. James remembered the mound, but it looked different in the stark sunlight. A square, flat slab of darker stone dominated the center of the circle, about a handspan higher than the bare earth around it, and Hugh Graeme stood stolidly beside it with a quaich in his hand.

Of more immediate concern were the six remaining men waiting just outside the circle, three to each side of a vee formation that funneled James and Graeme toward a gap that opened between two of the standing stones as its occupant stepped aside. The blades of the six flashed in the sunlight as they came to attention and saluted, holding in a sword arch as Graeme paused just outside the circle to remove James's gillies. They followed by twos as James and Graeme passed between the two standing stones and into the circle, and the wind suddenly seemed to fall off as a cloud scudded across the sun.

In silence the Graeme led James to step up alone onto the center slab. The six escort knights, all of them older men, ranged themselves evenly around the slab, saluting with their swords again and then going to one knee as they grounded their blades, heads bowed before him.

That seemed to be the cue for the twelve between the outer stones to raise their swords in salute as well, though they turned on their heels when they had finished and marched silently off into the bracken, swords held before them, doubtless to prevent the approach of unwanted witnesses or would-be rescuers. Their departure left the six kneeling around him and the four at the quarters—who now also made him low bows, though they did not kneel. Sir John the Graeme was the next to give him salute, standing diagonally opposite Sir Hugh, and then Hugh himself, bearing the quaich, which James now could see was made of horn and silver, and filled with a dark, potent wine.

"Sir James the Rose, heir of Loch Laggan," Hugh said, offering the quaich to him. "It is meet that ye now give salute to the four airts and to the man whose life ye took untimely, before offering yerself as a fitting substitute and an expiation for what ye have done—if that still is yer will."

James only allowed himself a small, bitter smile as he took the quaich and inclined his head in a stiff little return of Hugh's bow. It was not his will to die, but given that he must, did they really think he would go back on his pledged word? Besides, it was too late to change his mind now. It had been too late from the instant James spilled the blood of the squire called

Angus Graeme. James did not know why he had been fated to take Angus' place, but he would make the best job of it that he could.

Letting fall his brechan, then, he straightened proudly before them and raised the quaich to the east, tipping it to spill a little of the wine on the ground beside the stone slab, remembering how his father and the Laird of Marr had raised their cups at innumerable feasts and banquets—though never in such important salute as the ones he was about to make.

"I give salute to the airt o' the East, where rises the Sun in His splendor," he said, well aware for Whom this rite was about to be enacted.

Turning to his right, he spilled wine again, looking beyond the dour Graeme clansman who stood in the southern quarter.

"I give salute to the airt o' the South, where arcs the Sun in His turning."

Again he turned to his right and tipped the quaich, this time in tribute to the West, where the piper waited—and where once had come a Woman clothed in the sun. . . .

"I give salute to the airt o' the West, the Sun's rest at end o' day." *An' mine, in Her,* he though, closing his eyes briefly before turning right again, to tip the quaich once more.

"I give salute—to the airt o' the North, the place o' the passin' o' the night in darkness." *An' the place o' my passing into darkness, too,* a part of him yammered, fearing it.

But he pushed down his fear and made himself turn to his right again, now facing east once more. He chose his words with care as he raised the quaich in steady hands.

"So also do I hail th' Mighty Ones, the Sun Lord an' the Lady, Whose children we are an' Whose power an' bounty we honor in this sacred place." Lowering the quaich, he sipped from it briefly and then raised it for the last time.

"Finally do I give salute to the gallant squire, sealed to the gods, though I didna know it, whose life's blood I spilled in violation of sacred law. I drink to Angus Graeme an' I offer myself in his stead, in expiation for my crime and in hope that I may carry part o' his burden directly to the gods. So mote it be!"

As they echoed his words, "So mote it be!" he brought the quaich to his lips and drained it to the dregs, lifting his eyes to the burning sun when he had done. He heard the rustle of their brechans as they rose to their feet around him, and started at the touch of Graeme's hand on his elbow, almost hoping they would do it now, before he had too much more time to think about it.

"Step down now," Graeme murmured, guiding him off the slab toward the stone in the north quarter—the place James somehow had known would be his final destination. Hugh came with them, taking the quaich from him and tucking it inside his shirt as he moved to the right of the stone. The six swordsmen followed, swords held at salute, basket-hilts at chest level.

It was fairly clear now how they would do it. The man guarding the northern quarter was already kneeling at the left of the stone as Graeme guided James to stand with his back to the stone, facing toward the center and toward the sun. Hugh Graeme came to take up a similar position on the right. The stone was smooth and cool against James' bare back, curved to fit the arch of his spine, reaching just to his shoulders. He had noted the slight depression in its top as he approached, and he tried it briefly as he lifted his gaze above the heads of the six swordsmen.

"Will you be held or shall you stand alone?" Graeme murmured in his right ear, as the piper in the west struck up a *coronach*. "If you flinch at the final moment, the blow may be sure. You are not meant to suffer."

The words brought home the purpose of the two

men kneeling to either side of him, waiting to hold him. For a moment James wavered, as the sad lament of the *coronach* brought unbidden tears to his eyes, but then he shook his head, dismissing them with his gesture, and purposefully stretched his arms around the stone and behind him, pressing his splayed fingers hard against the cool granite for courage.

"I shall stand alone," he whispered, as the two gave him salute and withdrew beyond the ring of glittering steel. The eyes of the six were averted, but their swords burned in the noonday sun. "Will it be your blade or theirs?"

"Does it matter?" Graeme replied.

"It does to me."

"Mine, then," Graeme said softly.

"May I see it?"

"Perhaps later."

At his minute nod toward the man in the east, a soft, slow drumming began: a simple, almost inaudible rhythm just on the pulsebeat, tapped out on a small, skin-covered drum. It gave eerie counterpoint to the *coronach* as the six swordsmen brought the tips of their blades together in salute above his head and then began a slow, intricate dance around him and Graeme and the standing stone.

The sunlight caught the steel and his fascination. In time to the beat of the drum, the six paired off in every conceivable combination to cross or clash their blades, sometimes grasping another's sword-tip to turn or dip or weave a pattern of flashing steel. James was aware of Graeme easing around behind him, withdrawing something long and shining from inside his shirt, but he tried to keep that image out of his mind, concentrating instead on the dancing swordsmen.

Time and again they closed, making mock menace with their blades; time and again they retreated. Again and again the swords clashed above his head as the tempo of the dance increased, drawing his attention, holding his gaze, jangling at his nerves. Until finally the six spread wide their arms and stretched their swords behind and to their right, each man's left hand reaching behind to grasp the point of his neighbor's sword two places away—lifting up, over, wrists crossing—

Suddenly, in a slither of steel, the blades were interlocked above him in the knot, the six-pointed star, its open center just large enough to admit his head. He caught his breath as it was lowered almost to his shoulders and then miraculously raised again—three times—gasped as the interlocking symbol then was tilted before him by just one man holding it aloft, the opening now framing the Sun in Splendor, high above his head.

James flung his head back to see it, squinting against the glint of sun on steel, awestruck at the image of the Sun viewed thus through the magic of the interlocked swords. His eyes streamed with tears as he tried to focus on a vague, brighter shape that *almost* could be coaxed into resolution. He strained to see it, starting to reach with one hand to grasp the vast, elusive prize.

Only in that final instant but he catch the glint of what he now knew to be another blade that suddenly was in Graeme's hand, flashing toward his upturned throat, and feel the tug of fingers locked in his hair, holding him steady—and then the brief, sharp kiss of the Sun at his throat, of the Woman clothed in the Sun, of the blinding light lifting him out of his body and into his destiny.

Later, much later, as dusk was advancing across the purpled moors, Sir John the Graeme rode back to the House of Marr with four and twenty belted knights. Twenty-three of those who rode with him wore the colors of the Clan Graeme, but one was wrapped in a different brechan, and rode tied across the saddle rather than astride, his blood staining his pony's sides. Sir Hugh Graeme led the dead man's mount, and six more Graeme men gave them escort, bearing torches rather than the swords they had brandished earlier in the day.

The Graeme himself bore an even more awe-ful burden: a bloodstained shirt of white linen wrapped around something stuck on a boar spear. There was blood on his own shirt of saffron, spattered on the sleeve shoved back to bare his arm to the bicep; and blood had run down his forearm like scarlet ribbons. His face was grave as he drew rein outside the castle gate to nod greeting to the woman who waited, a plaid of Graeme tartan covering her loosed red hair.

"It is done, then," she whispered coming to set a hand on his stirrup, her face white and taut as she searched his eyes with hers.

"Aye. And it was done well, lass," he said quietly. "You—may be proud. He carried his burden like a true messenger of the gods."

"*His* burden—aye," she whispered. "He made payment for his sacrilege and carried Them his remorse, but Angus still is dead. Who will carry *his* burden, come next Beltane?"

Graeme smiled an odd little smile as he handed her the spear. "Why, a new *carline*, of course. We ride back now to choose him. No man here would refuse the sacred charge. The bannock will be broken, and the gods will make Their will known. Perhaps the willing victim rides among us even now."

"Aye, perhaps he does," she whispered, looking at him strangely. "Do nothing for *me* in this regard, John."

With a shrug, he backed his horse a few steps and made her a little bow in the saddle. "I do what I do for Them," he said lightly. "Take care that you do the same. Until next time, then."

"Aye. Next time."

She clutched the spear and its grisly burden next to her heart as he and his men rode off into the light of the rising moon, remembering another moon, and the divinity that had come upon her and upon the young lover who lay with her that night.

But for now, she must play another kind of priestess and bear his final relic back inside the castle walls, where a heart-shaped casket awaited filling. She held her head high as she turned back through the gates and headed slowly across the yard, and allowed herself no tears. The men of the yard doffed their bonnets and the women curtsied as she passed, as they always did, but this time she knew that the reverences they made were not for her.

LORD OF THE BRITAINS

It was several long moments before the young god pulled his eyes off the now blank screen. "I would prefer my heroes to survive," Tek observed dryly. Even as he said it, the young god realized the remark was unnecessary and it showed just how strongly he had reacted to the story.

"Not all my heroes die," corrected a deep voice from someone standing to Tek's side.

Tek, already nervous and not sure why, literally jumped. He decided that for a war god he was being snuck up upon much too often.

Mentor grinned. "May I introduce the Lord of the Britains and guardian of their isle."

"You can," Tek spat out the two words nervously. Something told him he was in danger. But when he faced the old man that had just appeared, there seemed no threat to him. Still the feeling he was missing something important bothered the new god.

"Welcome to existence," the new intruder offered in a resonant, comfortable voice. "I did not mean to startle you. Has this one not explained the effect of Names upon this plane?"

Tek transferred his annoyance from the stranger to Mentor.

"I've hardly had time," the teacher sputtered, backing away half a step when he noticed the static sparks surrounding Tek's hand. "Nor did I expect so rapid a response, Lord Lugh."

The old man smiled, then looked puzzled and stood with his head cocked to one side staring at nothing. Finally he spoke.

"There is something amiss with the feel of this place."

There sure is, Tek thought to himself. My security stinks. But a distant feeling of urgency made the war god feel the need to assert himself.

"Then tell me why you are here?" Tek demanded. Then turned to Mentor for confirmation. "I doubt you appear anytime you are mentioned in a tale."

"True," Lugh agreed, "but rarely is the tale being told to the newest of mankind's gods."

"So you were just curious." Tek was suddenly annoyed. Was he so pitiful as to be nothing but a curiosity to the established gods?

"I did not mean to give you that impression," the older god replied placatingly. "I came because we gods often help each other."

"Or stab each other in the back," Mentor added. Both of the gods looked at the small teacher in surprise.

"How?" Tek asked after yet another awkward silence.

"To show an event that took place during one of my children's finest hours. So you understand that a hero is not a sacrifice, though some of the other gods like to think so."

THE LONG HAND

by Terri Beckett

The island is mine. Has always been mine, since the first men lifted their eyes to the sky and blessed the warmth and light I give them. The fresh summer green, patchworked all over little fields that hug the contours of the land; the hedgerows, and the darker greens of the woodlands—oh, it is fair, this island. And precious—more than they know, those who fight to keep it from the enemy. It is mine: my heritage.

The battle nears. It is the Lugnasad, my time of power; and in other older days my children knew it and did me honor with festivals. Those festivals have other names now, but it does not matter—still they serve me, my sons and daughters, the children of Lugh. This is no mere mortal war. Loki and his

*minions ride the storm. It is time again for the Old
gods to go into battle, for our very lives.*

The high summer noonday was breathless with heat,
unstirred by wind, scented by bruised grass and the
heady almond fragrance of meadowsweet. The only
sounds were the hum of a wandering bee with a heavy
payload of pollen, the rustle of a turning page, the
murmur of desultory conversation. The sun burned
red and purple through the closed eyelids, and under
the bulk of battledress blouse and flying jacket, skin
prickled with sweat. It was an illusion of peace. Within
a few paces the ranked Spitfires waited, noses canted
skywards. The airfield drowsed under the August sun,
and the tarmac shimmered with heat haze.

"You readin' that then, Taff?"

"Get your own Sunday newspaper, English." Pilot
Officer Llewellyn Laurence Griffith, inevitably known
as Taff to the rest of the 152 squadron, and Black
Welsh to his fingertips, folded a protective arm across
his copy of the Telegraph. "One with the short words
in, is it?"

"Bloody dog-in-the-manger Welshman ..." The
grumble subsided as the importuning colleague tried
for reading matter elsewhere. Taff cracked an eye and
squinted into the hazy blue. He supposed he could
write a letter to Blod—he owed her one, or maybe
two. That would mean finding paper and pen. Using
the brain. Too much like hard work. He turned his
head to where Tommy Markham reclined beside him,
head pillowed on his lifejacket.

"What are we on, bach? Still 'available'?"

Markham grunted assent, more than half asleep. He
was the baby of the squadron, having come to them
straight out of flying school with eight hours flying
time on Spitfires. Within a fortnight he had increased
this to forty-five, and practice sorties had given him
much-needed experience. He also had the kind of luck
that new pilots rarely survived without. One of his

predecessors had arrived on a June morning and died that same afternoon, before many of the squadron had even learned his name.

"We got time for a pint, then. It's your round."

Markham groaned good-naturedly and sat up, his tousled fair hair flopping over his eyes. The sun had freckled his fair skin, and he looked like the schoolboy he had been only months ago. "It's always my round," he said, stating a fact rather than making a complaint.

"That's because your da's filthy rich," Taff told him kindly.

"And because Taff's a tightfisted Welsh bastard," someone else said, grinning. The jokes were ancient— 'last time Taff opened his wallet, moths flew out'— and untrue. Taff swore happily at the insult and tossed the discarded newspaper into the nearest grasp. Then, slinging an arm across Markham's shoulders, he started across the dusty green of the airfield towards the Officer's Mess.

It was darker inside, and marginally cooler. Markham ordered two pints—when it came Taff lifted his in a genial salute. "Cheers, boyo."

The froth of the head had barely touched his lips when the shrill belling of the telephone froze everyone in expectation, and the cry of "Scramble!" came almost as a relief from the tension. Taff set his beer carefully down on the bar and grinned at the barman. "Be right back, laddie," he said, with a coolness he did not feel. It didn't matter how many times this happened—the rush of adrenalin made his heart thud harder and sank a cold tight knot in the pit of his stomach. It wasn't fear—well, he didn't think it was entirely fear, anyway. At first, when he had time to think about it, he had guessed that any warrior, in any time, must have felt the same way when they went into battle. It wasn't something you talked about. It was something you lived with.

He and Markham were neck and neck in the dash for their aircraft. The mechanics had already started the engines, the roar of the Rolls Royce Merlins beating at the ears—others held the parachute packs ready for strapping on. Taff shrugged into his, clambering into the tiny cockpit of the Spitfire, fastening the seat straps and giving a quick thumbs-up to signal the man to shut the side door. Straps tightened, he pulled on the helmet, plugged in the R/T lead, and checked the engine. It was a routine as natural to him as cleaning his teeth now—he waved to the groundcrew for chocks away, opened the throttle, and taxied out onto the runway to take his position behind his Squadron Leader, Jon Brittan. From alert to take-off, the procedure had taken just ninety seconds.

It took only minutes to reach 20,000 feet in a climbing turn above the base. The haze was more obvious here, cutting visibility in the deep summer blue—Brittan took a roll-call of his squadron, getting the "A-OK, Skipper," from each of them before lining them up in formation. Taff settled himself more comfortably in the tiny space, and trimmed his Spitfire so that it responded to the least pressure from hands or feet. The clean sky wrapped him round. There was no movement in the cockpit, save for the slight trembling of the stick that made it seem alive and not merely the central control of the machine he flew. The ever-present nervous tension engendered by the interminable waiting had been changed into a cool alertness.

Once my children fought with weapons of stone, of bronze, of iron. Now they go into battle in the very air, in frail constructions that defy the pull of earth, and the weapons at their command are terrible. Swifter than eagles, they hunt their prey, and strike— or die.

The static in the headphones was reassurance of the squadron's presence—each sealed in the confined space of the cockpit the pilots felt the invisible threads that bound them into one unit, the brotherhood of warriors that transcends differences.

Taff checked his armament, the eight Browning

.303 machine guns and the Hispano 20 mm. cannon—
he could need both in a hurry. As if on cue, the enemy
came into sight, seeming to hover like so many midges
over the south-east horizon, too far and too many to
count. Brittan's voice crackled tensely over the R/T.
"Bandits ahead. A whole gaggle of 'em, four o'clock.
Tally-ho!"

A head-on engagement, the reasoning went, could
break up the enemy formation—the German crews,
sitting as they did unprotected in their glass-fronted
bombers, would have to have nerves of steel to continue undaunted by a frontal attack. Those who broke
formation would be sitting targets.

But these were Stukas, dive-bombers, heading for
the vital radar installations along the coast, with an
escort of Me 109s. The Spitfires smashed into the
Stuka formation as they were manoeuvering into line-
astern for their dives. Taff and Markham broke right
and left on command, opening fire on the Stukas,
seeing their rounds hitting, breaking off when the
escorting Me 109s came stooping out of the sun to
protect their charges. Taff hit the firing button of his
cannon, jolted in his straps by the force of it, its angry
chatter making his ears ring, and saw the Stuka that
was his target attempt a crabbing side-slip, trailing
smoke. He abandoned it to its fate—they were over
water now, and the chase was on. The R/T was a
babble of voices, shrill or hoarse or obscene, no longer
remembering or caring that every word was logged
back in the ops room.

"Jaybird to Red Team. We're going down low."

*As the hounds course the hare, as the hawk stoops
on the rabbit; chivvy them, drive them, strike them
down!*

From one hundred feet above the waves, the white
caps seemed stationary, and the cross-shaped shadows
fled across them like clouds. One Stuka, streaming
flame, touched down on a wave top, digging in and
flipping over onto its back in a welter of foam. Another

throttled back into a steep turn, and Taff, on its tail, overshot. The air was alive with tracer, coming from behind—it hit the flank of the Spitfire with a noise like hailstones, but everything still worked, and Taff deduced the damage was light.

"109 on your tail, Taff. Break right."

"OK, Skip, I'm on him." Markham's voice, and a jubilant: "Got the bastard!"

"Good show, Tommy," from Brittan.

The 109 split apart as it hit the water—Taff pulled into a steep turn and got altitude, looking for another target.

He did not have long to wait. Another 109 was abruptly in front of him, so close that Taff could see the square wingtips and tail struts, the dirty grey-black camouflage, even the goggled and helmeted pilot. For a split-second the two were staring at each other before Taff swung the Spitfire to get dead line astern and opened fire with all eight guns. The Spitfire juddered, rattling his teeth. He kicked the bottom rudder and skidded inwards, down and behind the stricken enemy. It twisted out of control and into the sea with the fire blooming in its belly like some monstrous flower.

Taff turned again, a steep g-pulling climb that greyed him out momentarily as the blood drained from his brain. Out of nowhere, a 109 came to him, guns spitting—Taff managed to side-slip, but felt the rounds hitting the fuselage in a series of rapid hammer blows. He had no control, everything was dead, and the Spitfire was screaming seawards in a dive. He couldn't pull out of it. He struggled with the canopy, but something had jammed it. God, he thought, this is it . . .

This is the one. Even the name fits my purpose. There are magicians in your ancestry, boy-bach, but they were children at play. Witness my power—now!

And suddenly he found himself alone in the sky, in level flight. "Damn, that was close . . ." He sagged against the straps, limp with relief. The cloudless blue around him was silent. The high-speed battle was out of sight. All the instruments were haywire. This was something that happened in the mayhem of the dog-fight, but it was unnerving since it would take several minutes for them to become operational again. The sun was hot through the perspex canopy—below, the sea was a sheet of hammered silver. The curve of coastline, palely fringed with beaches, might be the Isle of Wight, or France. Abruptly, he realised he wasn't sure which it was. Surely, if he was over France, there would be the telltale bursts of flak?

"Red Two to Jaybird," Taff said. The R/T hissed, but there was no answering hail. "Jaybird, come in. This is Red Two." Nothing. And besides the non-functioning instruments, there seemed to be something very wrong with the controls—the stick was dead, the rudder pedals frozen. By rights he should still be in a sickening tail-spin for the chill embrace of the Channel. That he was still, amazingly, airborne, had to be some kind of a miracle.

"Something like that." The voice seemed to be directly in his ear, bypassing the R/T. "Tommy?" he croaked. "Skipper?"

"Neither. Try again." The thread of a chuckle. "Ah, once you'd have known my name . . . Riding the air as you do, Llewellyn Laurence Griffith, pure-bred Cymru out of Dolgellau, can you tell you have never heard of Lugh the Long Hand?"

I'm hallucinating, Taff thought. My oxygen's gone, and I'm hearing things.

"Not quite," said the laughing voice next to his ear. "Well, child of mine, are the old stories still told in Wales, or have we faded altogether from the memories of men?"

The brightness outside was making his eyes burn and tear. It did not exactly dim, but it did change. Coalescing out of the sunlight, a man-shape formed in the air. A golden man. Taff blinked. The vision didn't go away. "My Uncle Gwydion told me tales, when I was small," he said aloud, "about the Children of Don." He had not thought of that wealth of legend for decades, but they were clear in his memory as if it had been only yesterday that he had sat at his uncle's feet and heard wonders. Except that those were children's tales. The reality glowed at him, almost too bright to look at.

"My blessing on him, then, that we are remembered." The golden man smiled.

"Oh, you are remembered, lord. In stories, like."

"In whatever fashion. It is only when men forget us that we . . . fade."

"Lord . . ." What impulse prompted him to use that title? But it felt right. "Lord, where am I? I mean . . . am I dead?"

"Not yet, my son. You are between worlds. Below you—that is my country, the Summer Country, Tir-ran-Og."

"The Land of the Ever-Young . . ." *They shall not grow old,* whispered a memory of a once-heard poem, *as we that are left grow old . . .*

"Yes. And you will take your place there, with the other heroes, when it is your time."

It occurred to Taff that he ought to be afraid. He was out-of-control, several thousand feet above an unknown landfall, with an hallucination—if it was an hallucination—talking at him. He didn't know why he wasn't afraid. He felt very calm, quite at ease. Perhaps he was dead and hadn't realized it yet. A wave of regret swept over him. Things he had yet to do, places he had yet to see—people he did not want to leave. Uncle Gwydion, who had raised him after his parents had died, still as black-haired as his nephew and with the same blue far-seeing eyes, caring for the sheep as he had done all his life as if they too were his children; and Blod, with her primrose hair and violet eyes and apple-blossom skin . . . he and Blod had an understanding, and he'd meant to speak to her next time he went home on leave . . . His friends and colleagues in 152, bound closer than brothers . . .

"They are worth fighting for, are they not, my son?"

Taff supposed he should be surprised that the apparition could read his mind. He wasn't. If he was dreaming this, or hallucinating, it was better than floating helplessly in the cold Channel, waiting for a rescue that might or might not be in time. "Well, if we don't fight 'em, the buggers'll win, see . . ."

The god laughed, and the air rippled. "Then we shall hunt them together, you and I, harrying them like Annwn's hounds!" He made a gesture, and the controls were alive again under Taff's hands. "'Ware, son of mine! See, they come!"

Me 109s, in tight formation. But not only them—with a weird kind of double vision, Taff could see a dark mist about them, and spectral shapes that shifted and changed.

This was the Enemy, indeed.

Exultation pure as sunlight ran through his veins, an impulse of delight. With a yell that owed nothing to R.A.F. slang, Taff dived into battle, scattering the 109s like sheep. He could see their tracer streaming past, lines of sullen fire. Nothing hit him. One swung and turned to him. Lips drawn back in a savage grin, Taff thumbed the cannon button, and a shaft of brilliance speared the attacker. Shadow and substance both together vanished in a fireball. He had another in his sights now, took it in a raking burst that gralloched it like a deer. The Spitfire was answering to hand and eye as if it were a part of himself, or he was part of it. The sunlight bathed them both, wrapping them warmly. Enemy fire spilled off the Spit's flanks, as from a shield, but his lances of light found mark after mark.

As he destroyed them, so the core of their formation became visible. A darker mass loomed ahead. No thunderhead this. It was thick as the black smoke from a blazing city, but living. Aware. And angry.

"Duw Mawr—what's that?"

"Loki's creature." The god burned brighter by contrast with the darkness.

"Can we kill it?"

"Kill—no. But we can hurt it, wound it. Each thing of his we injure weakens the whole by a little."

Taff squinted into the radiance. "Right then," he said. "What are we waiting for? Let's get the bastard!"

They struck the rolling mass in a sunburst before the dark swallowed them up. Even Lugh's light was dimmed by that hungry darkness, but there was no turning back. Taff felt as if he was trying to fly through a thunderstorm. Except that this was worse.

Lugh was the only light, and the darkness was shrivelling about him. But there was always more of it, bred by the seething core of the thing.

"You are my spear, my son. Fly straight, strike true!"

Taff tossed him a salute and set the Spitfire on course for the black heart of the creature with a howl of challenge. The murk sucked him in. He was flying blind.

No, not quite. Ahead of him was a blacker blackness, if such a thing were possible. It drew the Spitfire like a magnet.

"Now, my son!"

Taff jabbed down at the firing button, and incandescence blazed from the cannons.

The shriek was beyond sound. The blackness writhed, shredded apart, whirling around him insanely. He pulled the stick back for a steep climbing turn, laughing . . .

. . . the grey-out following the steep turn faded, and the high-speed battle was out of sight and all instruments haywire, which happened in the aerobatics of the dogfight but which was unnerving because it would be precious minutes before they were operational again. "Red Two to Jaybird," he said urgently.

"Jaybird, this is Red Two. Are you receiving? Anyone?"

Nothing but a soft hissing. Taff glanced down, oriented himself by the coastline of the Isle of Wight. Suddenly there was a 109 bearing straight at the vulnerable lone Spitfire, coming in for the kill.

No one now to fly cover, to dive in on the enemy's tail and take it out with a swift accurate burst of fire. Taff swung the Spitfire up and up in a spiralling climb. The g-force tugged at him as he forced the aircraft to her limits. He had the throttle wide open, and was in the tightest of vertical turns, but the 109 hung on like a Rottweiler. Stick over now, full forward—and Taff plunged into a near vertical dive, pulling out of it just above the sea. As he came back up at the enemy, he fired a burst into the underbelly. The tracer ripped home, and Taff spiralled away as the crippled thing faltered and went into a spin.

Taff's whoop of jubilation had another and unexpected echo.

"There's a Spit behind us, Jaybird. 2000 yards."

Taff whooped again, because now he saw them, the little cluster of aircraft with the lovely curving wings that only belonged to Spitfires. "This is Red Two, Jaybird. Your little stray lamb."

"Thought we'd lost you, Taff," Brittan said warmly. "You okay?"

"A couple of nasty moments, Skip, but everything seems fine now."

"We'll orbit for you, Taff. Pick up on the right wing, and let's go home."

The dearly familiar landscape over the base beckoned as the returning fighters circled and, one by one, landed. There was no fuss, no aerobatics. Until on the ground there was no way of knowing if a stray bullet had struck a control cable. Just an ordered, easy landing, with the mechanics swarming over before the aircraft had taxied to a halt.

Taff climbed stiffly out of the cockpit. There were

holes all over the fuselage, as if someone had tried to turn the Spitfire into a pepperpot. Somehow she had brought him through it and safely back to earth. He laid a hand on the pitted skin briefly, in silent thanksgiving.

"Taff! Thought you'd bought it back there! What happened?"

"God knows, Tommy. They were coming out of the woodwork, weren't they?"

"Five kills confirmed, lads." Brittan strolled over, the Group Captain at his side. "One of 'em is mine, one's yours, Tommy. And Taff got three. Bloody well done!"

"Three!" Tommy crowed, slapping Taff on the back. "You jammy sod, Taff!"

"Just my lucky day," Taff grinned at him.

"You can say that again! Come on, this deserves a drink!"

"I still got mine waiting for me," Taff grinned, "Unless some bastard's drunk it. Let's get one in before we go up again, is it?"

They are frail, my children. Yet they strive to their utmost for what they believe. They are mortal, but they have a courage that even a god, sometimes, must marvel at. For that reason, we aid them. As my brother Manawyddan ap Llyr, when he smoothed the sea for the passage of their little ships across to Dunkirk. As DianCecht inspires their healers. As the Blessed Bran protects them. They are our children, and our continuance, and they carry at their heart's core the seed of immortality. Not theirs alone, but also ours. It is only when they forget that we, too, begin to die.

Loki shall not prevail against them. Not this time.

JUSTICE

Tek noticed that for a brief moment Mentor seemed upset at the story. It was almost as if he too had learned something new. The new god found that gratifying. He also noticed that they had been joined by a number of new visitors. The first were quickly introduced as companions of Lugh. They seemed friendly and, well, earthy. Tek found them easy to talk with, if woefully ignorant of the latest technology.

While he spoke with one of the earth goddesses, another of the newcomers began changing the landscape. The barren field rose up and formed itself into columns and buttresses. Ethereal dust whirled and Tek found himself standing at the entrance of a garden. It wasn't a very neat garden, not like those Tek had seen on military bases. This was a wild jumble of exotic plants and blossoms, cut only by a wide path which began a step ahead of the war god and his teacher.

"A peace offering from Diana," Mentor explained. "It might be best if we accepted."

"How would we do that?" Tek asked. He wasn't sure if he wanted to accept a "peace" offering or not. Diana and her companions had been less than friendly until now. Something was still bothering him, but the garden didn't seem menacing.

"Come, let's enjoy the views," Mentor said cheerfully as he took the first few steps into the garden and then looked back.

With a slight shrug, Tek followed. The two walked in silence for some distance. Occasionally Mentor would stop and examine an unusual flower or watch and insect scuttle among the debris beneath the plants. Out of courtesy to someone who was aiding him, Tek tolerated this wasted time. Finally the sense of urgency, a fear that he was missing something, drove him to comment.

"It might be best if we continue as we walk," the young god said to Mentor.

The old man had been amusedly commenting on the efforts of an ant to move a piece of sap much too large for even its strength and seemed surprised at Tek's insistence.

"You are a god," he reminded. "You have, in effect forever."

"But something needs me elsewhere," Tek observed nervously. "My followers must be calling on me."

"But you are not ready to aid them," Mentor pointed out. "That's why I'm here: to get you ready. To teach you how to be a god."

"So teach," Tek almost roared, "here. Now! I want to begin."

Mentor kept his half-amused smile, even when Tek bellowed, a sound that resembled nothing so much as the screech of a diving Stuka. Then he turned and slowly transmuted some of the nearby plants into another wide screen, high resolution television.

"It is now time," the teacher explained as the screen lit, "to teach you another face to war."

Tek nodded his approval. A sense of progress allowed him to ignore other concerns. You had to have the proper training and intelligence to successfully complete any operation.

The clouds that covered the conjured television's screen formed themselves into a new image, one of a beautiful oriental woman. She wore white silk robes embroidered with gold thread. Without question, even among the gods, this was one of the most lovely of all creatures.

"Kwan Yin," Mentor introduced. "Not exactly your type, but wise and in her own way powerful, a mercy goddess." Tek nodded a third time, unwilling to look away.

As they watched, the woman smiled, giving the impression she could see them. It was then that Tek realized there were other people on the screen, walking behind Kwan Yin. Concerned, the goddess turned to hover over an U.S. Army issue cot. As she turned her silken robes became the simple cotton gown of a peasant woman. On the cot was a Caucasian male in a thrown-together uniform. He was clearly near death.

WHITE LADY

by S.N. Lewitt

Langley Field, Va. 1919

"He's not going to make it," the doctor said to one of the orderlies. "Put him in with the others. No good infecting anyone else." He was put on a stretcher and taken out to the overflow facility, a small shack near the morgue. Half the patients there seemed to be dead already.

Anger burned hotter than fever in the young pilot. All his life things had gone stark screaming wrong. He had been just too young to fight in the War, and he had begun to understand the secrets of the fierce little biplanes just as they were being replaced. He had expected to die fighting. He was a fighting man and a pilot. He never expected to die old.

But to die in his own country, in Virginia, for God's

sake, that was bad enough. But of influenza? No matter that the country was under epidemic attack, that thousands had already died and that there was nothing that could be done about it. That something as civilian as influenza could do what a uniformed enemy had never had the chance to do made Claire Lee Chennault more furious than the fact of dying.

The little shack was dark, dissolved, and he was aware of the morgue next door. Where he belonged, most likely. The whole place filled with an eerie light and he could see his sweat-soaked body lying on a makeshift cot near the door. He became sad for a moment, all the half-schemed ideas in his head becoming solid and taking on shape.

He could see so clearly from this height the patterns of planes and how the older men were misusing them. How they just didn't understand the potential there, ready, straining, eager to pounce on their foxholes and infantries. In that one single flash of comprehension and death he could see it all so very clearly and he knew how to make it all work. And he knew he was dying and wouldn't have the chance.

He saw a friend open the door of the shack. Pale moonlight spilled through the door and onto his face. His friend went to where he lay with a bottle of cheap bourbon, looked at his glazed form and tucked the bottle under the blanket with what had been Chennault's living body.

Then his friend left and Chennault followed into the dark night of epidemic. There were tears on his friend's face. Chennault knew that he was truly, really dead.

"This is the one," he heard a voice say. Then he saw a lady dressed all in white, more beautiful than he had ever imagined any woman could be. She reached down and touched the bottle at his side, touched his forehead. And he woke up with the fever burning to drink the good whiskey his friend had left.

*   *   *

Amaterasu had invited all the Celestial Beings to her great cave in Heaven. The ancient Tiger of China appeared and was given a seat of honor on a silk cushion under a blossoming cherry tree, which all guessed was a bad omen. Amaterasu was planning something, and she had never given such precedence to the Tiger before. So there were whispers and speculations among the lesser gods, but none said anything aloud.

The gods of Korea and Burma, all the Buddhist saints and demigods arrived and were seated at the lower end of the table, and below them were the million local spirits and revered ancestors. All the gods of the Heavens and those who had descended to Earth, and those of the Sea and the Underworld all arrived, one after the other, to be seated in Amaterasu's Great Hall. The chamberlains kept careful count as they appeared, and each was guided to a place in the elegant chamber. For Amaterasu's cave was beyond the beauty and harmony of any Palace on Earth.

A great feast had been laid, rice and fish and shark's fin, fugu and eel all perfectly prepared and splashed with the lightest flavoring of soy and the most delicate sprinkling of ginger and onions. Even the gods appreciated all the delicacies laid out before them, the platters made to look like peacocks and mountain landscapes and fat carp swimming around lotus. After the feasting came the tea, and after the tea came the poems to the Sun Goddess thanking her for her hospitality, her beauty, her impeccable taste.

Still, as all this went on, the chamberlains were distressed. One single goddess had not appeared. She was a very humble goddess, but popular in both China and Japan with very many followers. Kannon, or Kwan Yin, was the only one of Amaterasu's guests not to appear. The chamberlains could not understand why this meek and quiet Goddess of Mercy, surely not a very powerful or noble lady in the great assembly, would scorn the power of the Goddess of the Sun, the Imperial Ancestress of Japan. So they did not tell Amaterasu that her last guest had not arrived.

After a polite interval the Sun Goddess arose. She was splendid, wearing the jewel that her father had given her when he had also given her the heavens to rule. Her brother the Moon God and her brother the Sea God stood on either side of her. All three of them were in the bright silks of Heaven, black and silver and gold and blue, all delicately woven with patterns of birds and cherry blossoms and butterflies all over. Surely there were no more magnificent gods anywhere in the universe. Even the great Tiger of China in his stripes and claws was not so dazzling as these.

Amaterasu cleared her throat delicately. There was complete silence in the hall. "Many have petitioned me, many have prayed to me with their deaths," she began. "The people of Japan have long desired to grow, to take over the leadership from the weary, Westernized Chinese. Burma has fallen to the British, China is under the influence of a million different round-eyes who speak unpronounceable tongues. Only Japan is left, only Japan is pure. And it is the Japanese destiny to throw the Westerners out of our homes, our countries, our world. Let them return to their own homes, their own people. Let them leave our people forever. My children are strong enough to eliminate them."

There was cheering in the great hall, for all the gods of Japan were in attendance and at the highest places. They all rose and yelled and stomped their support of Amaterasu's announcement.

The Tiger of China looked alarmed and circled the Japanese gods, his great tail making a barrier behind them. "Will no one speak for the Chinese?" he asked softly, hissing through his teeth. "Will the new Buddhists and our ancestors protect us from these people?"

But no one heard him. There was only laughter and cheering in the rafters among the assembly. The cheering was so loud that it could be heard outside the great cave of Heaven, where a single wanderer stood at the gate.

She was not a magnificent sight, she had no jewels or bright silks. She wore only a simple white cotton robe like a peasant woman. And like a peasant woman she carried an infant in her arms.

She heard the cheering and the cries, and under it all she heard the hiss of the Tiger. She was too late. Kwan Yin, who could not help but listen to prayers, had stopped on the way to Amaterasu's cave to help a family whose house was burning put out the flames before the baby died. She could not ignore the old man who wanted to see his grandson, she could not pass by the potter who had been robbed and all his clay tea cups and bowls scattered broken on the ground.

She did not know if these people were in China or Japan, if they were in Burma or Korea. She was ignorant of boundaries and the language she understood too well was pain. That did not need translation.

So she had been delayed on the long road to Heaven, and had missed the pronouncement of the Sun Goddess. Slowly she glided into the great hall. Already those who had feasted were drinking rice wine and were praising the Goddess Amaterasu for cleansing the whole of Asia. Only the Tiger of China noticed the small, white-clad goddess arrive.

The Tiger padded quietly through the celebrating guests and nuzzled her arm. "Kwan Yin, this is a very evil thing," he muttered under his breath.

The doe-eyed goddess of mercy stroked his great spotted nose. "Our people have suffered from Western ways," she said gently. "I hear so many women calling in the night, begging for help with a father, a husband, a brother who is lost to the opium forever. To destroy that alone will be a great good."

The Tiger snorted softly. "You are too soft, Kwan Yin," he said. "You don't understand these things at all. The Japanese have always wanted to take China.

Now they have all the gods with them and China is abandoned. It is already done. I am the only one who will stand for China. Will you stand with me?"

Kwan Yin looked out at all the celebrating gods. Her long thin fingers tangled in the ruff around the Tiger's neck. "I cannot chose China or Japan or any one place," she said very quietly. "I am not sure I understand it. These countries have nothing to do with helping those in need."

The Tiger moved back carefully and looked at her full in the eye. He was far larger than most tigers and she was not so tall as many of the goddesses, and so well back they were of a height. "Even you," he said, and Kwan Yin saw the glittering harshness in his eyes. "Even you will abandon me and my people. We will still fight even without mercy."

Kwan Yin wanted to protest, but the Tiger was gone. The joy in the great hall of the Celestial Cave turned her stomach. They were celebrating something that would bring only more pain to the mothers, to the elders, to those who cried out to her. There was nothing at all here that Kwan Yin wanted to see. And there were already petitioners at her ears, women of Japan who did not rejoice as the gods when their sons volunteered for war.

Amaterasu sat in her cave in the place of honor she had given to the Tiger of China. The cherry tree had lost its blooms in the great cavern, and the stream that ran under its dripping fronds reflected not the leaves of the tree or the delicately arched ceiling of the cave, but something that happened far away on the Earth below.

The stream showed her a great city. Overhead were a cloud of airplanes with the mark of the Rising Sun on them. Her mark. They flew dark and heavy, laden with bombs. Amaterasu clapped her hands in delight. She knew enough about modern war to know that bombers were invincible. They soared over a city like a flock of birds and the whole town blossomed with red flame. There was nothing at all anyone could do.

She watched for the pleasure of it. And then she saw other planes, smaller and faster approaching out of the West. The West, the evil direction that had brought far too much foreignness already. Now it was bringing planes.

They weren't large, though, the Sun Goddess realized. They were tiny things against the bulk of her bombers, and there weren't many of them. As few as she could count on her fingers. Nothing to fear. The Tiger of China was large and fearsome, but he was also old and weary and without friends.

The little planes approached and did not run away. They moved in a complex dance pattern, two together, each group diving from above the bombers and cutting through them with machine guns. The little guns, she couldn't even see the damage they did to her great birds of death, and yet her own here falling. Falling, failing, some turning and running back to sea. Where they plummeted into the water, to the embrace of her brother.

Amaterasu was angry. She did not like to lose. She had rarely done so. This was humiliation. These metal birds had worn a talisman of the Sun, the painting of the jewel her father had given her as he had given her the Heavens to rule.

She cursed under her breath and blew hard on the stream. The water rippled and clouded. She was in charge again. The coastal cities of China would be cleansed of the aliens. The millions of round-eyes who thought of Shanghai as home were learning the hard way, the very hardest way, that they were not welcome here in Asia. They were not wanted at all.

1937, Nanking, China

A single man left Nanking in an airplane on the orders of Chaing Kai-shek. He did not want to go but there was nothing at all here he could do. The planes he had been promised had been sunk when the Japanese bombed the harbor at Shanghai. No, there was nothing Claire Lee Chennault could do to save the city. The Japanese had begun the ground offensive four days ago. Now they had won. He looked down as he lifted off over Nanking. The sun was rising and the buildings looked rosy in the dawn. The brilliant pink deepened into a blood red. He had not been the head of the Chinese Air Force very long, and now there was little enough left of China and less left of their ability to fight.

Not that they hadn't tried. With the ninety-one airplanes in the Chinese Air Force and the Italian-trained pilots, Chennault had sent groups against the Japanese bombers who flew over the coastal cities every day. Fighters against bombers. Insane, Chennault's old cronies would have said. They did not see the fast, tight-turning fighters rip into the heavy-laden bomber squadrons, shredding their thin wings, piercing their armor with machine guns.

Ninety-one airplanes, of which only half were reliable. And some were gunned down. A Chinese pilot, shot out of the sky, managed to escape and recover his machine gun. He asked Chennault for a new airplane for his gun. Only there were no more airplanes. The Japanese had hundreds, thousands, more than the sky could count. They flew heavy bombers.

After the first raids by the Chinese, the Japanese never flew without fighter escort. Only there were so many days, there were so many bombs, there were so many planes. And by October, Chennault didn't have a plane that was skyworthy. Human courage and blood alone couldn't prevail against the dark clouds of bombers that appeared daily over Shanghai and Nanking.

So now he was leaving. He was under orders from the only man who could give him orders, the only superior he had never offended. He took off and looked below where the Japanese were beginning to celebrate their days of victory in Nanking, celebrate with Amaterasu at their first conquest in China.

Three hundred thousand voices were raised together. Three hundred thousand pleading, crying, screaming in a single chorus. And those were only the victims, not their families and their relatives, not those who had died quickly in the massive bombing of the city nor those who had been cleanly shot by Japanese soldiers.

Kwan Yin was overwhelmed. Never before had she heard so much misery, so much sorrow all in a single month. Not in the tens or even hundreds, but thousands every day crying out. The women who were raped and then gutted on bayonets, the old men who were dragged into the street and made to perform obscene acts before they were decently killed, the children who were thrown against a wall or stomped in the street by polished leather boots until their brains ran pink-grey over the stone.

Never, never in any defeat had so many been tortured and murdered for the sheer pleasure of it. The numbers were more than Kwan Yin could bear, more than she could attend. There was nothing anyone, no god nor being of celestial might, could do to stop the insane victory tide of the Sun Goddess' chosen.

This was not war. Kwan Yin had known wars before. She had seen villages lost to the Mongols. She had heard the screams of the poor when her children, undefended except by faith and fury, attacked the British gunboats and the troops of the Empress Dowager. She had seen the British sail into the harbor and hold Shanghai, forced China to accept the opium trade. She had seen all this and bled with all the people who had bled. But she had never seen the like of the victory in Nanking.

What was once a great and prosperous city became a charred waste. The only color was the blood that ran in the gutters, that stained the houses. And the blood rapidly faded from red to rust-brown, ugly like the city had become.

Surely they would come to their senses. Surely Amaterasu wasn't finding pleasure in this outrage as a victory. The gods themselves could not enjoy the fruits of triumph with this noise assaulting Heaven.

And yet it went on. Kwan Yin silently haunted the streets of Nanking. She could hear no other voices. Only these, where there was not one person alive who did not plead with her to come to them.

Come she did. There was little she could do. She could touch one officer here and recover his decency enough that he would try to discipline his troops. She could hide one ten-year-old girl from the men who would rape her, give this granny a heart attack and quick death before the invading army could drag her into the street and urinate on her respected elderly body. She could make the walls of a bombed-out shop tumble in on the looters who had carelessly killed the owner when they had gouged too deep cutting out his eyes.

But there was too much and she could not do it all. She was a goddess, but she was too small for the task of Nanking. She took no comfort in the horror of humans throughout the world. She took no pleasure in the outrage other gods might feel. She knew only that she had been called here to the greatest calamity ever in the universe, and she had failed. Amaterasu had won this time, won far too much. And Kwan Yin was angry as she led survivors to safety. Then back in the bloody looting of the city, the white-clad goddess of Mercy raised her hands and screamed in fury, her first fury. "No, Amaterasu," she said to the burning sky that answered with laughter.

Finally there was nothing left to take in Nanking. There was no more blood, no more rice, no more pleasure for the place. And so the invaders became quiet, behaved like other invaders.

Kwan Yin was not appeased. She knew this was the

work of Amaterasu and that the Sun Goddess would be happy for her children to rape all of China as they had Nanking. Hadn't the Japanese always had a great love and admiration and a far greater hatred for China? She, Kwan Yin, who was worshipped in Japan as Kannon, knew them both. She had always had compassion for both. But this time she had been pushed too far. She had seen too much. And she could not forget.

She walked out of the wreckage that had been Nanking and vowed that she would somehow stop this slaughter, stop this evil. This was what Amaterasu had wanted in her war. This was no cleansing of the Westerners from Asia, this was the annihilation of all that was not Amaterasu's own domain.

Outside the city there was a mountain that had not been touched. The forest here was still green and smelled of early morning and shade, though even this freshness had been touched by the perfume of cordite. Here Kwan Yin sat on a fallen pine tree, her long white robes covered in scented needles in the deep shade. She wondered what to do.

She was no goddess of war or of thunder to scare and kill the enemy. She was no goddess of the tides to wash their ships from the sea, nor of the air to tear their airplanes from the sky. She was only the gentle goddess of Mercy. And she try though she did, she could think of no way that Mercy could protect her people from the scourge Amaterasu had let loose on the world.

As she sat thinking a great Tiger came up and lay his head in her lap. He was at least as large as she and his head alone was heavier than her whole body. His fur was grizzled and faded, its markings no longer strong and fearsome. And he was more than weary. He was limping, hurt, as if he had been crippled but not killed by a hunter.

Hunters should know not to cripple tigers without killing, she thought idly. Everyone knew that hurt tigers were far more dangerous, would attack anything that moved. Everyone knew that a tiger in pain was more terrible than anything on this world. Except the army of Amaterasu.

"Kwan Yin," the Tiger said. "It seems that you and I are alone against Amaterasu and brothers and all their children, and all the spirits of Japan and their armies. We must do something."

The goddess of Mercy wiped her eyes. She knew this was the Tiger of China, so different from the powerful god she had seen in the great feasting cave not so long ago. "I know. But I don't know what. You can attack and kill, but I am a goddess of Mercy and I don't know how mercy can defeat invaders like these."

The Tiger closed his eyes. Kwan Yin understood. Mercy had never been a weapon. How could she stand against these invaders, what power of hers was useful to her people in this war? Her heart cried out but she knew only despair. Against such things as bombers and machine guns, what could mere Mercy do?

As the men appeared, Col. Chennault was worried. He had wanted younger men, in their twenties and with three hundred hours of flying time. After all, the American Volunteer Group was paying well. Better than the Army paid, six hundred dollars a month and high bonuses for each enemy plane shot down.

He was disappointed. He was used to being disappointed, that had never stopped him before. It had not stopped him when the Russians were in charge of the Chinese air defense after the fiasco in Nanking, it had not stopped him when he went to Washington to request bombers and came back with a hundred P-40 fighters that no one else wanted.

In fact, even with the volunteers he was getting, Chennault realized that he could prove the points he had tried to make for an entire decade before. The points that had gotten him kicked out of the War College and passed over for command. He was a brilliant aerial strategist, was Claire Lee Chennault, and a lousy politician.

But in this war China needed him. Chaing trusted him. The mere hundred P-40s might not win the air war, but they were a start. He could prove what fighters could do against bombers. The two-plane element working together could trap the fat, slow bombers and then climb away faster than the bombers could follow.

He had seen it, seen it all so clearly on the night almost twenty years ago, the night he should have died. And he would have to make do with these men. Not the fine young fighter pilots he had envisioned recruiting, but these older, harder, more mercenary fliers who were all misfits in the U.S. Army. Just like himself.

Their assignment was to protect China from invasion from the south by protecting the Burma Road. It seemed simple and straightforward, flying out of Rangoon in the P-40s while the Japanese were testing out their Zeros. Every day over the hills of Burma the men of the AVG, their planes painted with angry looking shark mouths and eyes, went on the prowl. At least those who were not too hung over.

The things China needed came over the Burma Road. Convoys full of food and rifles, ammunition and warm winter coats came over the sharp hairpin turns through the mountains and gorges. And over the passes came the Japanese bombers, trying to get through into the interior of China to Chaing's headquarters in Kunming.

The bombers did not get through. The AVG flew over the high passes in their shark-painted P-40s. They wore jackets that had a patch with, "I am an American flyer and a friend of the Chinese," written in Chinese on them, so when they were shot down they were not taken for the enemy.

The American media loved them. Claire Boothe Luce wrote stories about these brave young clean-cut American boys who were fighting to keep China free.

The image caught on, and if it wasn't quite the truth, well, it roused spirits and was good for public morale. Who in the States needed to know about the rickshaw races in the streets of Rangoon, about American pilots whistling derision at British Army officers in their tropical shorts, about the Zeros and bombers by the hundreds massed over Burma day after day after day?

Day after day Rangoon was battered. The British troops were worn down and needed on other fronts. Day after day the three squadrons of Flying Tigers went out against the enemy in their hundred planes.

And the planes were shot down. Planes came back with holes in the fuselage and the wings, with leaks, with shredded tires. The tires were the worst, the hardest thing to replace. There were no parts coming in. And so, bit by bit, there were fewer and fewer planes for the AVG to fly.

The ancient Tiger turned his head on Kwan Yin's lap. "What can Mercy do?" he repeated, the rumble deep in his throat like the throttle of the planes taking off in the hills. "Can Mercy spare one life? Can Mercy go and do one single deed, save one man?"

Though her mouth still seemed sad, Kwan Yin smiled in her eyes. And her smile was great enough to make the whole world shine, brighter than a thousand suns. "Yes, surely I can save one man," she agreed quickly. "But tell me what to do, tell me that my people will be saved, that this terrible thing will not happen again."

The forest above Nanking was deep and full of shadows, the smell of pine perfumed them more luxuriously than the richest incense in Amaterasu's Cave. Here they were hidden from the sun, from the fury of the fire and the screams that had settled below. Kwan Yin was a sliver of silver-white against the deep moss, shining as the great Tiger of China gained strength from her care.

"Would you go back and prevent this thing from happening?" the Tiger asked gently.

Kwan Yin drew in a sharp breath. "Prevent it?" she asked, with a great hush. Then the silence took over. The scent of blood hung just under the dampness. "No," she said finally. "This is a truly evil thing that has happened. I do not have the power to stand against all the evil in the world. Perhaps someday people may learn from this, and that will be well. And the people of Japan, they are my people too. I want only to help defend the one, not punish the other."

Her perfect almond-shaped eyes were as soft as snow, her touch as cool as the mountain air. The Tiger looked at her and took heart. He was over five thousand years old. He had prevailed against invasions and epidemics, famine and foreigners and opium. He remembered the time before the gods of Japan had been born, the time when only the small tree spirits and animal ghosts and ancestors ruled there in schism and anarchy. He was the oldest of the ancient ones, and this war was no new thing to him.

Time, he thought, was all that China ever needed. China had always prevailed in the end. What was Chinese lasted forever, once it had roots in the earth.

"Can you save one foreigner who will defend us?" the Tiger asked softly.

Kwan Yin nodded solemnly. And then the forest north of Nanking dissolved and the black air of night rushed around them and time dissolved. She could see the years melting back, time turning in on itself. Then they were in a hot foreign place that was damp and smelled evil. Smelled of death.

The Tiger led Kwan Yin to a small hut, a place that reeked of disease and dying. He touched his great paw to the head of a young lieutenant who lay dead on a cot, a bottle of whiskey tucked under his arm.

Kwan Yin looked down on him and felt great pity. She reached out one white hand and touched his forehead. She felt the destiny written, that this was one of the brilliant and cursed ones, and it was his time to die.

But Fate was her sister, and Kwan Yin had delivered others from Fate before. So she touched, and the life entered the young man again. She touched the bottle and it became a blessed thing, filled with the pure livingness of the Lady of Mercy.

The young man drank. He drank until the bottle was empty, until he was so drunk he didn't care anymore if he died. But he wasn't going to die. He was chosen for China.

Finally Rangoon was abandoned. The British packed up, the foreigners left. Millions of Burmese crowded the Burma Road to escape into China. Families loaded their pots and pianos on top of ox-drawn wagons and tied suitcases onto the trunks of their cars as they made their way over the torturous road up the mountains. Steep grades, unpaved, led to treacherous hairpin turns that brought travelers to a narrow bridge across the Salween Gorge.

The refugees pushed into China, a long slow caravan that took forever to cross the mountains. The British had left, the AVG was leaving and the Japanese were following behind, columns and columns of infantry and artillery coming up the Burma Road. The luckiest of the refugees made it across the Hweitung suspension bridge, hanging high above the Salween River. The unfortunates were those caught on the other side when the Chinese blew it into the muddy water below.

The Americans were among the last out. In their planes the Adam and Eve First Pursuit, the Panda Bears Second and the Hell's Angels Third brought their battered P-40s out of Rangoon. Below them the ragged refugee column crossed the bridge, and the last across set fire to it.

The Japanese were less than a day's march behind. Up through the Salween Gorge, across the pass, then there was nothing between them and Kunming. No army garrisoned the south, no Chinese troops guarded against the Japanese coming up the Burma Road. Once through the gorge, the Japanese would be in control of China.

Men and material stood bottlenecked on the hairpin turns of the Burma Road down the Salween Gorge. The Japanese waited for the engineers, for the pontoons to float a bridge across the river. They were out in the open, unprotected, the victors. There was nothing at all they feared and nothing that could stop them.

Amaterasu laughed with them. Finally China would be hers. She had desired this day above all others. The Chinese had invented civilization, but the Japanese were the rightful masters of it. She had nurtured her children well, grew them anxious to fight for her many-times great grandson the Emperor, to fulfill their true destiny. The destiny she had chosen and for which her father had given her the jewel to rule.

So she watched in the silent pool the masses of men, of tanks and mortars and armored vehicles, all waiting on the arrival of the engineers. She saw them arrive, the pontoons ready mounted on trucks. She licked her lips and drops of ruby blood fell into the pool.

And the planes came. Four tiny things with painted teeth and tongues spitting out bullets emerged from the mountains and dove. Piloted by four ex-Navy dive bombers, the new P-40Es had bomb racks under their wings. And like the birds of Amaterasu's Cave, they plummeted toward their prey shrieking in the wind.

And the whole column began to burn, burning like Amaterasu's sun. Burning red as the incendiaries rained down on the twenty-mile column. The planes turned, low on fuel. The Japanese felt false relief, for once the planes had been refueled they returned and wrecked vengeance on the trapped column. Their own gasoline and ammunition became the enemy as the fragmentation bombs of the AVG hit the invasion force.

The Japanese had no air cover. They were too far from their own air bases, out of range for the fighters in their Zeros who could shoot the bombers down. In the deep gorge there was no place to hide. There was no place to run. There were sheer rock walls and a burning road into the thick river. Smoke rose thousands of feet into the air like the incense at a great festival or a mass cremation.

Claire Lee Chennault pressed the attack further. For four days the skies over Salween bloomed with bombers, with fighters strafing targets left on the ground. Nothing at all was left of the force massed on the Chinese border.

Kwan Yin looked over the destruction at Salween. Nothing was unburned, nothing was alive. There was nothing at all to call out to her for pity. And she cried for the ones who were the enemies, knowing that too soon they would be calling on her as well. Against all the evil of men what could Mercy do?

But at least Amaterasu was no longer laughing.

ATTACK

The creature came out of nowhere, even as the image of wreckage and fiery death faded from the screen hovering over the jungle path. Tek had been enthusiastically approving of the use of technology to overcome numerical inferiority. He was still smiling when it hit.

It came out of the foliage without a growl or any warning. The creature's claws resembled those of a tiger and they dug painfully into the war god's shoulders as it struck. Even as he fell Tek summoned the latest design in commando knives and stabbed at the half-tiger, half-dragon abomination. He and his attacker were thrown into an area of rubber plants, scattering thick leaves and blood in every direction. Mentor retreated a few steps and then watched with interest.

The monster was easy to see now. It had the body and head of a small, wingless, oriental dragon and the legs and tail of a tiger. Over ten feet long, it dwarfed the current form of the young god as it tried to drag him into its massive jaws.

Tek changed one hand into a powerful waldo and forced the creature's head away. It breathed flame, but before the gouts of orange reached the bleeding war god a sheet of the latest ablative tiles interposed itself. Then Tek struck back, summoning a forty-five auto and pressing the gun into the scaled chest as he fired. Bullets whined and tore through the plants as they ricocheted off the suddenly thickening scales on the dragon's chest. But the force of the weapon's blast threw the two combatants apart.

Breathing hard, Tek took stock. His left arm was badly torn at the shoulder. Below that he had been slashed by the monster's rear legs until bone showed on the front of one leg. The first wave of pain penetrated and the godling wavered and nearly fell. His face twisted with agony and Tek recalled that painful crash into the Sinai. Instantly he summoned and injected a vial of RPR 45. The drug had been developed for the US special forces, but ruled too dangerous to use. Every volunteer who had tested it had sustained major or mortal injuries during the trial. This top secret anti-pain formula took only seconds to act. Responding to the activity level of the nerves themselves, anywhere the damage was too painful, it dampened all electrical output. Tek found he was numb almost everywhere but his hands and head.

The Dragon-Tiger circled, looking for a chance to jump the young god. Twice it lashed out, but Tek avoided the blows. Then, almost as an after thought, the god summoned his own dragon. The whop of the helicopter's blades met the half dragon's roar when it perceived this new foe. The roar ended with the deceptively soothing tone of the gunship's twin gatlings firing six hundred rounds per minute into the creature. The heavy caliber rounds tore the monster apart. Within seconds nothing remained but scraps and a wide gout cut by the massive firepower into the forest behind where it had stood.

Tek almost waved his thanks before dissolving the helicopter. He then turned toward Mentor and managed a weak smile.

"Someone's upset," he managed before collapsing at the teacher's feet. You can't kill a god, but especially on the ethereal plane, you sure can hurt one.

Tek revived to a soothing cool touch on his forehead. It took a moment to realize he no longer hurt. How long had it been? Why did this concern him?

It was a struggle to open his eyes, but the reward made the effort worthwhile. A few inches from his face was that of Kwan Yin, wearing a most concerned expression. When she saw he was awake, she smiled.

It took Tek some time to find his voice. Finally he settled for looking confused.

Kwan Yin had been treating injured warriors for several millennia and understood his confusion.

"You were badly hurt," she explained. "Too badly to will yourself to heal or into another form. I noticed you when this imposter of a teacher," she gestured toward Mentor who sat nearby, "began spreading tales about me."

Tek noticed that he was back in his bunker.

"The other gods: have they left?" he asked Mentor. There had been over a dozen gods in the area when he had entered that jungle path. The one who had fled would be the culprit that sent that creature.

"All are still here and more have heard and arrive every few minutes," Mentor answered almost happily. "Seems it's been quiet lately, and you are the most exciting thing happening anywhere on the plane."

Tek grunted. He didn't feel very exciting. What he wanted was to pay more attention to the ravishingly beautiful goddess at his side. He tried to sit up, and a wave of dizziness and nausea rose inside him. Tek fell back and could feel a new dampness on his forehead.

"Too soon." Even Kwan Yin's voice was soothing. "Rest and in a short time you will be restored." She began to croon softly and Tek found it hard to stay awake.

"No!" the war god protested with more conviction than he felt. He would not have this woman think him a weakling.

"Very well," Kwan Yin acceded. "If you will remain still, I'll show you a more accurate picture of war. The one I see."

Within seconds the television appeared and with a gesture Kwan Yin began her tale.

ORDER IN
HEAVEN

by Jody Lynn Nye

Szih Mei was hardly aware of the cold of winter while she knelt in the sheltered warmth of the temple. The brightly painted ceremic images of Buddha in his many aspects stared benevolently down upon her through their wreaths of incense smoke. There was an air of peace, if not quiet, since the hum of the monks' chanting provided a constant undercurrent of sound. She sat before the image of the bodhisatva goddess Kwan Yin with a handful of incense sticks and a photograph of her young son clutched between her palms.

She put away thoughts of the day as she knelt before the shrine. The gods didn't need to hear her worries, nor to have her waste their time with unimportant entreaties. Incense sticks, their tips orange, burned in the sand-filled urn on the floor before her, and in the fragrant bundle between her hands. She dipped her face into the smoke, and let her prayers float on high with it. The year was growing old. Soon would come the new year, and with it, she hoped, better things.

"I am so grateful for Your intercession, benevolent one," Mei said over and over again. "The doctors did not want to tell me I could never bear another child to term, but with Your aid, he is safely born. It is not that I am ungrateful for my daughter, but my husband has been longing for a son. Do You see how fat he is growing? And how strong! His legs are so strong he thinks to stand already, forcing his little heels against the ground! I will bring him when the season grows warmer, and there are fewer soldiers around. You will say that he looks like my uncle Szih Sun. I think he will be handsome."

She heard the gentle sound of a chuckle to her left. Mei started. When she had arrived, she hadn't noticed anyone else, but in her haste to make her devotions and get back to work at her parents' shop, she might not have noticed the nine sons of the dragon if they had been standing in a row.

She glanced sidelong and caught the eye of another woman who seated not far from her amidst the incense smoke. The woman was smiling indulgently at her, but without disrespect. No doubt she had heard Mei's one-sided conversation, and found it charmingly childlike. Mei smiled shyly back. The woman dipped her coiffed head gracefully, and rose from the woven mat spread before the image of Buddha and swept over to where Mei was sitting. Her long embroidered silk robe whispered coolly over the woven floormats. It was an expensive gown, shining white as if it was completely new—incredible in these hard times— bordered with a thick frieze of flowers done with delicate skill, and bound around the woman's slender middle with a shimmering, green silk tie, catching long-stemmed flowers against her body to make the whole outfit seem an out-of-season bouquet. Mei realized that her own carefully preserved robe was far more shabby, and that a fold of it had fallen open to reveal the edge of soiled, dark blue trousers and jacket, her working clothes. Probably this stranger was a sophisticated woman, who paid visits to the temple out of duty. What she was doing still in Nanking with a Japanese threat of invasion imminent, Mei could not guess.

"He *is* handsome," the lady said, bowing like a willow dipping in the wind to pick up the little black-and-white photograph. Bestowing another kindly smile upon Mei, she returned the snapshot. The woman vanished around the carved screens which shielded the room from the blasts of winter cold that whistled in through the doors from Nanking's streets.

Mei sat for a few more minutes with the incense sticks warming her face. It probably did seem atavistic and backward for a modern woman to be sitting before the images of gods, asking for favors and comfort. Times had altered since her grandmother's day. It was no longer clear where to go for guidance. Government in China had changed a dozen times in the last forty years, and now the two principal powers, the Kuomimtang, based in her own city of Nanking, and the Chinese Communist Party, threatened to tear apart the country while jackals such as Japan, Britain, and the United States waited outside the boundaries waiting for the carrion. Japan was not even troubling to wait. It had invaded Shanghai months ago, and cut off its contact with the rest of the Chinese world. Mei was an educated woman, but she was terrified of the forces she could neither see nor control, and had no faith in either of the parties to protect her from them. Although there was supposedly an alliance between the GMD and the CCP, each guarded jealously its territory and doctrines. If one turned to religion, despised so by the Communists and only tolerated by General Chiang's centrists, could any thinking person be surprised? There was order in Heaven, at least.

Two monks in saffron appeared and replenished the incense sticks burning before the great statue of Buddha. One spun the prayer wheels with the heel of his hand and glanced at Mei. Suddenly aware of how long she had remained, Mei rose hastily and left through the temple's second door. She made her way quickly back through the cold streets to her parents' cookshop.

When she arrived, her father was arguing with an old customer. He glanced up at her long enough to gesture impatience, and went back to the discussion. What with having had to return to her own home to feed the baby and the visit to the temple, Mei had been gone a long time. Silently, she put away the silk robes in her parents' living quarters and came out to the front with an apron tied over her shabby clothes. The big, bakelite radio on the counter blared European jazz music, interspersed with brief news reports from the announcer.

"Wuxi has fallen, a week ago now," her mother informed her, laconically, pushing rice around a vast wok with a spatula. "Blessings upon General Chiang for insuring that we will be safe here."

"Blockhouses and garrisons are not a guarantee of victory against an attacker," her father shouted. "Especially not against those Japanese capitalist devils. Why must we continue to act as if all is normal here? We are in danger, too. Like any tower which stands too tall, Nanking has always attracted the lightning."

"The General has said that Nanking will never fall," Mei's mother argued, as if that ended the matter. With a toss of her head, she dismissed the Japanese and all other invaders. Mei wished she could share her mother's complacence, but her precious General Chiang had waited too late to sue for peace. He had taken the winner's part of taunting the enemy until, like an enraged tiger, it could no longer be held back.

After closing time, Mei went home to her family with food from the cookshop. Her fourteen-year-old daughter, Jinyiang, met her at the door with the baby, Sunli. The two-month-old infant fussed and kicked, his tiny face screwed up and red. Jinyiang, a shy teenager, was apologetic.

"I'm sorry he isn't calm, Mama. I changed him and played with him," the girl said, "but he wants you."

"I'm glad he's hungry," Mei said, with relief, setting down the fragrant bamboo containers. She took the baby and kissed her daughter on the cheek. "I'm ready to burst. It took longer to get home than I feared. Will you dish up the food? I don't want your father to have to wait while his son dines."

"Of course, Mama," the girl said, picking up the packages. "Papa is home. He is in the kitchen listening to the news."

Mei was proud that between Sunyi's salary and her thrift they enjoyed serveral modern amenities. One of them was a new crystal radio set. It cost the equivalent of a month's pay, and was quite a status symbol among their neighbors. When music programs played in the evenings, they invited in others who lived in the building to listen with them.

"Good evening, sweet flower," Sunyi said, turning away from fiddling with the huge bakelite knobs and smiling at her. He was a thin man, not much taller than Mei herself, with a sharp nose and chin, and cheekbones to match. Mei's mother had always said her daughter's intended looked like the son of a half-starved fairy. Mei felt her own round, little face reflected her practical soul, as Sunyi's did his energy and enthusiasm. "How was your day?"

"The same," she said, rummaging one-handed through a low cupboard to find bowls. The baby nursed contentedly, kneading a hand against her side. "Father is afraid everything will fall on our heads, and Mother still holds faith in General Chiang."

"I hope his army is as strong as his words," Sunyi said. "Did you hear the last radio report? The Japanese have claimed more territory east of here, as buffer zones, they say. General Chiang breathed out dragon fire. The editorialist is afraid to say anything for fear of being dragged out and shot, but we are all worried that it has escalated past the point where peace can be established."

Mei clapped the bowls down suddenly on the table, and Sunyi moved his arms out of the way. "I want to leave Nanking," Mei said firmly. "We have children to protect. This is becoming serious. We can go live with my brother in the country until this is all over. My father is right. Nanking is like a rod drawing lightning."

"But my job?" Sunyi asked. "I'll lose it if we flee."

"Would you rather lose your life?" Mei demanded, gesturing at the shrinking girl and the baby. "Think of these two if you won't consider your own safety. We must go immediately!"

Sunyi nodded woefully. "Tomorrow," he agreed at last.

At dawn the next morning, they were awakened by explosions that sounded directly over their heads. Mei sprang upright and pushed aside the thick quilt. Cold air shocked her fully conscious. The small coal brazier beside them had gone out overnight. Sunli, the baby, awoke at the noise and began to cry. Sunyi lay gasping at the ceiling like a beached fish.

"What is happening?" Mei asked him. She picked up the fussing baby from the cot beside their bed and put him to her breast. More explosions came. The floor rocked beneath them. Unhesitatingly, Mei rolled out of bed and onto the floor, sheltering the child with her body. Sunli shrieked in fear at the sudden movement, and beat against his mother's body with tiny fists and feet. Through the walls Mie heard her neighbors screaming.

"Shells. We're too late to leave." Sunyi slid off the mattress and crept on knees and forearms to the window. Lifting a tiny corner of the thick drapes, he peered out. Mei cooed soothingly to her son, and crawled to the archway of the door, the most stable structure in the room.

"What is there?" she called.

"Nothing but smoke," Sunyi replied. "I don't see any damage. Perhaps it's far away. There are Zeroes in the sky. They're coming around again!"

The harsh racketing of small combat plane engines close by interrupted him. He had time to dive into the doorway with Mei before the next round of explosions hit. These were much closer. Jinyiang crawled weeping out of her small chamber and joined them in the hallway.

"Will we die, Mother?" she asked, in a breathless gasp. Jinyiang had a timid voice, scarcely audible at ordinary times.

Her mother studied her small, tear-stained face. "I swear you will not," Mei said, strongly, and put her arm around the girl. An explosion shook the house, and she shrieked, pushing the children down. Sunli let out a frightened wail. Mei cuddled him fiercely while a rain of gravel pelted their roof. "Oh, we should have left weeks ago and gone to stay with my brother in the country!"

Sunyi shook his head sadly, his sleep-mussed hair tossing like windblown grass. "We couldn't. I've got to do my job."

"Your sense of duty is an obsession," Mei complained.

The bombardment continued. Pieces of plaster fell from the ceiling and peppered the family with shattered grains of white. With every fresh impact, ornaments and books vibrated off the walls and crashed to the ground. Mei was sure some buildings in the street had been hit. She could hear screams of pain and grieving wails rising and echoing throughout the long, brick canyon.

Then, mercifully, the bombing stopped. In the sudden calm, Sunli emitted a noise that was almost an interrogative. Mei sat up and put the baby over her shoulder and patted him. Sunyi started across the room on his knees to look out the window.

Before he got past the bed, the sound of airplane engines roaring overhead caused him to flatten out on the rough, board floor. Mei threw herself over the children to protect them. Instead of explosions, she heard a fluttering roar, like a flock of birds rising. She coughed, spitting out plaster dust, and looked a question at her husband.

"After the thunder comes the rain," Sunyi said, picking himself up. He peered out of the window. "Very strange. There's paper falling from the sky. They're dropping pamphlets on us."

Before Mei could stop him, he leaped to his feet and dashed past them toward the stairs. Mei sighed, and realized that she was very cold, and the baby was wet.

"Your father is impetuous," Mei told Jinyiang. "Come into the kitchen. I'll make us some breakfast."

"The Japanese demand our surrender!" Sunyi announced, emerging into the kitchen waving a thin sheet of rice paper. "They promise decent treatment of all civilians."

"Hah," Mei said, poking at the banked fire in the stove to rouse the embers. "I hope you don't believe it so much you're going to go open the city gates to them."

Sunyi shook his head. "I'm a journalist. One never believes enemy propaganda. Many of our neighbors want to believe in the benevolence of the Japanese, but they are afraid." A wisp of hair settled over his eyes. He ran a hand over his head to smooth it out. "I'll go and find out what the city's defenders think of this."

*   *   *

The December cold permeated Mei's bones on the bus and the long walk home from her stop. Her parents' shop was full of anxious men and women eager to gossip about the morning's attack. The radio reported a speech by General Chiang that sought to reassure all citizens of Nanking.

To their dismay, General Chiang threw the offer to parlay back into the faces of the Japanese High Command. Most people were now waiting only for the sword's edge to fall upon them, but the Generalissimo insisted that they were protected against all harm. They were to continue with life as usual, because the defense of the city was in good hands. Chiang himself had put that task into the hands of Tang Shengzhi, who followed the teachings of Buddha, and now added his vow that he would loyally defend the city of Nanking to the last drop of his blood.

She clutched close to her chest the paper bag of soup, rice, and steamed duck with vegetables, grateful for its warmth. It was a cold walk, and she was afraid of getting lost when the last of the winter light had gone. The city was now officially under siege, and blackout regulations were in force. She and her family lived in a more prestigious part of town than her parents did, closer to the foreign concession areas, but farther from the stop for the local bus. Many of the foreign nationals with whom she and her husband had become friends—Sunyi worked for the chief Nanking newspaper and had many connections among British shippers and American industrialists living nearby—had already been evacuated by their governments in the face of the Japanese advance. The besieged neighborhood seemed empty, its big, brick buildings leaning over her with black, dull eyes. Perhaps it was just that all of the other women were already home cooking supper, and no one was left in the street at this hour. Everyone was hiding behind thick, dark drapes.

Mei suddenly felt eyes on her back. She spun on

her foot, seeking the source of her discomfort. There was no sound but the wind.

"Who's there?" she asked. The wind whipped away her words. She repeated it, louder. "Who is there? If you do not show yourself, I will scream for the patrol."

A filthy hand circled around her throat, and another planted itself across her mouth, cutting off her last words. Terrified, she dropped the bag of food and clawed at her captor's arms. The hot soup flooded out of the container and splattered her feet, and, she hoped, those of her assailant. Where were the soldiers on patrol?

A harsh command barked in her ear. More hands pulled down her clawing fingers and pinioned her arms at her sides.

Merciful Goddess, she prayed. Free me, don't let me be harmed! My children, my husband!

"Don't scream," the man's voice in her ear said. He had a rough, uneducated man's way of speaking. Her heart was pounding, and she had to bite back the cry that almost escaped. "We're Chinese, like you. All we want is food and clothes, and we'll leave you alone." He turned her to face him, his hand still covering her mouth. There were four men in all, armed and dressed in the uniforms of the New Army. "If you don't scream, we'll be gone as soon as you help us."

Watching them all carefully, Mei nodded, as aware of every movement as a tiny bird trapped amidst a crowd of cats. She stooped to pick up the bent and crumpled bags of food lying on the pavement, but the man who had been pinioning her arms knelt first. She held out her hands for her parcels, but he shook his head, holding them away from her.

His voice was thin and exhausted. "We haven't eaten anything in a week. We come from Wuxi." There was an expression of dangerous determination that warned Mei not to argue with him. He pried open the carton of steaming rice and began to eat it with his fingers. The other two soldiers, who had stood in the shadows, pushed forward and shouldered their guns. They grabbed handfuls of rice and stuffed them into their mouths, catching stray grains with fingers and tongues. The first one elbowed his companions away from the food, and they poked him to get him to drop his guard. Mei noticed as they chewed that the lines of their faces were pared very thin. Under the baggy uniforms, there was bone and muscle only, no meat. She felt sorry for them. Not one was older than twenty or twenty-two. The dirt concealed only the barest trace of moustache hair.

"The Japanese pursue us," their leader said. Mei judged him to be nearer to her age, thirty or so. He wore a corporal's uniform, rumpled and torn, with rag ties holding the sleeves closed over his chilblained wrists. "If they spot us dressed as soldiers, they will shoot us on sight. Give us your husband's clothing. As civilians, perhaps we can escape to the west."

"My husband is a reporter," Mei said, sizing them up critically, watching them squabble over the last of the rice. "You might pass, dressed in his clothing, but these others won't."

"They're only country boys," the corporal smiled fondly, then the expression turned grim. "They will pass, or lose their lives." He let go Mei's arm to work open the container of duck. She watched resentfully as he picked out meat and vegetables and shook them, steaming, in the air to cool them down before popping them into his mouth.

When he had eaten his fill, he handed the container over to his men, who exclaimed between them over the feast, laughing, hissing and batting at the air at the heat of the food on their tongues. Mei's eyes flashed with anger, but she held back sharp words. They had treated her with respect so far.

"They're only boys," the corporal repeated, but there was a warning in his tone this time.

"Where are the soldiers of the garrison?" Mei

demanded. "They are all around the city walls. General Tang has them marching patrols everywhere. They should have stopped you entering the city."

"So where are they now?" he asked. "We came in through the gates before dusk, and no one challenged us."

"I don't believe you."

"Believe, sister," he said, wearily, taking her arm and urging her up the street. "We were not alone. Thousands of soldiers, fleeing Wuxi, and some, on the road even longer, from Shanghai, came in with us. They're looking for the same thing I think—food and a place to hide. If you're smart, you'll get out of town."

"General Tang has sworn he would defend Nanking to the last breath in his body!" she retorted.

"Hah! No one is that self-sacrificing." His cry was bitter, and he thrust her along with a push of his hand behind her upper arm. Mei's shoes slipped on the pavement. She windmilled, trying to keep her balance, and her kidnapper grabbed hold and righted her just as she tipped over. "You kept silent. Good. You seem to be an intelligent woman. Remain so."

"I have a degree in international economics," she hissed, furious at being treated like chattel.

Her captor was unimpressed. "Good. Tell that to the Japanese bombs when they fall on your house."

They skirted the crumbled ruins of the two buildings at the corner of her street. Only one man had been killed that morning, but twenty families were rendered homeless. Friends and kin took them in, wondering how long it would be until they too lost their homes or their lives. Mei shivered. Once they reached the apartment building, the corporal stayed close by her while she felt in her pocketbook for her latchkey, and kept his gun in her ribs all the way up the stairs to the first floor.

"Mei? Is that you? You're late, sweet flower. Was the bus crowded?" Sunyi came out of the kitchen with a baby bottle and a drying cloth. He stopped short when he saw Mei's escort. For the first time in all the years they were married, Mei regretted that Sunyi was not a bruising stevedore. His intellectual's shoulders were thin, his reactions wary but predictable. He had no defense against soldiers; they knew before he did what moves he might make.

"Give them clothes and they will go away," Mei said tightly, her jaw set against the tears of frustration she could feel welling up in her eyes.

"The Japanese are coming," the corporal broke in. "Flee for your lives, but give us clothes first so we can disguise ourselves."

Sunyi opened his mouth to protest, but Mei's pleading gaze reminded him that there were children in the next room. His face became expressionless; his hooded eyes gave no clue to his thoughts. With a silent nod, he went into their sleeping room with two of the soldiers in attendance. They emerged with armfuls of clothes. The corporal stood on guard while the others changed, then doffed his uniform for Sunyi's best suit.

"We thank you, and in our gratitude, leave you your lives," the soldier said, cynically. "You would be wise to destroy those uniforms, not merely throw them away. Is there more food?"

"No," Mei said quickly. "I was bringing it home for my family. You have eaten it all."

With a nod, the corporal covered them with his rifle barrel while the other three men, ill at ease in Sunyi's Western clothing, slipped out of the room and into the dark hallway.

The tension held until the door at the bottom of the stairs closed behind the last man. Mei's shoulders slumped, and she felt the tears overflowing down her face. Sunyi ran to hold her.

Mei wept for a while, trembling against Sunyi's chest. He kissed her smooth black hair, and murmured little baby words to comfort her. "We have to get rid of the uniforms," she said, her voice quavering. "They must not be found here."

"How did they get into the city?"

"They said they were not challenged," Mei said. "Where are Tang Shengzhi's troops?"

"On guard," Sunyi assured her. "I interviewed a high officer close to him this afternoon. My report is in the evening paper. Perhaps when the sentries saw them, they assumed these men were joining Nanking's defense. I will ask them tomorrow."

"Don't go," Mei pleaded with him. "You heard what that man said. The enemy is coming. I don't want to be separated from you."

"We are quite safe," Sunyi said, confidently planting his hands on her shoulders.

"Mama?" Jinyiang stood in the doorway, cradling Sunli. The baby stared, wide-eyed but quiet. Mei and Sunyi opened their arms to the children and held the girl and baby between them in a tight embrace. "I hid when I heard the strange men talking."

"You did right, blossom," Sunyi assured her, stroking the girl's shining black hair.

"We should leave, too," Mei said.

"I will find us a way out tomorrow," Sunyi promised. "Someone will give us a ride to the country."

Feeling uneasy, Mei went to the kitchen to prepare the second dinner that night, to replace the one stolen by the soldiers. She flipped spoonfuls of rice resentfully around the inside of the wok, seeing the grinning faces of the men as they ate her family's dinner. No apologies, no words of thanks, only the mannerless exigencies of war. And yet, they were all so thin, so scared, running from their own army as well as that of the enemy, that a part of her heart was with them, erasing most of the anger she felt.

"For the duration of this action against the enemy, no hoarding of valuable supplies will be tolerated. Severe penalties will be visited upon persons who defy this order. By order of General Tang Shengzhi."

Notices and radio announcements about food hoarding

began to appear and were repeated more and more frequently as the days went by. Mei's parents' cookshop was broken into several times by desperate townsfolk looking for supplies. At last, her parents closed it and came to live with Mei and Sunyi.

"Thirty-five years we worked in that place," Mei's mother complained bitterly, her wrinkled face pinched around the mouth. "You think you can trust your neighbors? I recognized old lady Yao's eldest boy climbing in the back window. I thought it was more of those soldiers looting and killing. It isn't enough that we must guard against our own militia. Now we have to hide from thieving neighbors. I loathe Mrs. Yao and all her brood." Her mother spat to rid herself of the evil taste of the Yao family name. "Anyhow, we brought what was left in the storeroom. Our customers bought most of what was there. We haven't got much: rice and dried fish, a chicken, a few vegetables. But we were not hoarding them!" Mother glared as if defying anyone to accuse her otherwise.

"You are welcome with your hands full or empty," Sunyi assured them warmly.

"Well, I hope it will not be for long," Mother said, somewhat abashed at her display of bad temper. "I want to be in my own place again as soon as possible."

Sunyi set up a pallet for them in the kitchen next to the stove. Mei, the children, and he were already sleeping there, since it was the warmest room they had, and it was away from the windows. Japanese planes occasionally strafed the area, throwing metal shrapnel and shattered stone everywhere. Every window was broken, by direct hit or sonic boom from nearby explosions. The neighborhood, with its privileged location near the concession area, was more fortunate than the areas to the south and west, and avoided the constant bombardment suffered by the rest of the city, but they could not avoid hearing the sounds of battle. General Tang's planes seemed to have little ability to deter the enemy's air attacks.

Fortunately, wherever the Japanese troops attempted to breach the walls of the city, they were turned back. Thousands of citizens left every day, fleeing via the river, or on foot. Sunyi attempted to find them a ride out of Nanking with friends, but the friends left sooner than expected during a barrage by Japanese bombers. Mei despaired of being able to leave the city on foot with the baby. It was too far, and the weather was against them.

"I blame myself," Sunyi said sadly. "I should have abandoned my job and taken all of you away at the first sign of trouble."

"Heaven will provide," Mei assured him, inwardly doubting her own words. She had gotten over being angry with her husband's obsession with his job, and now felt only despair.

Supplies ran short in Nanking sooner than anyone expected. There were riots, which were put down by the military. More break-ins occured as hungry people suspected their neighbors of having more than themselves. The frozen remains of edible plants were uprooted in the night from public gardens. Houses abandoned by the foreign nationals were looted in search of supplies. Mei husbanded her meager pantry, and doled it out to her enlarged family in the evenings only. The only one being fed regularly was the baby. Mei was getting so little to eat that she felt lightheaded each time he nursed, but she couldn't deny him sustenance.

To keep her mind off the hopelessness and fear around them, she told her family stories. Cuddled up by the big iron stove, she smiled at the kitchen god's paper image, and reached far into her memory for tales of Pangu, the giant whose body filled all the space up to heaven and eventually formed all of the features of the Earth, and of the great tortoises who carried the islands of the immortals in the Eastern Ocean.

"... There were five at first, but in the end, only

three, and all because of a curious giant," Mei concluded, sitting with Sunli and Jinyiang against the side of the stove. "The giant was punished by the August of Jade for his carelessness, and the three islands which remained were called Penglai, Fanghu, and Yingzhou. They became the refuge of immortals and other unusual men and women who find peace there from the turmoils of the human world."

Jinyiang sighed. "I would love to see an island carried by turtles. I wish we could go there, don't you, Mama?"

"I'm afraid we are not unusual enough, child," Mei said, with a smile. "I think we'll have to settle for the human world. Things will be better soon. You'll see."

Her mother stirred. "You tell the old stories better than I do, daughter. I wish your brother was here with us. He loves the magical tales."

The five of them stayed together in the apartment during the days. Sunyi continued to seek out his stories for the now much-reduced Nanking newspaper. Many of the employees had fled, so he worked at whatever task was needed, including running the great presses to keep the paper on the streets. He came home later and later every night, forced to walk for miles when the few buses left in the city were too crowded to carry one more man.

"I'm ordered to write of high morale in the garrisons," Sunyi told them one night, "but it's a lie. If it wasn't for fear of being shot by their own commanders, most of these young men would desert in a second. The monk who advises General Tang exhorts the troops to think of others than themselves, but these are no philosophers. They're children. To give them deserved credit, they are holding the defense valiantly. That small bit of hope at least I can give our fellow citizens trapped with us in Nanking."

Early the next evening, Mei heard the sound of feet galloping up the stairs. Fearing that it was more soldiers breaking into the house, she pushed the children into the kitchen and made Jinyiang squat down behind the stove with the baby's mouth muffled against her shoulder. There had been reports daily of people murdered and robbed by terrified troops retreating through the city. Mei counted herself lucky that her encounter with runaway soldiers had been so peaceful. She took up the kitchen cleaver to defend herself.

The door flew open, letting in a gust of cold wind. Her heart gave a tremendous jolt as she summoned inner strength to make the attack, and returned abruptly to its normal pace when she realized the intruder was Sunyi.

"You're home so early!" Mei exclaimed, putting down the cleaver and running to him. She was frightened by how exhausted and haunted he appeared. The hollows under his sharp cheekbones were touched by black shadows. "What's wrong?"

"The garrison is empty," Sunyi croaked, dropping into a chair. At the sound of their son-in-law's voice, Mei's parents crept out into the room.

"What?" asked Mei, her mouth dropping open. She ran to the stove for the kettle of hot water on the hob and poured it out over waiting tea leaves.

"The barracks are empty. The walls are unguarded. Even the airstrips are unmanned."

"How long?" Father asked. Sunyi shrugged his shoulders.

"What happened to Tang Shengzhi?" Mother demanded.

"Gone!" Sunyi gulped, accepting a cup of tea from his wife.

"But he swore he would defend us," Mother wailed. "He swore an oath to Buddha. Where has he gone?"

"No one knows. They are not here, that's all. We've been abandoned."

"We must flee," Father said at once.

"It's too late to flee," Sunyi said very quietly.

Before dawn, the Japanese, too, had discovered that

the city was defenseless. Troops streamed in, destroying defensive structures and taking over the abandoned arsenals, but instead of leaving the civilian population alone, they attacked them with astonishing ferocity. The few townsfolk that approached the platoons that marched in were savagely gunned down. After neutralizing the garrison, the bombers fell to attacking purely residential districts. Civilians fled, only to be cut off by troops entering from the river gates. Very shortly, no more radio reports came from the center of Nanking, meaning that the communication centers had been taken over or destroyed by the Japanese invaders. Sunyi mourned for his lost colleagues, and feared what would happen to them.

A squad of bombers made a run over their neighborhood. The front half of Mei's apartment building was destroyed, caving in half of their rooms. They cowered in the kitchen, which remained intact, in the shelter of the stove.

What followed was almost incredible in its barbaric intensity. Those who fled the explosions were mowed down in cold blood by the Japanese soldiers. Men, women, and children were shot whenever they appeared in the streets of Mei's neighborhood. Children, sent out to scavenge for food, were used as moving targets by whole squads of soldiers. To her horror, the troops made wagers on whose bullet would fell a particular victim. Some of the soldiers held murder contests, seeing how many people they could kill within a time limit. Bodies lay everywhere, steaming faintly in the cold air before becoming no more than part of the horrific landscape. In days, there was no movement whatsoever in their street except the creeping of rats. Mei hoped that some of their neighbors were still alive. No one came forth, and she did not dare to seek them out, fearing the bloodthirsty soldiers. Jeep patrols rode through the ruined lanes several times a day, killing anything live they saw. Mei hardly knew how to deal with the grief and fear she felt.

Women found outside were dragged screaming into the nearest alley, where they were forced by numerous soldiers until they slumped, bleeding, to the streets. Mei and Sunyi could do nothing for their neighbors. They were afraid to move from the intact room left in their apartment. Gunfire and explosions echoed to their ears from all over the city. They dared not even venture out to forage. What little rice they had left was left to soak and grow soft enough to eat, a cold porridge that satisfied no one, but at least it was a form of sustenance.

Jinyiang grew more silent every day. She shuddered when she heard female screams of terror. Dead women lay strewn all around them. Some were only shot to death, or had died of wounds sustained in blasts. Others were naked or partially so, battered around the face and ribcage, bloody between the legs. Those had been murdered after multiple rapes. Mei wanted to shelter the girl from the horror, but couldn't figure out how. It was difficult enough to keep her safe.

In the dark of night several days after the invasion began, Mei rose from her huddled blankets beside the barely warm stove. There was a sound somewhere below. Ever since their siege began, she had been sleeping badly, and blamed it on the lack of food. She poked Sunyi, then slid silently back into the recess behind the stove with the sleeping baby. Her husband sat up and armed himself with a chair leg which was all that remained of their handsome furniture. The rest, along with the four Chinese soldiers' discarded uniforms, had been burned for warmth.

"Mei?" A whisper in the darkness.

"Who is there?" Sunyi hissed back. He and his father-in-law rose and silently glided to places behind the broken door.

"It's Chi'en," the voice replied. "Where are you?" Soft footsteps sounded on the floorboards, stumbling a little as they hit a piece of fallen plaster or shattered brick.

Sunyi and Father grabbed the intruder and dragged him in, forcing him against the side of the stove. Sunyi clapped a hand over the figure's mouth to keep it from calling out. Mei opened the stove door to let out a little of the embers' glow. Mei's father raised a chair leg to deliver a killing blow, and stopped short only just short of murdering his own son. In the orange light, Chi'en blinked up at them, and pulled his brother-in-law's hand away from his mouth. Mei let out a little cry of joy, which she immediately stifled. Who knew how well the Japanese could hear?

"You're alive," he croaked, beaming at his parents, and hushed his voice further as they gestured desperately for silence. "I hardly dared hope when I saw what happened to the shop."

"Is it standing?" Mother asked, almost pathetically.

"There's not one brick on top of another," Chi'en admitted, sadly. His mother pressed her lips together as tears dripped from her eyes. Mei knew her parents held on to the thought of returning to their shop one day as a way of surviving. This was the end of their hope.

They all wept together, softly, so as not to draw attention to themselves. Chi'en recovered first.

"Look here," he whispered. "I brought food. I killed this duck myself in the marshes only sixteen miles from here. These greens are from there, too. I also have a small bag of rice." He took the foodstuffs out of his pocket and piled them in his sister's lap.

"Everything else was taken from me on the way here," he said, a little embarrassed.

Mei regarded them as if the small offerings were the riches of the Yellow Emperor. "Chi'en, this is better than silks and jades," she said, her eyes shining.

"Will you cook for me, sister?" Chi'en begged. "I'm half starved. The street is empty, and it is still full night. I'm sure there's no one around. Please?"

It had been days since they had had a hot meal. It seemed worth the risk to have decent food again. "All right," Mei agreed.

Taking precautions to channel the wisp of smoke down under sheets of old newsprint, so that it might be mistaken for mist over the icy ground instead of spiraling out of the chimney where it could be seen in the frosty air. Sunyi built up the little fire. Mei didn't realize until the flames began to crackle how cold she was. Even the baby showed more animation as he warmed up. The sizzle of the wok was music in the fearful silence. Cooking odors were heavenly perfumes. Quietly, Mei cut up the offering of meat and set it in with the rice so that its strong aroma would be muffled while it simmered. The one burner was all they dared risk.

"Please may we come in?"

Mei recognized the voice immediately, and gestured to her father to put down the chair-leg club. "It is old Mrs. Wu Tien," she said. "Come in. We feared you dead."

The old woman sighed. "Not yet. My son's wife is with me."

"Come ahead. Be careful. The floor is not safe."

Two faces appeared in the darkness. Far behind them, Mei could see the black of the sky beginning to change to midnight blue. False dawn was coming. They had better be finished with their meal and all traces cleared away before the Japanese began their morning rounds.

Mrs. Wu warmed her hands against the side of the stove and said a blessing for the kitchen god. "We smelled cooking, and thought at first it was a beautiful dream. It is an imposition, but may we beg you for a small portion of rice? We ran out of supplies days ago."

Even in extreme need, Mrs. Wu was still an admirable lady. Her request was not a demand nor a groveling plea. Mei could see how weak she was, and her heart went out to the old woman. The daughter-in-law proudly held her husband's mother erect, not daring to add her own voice.

"I will share with you," Mei assured them.

"Not all would do so," the old woman said, gratefully. Jinyiang sprang to help the old woman to sit closer to the warm stove, with a fold of thick quilt brought up to support her back. Mei was proud of her daughter. The girl seemed to be handling the isolation and privations heroically. No child, especially not one whose parents brought in an income that was well above average should have had to live like a scavenging rodent, living in silence during the day, in utter darkness when the sun went down, and cold and hungry all the time. The girl should have been thinking of young men, and pretty clothes, and a college education.

A few more neighbors, who had hidden in broken walls, in closets, or in cupboards underneath stairs came to join them as the aroma of steaming duck and rice permeated the chilly building.

"Whatever I have you may have also," she told them, as they appeared, one by one, pale and ragged wraiths around the fire.

"After I struggled to get this food here for you? After I carried it in on my very back?" Chi'en exclaimed, in disgust.

Mei dragged him aside. "What does it matter? If this is the last day of my life, I don't want to be reminded before the Jade Throne that I watched others starve while I had plenty."

"You're a fool," said Chi'en, throwing up his hands. "Now you will be hungry sooner. That is reality."

"Everything seems unreal to me now," Mei snapped. "Will you help, or will you get out of my way so I can finish cooking?" She shoved Sunli into his hands and put the two of them closer to the stove so the baby would stay warm.

Every dish in Mei's cupboard, every cup was used

to hand around the meager meal. Mei ate slowly, hoping her shrunken stomach wouldn't reject the only substantial meal she could see for the near future.

Footsteps resounded in the hall and the door opened again. Mei clutched her children to her, huddling in the shadow, fearing that Japanese soldiers had found them. The sun was nearly up now, fingers of light reaching across the leaden dullness of the winter sky. There wasn't time to scatter to their many hiding places. It was a vain hope that her family and friends could escape being seen. Twenty people could not be invisible in the corner of one small room. It must be the last moment of her life. She braced herself, determined to take the bullets before they could touch her daughter and son. Sunyi and Chi'en interposed themselves between the knot of refugees and the door.

Instead, she who entered was the beautiful woman whom Mei had seen in the shrine. Mei was amazed. The woman's exquisite costume was still spotless, a fantastic picture of calm against the destruction of Mei's home. She looked worried.

"Forgive me if I have surprised you," she said, bowing in a graceful fashion. She had not only the clothes of an ancient court lady, but the manners as well.

"Do not fear you have intruded," Mei said, standing up with the baby in her arms and extending her hand. The woman probably had smelled the steam from the wok, and had come, hoping to be invited to partake. Their efforts to conceal the cooking odors was probably not as successful as she had hoped. "Will you share our rice?" Mei asked.

The tiny smile spread across the lady's face. "Thank you, no. I do not need food. You are most generous."

Bursts of gunfire erupted in the street outside, breaking the stillness, and Sunli shrieked. His mother, frantic, grabbed him from his father's arms and clapped a hand over his mouth.

"Oh, my love. Please be quiet. Please, my love,"

she whispered fearfully, rocking him. The people around her cowered back. The shaft of light at the door was interrupted by a squat, dark shape.

Framed by the doorway, a Japanese soldier appeared, and leered at them with a greedy glint in his eyes. He called out something over his shoulder in his harsh voice. The baby's cry must have attracted his attention. They were discovered. It meant death.

"No!" Mei screamed, throwing her body over her son and daughter. "Get down!" she called to the visitor as the soldier raised his rifle.

Instead of recoiling, the woman swept out an arm, her broad silk sleeve nearly touching the floor. The soldier was hidden from view, but Mei could hear his gun fire again and again. The report sounded loud in her ears, but no bullets tore through her. The shining silk quivered, causing the embroidered figures upon it to appear to dance. Nothing passed through it. Like crystal raindrops, little balls of dull metal fell ringing to the ground. Mei stared at them.

"Do not cry, children," the stranger said, then swept out, an illusion of smoke on the air. Behind her, the soldier was gone, and the ruined hall was empty.

"I think we are all going mad," Mei's husband said.

"Who was she?" asked Mrs. Wu.

Mei raised her shoulders once and busied herself settling the baby, who had stopped crying when the noise ceased. "I met her in the Hall of Ancestors."

"She's no ancestor of *yours*," jeered her brother.

"She's a goddess," Mei said, without the least trace of doubt, remembering the tiny smile.

"Impossible," said her mother. "Why would a goddess stoop to rescuing peasants from soldiers."

"That was Kwan Yin," Mei breathed, marveling that she hadn't recognized the calm smile of the statue in the Buddhist temple the first time she had seen the strange woman. "The Goddess of Mercy saved us." She cuddled Sunli, who cooed.

"Oh, nonsense!" Chi'en protested. "Superstitious nonsense at that."

"But those are spent bullets on the floor."

Jinyiang sat up straight. The girl's eyes were fever-bright. "Mother, she can take us out of Nanking. You said if we had a safe escort we could go out to Uncle Chi'en's farm."

"Darling blossom, what just happened was a fluke," Sunyi said. "The soldier missed us, that is all. The woman ran away. She is no goddess."

"No, Mama is right," Jinyiang insisted. "I'll ask her." She stood up. Her gaze was fixed on something far away. Mei was frightened by her expression.

"The child is deranged," Father said, reaching for Jinyiang's arm. "Come here, blossom. It was an illusion, that is all." The girl slipped his grasp and ran down the stairs toward the street.

"Kwan Yin! Mother of Mercy! Take us with you!" she cried.

"It's those stories you told," Father said, glaring at Mei. "She believes them, and she will get us all killed."

Not bothering to defend herself, Mei sprang up, baby in arms, and dashed after the girl.

"Jinyiang," she called softly. "Jinyiang, the soldiers might hear you! Be quiet. Come back!"

The sky was brightening in the east, casting a long shadow behind the girl as she ran down the deserted street, looking wildly about for the silk-clad woman. Mei felt the teeth of the wind biting at her cheeks and ears as soon as she emerged from the protected alcove.

"Take us with you!" Jinyiang wailed, her voice thin and childlike. Her mind had broken. Mei dashed after her.

To her horror, there was a patrol jeep driving along the ruined streets not a hundred yards away. The Japanese in the front passenger seat pointed at Jinyiang. Mei couldn't understand his words, but the intention

was obvious. He was ordering his men to capture the
pretty young girl and bring her to him. Jinyiang, distracted, realized her danger only when the soldiers
grabbed her arms and began to drag her away. She
struggled, planting her heels down, and was hauled
unceremoniously over the stinking, decaying bodies in
the street, still calling for help from Kwan Yin.

Mei screamed, "No!"

Her family and neighbors crowded out behind her
to see where the girl had gone. The officer looked up
at the interruption, and pointed up at them. One of
the men sprayed the stairwell with a machine gun.
Out of the corner of her eye, Mei saw some bodies
fall, but had no idea whose they were. There wasn't
time to think. She had to free her daughter.

She and Sunyi flung themselves between the men and
the jeep, clawing at the soldiers. Weak from hunger and
long disuse of their muscles, they were easily pushed
away by the soldiers. One of the Japanese let go of
Jinyiang and unshouldered his machine gun, aiming it
at her parents. Mei dropped to her knees. She heard the
shots and her daughter's scream, but she felt nothing.
Incredibly, he must have missed. She felt instead the
cool brush of silk on her cheek. She turned, and saw
the goddess standing behind her, shielding her with the
broad, white sleeve.

"Kill them," she screamed. "They are murderers!"

The goddess didn't lose her holy smile, but her eyes
were sad. "They have mothers, too," she said. Mei felt
ashamed.

Sunli was sobbing in her arms. Jin was pushed
against the hood of the jeep, and the officer tore at
the child's ragged, sooty clothing. The girl cried out,
pulling weakly, failing to free her arms from the grasp
of the unsmiling soldiers who pinioned her.

"Mercy, lady," Mei begged Kwan Yin on her knees.
"She is too young. She will never heal of the scar.
Spare her."

The calm smile assured Mei that all would be well.

She reached between the men and the jeep, drawing the girl out. The men continued their actions, never realizing that their prey had escaped, that what they held, laughed at, thrust against, was empty air.

Mei felt as if she must be going mad, watching the rape go on. The soldiers paid no attention at all to the little crowd standing on the steps of the building. She stroked her daughter's hair and settled the torn rags of her clothing around her body in a seemly fashion. The girl wept with deep, tearing sobs.

"Come with me now," the goddess said to Mei over the girl's head. "It is time to leave this place. I promised your son a long life. He will be a remarkable man, born in war but fostered in peace. He will be safe where I take you."

Mei glanced up at her friends and neighbors clustered on the exposed stairs of her home. "But all these? You can't leave them. They'll die."

Kwan Yin's smile included them all. "To lose one's body is an important step on the road to enlightenment. But they shall come, too. There is plenty of room on the Islands, where we are going. We have others to gather. Come with me."

In a dream, Mei gathered her family and followed the goddess. Sunyi joined her, taking his wife's elbow and wrapping a protective arm around his daughter's shoulders. The baby in Mei's arms drowsed or suckled placidly. Though they must have walked for miles over the next hours, Mei never felt tired or hungry.

Nanking was a charnel house. Among the shells of burned and bombed-out houses and shops, tens of thousands lay dead in the streets, discarded like spoiled vegetables in drifts of soiled snow. Wounded people, their numbers unguessable, huddled in the ruined alleys and derelict houses. Kwan Yin chose from among those she found, and bid them join the ranks following her.

Occasionally, someone would see them, and stare

fearfully at the procession with the shining lady at its head. Once in a very great while man or woman would cry, "Mercy, lady," and stretch out a hand to the goddess. Their hands she would take, and pull them up, giving them the strength to follow her.

"Why can't you take them all, Great One?" Mei asked, watching with horror as the goddess passed by a horribly wounded mother kneeling in a gutter mourning the death of her husband and child.

"Some of these have karma to play out," Kwan Yin explained. "They are fated to pay for actions which they committed in earlier existences."

"It seems cruel," Mei shuddered. "I thought you were a goddess of peace."

"Every death is a lesson," the goddess replied imperturbably, the serene smile never leaving her lips. Mei reddened, realizing she had questioned the goddess's judgement. "My brother The Tiger battles against Susano, Japanese god of the Earth, who is greedy for more land over which to rule. He is unconcerned with what is left behind after the confrontation. All he cares is that he must win. I am involved with war also, because where there is killing, there is also mercy. Where there is pain, there is relief. The balance is maintained. All things move toward their appointed place. That is the essence of order. Soon, one abandons the body entirely and moves toward enlightenment. I ask you to trust in me, but only you can decide if you will or not."

Mei hoped she understood the goddess's lesson. Kwan Yin's task was certainly one she wouldn't want to undertake.

"Where are we going, Mama?" Jinyiang asked, squeezing in between her parents and slipping her hand through Mei's elbow.

"I don't know," Mei said. "She promises we will be safe. I trust her. Will you?"

"Yes," the girl said, eyes shining.

They reached the waterfront. Holding Jinyiang

firmly by the hand, Mei followed Kwan Yin onto the rough, wooden pier. The goddess's steps never stumbled over the planks as her own, mortal feet did. At the edge of the pier, Kwan Yin continued walking, supported by the very air. Mei stopped, staring.

The goddess turned back and stretched out a hand to her and the others following. "Come with me."

"I will fall," Mei said, glancing at the black, tossing waves a *li* below her.

"You will not," she said. "Trust. You have a long way to go yet."

Timidly, Mei put her foot out into the air. Incredibly, there seemed to be a surface strong enough to support her. With her arms wrapped firmly around the baby, she stepped out onto the air. Sunli cooed and chuckled. Mei smiled at him and looked back at her family.

Sunyi's eyes opened with wonder, and he came forward through the crowd on the pier. "The old stories are true, then," he said joyfully, leaping out to do the impossible. His fairy's face seemed to light up as he stood beside his wife. "Come, friends!" he cried.

The crowd surged forward, their eyes upturned to the bright figure hovering in the sky now many feet above them. Both parents stretched out hands to Jinyiang, steadying her as she took her steps into the infinite. Mei's parents came behind. The old woman nodded with sage acceptance, watching the sea toss far below her feet.

"Just like in the stories. You tell them better than I do," she told Mei. "Perhaps it is because I never thought they were real."

"Neither did I," Mei admitted. The sun was fully above the horizon now, outlining the goddess with blazing light but incredibly not blinding her followers. Mei and a hundred thousand others trailed behind her, floating toward the eastern sky.

"They will never know where we went," Sunyi said,

glancing back at the darkened mainland, now very far behind them.

"Look, Mother," Jinyiang said, full of excitement. She tugged her mother's sleeve and pointed straight ahead. "Do you see?" Mei squinted into the glare, realizing what she was looking at with a gasp of wonder. "There are three islands out there in the water. And they are on the backs of *turtles!*"

MYSTERY

To Tek's frustration, once his strength was restored Kwan Yin announced she had to leave. There were other places where those in need called for her and she had to go to them. This upset Tek more than he understood.

The Chinese goddess's departure left the war god and Mentor alone in his bunker. Outside he could hear the sounds of the other gods talking and laughing. But Tek was in no mood to return to the party.

"Who summoned that *thing*?" Tek demanded.

"The question is not who, but why," Mentor corrected. "Most of the gods gathered here have no cause to fear you or your followers."

"The old war gods," Tek suggested. He certainly was a threat to them.

"None are here," Mento answered, "and even a god would need to be somewhere nearby to create that monstrosity and send it to attack you."

"Where are they?" Tek demanded.

"Er, back on the earth watching something . . . sports perhaps or one of those ever present ethnic wars they have there. I believe the Olympic Games are near and they used to be a military competition."

Mentor seemed hesitant to discuss the subject and quickly changed it. "You should appear before your guests. With Kwan Yin leaving they will know you are well and you don't want them to think you are afraid to face them."

"Afraid?" There was a touch of outrage in Tek's voice as he rose menacingly from his seat.

"Then let's mingle," Mentor choose to misunderstand the gesture and moved toward the bunker's metal door. It opened before he reached it and the sound of voices and laughter became louder.

With a sigh Tek followed.

The party was festive, and there was even a slight cheer when Tek appeared. He wasn't sure why the other gods cheered, but smiled politely in return.

There were garlands on the sand bags and oriental lanterns hanging from the radar masts. Someone had willed it to be early evening and there was a cool breeze. The music, a slightly jazzy rendition of the music of the spheres, was just loud enough to dance to. A table had been spread and a heavy god who introduced himself as Mammon had taken charge of the snacks. He boasted that he had arranged for them to be appropriate for the occasion. Tek was amused to see most were taken from U.S. Army field issue MREs. He took a piece of the cherry cake, which the plump god recommended and had to agree it was tasty, if a little dry.

Mentor stayed close, making introductions. The Aztec gods stayed to themselves at the edge of the compound, drinking something whose smell drove most of the other gods away. The only outside god who ventured to drink with them was a loud, gruff figure that Mentor introduced as Thor. Judging from the weight of the war hammer the god carried, Tek assumed he was another war god and watched for any sign of trouble. After a long time he had to accept that the cheerful, drunken Northman seemed seriously concerned only with getting more drunk. The bearded

Norse god even took a swipe at Mentor with his hammer, but the old man nimbly dodged the blow and swore under his breath as he backed away and gave the hammer wielding drunk a very dark look.

The Egyptian gods made Tek uncomfortable at first. Most had retained their animal heads. That reminded the godling of the hybrid beast he had just been mauled by. After a short time the Egyptians' exquisitely polite manners appealed to his sense of structure and he relaxed. After a long conversation he was pleased to receive an invitation to visit them in their land of the dead whenever he had a chance.

As they walked among the other gods, Tek wondered why he was doing this. He was a war god, not a party god. He finally dragged Mentor aside and asked.

"Even wars do not happen in a vacuum," the old teacher explained. "You need to be able to deal with the gods your wars effect. Just as they have to calculate your effect on their plans."

Tek soon realized this gave every god a motive to have attacked him. A conclusion that made him even more uncomfortable as he walked among the dozens of divine guests that had now appeared for the party. Casually he wondered how they all were made aware of the event.

The real hosts of the party were obviously the Greek gods. From what he could tell, this was traditional. Isis had commented that Greeks were always organizing and politicking. She viewed this as a personality flaw. Only a handful of the Greeks were here, but those that were always took the lead in conjuring up new treats or entertainers. As he was introduced to her, the war god remembered that Diana had also been responsible for creating the garden in which he had been attacked. Diana may have sensed his suspicions and was less than cordial. Their initial greetings were almost insults and Tek's thanking her for throwing the party here led only to her snapped comment that *she* could hold a party anywhere, even in a "khaki nightmare."

Mentor tried to pass off her attitude, but Tek persisted in his suspicions. Finally he became so concerned that he almost dragged the teacher back into his bunker.

"That goddess Diana seems quite hostile," he said as the heavy steel door swung silently shut behind them. It wouldn't keep a determined intruder out, not a god, but it discouraged casual interruptions.

"Her favorite brother is Mars. He's probably the most popular of the old war gods," Mentor admitted. "He's also the prime god of heroic warriors and you are likely to be a major threat to his power."

"End it, most likely," Tek said smugly.

"Nothing is everything," Mentor corrected ambiguously. "Still, she may have been testing you. To see if you are a threat to Mars."

"Then she found out I am," the new war god finished, almost smiling.

Tek pulled himself up to a control panel and watched the radar display. The lanterns had only degraded the signal slightly. With a few miraculous enhancements he could easily see the locations of all the other gods. Several were now clustered around or in what appeared to be a swimming pool. Looking over the war god's shoulder Mentor commented that it probably meant that Neptune, or Poseidon as he preferred to be called, had arrived, as that god needed water nearby to support the sea nymphs he always had with him.

They watched the impersonal screen for several minutes. Tek enjoyed the illusion that he was watching the others without being seen himself. Finally he found himself nervously following the blip that represented Diana. Pulling himself away from the screen, he turned to Mentor.

"Your magic TV can show almost any incident," Tek demanded.

"Anything that has happened, and a lot that hasn't," Mentor agreed.

"Then show me what Diana was doing just before she came here."

"If you wish," Mentor agreed. "But she will know of it. All the gods can sense these things."

"I'll take that chance," the young god insisted. He half expected the screen to brighten with an image of the goddess summoning the dragon tiger from some demonic plane.

UPSTART

by Jane S. Fancher

The room was growing a bit tawdry around the edges—curtains fraying, cracks in the stained-glass windows, a stain on the couch the maids *could* not get out—still, Diana called it home.

Far more dismaying was her own physical state. It had been such a long winter.

"Getting downright anorexic, darling." Mammon came up behind her, examined his own face for wrinkles or (worse) spots, winced at *her* reflection, and retreated from the mirror.

"For gods' sakes, man, remember the year. That term won't be in vogue for another—" Oh dear, what *was* it? '68 . . . '78 . . . '88. "—at *least* fifteen years. I'm—twiggish. Quite fashionably thin."

"You look like a rail."

Difficult to argue with the truth. And speaking of Truth . . .

Sweeping her voluminous robes into an elegant swirl around her feet, she turned full about on the vanity stool to smile sweetly across the posh Hilton suite. "And you, my dear, look like a fat—you should pardon the expression—toad." With the grace only eons of battles (verbal and otherwise) lost and won could achieve, she rose to her feet. "I'm starving. Shall we go?"

And as they strolled arm in comfy arm through the suite to the door: "What are we doing today?—American tourists?—Oh, *good.*"

Mammon opened the door and the cool draft from the excessively air-conditioned hallway brushed her bare knees.

The daily squeeze in the Hotel Diana lobby was well underway by the time they arrived.

"I don't know *why* you always insist on eating *here,*" Mammon grumbled, turning sideways to avoid a tourist armed with 50 pounds of camera equipment. "The food is mediocre at best."

"Only because you've developed a taste for American grease-burgers, darling." Diana paused, admiring the tall statue holding court at the far end of the lobby, an admirably accurate recreation of one of the ancient statues excavated from the nearby ruins of Ephesus. "Do you honestly wonder, my dear? How many of us have been so honored in this century?" She cocked her head, trying a different angle on the many-breasted statue. "Goodness, that would be painful at *that* time of the month. My male worshippers always did get a bit—carried away. Seems to me four would be sufficient to make the—" Across the jammed lobby, at one of the coffee shop tables: "Oh, *look.* He's here. Somehow I knew he'd be."

She pulled Mammon through the crush as smoothly as his girth would allow.

"Just a minute," he growled, and dug in his heels beside the news stand.

"Isn't he *sweet*!" she murmured, tapping her foot impatiently, while Mammon negotiated the price of the Wall Street Journal. "I think, perhaps, it's time I approached him. What do you think?"

He ignored her, involved in arguing over the cover price. Why, just this *once,* he couldn't simply *pay* the man . . .

"Find us a table, will you, darling?" she said, and drifted away, slowly fading as she approached the crowded table.

More crowded than usual. The new one was tall, blond, definitely middle-aged and decidedly out of place in the abundance of dark native elegance. Swiss, unless she missed her guess, and not to her taste—today.

Today, her taste ran more toward eighteen—*ma-a-aybe* nineteen—slim build, golden skin, and bl-l-lack cur-r-rly hair.

And equally out of place among his co-conspirators, though his differences were more subtle than yellowhair's. His dark sweater and form-fitting slacks, of good quality and excellent taste, were a bit frayed about the edges. Nothing overt, but the least his excessively well-heeled 'friends' could have done was lend him a cast-off or two for their frequent meetings in this exclusive hotel.

Sweet. Terribly sweet, the way he gazed wonderingly upon her monument. Of course, he wasn't the only one to do that—a half-naked woman with about a million and one breasts tended to have that effect on male mortals—but this mortal was different.

His name was Kemal. She'd first seen him a year ago, and with increasing frequency as time passed. At first he'd been alone, standing just inside the door while the tour groups he guided took their lunches at the feet of the spotlighted statue, waiting for them to rejoin him at the bus, as though he would not be welcome in the posh, European-style hotel. Then, barely a month ago, here he'd been. At this same

table. Always with this same group. Always slightly out
of place.

She came up behind him and brushed an invisible
finger along his rounded cheek. He started and
glanced over his shoulder, his smooth brow wrinkling
with puzzlement. She chuckled silently and waited
until his companions called his attention back to the
conversation. Then she ... let her fingers do a little
walking ... until the poor boy was flushed and quite
thoroughly confused. With a final brush of her lips
across his, she whispered in his ear ...

"It was wonderful, darling."

... and drifted back to Mammon's table, fading into
Reality until, when she sat, she was quite as visible as
a mortal woman.

"Have fun?" The question rose from behind the
paper.

She pressed the paper down, smiled sweetly into
his irritated face. "Wonderful, darling."

He flipped the paper free, disappeared again.

She smiled as the waitress delivered her usual:
steak (Diane, of course), with fruit macedonia, a dozen
croissants, aubergine parmesan, haricots abeurre,
pilafi, and squid etouffe aux pelits champignons ...

... plus a six-pack of Coors. One at a time, of
course, and specially imported for her. *Terrible* habits
one picked up in one's travels.

"You're wrong, you know," Mammon said.

"Wrong?" Kemal's eyes, making a surreptitious scan
of the lobby, met hers. She smiled. "About what?"

"The statue," Mammon said. "It's not to honor *you*.
The sign on the front door might read the Hotel
Diana, but the whole establishment is a monument to
moi."

"Never!"

"Oh, but it *is*, darling. The people come here to
gawk at the statue, but they spend money. Lots of
money. And *that's* why the finance company loaned
the money to *build* your statue." His Cheshire Cat

grin appeared over the top of the *Journal*. "Mine, darling. All mine."

She wrinkled her nose, and carefully trimmed the fat off her steak.

Asker, Deniz, Cahil, Mart and Kabil. No family names; likely not their real given names, either, but Kemal Dunman hadn't known that when they'd introduced themselves, had naively exchanged his own truth for their prevarications. Now they used his true name casually—and frequently—in the presence of this ... foreigner ... ensuring that he, and anyone (or *anything*) listening, would remember it.

He ran a finger around the rim of his glass, sipped the ten-year-old Glen Kinchie within, resisting the temptation to gulp. He couldn't really afford this one. Another would mean going hungry two nights running. But he wasn't about to sit in this elite company swilling rakhi.

Six weeks ago, Kabil had been a stranger, one of many thousands he'd herded through the ruins of Ephesus. But then Kabil had casually invited him to join him and his university-educated cronies for drinks here in the shadow of *her* statue, where the scent of flowers filled the air regardless of the season, and the fountain's gentle spray drowned out the racket of the traffic outside. Initially he'd felt ignorant and foolish among the students, but soon Kabil had had him pouring his heart out—about his fears that the Turkey he loved, a land rich in history and pride, was disappearing into the hands of Western developers who would destroy that history's relics in the name of socio-economic 'progress.'

Now, six weeks later, Kabil was still a stranger to him, as were these others, but their 'scholarship' and their sophisticated airs no longer impressed him. He didn't know *what* they believed or wanted. They *claimed* similar gods to his. They *claimed* that they wanted Turkey for the People, not the Americans or the British, or any other nation with money for development.

But their methods had grown increasingly suspect in his estimation. Even now, Kabil smiled and reached across the table to shake this foreigner's hand: a business transaction completed. Not an uncommon occurrence in this lobby, excepting the commodity in question.

"So, Duman," Kabil said, once the foreigner had left. "When did you say you'd have the bus ready?"

Kemal pressed his lips together, smothering objection. Kabil had slipped *that* part of the deal past him when he'd allowed his imagination to ... wander. He'd subsequently resisted the statue's haunting presence, but by then, it had been too late, the transfer arrangements made. Besides, if they were caught, losing his job would be the least of his worries.

"Eight-thirty, no later. And wear light clothes: it'll get hot in there. We can change into the blacks later."

"I *still* don't like this," Mart whined. But then, Mart whined every time he opened his mouth. "I don't *want* to spend all morning in a baggage—"

A soft *thud* from beneath the table. Mart cursed and glared at Kabil, but he shut up.

"Well, we'd best get going. Tomorrow morning, then." Kabil rose, the others followed suit. "Cover it, will you, Duman?"

And they were gone before Kemal could object.

"Damned upstart."

"Who's that, darling?—Why, those scum! They've left the poor child with the tab. He looks positively ill. —Who's an upstart, darling?"

"Tek. Thinks he's so important. Look at this."

He slapped the paper down on her plate. She stifled complaint—this being a class hotel—and obligingly inspected the article on the 'New Look of War.'

"Good PR—that's all. I tell you, Diana, *he* only fights the wars. *I* make them."

"Yes, darling, I'm sure you do." Having made desperate peace with the waitress, (who surreptitiously slipped a bill in to cover the balance—curious behavior in a waitress, but this one was Kemal's *special* friend), the kid was leaving. "—Oh, my, such a view."

As the painted-on slacks passed their table, she blew a gentle breeze into his ear—

He stopped abruptly, rubbing his ear.

—and with a second breeze, she wafted a fifty into his back pocket, carefully smoothing the fabric afterward so as not to disrupt the pleasing line, all without removing her hands from the table.

He jumped. She met his eyes and smiled. He blinked and bowed politely, his dark eyes flicking to her hands folded demurely on the table, blinked again and moved quickly (from his mortal viewpoint) out of range.

She chuckled and let him go. "Oh, he *is* sweet."

"He was had, you know." Mammon was back behind his paper.

"Who's that, darling?"

Mammon's hand waved vaguely in the direction of the momentarily empty table. "Shouldn't have gone over seven per, US."

Mammon insisted these days on using the New World currency, convinced it was the way of the future market; Diana didn't bother figuring the exchange. This began to sound as if Mammon knew more about her newest conquest's business than she did. And if it affected Kemal's future, she wanted to know it, too.

She double-checked the numinous disruption wall that turned their voices into white background noise even for the nearest mortal ears, then asked:

"Seven per for what, darling?"

"Guns. No overhead. Bulk quantities. Hell, *I* made it easy for the bastard to get them out of Israel in the first place. —If this is any indication of the next generation's business sense, I'm sure I don't know what the world is coming to. Appalling, I say."

Diana didn't bother reminding him he knew exactly what the world was coming to—or could, if checking out specific Futures didn't take all the fun out of living the moment's Possibilities.

"Which 'bastard'?"

"The 'banker,' naturally."

"Banker? You mean Yellow-hair?"

A grunt from behind the paper. "Deals contraband. Front man. Arms, mostly. His newest commodity is a rather lovely lot of fresh-from-the-factory Uzis."

"*Uzis?*" Such names these boys came up with.

"New version of the Israeli automatic. I suspect that's the shipment your boy's friends are after. Funny, I figured he'd go for Korudan's crowd in Greece. They're much better organized, ready to make their move on the Junta—and these guns could have tipped the balance. But they were *too* canny this time. Kabil paid too much, but he'll get the guns."

"What did you mean, you made it easy? What did you do?"

"Nothing much. Just a little temptation. A single truck can carry a lot of these little suckers. Slip the necessary clue to the Banker, run the transport truck out of gas at the properly isolated point, tweak the driver's greed at the right instant. *Voila'.*" He took a sip of coffee, never taking his eyes from the paper. "All in the timing. But the banker had deeper laid plans than I gave him credit for. This Kabil is so delightfully ignorant—very easy to influence him."

She frowned at the paper. "Influence? Kabil? Just now?"

The paper slipped until she could just see Mammon's face. "He's terribly anxious to take over Turkey, lock, stock and barrel. And he's so delightfully certain of his own power. He can't possibly succeed, of course, but that unforgivable price he just paid will generate flux in the world black market, open up avenues for those who seek wealth and power." He smiled tightly. "My kind of people."

"Which? The Banker? Or Kabil?"

The grin widened. "Both, darling. Obviously, both. Power on that scale doesn't happen without the fools to support it."

The paper snapped back into place.

Well, Mammon could have his followers. She didn't want them. Could care less what happened to them. It was her Kemal she worried about. Kemal was not one of Mammon's fools, nor was he a shark. He couldn't be.

Could he?

Without a word, Diana faded out and floated out the Hotel Diana's front door.

Kemal throttled the motorcycle's engine back, let the smooth-running machine coast up to the guard's station. Berk came out, the frown on his face clearly visible in the moonlight, and Kirsi's arms tightened around Kemal's waist, her face pressed against his neck.

Kemal murmured reassurance, had that confidence rewarded when the frown lightened in recognition.

"Kemal!" Berk cried, grinning. "What are you doing here? And where'd you get this?"

A wave of the hand which might mean the cycle— or Kirsi.

"This—" Kemal tapped the leather-covered hand grips. "—was a gift from Mr. Simons."

"The man whose daughter tried to investigate the sewers the hard way?"

"That's the one. He was—grateful. I was going to sell it, but Mama—"

"And right she was, Kem," Kirsi interrupted him, arms tightening for a different reason. "You deserved something nice for risking your foolish neck. You send *everything* to her and your sisters. If I hadn't covered for you this morning—"

"And who is this pretty thing?" Berk asked, giving Kirsi his most lecherous smile.

"Mine," Kemal said firmly. "Keep your hands to yourself. I wanted to show her the temple by moonlight. —Mind?"

"For you, kid—" Berk stepped back a pace and waved them through the gate.

"Thanks. I owe you one."

"Hell, just put in a good word with the Lady for me and we'll call it square."

Kemal laughed and put the cycle in gear. "I'll do that."

As a tour guide, young Kemal was good, exceptionally good with his attentive audience of one besotted girl. Kemal knew his history and told it well. Kirsi, the waitress from the Diana, seemed to hang on his every word, and, from the intelligence of her occasional question, it wasn't just for Kemal's good looks.

But to Diana herself, it was all just—ancient history, and she soon wandered off into her own memories. The white marble ruins of Ephesus glowed in the moonlight, even to the marble street down which she floated. Memory filled in the lines, the larger than expected scale, and memory populated the wide road. The vast majority of the traffic had been tourists, even then, visitors come to experience *her* city, to worship at *her* temple. The temple to her Mother Earth aspect: so much more interesting than Artemis. That virgin goddess aspect was a bitchy bore.

Too bad, really, that she daren't reveal herself to the lad. The stories she could tell him of this place . . . far more personal and exciting anecdotes than he could possibly know. But he'd never believe her. That level of faith had vanished in this age of skepticism; gone to ruins like the marble rubble surrounding them.

All the beauty and the grandeur—gone, thanks to the arrows of Apollo and the damned, disgusting little bugs they carried.

Apollo and Diana. Day and night. Life and death.

They'd shared Ephesus once upon a time. Too bad they hadn't seen the truth sooner, that they hadn't known which Possibility to explore. Perhaps they could have saved the city from its decline. Perhaps they might have planted a careful suggestion in a ready ear, as she'd planted the fifty in Kemal's pocket. Drain the marsh. Get rid of the mosquitoes.

The future was flux. So many possibilities. Some—like the one which had Happened—had led to an understanding and cure for malaria. Others—well, none would have found it soon enough to save Ephesus, and while the Future was flux, the Past was singular and done.

Too late now. She missed the Sun God aspect more than she cared to admit. Mammon was another bore. Perhaps, one day soon, conditions would favor Apollo's return.

The couple had worked their way down to the temple—*her* temple—or what was left of it. Time had been cruel to them both. She was thin and wasted; her temple, seventh wonder of the world, reduced to its marble foundations.

". . . They're talking about rebuilding it." Kemal's voice, drifting to her on a breeze. Diana pricked up her ears, glided back to the temple.

"Would you like that?" Kirsi asked, sensible, insightful question.

"I honestly don't know." The lad walked out into the middle of the vast, rectangular foundations, head thrown back, eyes glowing in the moonlight. "It must have been wonderful. Largest pillared roof ever built . . . all in white marble . . . I'd love to have seen it. But—" He turned to her, biting his lip. "It's for all the wrong reasons, Kirsi. They want the money—the tourism. That's not right."

"Not all of them, Kemal." Kirsi walked up to him, took his hands in hers. "Some love the past as much as you do. There *are* others who would like to rebuild the glory that was."

"Do they? I wish I could believe that."

"*I* do."

His eyes were swimming between the long lashes. His head bent above Kirsi's. The kiss lengthened and deepened until Diana felt obliged to leave the temple's aura for the cool breeze coming off the sea and up the hill. When she'd regained control, she drifted back to the temple and silently urged the youngsters off the immediate premises. Some spots were *too* ripe with past energy, and she had the present to worry about.

Kirsi had sensed Kemal's upset and was probing gently regarding the arms deal. He was resisting explanation—possibly for good reason.

On the other hand, a little pressure at the right moment might just give her the information she sought.

Kirsi . . . she'd worry about Kirsi later.

The great theater of Ephesus stretched out around them, row upon semi-circular row. The round marble spot marking the acoustical focus glowed moon-white in the dark, grassy stage far below. Beyond the stage, rows of cap-stoned pillars, was the prop-storage and beyond that, the straightline demarcation of the theater gateway, lying at a perfect perpendicular to a wide marble road that vanished into the misty flat distance.

Once upon a millennium ago, some other young man had sat, hour upon hour, on these stony seats, as Kemal did now, with his sweetheart wrapped in the circle of his arm as Kirsi was in his, watching, listening, learning . . . "Imagine the plays they must have seen from here," he whispered into her soft, wavy hair. "Oedipus Rex, Antigone, the Oresteia . . ."

"Ugh, king-sacrifice." Kirsi giggled and pressed his arm against her side. "Morbid taste you have, Kem. Give me the comedies, thanks anyway."

"They're all right, too, but think about it. Oedipus, Agamemnon, Orestes—and all the other powerful kings whose deaths brought prosperity to their people. We need kings like that. Kings willing to sacrifice all for *our* people, *our* country, not for someone else, and not for their own wealth."

"Agamemnon didn't exactly jump under the knife, Kemal."

"You know what I mean."

"I suppose so. But do you honestly think Kabil will be such a leader? A man who spends the equivalent of your monthly salary on a sweater he'll never wear, then leaves you to handle the bar tab?"

He blushed. "Not really; I don't believe in him. Not any more. Once . . . but he's not what I'd hoped. Now, I'm sort of stuck."

"Why? Why not just leave them?"

"At the moment, they need me. And they know my family." He squeezed her arm. "And they know about you. They know I won't risk any of you. But once they have this stupid shipment, they won't need me any more and I'll be free of them."

"You don't really believe that."

He shrugged, setting his personal future aside as he'd learned he must: in it there was little cause for wonder, only gratitude for surviving each day. But wonder was far from dead in his soul as his eyes tracked a moonbeam to its source. He leaned back, resting his elbows on the stone. The moon was almost full tonight—would be tomorrow. . . .

"You know, the Americans say they'll land a man up there next year. Another of Diana's secrets revealed."

"I don't think she'll mind."

"I'm certain she won't. I think she'll be waiting to greet them. I wish I could be there. Touch her with them. And if not me, one day, my son . . ."

"Or daughter."

He smiled down into her moonglow eyes and kissed her lightly. "Or daughter," he amended, willing to accept even the most outrageous tonight.

She returned his kiss, less lightly, then snugged in

against him. "I don't think you really hate the Americans enough to be a part of Kabil's coup."

"I don't know what I want any more. The Americans give us tractors—and our people use them to pull drag boards around the threshing floors. Might as well go back to using oxen."

"At least some of them *have* tractors to pull the plows."

"I *want* our people to have all the good things the world has to offer, but I want them to understand what those good things are and to have the satisfaction of adding new ideas to the world pool. I *don't* want those good things to be owned by people who've never touched the soil of Turkey. I want us to be leaders in the world, not beggars. Producers. Inventors. Proud, as we've a right to be."

She shivered against his arm.

"It's getting cold," he commented generically, giving her an opening to bring the evening to a close he didn't personally care to suggest.

"We should count our blessings. This summer, the mosquitos would eat us alive."

"True." Thinking she was perhaps being martyristically accommodating: "Want to go home?"

"I . . . suppose."

But she didn't seem inclined to sprint for the parking lot, either. They worked their way slowly down the theater's stone steps, and through the ancient gateway. The ruins closed in on either side as they passed under the arch of Mithradates, bringing black shadows with them.

Fortunately, Kirsi seemed no more inclined toward senseless chatter than he was as they walked hand in hand toward the Temple of Diana. In the distance, the barely visible archaeological excavation tents were multiplying rapidly. Soon—very soon—the supply trucks would begin deliveries. And soon after that, this year's crop of foreign students would begin unleashing the secrets hidden beneath Turkish soil.

"It's tomorrow, isn't it?" Kirsi asked from a shadow.

Kemal bit his lip, fighting the urge to confide in her. She was a friend. A *good* friend. And an honorable man didn't pull friends into trouble with him.

"Where are you going to stash them?"

He turned his head away from her scrutiny, at a disadvantage in a shaft of moonlight.

"Here?"

He nodded briefly, then: "Please, Kirsi, let it alone. I don't *want* you to know. If I tell you, and something went wrong, they'd blame you. Come after you."

"Only if they knew."

"They'd know."

"Don't you trust me?"

"You know I do. It's *them* I don't trust."

She paused beside a crumbling wall, leaned her elbows on it, looking into the warren of walls, rocks and weeds.

"So many small rooms. What was this place? Do they know?"

He laughed, grateful for the change of subject.

"Well, let's see. The temple is just across the street. Lots of small rooms. What do you suppose?"

"Aha. Diana's priestesses."

"You might call them that. They undoubtedly gave a percentage to the temple coffers."

"They gave more than that."

"What do you mean?"

She turned and leaned her back against the low wall, tracing his arm with a fingertip. "Life. Death. Love. War. All different aspects of the same coin. Many of the ancient camp followers were priestesses. Before a battle, the men came to them, garnered strength from their—coupling. The good will of the goddess. Good luck in the battle to come."

He had a battle to fight tomorrow. God willing, it would be quick and clean, without bloodshed. A simple transfer of—merchandise.

Kirsi knew that. Knew the situation disturbed him

and tried to coax him free of the worry. And at the moment Kemal was more than willing to be coaxed.

He hung his head and said morosely, "I've nothing to give. No money left." He blinked up at her. "Do you suppose the goddess would like a used 'cycle?"

Kirsi smiled, took him by the hand, and drew him uphill into the weed-choked maze, into shadows, where moonbeams and wind would not reach them.

"We'll think of something."

Such sweetly naive coupling. Completed almost before it was begun. Diana smiled and brushed each young cheek with her lips, wishing them both gentle, restful sleep, surrounding them with a blanket of warm air to keep them comfortable until they were ready to return home.

Someday, she'd have to instill a bit of creativity into Kirsi's libido. For Kemal ... Perhaps Kemal would benefit from a bit more—*personal* instruction.

She caught the wind back to the Izmir Hilton. Mammon was still awake—on the phone to his broker in New York. He nodded to her as she drifted in through the window, but it was a good fifteen minutes before he hung up the phone.

"So. Did you have a good time?"

"They went to Ephesus."

"Oh, joy. Oh, rapture. That dump ought to be torn down once and for all. Clear the land for something useful." His bearded face lightened. "A factory, maybe. That would be nice."

"Kemal says they've plans to rebuild the temple— make it into the ultimate tourist trap. Make *lots* of money, it will."

Mammon snorted. "I'll believe that when I see the receipts. —Find out anything interesting?"

"Tomorrow. Want to go with me?"

He yawned. "Wouldn't miss it for the world."

She leaned over his shoulder and stroked his beard, became distracted by the ear next to her mouth and nibbled it lightly. Kemal and his sweetheart had her feeling quite energetic.

But:

"Not tonight, woman. I just lost a cool half-mil and my head is killing me."

"Scum." She bit hard enough to draw blood and floated away on a breeze before he could retaliate.

Predictably, Kabil was late.

"What's your problem?" Kabil asked as Kemal hurried him and the others to the back of the bus. "Your American tourists aren't even up yet."

"That's all you know about it," Kemal muttered. He threw open the luggage compartment and jerked his head toward it. "Get in. *Hurry.*"

"It *stinks!*" Mart groaned and complained. "The exhaust will kill us."

"The compartment is rated safe for animals," Kemal hissed. "I think you'll survive. Just get in and shut up, will you?"

"I still don't understand why we can't just pretend we're tourists." Mart whined.

"Because the bus is *full*, fool," Kabil answered for him. "And if the gateguard registers you going *in*, he'll expect you to come *out*, now, won't he?"

"Hello-oh, Keee-ma-a-al!" An adolescent female voice echoed down the narrow side street.

Kemal wrenched the door down just as Teresa Preston skipped around the corner of the hotel. He twisted the lock on the panel and jolted upright in time to avoid her rather personal greeting.

"'Morning, Miss Preston." He smiled tightly, dodging her groping hands with a practiced sway. "Are the others ready to go?"

"What have you got in there?" She tried to look around him at the luggage compartment.

"Nothing. I thought I'd left something last night. I was mistaken."

A smothered sneeze.

"What was that?" she asked immediately.

"What was what?" He gave her his best wide-eyed innocence, and taking her arm with a familiarity she'd sought for three solid days, he led her toward the front of the bus and helped her up the stairs, brushing his lips across her hand before releasing it.

Funny thing, she seemed to forget completely about the noise in the baggage compartment.

"But the agency *assured* me . . ." The woman's voice trailed off uncertainly, and Kemal felt an honest pang of regret when he had to say:

"I'm sorry, ma'am, but, as you can see—" He waved an arm toward the loaded seats. "—I'm full."

Her bright blue eyes followed that gesture, returned mournfully to his face. A momentary flash of recognition, gone with the next breath. Tall, slender, copious blond hair—if he'd met her before, he'd certainly remember, for all she was decidedly middle-aged.

"Oh, dear," she said, breaking the spell. "What shall I do? I was to meet my friends at Ephesus. They'll be waiting for me—"

Suddenly, from the seat behind the driver's niche:

"Mama? Mama, I think I'm going to be—"

A choking cough. An exclamation. A sudden flurry to get the window down. And a very surprised passer-by on the far side of the bus.

Thanks to the blond lady's skillful soothing, the passer-by laughed the matter off. But as Teresa Preston's mother helped the precocious teenager off the bus, Mr. Preston said loudly: "I shall, of course, expect a refund . . ."

"I haven't that authority, sir," Kemal answered quietly. "But I'll make a complete report to the office. If you'll contact them, I'm certain they will—"

"My daughter's *sick*! Probably food poisoning! You'll hear from my lawyers."

Kemal watched helplessly as Teresa's parents

bundled her—despite her loud protests—back into the hotel.

"Poor thing," a voice said solicitously at his back.

He turned to find the blond woman still there.

She smiled. "I'm sure she'll be all right. Probably something at breakfast . . ."

He grimaced. "Probably just too *much* of everything. On the other hand, it appears we have a seat available—if you'd still like it."

She wrinkled her nose at him. "I'll just grab a towel from the hotel to put over the wet spot."

Diana pressed her nose to the window, examining each passing vehicle carefully. Not that she expected a truck marked *Contraband*, but one never knew—which was why she'd *had* to be on this bus. She'd investigated the flux last night, but they were evidently close to a primary pivotal node, so numerous were the possibilities.

Without details, she'd just have to stick close to Kemal's rear all day long. Dirty job, but somebody . . .

They were among the first visitors to arrive at Ephesus. Kemal dropped the passengers off at the entrance, then took the bus to the far end of the parking lot: only polite, or so he claimed—Diana couldn't help but notice that in so positioning the bus, the baggage compartment was carefully aimed toward the brushy hillside.

Kemal then treated his tour group to a much modified version of the same spiel he'd given Kirsi last night, then turned them loose with information pamphlets and instructions to meet him at such and such a time, beyond the theater in the lower parking lot.

Diana faded out and drifted at his back as he returned to the bus.

His fellow conspirators emerged from the baggage compartment, sweaty and cursing, accusing poor Kemal of purposely forgetting them. Kemal swallowed any retort he might have made, halting their tirades with the simple expedient of stepping into the open at the back of the bus and raising the engine casing.

When next Diana looked, they'd disappeared.

The small transport vehicle beeped a protest and Kemal stepped aside to let it pass. Yet another load for the excavation team working the far side of the temple. The fifth such load today from the large truck parked in the upper lot.

Kemal wondered which, if any, of those crates contained *their* shipment. Which, if any, he'd be carrying up the hillside tonight, to a hidey-hole *he* knew and no one else did.

Yet.

After tonight, Kabil and all his cronies would.

He made his way slowly to the lower parking lot, where he'd left the bus, stopping occasionally to answer questions—some from his own group, some from lone tourists. It was an old routine, and one he generally enjoyed. Once someone proclaimed you an expert, other someones invariably emerged from the shadows armed with observations they simply *had* to share. Most of the questions, he'd answered a hundred times his first week on the job. But every once in a while, usually from the most naive visitor to the ancient city, an insight occurred which opened a whole new realm of historic possibilities.

Today, however, his interest waned rapidly, and he finally hurried past the crowds to the lower parking lot.

"What do you mean, the bus won't start?"

Sometimes, tourists were amazingly thick headed.

"Just that, Mr. Clark," Kemal said patiently. "I called for a replacement over an hour ago. He'll be here with a working bus in half an hour." He smiled placatingly, and knowing how fast Acayib could drive with an empty bus: "Maybe less."

"I know something about cars, son," Mr. Bierhorst said from the back. "Want me to take a look?"

No! Kemal wanted to say, but instead: "The mechanic will come tomorrow. He'd have been here today, but his sister's getting married and . . ."

"Nonsense. It will give me something to do while we wait."

"I really can't let you, sir. Company rules. It would be my job if—"

"Honestly, son, I'm a licensed mechanic." Bierhorst pulled out his wallet, handed over a card, but Kemal barely glanced at it.

"Sir, I—"

"C'mon, son." Bierhorst persisted. "I've worked for the bus company back home for twenty-five years. Maybe I can save *your* company some time and money."

Bierhorst had no reason to lie, and perhaps it was his own raw nerves, but the others in the group seemed to be casting suspicious glances at one another. Kemal sighed and murmured:

"Thank you, sir. I'd appreciate it."

Bierhorst, as Kemal had feared, found the 'problem' the instant he raised the casing.

"Why, it's nothing but a loose wire. Try it now, son."

With a silent prayer, Kemal pressed the starter. A working bus meant he took the tourists home—and left Kabil and crew stranded.

The engine turned over . . .

Kemal's heart sank.

. . . sputtered, and died.

"Try it again."

This time—nothing.

Which circumstances solved the problem of the tourists, but not Kabil's getaway vehicle.

"You're sure you don't want a lift back to the city?" Acayib, his replacement driver, asked, across the stream of tourists they were helping onto the bus. "I can drop you off here in the morning."

Kemal shook his head. "The bus is my responsibility. I'll feel better staying here until the mechanic can make it."

"Bad luck, the engine's going dead on you today."

"Can't blame Abi. Not every day your sister gets married." Which was why they'd chosen tonight—full moon and all—to make the transfer. "Do me a favor?"

"Name it."

"Go up topside and leave a message with the guard for me, will you?"

"No problem."

Kemal waved goodbye to his group, and climbed back into his own bus. He *had* to get it running before closing. He turned the key, one final attempt to start it.

Kabil would have his hide—

It caught without so much as a splutter, ran smoothly in the seconds it took to gather his wits and turn it off again. Then he dropped his head into arms crossed on the steering wheel and offered a silent prayer to the goddess.

A pleasant filling of the void inside. Diana smiled at her young convert, and passed a gentle, relaxing hand over his back. He did well to recognize his benefactress. Few would.

What she didn't know about auto mechanics would fill a library, but it took no genius to lift the wire free again, nor to replace it afterward. On the other hand, it had taken *exquisite* skill to trick Bierhorst into seeing otherwise.

The site closed down for the night, the guard, making a final run through, stopped for a word with Kemal before returning to his station. And as darkness closed around them, the others began filtering in from the ruins, slipping on the black clothing Kemal produced from the baggage compartment.

The last to arrive was (no surprise) Kabil.

"So," he said, without preamble, "Where's this digging going on?"

"You spent the entire day here and don't know?" Kemal asked, handing him black slacks and turtleneck sweater.

"I was—otherwise occupied."

Ribald laughter echoed through the bus along with comments of a personal nature in which Kemal, frowning toward the window, evidently found no humor.

Neither did Diana. She'd seen what Kabil called love-making; animals had more finesse. And the poor idiot tourist he'd lured into the ruins would have some heavy-duty explaining to do to her parents in about nine months. Not good to play those games in *her* territory.

"Let's just get this over with," Kemal muttered, and threw the bus door open.

Kemal led the way through the ruins, past the temple, to the excavation pit and its accompanying supply tent, where, according to the blond-haired foreigner, the single guard had been . . . taken care of. Certainly no one challenged their entry into the tent.

Inside, stack upon endless stack of crates and boxes of all shapes and sizes. Kemal despaired of ever sorting out those they'd come for, but Kabil pointed silently to one box. They worked it free of the stack and Kabil, producing a knife from his pocket, prised the lid free, revealing layers of packing material, evidently designed for shipping artifacts away from the site.

Kabil thrust a hand in among the shredded fibers, grinned and withdrew what had to be one of the submachine guns.

"It's so *small*," Asker said wonderingly, kneeling down for a closer look.

Personally, Kemal could see all he wanted from the far side of the tent.

Small, indeed. Not much more than a foot long. And light, if the overall weight of the crate—which must contain several of the hand weapons—were any indication. Frighteningly easy to hide.

Kabil tilted the Uzi this way and that, poking and prodding, finally, swinging the stock around and down, clicking it into place. Another bit of burrowing in the crate uprooted a box of clips, another examination of the weapon revealed only one way to load it—trial and error actions which made Kemal's skin crawl.

"How much training have you had with one of these?" he asked, morbidly curious.

Kabil sneered up at him. "Not exactly difficult to figure." He hit the bolt above the handgrip, and waved the loaded weapon casually about the tent, making soft *ack-ack* sounds. "Here we come, ready or not." He caressed the barrel, kissing the tip. "Seven pounds, 14 inches, 950 RPM. Hell of a baby, don't you think?"

"If you don't drop the spare clips on your foot!" Kemal controlled the urge to bolt from the tent. "For God's sake, man, put it *away!*"

Kabil laughed silently, and slung the weapon over his shoulder. "Let's get these condensed and stashed." He stood up and began singling out boxes, choosing unerringly, for all that no two were marked or packaged alike, until they had a stack sorted from the rest.

Of a sudden, from outside the tent:

"Hello there, Officer Berk. How's it going tonight?"

Kemal cast an anxious glance at Kabil. Kabil frowned, then gestured the others into the shadows between boxes, doused his flashlight, and grabbed Kemal's arm, pulling him into a shadowed alcove, keeping him there with a hand on his elbow.

A reflective flash beside him, a click of metal on metal: Kabil had the Uzi unslung and ready.

The voices came ever closer, exchanging pleasantries and rude comments. Berk was just growing bored.

Had discovered the empty bus and come looking for Kemal.

"Haven't seen him," the dig's night watchman's voice said, "but if I do, I'll tell him you were looking for him."

"Probably just out wandering. The kid loves this place . . ."

The voices faded again and the pressure on his elbow eased. But in his ear: "We're going out there, Duman. You're going to give that guard a convincing story, get him back in his little office, or he's gone. Do you understand me?"

A flourish of the expensive toy punctuated the threat.

"Don't be ridiculous. Put that away. I'll take care—"

"I'll watch. Just make it good."

It wasn't exactly difficult. Kemal intercepted Berk at the temple, promised to meet him later for coffee and donuts, but for now, he said, he just wanted to—commune with the stones of the city. Berk laughed, asked if he had Kirsi stashed in the ruins somewhere, and left him without waiting for an answer.

Sighing with relief, Kemal returned to the supply tent with Kabil. The others had three crates ready and were still working. But what they packed now were very definitely *not* Uzis.

Kemal leaned for a better look, got a sick feeling in the pit of his stomach. A glance discovered Kabil looking speculatively down his long nose.

"Explosives?" Kemal whispered, not trusting his voice.

"Naturally." Simple, straight answer.

So why did it make his skin crawl?

"Mart, you and Cahil continue packing. —Deniz, Asker, you come with us. —Duman, where's that stash-point?"

The hike to the far side of the hill was a nightmare. A half-dozen of the little guns was no weight at all to shift about the inside of a tent. Four times that number, on a long hike across rough ground, made the crate's rope handle bite painfully into his bare hand, made the muscles across his back burn.

"How much . . . further?"

He was glad to hear the breathlessness in the superior Kabil's voice. He pointed up the hill and replied, with somewhat less difficulty:

"Just past that cap-stone."

"Thank God."

From the two following them, only the sounds of labored breathing.

The ancient cellar was quite clear. Kemal had found it during his childhood explorations of this place, had cleared it out one summer for his special place. Recent development of the site had cut him off from it, but no one had yet disturbed his 'lock rock.'

Not that it really kept anyone from getting into the cellar, but the entryway couldn't be cleared without moving it, and replacing it required a special touch.

They stowed the two crates, then collapsed onto rocky benches to catch their collective breath. Suddenly, from down the hill, a scream. Gunshots. Single shots, not the staccato spray of the automatic weapons.

Asker swore, and bolted down the hillside toward the temple, stumbling over the rubble. Deniz followed at a somewhat slower pace. Kabil jerked his head after them. "Let's go."

Without a word, Kemal worked his way down the rock and brush-strewn hillside, quickly, but with careful attention to where he set his feet. They caught up with Deniz and Asker just short of the marble roadway. Asker was sprawled on the ground nursing his foot.

"I think it's broken," Asker squeaked.

Kabil grabbed him by the arm and hauled him to his feet. Forced him to walk the few steps to the more even ground of the road, then thrust his arm at Deniz. "Get him to the bus. Now. Wait for me there."

Deniz and Asker began hobbling up the long hill toward the parking lot. Kabil gestured with the Uzi in the opposite direction and Kemal led the way toward the supply tent, that singular 'me' not getting by him unnoticed.

The archaeological site had been silent since that initial scream and the crack of gunfire. But in the distance, clear to see in the moonlight, and well down the slope toward the theater: four figures. Two grotesquely twisted pairs, bent with the weight of the crates swinging between them as they hurried down the slope.

Kabil swore, aimed the Uzi at the fleeing bodies, and fired.

The barrel climbed wildly, throwing Kabil's aim (such as it was) off, and the figures hardly even hesitated in their staggering dash.

Behind them, a shout.

Berk: gun out and feet planted.

Kemal whirled. Shouted a warning. Threw himself at the old man, taking the bullets meant for Berk.

Kabil was a fast study.

The strangely calm analysis ran through his mind even as Kabil fell, Berk's better aimed bullet making short work of the would-be terrorist.

And then it was Kemal's turn to stare down the guard's gun barrel. He froze, one leg numb, the other throbbingly alive.

"Don't even think it, Kemal," Berk hissed a warning and worked his way free. Wavering to his feet, he called out to the dig's watchman.

Nothing.

Then, of a sudden, rapid fire, and, as if in slow motion, Berk stumbled backward, spraying black-in-the-moonlight blood like a fountain.

Confused, horrified, all Kemal could think of was escape from the unknown attackers. Turkish police, American CIA, Israelis, or even Mart; whoever had killed Berk would be after him next, he was certain of it. For the moment, he didn't care who that was, certainly did not count him a friend.

Not even sure his legs would work, he rolled down the marble street and into the shadowy ruins, where, ignoring the pain in his leg, dragging the other limply behind him, he wormed his way among the stones and brush, intent only on avoiding the inevitable pursuit.

From down in the parking lot, he heard the familiar rev of the bus engine, wondered vaguely who would escape, knowing it wouldn't include him. Not tonight.

Black haze fogged the moonlit marble. His world reduced to an instinctive fight for survival. Layers of stone shielded him, now. He pulled himself to his feet, found marginal support in the numb leg, a little more in the other, and an arm that grated ominously when he leaned on it. Blind with pain and shock, he staggered deeper and deeper into a honeycomb of low walls and half stairs, thick brush and thicker shadows.

The brothel across from Diana's temple.

With a smothered sob, he realized instinct had led him to the best possible cover. He sought a partial staircase he knew well, staggered and fell, his right wrist collapsing with a nauseating snap as he tried to buffer that fall. The world greyed out for an undetermined time, but that survival instinct roused him and he tucked in under the stairs, pulling his numb leg up with his working hand.

Silence, save for the pounding in his ears, the rasp of his own breath.

The bus was gone.

No evidence of pursuit.

Free.

Free to feel the pain.

Free to feel the blood slowly soaking his pantleg, creeping up his sweater from the shattered wrist.

Free to wonder . . . why?

Curious dilemma.

Diana perched atop a tall pillar, knees clasped to

her chest, and watched the mortals blithely eliminate each other without regard to motivation, waiting to see what shook out of the chaos.

On the one side, her Kemal and a pack of fools. On the other, equally foolish Greeks armed with an honest desire to get the guns to roust the Junta regime holding their homeland hostage.

In the middle, one old man who'd befriended a kid and trusted too much.

Mortals. Thousands of years of observation, and their capacity for stupidity and waste still held the power to amaze.

But the shooting had ended. The bus had departed with the two surviving Turkish fools. The Greek fools quickly collected the contraband weapons and loaded them into a truck in the lower lot. Even the two crates Kemal had stashed.

As for Kemal himself . . .

"Kem?" Soft whisper out of the shadows. *"Kemal Duman, are you in here?"*

Kemal bit his lip on a sob. Denied that voice out of dreams.

"Kem?" She appeared out of the shadows, and it *was—*

"Kirsi?" He got her name out on the front end of a gasp.

"Kemal!" She dropped to her knees beside him. "Oh, my gods, you're hurt. . . ."

His breath caught on attempted laughter. That was an understatement if ever he'd heard one.

"What . . . are you . . . doing here?"

"I came to find you. I was worried. . . ."

She slipped an arm beneath him, pillowed his head in her coat.

But there was a smell . . . an all too familiar oily smell, which belied her statement. He reached his good hand to brush that coat-pillow, hooked a fiber and brought it close to his face.

Packing. Like that the archaeologists used to protect delicate artifacts. Or contraband weapons.

He let his head fall, bringing his injured arm up to hide his face, perversely grateful for the jar to the wrist which could account for the tears in his eyes.

"Wh-who are you?"

Her hand, encased in a black glove, brushed the hair back from his face. "Such a strange question, Kemal. You know me."

"Do I?"

Her hand swept gently, but thoroughly, down his body, tenderly rearranging his wounded limbs.

"I haven't a weapon, if that's what you're looking for. Anything else—" His breath caught. "—I fear I'm not quite up to tonight."

"Kemal, I'm so sorry." She sat back on her heels.

He stared up at her, wishing the blackness didn't obscure everything, knowing it wasn't the blackness of night he fought.

"My name, sweet Kemal, is Kirke. I was born and raised on Cyprus, and I, like you, love my country and my people."

Cyprus. Half-Greek, half-Turk. A millennia old conflict in microcosm. You've been had, Kemal Duman, he thought. Aloud, he whispered: "No wonder you speak so well."

"Many of my childhood friends were Turks, Kemal. — A fact I'd forgotten in my college years in Athens. Until you."

"Am I—" He gasped. "Am I to take that as a compliment?"

Her fingers brushed his face. "As a thank you. For reminding me not all non-Greeks are enemies."

"What—" He had to pause as a wave of pain shot through him. "—do you people plan ... to do ... with me?"

"The others have left. They've got to get the shipment loaded onto the boat before dawn. They left me to find you."

A chill went down his spine. "And what are your instructions, once you found me, Circe?" he asked, giving her Greek name the Anglicized pronunciation. "Turn me into a toad?"

A long pause. Long enough to make him regret that barb. Whatever she was, alienating her further now gained him nothing. Finally, rather than answer, she asked, "What do you suppose will happen to you when the police find you in the morning?"

"I won't lie to them. I was a fool. They should know the truth about what happened tonight."

"I thought so. And do you think the Turkish army will buy that—truth?"

"I—" There was no answer to that. Even had—Kirke—not shown, he hadn't the strength—nor the will—to escape. And the evidence was too strong against him.

"I can't take you with me to Greece; my companions would be as anxious to extract information from you as the Turks—and as ruthless in their methods. I can't leave you here to point me out. My job here is not yet completed."

His breath caught. "Have a problem, don't you?"

A sharp point touched his side.

"Do you trust me, Kemal Duman?"

Of a sudden, Kirsi's voice sounded different. Perhaps it was the increased fear pounding in his ears. But Kirsi's features seemed ... fuzzy ... around the edges, her dark hair glinting moonlight pale under the black scarf holding it back from her face.

"Do you trust me?"

"How can I?" His cry withered and died in the night breeze.

"Do you love Turkey?"

"Of course—"

"Do you love Ephesus?"

His breath caught. Tears fractured her hazy image.

"Do you love the goddess?"

"Yes-s-s."

"And would you, like the true Kings, give your life that the land you love might live? That your daughter might one day walk on the moon?"

"I have no daughter—" His mind grasped for stability at that one absolute truth.

"You will have, darling. Nine months from last night. The powers here are still quite potent."

"Why are you doing this to me, Kirsi?" he whispered, close to sobbing. "Just finish and be done. —Please."

Soft lips brushed his. He found his senses lost in that kiss. Felt the pain of his wounds vanish.

Sharp, sudden agony in his gut. Hot flow of blood down his side. And then—

—Quiet, gentle ecstasy as that heat flowed into the earth beneath him, drawing him into the goddess' embrace.

The room looked a little less tawdry today. The stain was still in the couch, but curtains hung like new, and the stained glass sparkled in the Olympian sunshine.

As for herself . . .

Diana turned slowly, viewing her reflection from all angles.

She had curves again. Curves even Mammon appreciated from the look on his lecherous face, not so full as he generally preferred.

Mammon crossed the room, holding out his arms, his intent quite obvious. She avoided him with a smooth sway, drifted on a breeze across the Hilton suite. Mammon was quite talented. And in a pinch, he'd do nicely.

Fortunately, for now, there was no such lack.

"There he is," she said, seeing dark curly hair gleaming in the Olympian light. "—Looking a bit bemused at the moment he is, but he'll come around. One thing's certain, *he* won't have a headache." She turned to Mammon, brushed his furry cheek with one hand. "Goodbye, darling. Enjoy your war. I'm sure it will prove quite profitable for you."

The curly young head turned, framed in a flowering archway. Dark eyes gleamed as work-calloused fingertips gently stroked the glowing marble. Closed as he sniffed a blossom.

She smiled indulgently. They were always so charmingly bemused at first.

Meeting Mammon's resigned look: "By the by, darling, you've not quite got it straight, yet. Tek is not an upstart. Tek is but a child—a babe in the woods. You, my dear, are the upstart. You make wars. Tek fights them. But I, darling godling, win them. And when all the gold is used, all the jewels ground to dust, when all the techno-toys run out of batteries, my devoted worshippers will still thrive. I was the first to arrive and I shall, most assuredly, be the last to fade."

She smiled sweetly . . .

. . . and walked into the mirror.

as his girth would allow.
Just a minute, he growled, and dog in his heels
beside the tree stand.

ALLY

The party had ended and Tek found himself still without any idea who had planned the attack. For a long while he had sat in his bunker carefully filing and analyzing data. For a longer time he had simply sat confused, unable to categorize and file all the data he was receiving. During all this time Mentor sat quietly, appearing pleased by the contemplation. Finally, the war god had to admit there wasn't any way to solve the problem with the information he had.

"I cannot determine who caused the attack." Tek broke the silence.

"Why?" said Mentor.

"Because I have insufficient data," was Tek's frustrated reply.

"No, I mean the information you need is now is 'why.' Knowing 'why' will tell you the who."

"But there seems to be no reason," Tek protested. "Jealousy? Would a war god send such a creature?"

"Most would prefer to face you in person," Mentor agreed. "This kind of attack would mean a loss of face, but there is no guarantee it wasn't one less concerned with honor."

"Except there weren't any of the other war gods at the party."

"Which does leave them out, excepting Thor perhaps," the teacher speculated.

"Not really," Tek said in a flat voice. "I saw him arrive after I was up and about again. Quite an entrance being pulled through the sky by that glowing hammer and all."

"That lug was always a show-off," Mentor agreed.

"Which still leaves me no closer to a solution."

"So then, why would anyone have made that attack?"

"Gods can't die," Tek said looking to his teacher for confirmation.

Mentor nodded. "But they can feel pain, as you have noticed." Tek had most certainly discovered he could feel pain. It seemed to him that he was rediscovering this particular fact much too often. Tek glowered. The reference to his injuries caused another long silence. Mentor wasn't sure if the war god was remembering the pain or calculating something he hadn't shared with his teacher.

Actually Tek was wondering why, if the attack was what he had been sensing approach, it was over. But he still felt a sense of urgency. It had to have been the sense of urgency he was feeling since he awoke. But if this was so, why was the feeling he should be doing something different still nagging at him? What was driving him? Why was there a growing sense of need and what was Mentor helping to prepare him for? For the first time Mentor broke the silence.

"What you need is some light relief."

"Hardly," Tek protested. The last thing he wanted was to relax. The last time he had relaxed was in that garden.

"Check your files for references to battle fatigue and the morale value of entertainment," Mentor urged.

Accessing the files, Tek had to agree that the

teacher had a point. Still he was a god, not an ordinary
soldier. He didn't need such things. Before the war
god could protest, Mentor had summoned his screen.

"Allow me then luxury of relaxing, even if you are
made of sterner stuff," he insisted. "Besides, you will
find this tale most enlightening, as well as amusing."

THE B TEAM

by Mike Resnick

It had not been a good year for the Mau Mau.

The British had brought in their army, and what had seemed like a battle against a handful of white colonists had become something infinitely bigger. Thousands of insurgents were held captive in camps that lined Langata Road. Thousands more had been shipped to the Northern Frontier District and incarcerated there in the burning heat of the desert. The bulk of those who remained were spread throughout the Aberdare mountain range, where the British made three daily bombing runs in their planes, killing Kikuyu freedom fighters, Kikuyu loyalists, elephants, rhinos, and buffalos with equal facility.

It was time, declared Deedan Kimathi, the Supreme Commander of the Mau Mau, to take the gloves off.

Peter Njoro, the officer in command of one of the western slopes, made his way down the twisting path, alert to his surroundings. Twice this morning he'd been charged by fear-crazed rhinos. Another time a bongo had stepped on a land mine not twenty yards from him. He could hear gunfire to the north, and he knew that the colonials had recently brought his blood enemies, the Maasai and the Samburu, to the Aberdares to help hunt his army down in the thick forest.

He shook his head. He should be back with his men, fighting the enemy, rather than proceeding on this fool's mission. But Kimathi had issued the order, and it had fallen on his broad shoulders to carry it out.

He stepped over a fallen tree, waded across a narrow stream, jumped with surprise as a colobus monkey screeched overhead, and peered ahead. He must be getting close to his goal, he knew, but visibility was extremely limited, especially in the lower sections of the mountain, where the British didn't drop any bombs for fear of hitting their own commando units.

Finally he broke into a clearing and saw a row of caves ahead of him. Three old women sat around a fire, and a naked little boy, no more than four years old, was scratching designs in the dirt with a stick. The women looked at Peter as he approached them, but made no move to leave.

"I am looking for Matenjwa," said Peter. "I was told I could find him here."

One of the women nodded and pointed to the farthest cave.

"*Asante sana,*" said Peter, walking over to the cave and standing in the entryway. He waited until his eyes adjusted to the darkness, then took two more steps forward and stopped before the old man who sat cross-legged on a blanket, mindless of the snakes that slithered across the moist floor of the cave.

"You are Matenjwa?"

The old man nodded. "I am Matenjwa."

"I am Peter Njoro," said Peter. "I come with an order from Deedan Kimathi himself."

"I told Deedan Kimathi's other messengers that my magic is not strong enough to kill all the soldiers," said Matenjwa. "I tell you the same thing, Peter Njoro."

"I am not the first?" asked Peter.

"No," responded Matenjwa. "The first messenger was a man named Kanoti. His tongue was cut out."

"How could he possibly have told you what Deedan Kimathi wanted?"

"His tongue was cut out *after* he told General Kimathi that my magic could not defeat the British soldiers," replied Matenjwa. "Still, he was more fortunate than Sibanja, the second messenger. I believe Kimathi killed him and ate his heart." He smiled at Peter. "You are the third. I do not envy you, Peter Njoro; I have the very distinct impression that your General does not like to be given unhappy news."

Peter swallowed hard. "He ate Sibanja's heart, you say?"

"So I have been told."

"Maybe it was just a rumor," said Peter hopefully.

Matenjwa shrugged. "Maybe."

"I believe it, though," said Peter.

"So do I," agreed Matenjwa.

"I can't just go back up the mountain and tell him that you can't defeat the British."

"But it is the truth."

"What purpose would be served by it?" said Peter. "He'd just kill me and send someone else."

"Very likely," said Matenjwa. "He does seem to be a creature of habit."

"But I can't desert, either. Sooner or later one of his men would find me and kill me."

Matenjwa nodded thoughtfully. "That is true. General Kimathi has even less use for deserters than for the bearers of bad tidings."

"Then what am I to do?" demanded Peter.

Matenjwa shrugged. "I have no idea."

Peter turned on the old man. "You're a witch doctor! Why can't you destroy the British?"

"There are limits even to what a *mundumugu* can do," answered Matenjwa. "To summon the proper spirits, I would have to sacrifice more cattle and goats than there are on the entire mountain."

"Well, can't you do *something*?" persisted Peter. "Bring down a terrible disease on them, or something like that?"

"Certainly I could," answered Matenjwa. "But I would have to appeal to Sagbata, the god of smallpox."

"Then why haven't you done it?"

"The British are all vaccinated. The only people who would contract the disease would be ourselves."

"Think!" said Peter desperately. "If you can't kill them, what *can* you do?"

"I'm very good at circumcision rituals," said Matenjwa at last. "But of course there's no magic involved, and you would have to bring them to me one by one. Once they saw my instruments, a few of them might come over to your side."

"You're not being much help," muttered Peter.

"I told you I wouldn't be."

"Look!" snapped Peter. "I'm not going back up the mountain until we've exhausted every possibility."

"They are all exhausted."

"That's easy for *you* to say. You don't have to tell that to General Kimathi."

"Some of us are warriors and some of us are *mundumugus*," said Matenjwa with a shrug.

"You don't get off that easily, old man," said Peter, pulling out his *panga* and holding it to Matenjwa's throat. "The rules of the game have just changed. *Both* of our lives depend on your getting rid of the British, do you understand?"

"I cannot summon the warrior gods without sacrificing at least two thousand cattle," said Matenjwa, pulling back his head slightly as the edge of the blade pressed into his neck.

"Well, summon *somebody* who can make them go away, or we're both dead men," said Peter.

Matenjwa uttered a deep sigh. "I will do what I can."

"Good."

"Fetch me that pouch," he said, indicating a leather pouch that was lying on the floor at the far end of the cave. Peter retrieved it and brought it to the old witch doctor.

Matenjwa pulled two dead gecko lizards out of it and placed them on the floor in front of him. Then he reached into the pouch again, removed a small handful of bones, and, muttering a series of chants, cast them three times on the floor. Then he sat motionless for a moment, his eyes tightly shut.

"That's *it*?" demanded Peter.

"No," said Matenjwa, reaching out and grabbing one of the cave's resident snakes. "Now I must treat each lizardskin with one drop of the blood from a living reptile. Your *panga*, please?"

Peter handed over his *panga*.

"You understand," said Matenjwa, "that the snake's blood is a substitute for the blood of two healthy oxen."

"How much difference does it make?" asked Peter.

Matenjwa shrugged. "I don't know. I've never tried it before." He paused and looked up at Peter. "You're sure you want to continue?"

Peter nodded, and the old man gently pierced the skin of the writhing reptile, then squeezed out a single drop of blood over each dead lizard.

"It didn't work," said Peter after a moment.

"I am sorry," said Matenjwa. "I guess it really does require the blood of two healthy—"

He was interrupted by a puff of smoke and a sudden rush of air, and suddenly there was a tall, portly, bearded white man standing before them. He wore a blue pinstriped suit with a white carnation in its lapel. Atop his head was a bowler hat, hanging on one wrist was an umbrella, and tucked beneath his arm was a thin, well-worn leather briefcase.

"Good day, gentlemen," he said in exquisite English. "I'm so glad you've invited me here. Have you ever wanted to leave your dark, damp domicile"—he gestured around him at the cave with an expression of distaste—"and see the world? If you act promptly, a first-class passage to Bermuda aboard one of Britain's finest luxury liners can be yours for an unbelievable discount in price. Think of it, gentlemen! Five-star French cooking, three—count them: three—nightclubs, a casino, an Olympic-sized swimming pool, and a telephone in every stateroom!"

He paused and stared at them expectantly.

"Who *is* this man?" asked Peter, frowning.

Matenjwa shrugged. "I have no idea."

The man stared at them a moment longer, then snapped his fingers. Instantly his clothing vanished, to be replaced by a ragged loincloth. He still retained his bowler, umbrella, and briefcase.

"I beg your pardon," he said in Swahili. "I seem to have been misinformed. I thought I was to be dealing with a party of British gentlemen."

"Who are you?" demanded Peter.

"Don't you know?" asked the portly man, looking more than a little ridiculous in his new outfit. "I mean, after all, you *are* the ones who summoned me."

"*He* summoned you," said Peter, indicating Matenjwa. "I'm just an onlooker."

"Oh. Well, I'm Hermes, son of Zeus."

"And *I* sent for you?" asked Matenjwa.

"I was told that you have a party of Britons who wish to visit distant lands. Is that correct?"

"In a way," said Peter.

"Well," said Hermes expansively, "if anyone can expedite their journey, it's me. I'm the god of travel."

"You are?"

Hermes nodded. "I'm also the god of eloquence, as you have doubtless noted, and of trade."

"Of trade?" asked Peter.

"Absolutely. I'll swap you my umbrella for your *panga.*"

"I think not," said Peter.

Hermes shrugged. "Well, then, how about two Mickey Mantles for a Willie Mays?"

"I beg your pardon?"

"A *Batman* #9 for a *Captain Marvel* #6? A Lincoln Memorial commemorative for a set of Equidorian Roosevelts? Or a complete set of Jane Austen, bound in leather, for—get this now!—an illustrated *Fanny Hill!*"

"Perhaps we had better stick with travel," suggested Matenjwa.

"Certainly," said Hermes, opening up his briefcase, which was filled with travel brochures. "Where did you wish to go—Ocho Rios, Fiji, Samarkand? They say that Duluth, Minnesota, is exceptionally nice this time of the year."

"We do not wish to go anywhere," said Matenjwa.

Hermes frowned. "There must be some misunderstanding. I was distinctly told that I was to help arrange passage for a large number of Britons."

"You are."

"Ah!" said Hermes with a huge smile. "Now I understand! You are simply their Nubian manservants." He snapped his fingers, and suddenly his loincloth was replaced by his original pinstriped suit, although this time the carnation was red.

"Now, gentlemen," he continued, "if you would just point the way to your employers?"

"Well, they're not exactly our employers," said Peter.

"Oh?"

"They're our enemies."

"Then what in the world did you want a travel agent for?" asked Hermes. "You need a god of warfare."

"But you said you could make them all go away."

"I said I could expedite their journeys," said Hermes.

"There's a difference." He held up his briefcase. "I have here all the latest timetables, group rates, brochures, even passport forms. But I can't *make* them leave. I can just help them book passage." He paused. "Are you sure you wouldn't like to visit Buenos Aires? Not only can I secure rooms with an ocean view, but you will miss the war entirely."

"No," said Peter. "We must drive the British from our mountain."

"Why didn't you say so in the first place?" replied Hermes enthusiastically. "I have access to Oldsmobiles, Cadillacs, Chryslers, Volkswagens ... I even had a few Studebakers left. Though from the terrain, I'd say that you'll need four-wheel-drives. I can give you a rate on, shall we say, thirty Land Rovers?"

"You don't understand ..." began Matenjwa.

"He understands perfectly," interrupted Peter. He turned to Hermes. "Of course, you'll have to negotiate a price directly with the prospective passengers."

"Certainly," said Hermes. "Just point me in the right direction. Negotiating is one of my strong points." He paused. "Besides, there's nothing in my cash conversion tables on cows and goats. I really would much prefer British pounds."

Peter escorted Hermes to the edge of the cave. "Just follow that winding path down the mountain," he said, "and I guarantee you'll come to the British."

"Damned white of you," said Hermes. "And now, gentlemen, if you will excuse me, I'll be bidding you a fond *adieu* and be going about my business."

He tucked the briefcase under his arm, and, humming happily to himself, the god of travel started wandering down the mountain.

Colonel William Smythe-Roberts sat behind his desk, drumming his fingers on the plain wooden surface.

"Well?" he demanded.

"Well, sir," said Sergeant Michael Wilcox uneasily,

shifting his weight from one foot to another, "it . . . ah . . . it appears that . . . well, it seems . . ."

"Spit it out, man!" snapped Smythe-Roberts. "Twenty-seven of our men have deserted in the past two days. I want to know why!"

"This is most awkward, sir," responded Wilcox. "You know that old witch doctor who lives up in the hills? Matenjwa, his name is?"

"Yes," answered Smythe-Roberts. "Are you trying to tell me that *he* is responsible for this?"

"Well, indirectly, sir."

"You're trying to tell me indirectly?"

"No. I mean that he's indirectly responsible, sir."

"Explain."

"Well, sir, it appears that . . . well, that he's conjured up a god to help the Mau Mau."

Colonel Smythe-Roberts looked at his sergeant with compassion. "Poor chap," he said at last. "You've been out in the vertical rays of the sun too long. What did I tell you about always wearing your pith helmet?"

"I've *been* wearing it," insisted Wilcox. "I tell you, sir, the old man has managed to summon a god."

"Of course he has," said Smythe-Roberts in a soothing tone.

"I swear to it, sir!"

"What does this god look like?"

"From what I hear, just like you and me, sir."

"Does he breathe smoke and belch fire? Rend the earth asunder? Call forth the heavenly host to aid his cause?"

"No, sir."

"What *does* he do?" asked Smythe-Roberts.

"He . . . ah . . . he sells holidays, sir."

"You mean like Christmas and Bank Day?"

"No. He sells trips, sir. Excursions." Wilcox paused. "Some of them are really quite luxurious. There was one to New Zealand that—"

"That's *all* he does?" interrupted Smythe-Roberts.

"Well, no. He also trades French postcards for guns."

"I beg your pardon?"

"French postcards, sir. You know. The kind that—"

"I am well aware of what a French postcard looks like, Sergeant."

"Well, then . . . uh . . . I guess that's it, sir."

"And based on this, you have concluded that he is a god?"

"Well, not entirely based on this, sir."

"What other evidence have you?"

"He told everyone he was, sir."

Patience, Smythe-Roberts told himself. *The poor blighter has cracked from the heat. Somebody had to be the first. Pity it had to be Wilcox, but there you have it. I suppose the best thing to do is to humor him until we can get him sedated and shipped back to Nairobi.*

But *how* did one humor a man in this condition? Well, he believed that a god was walking amongst his fellows. That was obviously the starting point.

"Thank you for your report, Sergeant," said Smythe-Roberts.

"Are we going to do something about . . . well, you know?" asked Wilcox.

"Absolutely," said Smythe-Roberts. *"They've* got a god. *We* should have a god."

"Sir?"

"That's your assignment, Sergeant," said Smythe-Roberts. *Let's see. The medical corp officer ought to be back by sunset.* "I'm putting you in charge of it. Secure a god for us by 1600 hours."

"But, sir . . ."

"No, don't thank me, son. You're just the man for the job."

"But—"

"Dismissed."

"Corporal!" said Wilcox. "I need a witch doctor."

"A witch doctor, sir?"

"On the double."

"Private!"

"Yes, Corporal?"

"Sergeant Wilcox has requested a witch doctor."

"Bully for him, sir." The private shook his head. "Vertical rays of the run."

"Get him one."

"Where the hell does the corporal suggest I look, sir?"

"I don't know. We've got all these Maasai and Samburu fighting on our side. Ask one of them."

"You're kidding, right, sir?"

"Am I smiling, private? Now *move*! On the double!"

The tall, lean Maasai stood in the doorway to Wilcox's tent.

"You sent for me, sir?" he asked.

"Yes," said Wilcox, getting to his feet. "Thank goodness you speak English! Please come in."

The Maasai entered the tent.

"You seem a little young to be a witch doctor," commented Wilcox.

"I'm not."

"Then why are you here?"

"We don't have any *laibons*—that's witch doctors to you—in our unit, so they thought they'd send someone who could at least speak your language and find out why you wanted one."

"I need to conjure up a god," said Wilcox, feeling distinctly foolish.

"Well, I suppose it can be done," replied the Maasai.

"Good. What's your name?"

"Olepesai."

"All right, Olepesai—how do we go about it?"

"About what?"

"Conjuring a god."

"I never said *I* could do it," replied Olepesai. "I just said that it could be done."

"Haven't you ever watched any ceremonies?"

"Well, yes, but . . ."

"Good. We'll just have to do it without a *laibon*."

"It's been a long time," said Olepesai. "I probably couldn't remember all the words, or the right chants, or . . ."

"We have no time to worry about that," said Wilcox. "My colonel demands a god by 1600 hours. That's four this afternoon." He checked his wristwatch. "We've only got about ninety minutes. What will you need?"

"A *laibon*."

"Besides that."

"Well," said Olepesai, rubbing his chin, "the last time I saw such a ceremony, I think there was a fire, and the *laibon* sang the Chant of the Gods, and then he sacrificed three mice and a lizard."

"And that's it?"

"If I remember correctly," said Olepesai.

"This will be easier than I thought," said Wilcox. He stuck his head out of the tent. "Corporal, get me three mice and a lizard, and bring them back in a small box or a cage."

"What if it doesn't work?" asked the Maasai when Wilcox turned to face him.

"Then we've done our best, and I can report to the colonel with a clear conscience." He walked outside. "Let's start gathering some kindling."

They had the wood in about five minutes, but were forced to wait another thirty before the corporal returned with the animals.

"Here you are, sir," said the corporal.

"Thank you," replied Wilcox. "You may leave us now."

"You're sure you don't want me to stick around, sir?"

"No. Olepesai and I are quite capable of taking over from this point."

"As you wish, sir," said the corporal, walking off.

"Well," said Wilcox when he and the Maasai were alone, "are you ready to begin?"

"I suppose so."

"Good. I'll light the fire." He took out a match and tried to light the kindling, but the wind blew it out. Two more matches received the same fate.

"Perhaps that is an omen for you to desist," suggested Olepesai.

"Nonsense," said Wilcox. "It's just a windy day."

He pulled out a brochure for the fjords of Norway that Hermes had given him, lit it with a match, slid it under the kindling, and waited. A moment later the fire took hold.

"You really want to go through with this?" asked Olepesai doubtfully.

"Orders are orders."

Olepesai shrugged and began reciting the Chant of the Gods while Wilcox stood a few feet away and wondered if perhaps he *had* been just a bit too long in the vertical rays. Finally the Maasai finished and quickly dispatched the mice and the lizard.

Wilcox wasn't quite certain what he expected, but it definitely wasn't a disembodied voice:

*"It looked extremely rocky for the Mudville nine
    that day,
The score stood two to four, with but one inning
    left to play."*

"Was that you?" asked Wilcox.

"No," said Olepesai, stepping back from the fire.

"Well, it certainly wasn't *me.*"

"It was *me,*" said the voice, and now it was joined by a tall blond man wearing furs and a metal helmet.

"Who are you?" asked Wilcox.

"Bragi, of course."

"Bragi?"

"The Norse god of poetry, come to sooth your savage souls:

> *A bunch of boys were whooping it up*
> *In the Malamute saloon;*
> *The kid that handles the music box*
> *Was hitting a jag-time tune . . ."*

Wilcox stared long and hard at the blond god. "But why *you?*" he asked at last.

"Well, your friend here definitely asked for a god of poetry. Since there *are* no Maasai poets—no offense, friend—we needed a little direction as to just which god of poetry you wanted. There are quite a few of us, you know."

"The brochure," said Wilcox dully.

"Right the first time," said Bragi. He threw a massive arm around Wilcox's shoulder. "I can tell we're going to be great friends."

"We are?"

"You'll have your women clean and baste a few cattle for dinner, and after we've had desert, I'll recite." He paused. "I've been boning up on all the new stuff:

> *For they're hangin' Danny Deever, you can hear*
> *the Dead March play,*
> *The regiment's in 'ollow square—they're hangin'*
> *him today;*
> *They've taken all his buttons off an' cut his stripes*
> *away.*
> *An' they're hangin' Danny Deever in the mornin'.*

"That's all very well and good, but we've summoned you here to perform a task for us," said Wilcox.

"Tasks are for gods like Mercury and Atlas and the like," replied Bragi. "Me, I just do poetry."

"But we're at war, and the enemy has called down its own god."

"What is that to me?"

"We rather hoped to pit you against him."

Suddenly Bragi appeared interested. "How is he on iambic pentameter?"

"I don't know," answered Wilcox honestly.

"That's one of my great strengths," said Bragi with more than a trace of pride. "Though I can recite sonnets with the best of them. Does my opponent let his voice linger lovingly over rhyming couplets? Can he bring tears to your eyes? How is he on free verse?"

"What he's mostly good at is making soldiers desert," said Wilcox.

"What? You mean he can't even hold an audience?" bellowed Bragi with a confident laugh. "Lead me to him!"

"I don't think you understand me."

"Certainly I do. You've set up a contest between myself and this pretender."

"Well, yes and no," said Wilcox.

"Explain yourself."

"We'd *like* to set up a contest, but not the type you're referring to."

"Any type at all will do. I'll murder the bum. *Into the Valley of Death rode the six hundred . . .*"

"That's kind of what we had in mind."

"Tennyson?" asked Bragi. "One of my favorites."

"No—murdering the bum."

"I beg your pardon?"

"Don't you understand?" said Wilcox. "We're at war, and the other side has a god helping them."

"No problem," said Bragi. "I'll fill your men with such spirit that they will be unbeatable."

"They will?"

"Virtually."

"What does virtually mean, in this context?"

"They'll feel pretty good about themselves for at least five minutes after I've finished reciting."

Wilcox shook his head. "I'm afraid that's not good enough."

"If pushed to my limits, I can encourage them to look death in the eye and stare it down," said Bragi. "*John Brown's Body* comes to mind."

"What good will staring it down do?" asked Wilcox. "In the end, they'll be just as dead, won't they?"

"But they'll die happily," said Bragi. "A few of them may even be mouthing the same brave words they hear from my immortal lips, inspired to the very end."

"This is not working out," said Wilcox. He turned to the Maasai, who had been a silent witness. "Olepesai, send him back."

"But I just got here!" protested Bragi.

"You heard me, Olepesai," said Wilcox. "Send him back and we'll summon another one."

"I protest!" said the Norse god.

"Protest all you want," said Wilcox. "We're wasting time."

"*Wait!*" said Bragi with such desperation that both men froze in their tracks.

"You *can't* send me back yet," said the god, tears coming to his eyes. "Nobody up there listens to me anymore. They've heard all my poetry. They snicker when I get up to declaim, and they always leave before I'm through. Loki is the worst of them, but even Odin leaves the room the moment I enter it. Give me a chance to destroy this other god. Then I will write a great new ode to myself, three hours in length and filled with the most remarkable felicity of expression, and my peers will finally listen in awe."

Wilcox had his doubts that anyone, human or deity, would ever be willing to sit through a three-hour ode that Bragi wrote about himself, but he was desperate enough to give the tearful god a chance.

"All right," he relented. "As long as you're here, we might as well make the best of it." He paused. "I suppose the first thing is to find the other god."

"I can see him right now," said Bragi.

Wilcox turned with a start. "Where is he?"

"In a cave halfway up the mountain."

"You have remarkable eyesight."

"Gods can always see others of their kind."

"You can?"

"Well, there aren't an awful lot of us to begin with," explained Bragi, "and we do have an affinity toward each other. With all due respect, I am already bored to tears by the two of you."

"Then let's start climbing the mountain," suggested Wilcox, who was feeling much the same way about Norse gods of poetry.

"There is an easier way," said Bragi.

"Twenty-seven!" shrieked Peter Njoro. "There are tens of thousands of British soldiers surrounding us, and you only managed to get *twenty-seven* of them to desert?"

"It's the wrong time of year," said Hermes defensively. "There's no snow base at Aspen yet, and it's raining in Miami." He frowned. "And Cunard has got the Queen Mary in drydock for re-outfitting."

"Twenty-seven," muttered Peter.

"There's a bright side, though," said Hermes.

"Oh?"

The god nodded. "Yes. Starting next week, Pan Am is giving a thirty percent discount on its around-the-world airfare."

Peter turned to Matenjwa. "Two thousand cattle, you say?"

The old *mundumugu* nodded.

"I'm doing the best I can," whined Hermes.

"And your best is none too good!" said a booming voice from the back of the cave.

Peter drew his pistol and trained it on the blond, fur-clad man who suddenly appeared.

"Who are you?" demanded Hermes.

"I am the one who is going to bring you to your knees," replied Bragi confidently. "Listen, and weep:

> *There are strange things done in the midnight sun,*
> *By the men who moil for gold,*
> *The Arctic trails have their secret tales,*
> *That would make your blood run cold;*
> *The northern lights have seen queer sights*
> *But the queerest they ever did see*
> *Was the night on the marge of Lake Lebarge*
> *I cremated Sam McGee.*

There! What do you think of that?"

There was a stunned silence, which Hermes finally broke.

"Actually, I rather liked it," he said.

"You did?" asked Bragi excitedly.

"Definitely," said Hermes. "I hate all this new-fangled stuff. I don't know how people can call it poetry when it doesn't even rhyme."

"My feelings precisely!" agreed Bragi.

"By the way, that's a fine-looking helmet you're wearing," said Hermes. "I don't suppose you'd like to trade it for my bowler?"

"I don't think so," replied Bragi after some consideration.

"I'll throw in my umbrella. You never know when it might rain up here in the mountains."

"Done!" cried Bragi, removing his helmet and handing it to Hermes in exchange for the other god's hat and umbrella. "You know," he continued, "you're not such a bad guy."

"Neither are you," said Hermes. "I could listen to *real* poetry all night."

"Not in my cave, you can't," said Matenjwa disgustedly.

"We can go back behind the British lines," suggested Bragi, obviously eager to recite for a receptive audience.

"Nonsense," said Hermes. "We have the whole world to choose from."

"We do?" asked Bragi.

Hermes opened his briefcase. "Just this afternoon I saw ... now where is it? ... ah, here we are!" He held up a small brochure. "Why stay on this cold, damp mountain at all when we can take a five-week cruise to Tahiti and then transfer to a luxury lodge on Bora Bora? You'll have round-the-clock room service, a private bath, an electric overhead fan, and four miles of absolutely uncluttered white sand beaches."

"It sounds wonderful," said Bragi. "Tell me more about the boat."

"Well, we'll want first-class passage, of course," said Hermes, taking Bragi by the arm and leading him out of the cave and down the twisting path that paralleled the stream. "There's a pool, a dance floor, two night-clubs, a library, shuffleboard ..."

"Nightclubs? Possibly they might like to hear me recite."

"No reason why not," answered Hermes. "Every morning there's a breakfast buffet from eight o'clock until ..."

Then they were out of earshot.

"*Those* were *gods*?" asked Peter bitterly.

"Perhaps we expect too much of them," offered Matenjwa. "Or perhaps not."

"I don't understand."

"If our war god met *their* war god in battle, they would probably have fought to a draw, just as these two did," said the old man. "At least this way, the mountain is still standing, which is a good thing, for we shall wish to live on it after our war is over."

Deedan Kimathi was killed three months later, bringing the State of Emergency to an unofficial end.

Peter Njoro, after a brief period as a game ranger, converted to Christianity and spent the rest of his life as a minister in Nairobi.

Michael Wilcox returned to England, converted to animism, dropped out of college, and opened a poster shop in Soho.

As for Hermes and Bragi, they opened the very first travel agency in Papeete. With the profits from this venture, they formed the H & B Theater Company, where Bragi still declaims nightly before a devoted audience of Polynesians who never learned to appreciate the virtues of free verse.

JUST REWARDS

Mentor and the new god had been discussing ancient battles and tactical errors. The views and information were so accurate and fascinating that Tek was able to almost ignore his growing sense of urgency.

"So if Stalin had kept the army in their fortified positions instead of moving everyone forward to occupy Poland, Hitler's generals would have convinced him to not attack until 1943," Tek wondered.

"Yes, and even then the Wehrmacht would have taken major losses at the border fortresses," Mentor agreed. "So that war and millions of casualties were determined by a decision made in peacetime two years before the battle began. An excellent analysis."

"We have spoken of almost all the wars in man's history. You have shown me scenes of glory and defeat. Can your television show me the earliest wars, the ones fought by the gods?" Tek asked. "I have found files referring to a Ragnarok and of a battle against the Titans."

Mentor smiled nervously and did not conjure back his teaching screen. Instead he considered for a time and then spoke.

"Your favorites, the Greeks, were among the first of the truly self-aware gods. They wrested control of the Earth and its worshippers in a gigantic war against those gods who had come before. Later the humans, unable to understand the nature of these early gods, made them mere giants. The Titans were really the early Earth and sea powers. They were defeated almost without a single loss by the new gods."

"Were they so weak that young gods could defeat them?" Tek worried aloud.

"No," Mentor said. "They were actually quite powerful. The young ones defeated them with guile. Where the Titans depended upon their great powers, the gods found a way around them. Even Mars found ways to outthink, not just outfight his opponents. You see, reason and cunning can overcome even the most courageous and powerful warrior."

"Reason or technology," Tek corrected.

"If you say so," Mentor agreed quickly.

"And this Ragnarok?"

"It hasn't happened yet," the teacher explained. "It is predicted by the Fates, and the Norse gods must always prepare for it. It makes them dreadfully dreary company. Their enemy is the giants, who are themselves, again, minor Earth gods."

"Giants?"

"Yes, most are man shaped and of enormous size— hence the name." Mentor explained. "The most powerful today dwell in the deserts and appear in whirling clouds of sand or occasionally from inside bottles or lamps. Others are shaped like gigantic wolves, but a few are easily mistaken for human."

"Will we be helping the Norse gods in this final battle?" The idea appealed to Tek. He'd been looking forward to Armageddon.

"No!" Mentor almost screamed his reply. Then he continued more calmly. "It is not a battle you should be part of. Almost family business." There was short pause as the teacher was obviously gathering his thoughts. "Nor are the giants an enemy. In many ways they have justice on their side. They were put upon at every side by the upstart gods. Later, when they fought back, the ungrateful bards portrayed them as evil. Why, there is even a half-god and half-giant who is like a hero to them."

"Who would that be?"

"Loki," Mentor answered. "A brave warrior and a brilliant thinker. All the giants admire his courage and cunning."

"And this half-god will side with the giants at Ragnarok?" the war god wondered.

"Maybe," Mentor seemed unsure. "He might." Then he shrugged and looked self-conscious.

This was almost the only time Mentor had not been able to answer one of the war god's questions. Tek sat, suspecting Mentor was accessing obscure files and waited for a clarification.

"The Nordic gods are gathering warriors to aid them in the final battle. The giants will rely on themselves alone, and maybe the one heroic god."

"Recruit warriors?" Tek asked. He wouldn't have minded a bodyguard that day in Diana's garden. "Could I do that?"

Instead of answering the teacher summoned his screen.

DISPATCHES
FROM
VALHALLA

by Brian M. Thomsen

There are three lies about dying that every profes-
sional soldier knows: "You hear the bullet that has
your name on it," "your entire life flashes before your
eyes," and "you regret that you ever became a
mercenary."

Damn lies all of them.

I never heard the bullet, saw my life in retrospect,
or regretted a single thing in my entire life. I felt pain.
Not a short, sharp piercing pain like a pin prick, or a
sudden poke that leads to a deadening feeling of numb-
ness. I felt pain, pain like I had never felt before in
my life. Worse than the time I stepped on a punji stick
in the Ia Drang Valley, worse than the time I had to

remove twelve pieces of shrapnel from my leg after the fall of Saigon, and even worse than the time I was dragged behind a jeep down a gravel road by Salvadorian refugees. Worse than anything I've felt during my entire career as a contract soldier.

The minute the bullet entered my back, I was in agony. When the supply truck, theirs, ran over me I screamed, I cursed, I cried. I wanted it to stop. I wanted it to be all over . . .

. . . and it was.

William J. Frederick had been a professional soldier for thirty years. The first six years he spent with special forces in Vietnam as a clean-cut, all-American, killing machine. Then, after a disagreement with a chickenshit CO who deserved to be fragged anyway, he went AWOL, and hooked up with a Frenchman named Jules Martine who offered to find him work, doing what he did best. South Africa, Beijing, Guatamala, Saigon, Montreal, and Havana. Wherever there was action, Major Frederick was always just a contract away from service.

At the time of his death, he was leading a band of rebels in Central America, trying to overthrow an uncooperative political regime that was standing in the way of a joint U.S.-Japan business transaction.

He was forty-seven when he died, two-thirds of his life having been spent on some battlefield or other.

The pain was gone, but not forgotten. I didn't know how long I'd been unconscious, or where I was. I felt my legs that had been crushed by the truck, but they were whole again. I felt for the bullethole in my back, but it wasn't there. It couldn't have been a dream. Was I going crazy?

Then I saw her. She was tall, and slender with perfectly ripe breasts peeking out from her camo top. Her hair was raven black, and her lips were full and moist.

She looked like Sonia Braga, and she called me by name.

"Welcome to Valhalla, Frederick," she said. "My name is Freya, and this is your final reward."

"What's going on here? I thought I had been shot, and seen my last sunrise," said Frederick trying to make some sense out of his situation. She obviously didn't want to kill him, at least not now, or she would have done so already.

"Oh, you have been shot, *maricone*. And you died. It really was quite glorious, a hero's death in battle. That is why you are here with me now. This is your reward."

"My reward," he said, accepting her hand as she helped him to his feet.

"Your reward," she said, "forever and ever."

And then she kissed him.

After a night of lovemaking, no, more akin to rutting, like he had never experienced before, she lead him to what she called his camp, a well-stocked bivouac on a rocky hillside overlooking the barren landscape.

There, Frederick was treated to a reunion with some of his closest companions of the past thirty years. They were all there: Rico the Italian who had his balls blown off by a "bouncing betty" in Cambodia, Larry Spellman who had been shot by a sniper in Havana, Gary Butler who had been roasted alive in his tank during the burning of Montreal, and Spada the Greek, whose throat he had seen slit four short weeks ago, and many more.

"Geez, Will, it's great to see you. Sorry about your recent demise. I see you've already met the boss lady. Ain't this place great," said Butler, slapping him on the back just the way he used to.

"What is this place?" asked Frederick, slightly more

relaxed now that he was among friends, even if they were all dead.

"It's Freya's place, Valhalla. Because we all died as heroes, we now get our eternal reward, warring all day, and whoring all night."

"Who are we fighting?"

"You name it. Last week we successfully repelled a group of Redcoats under Lord Nelson, before that a horde of Huns, and before that Otto Skorzeny and his commandoes. It's great! And the best part is we can't be killed. Well, at least not for long."

"That's right," said Freya, rejoining the conversation. "Bam! You're dead. Wham! You're back again. Just like that. Now get ready, Chiang Kai Shek and his forces are entering the clearing, and let the battles begin."

It was great being back with the guys, though in all actuality we had never fought together as a group before. In fact, in all probability, we'd fought on opposite sides more than once during the course of our lives. But here, that didn't matter. We were a finely trained fighting machine, and we made Freya proud.

And Butler was right, we can't be killed. Last week, Spellman was beheaded by a Turk, and sure enough, he showed up for breakfast the next morning.

After about three months, we pulled up stakes, and moved camp.

Having come upon a village that looked like something out of World War II Sicily, they decided to make camp. The lovely ladies who came out at night provided them with wine, and cheese, and female companionship. Since they no longer required sleep, they would all regroup around the campfire just before dawn, and share a cup of java before the day's carnage.

"Did you ever notice the way a guy's eyes roll up into his head as you're strangling him? I mean, there's nothing like it. The lights are out and nobody's home. Nothing like it," observed Rico, puffing on a cigar.

"It's not my cup of tea," said Spellman. "The bad part about strangling someone is when his bowels let loose. Gawd, the stink."

"No worse than Rico," added Butler.

"Ah, your mother," quipped Rico.

"No, your mother. After all, we're in Sicily aren't we? And isn't this the place old whores go when they die? I probably had her last night. Now I know why you're so ugly. It runs in the family."

Rico had never known his mother, but wouldn't abide anyone bad-mouthing her. "Take it back," he warned.

"Make me."

The two drew their guns, and fired. Rico got Butler right between the eyes. Unfortunately, Butler's gun didn't go off till after he was hit, and Rico wound up with a belly wound.

The sun rose and set before he finally died. His screams of pain threatened to give them away to the enemy.

Freya brought them both back for breakfast the next morning. Neither held a grudge. It wasn't worth it.

One night, after a day of particularly heavy casualties, I asked Freya what our objective was.
She just smiled, and called me her hero.

Several of the group that Frederick had originally found himself with splintered off to form another group a few months later. There were always new replacements coming in, and more than enough weapons to go around.

Frederick noticed that his group had several new members who were barely teenagers. Three of them had not yet begun to shave, and one of them was too small to manage an M16. Despite their size and age, their faces reflected the hardness and cruelty of war.

One morning Freya announced that the enemy had fallen into a deep sleep, and that they must sieze the opportunity to slit their throats.

Frederick, Rico, and Kim, the Korean kid who couldn't manage an M16, were dispatched to the enemy's camp, under the cover of fog. There, they quickly slit the throats of their sleeping prey, collecting ears as souvenirs of their mission.

When they got back to camp, Frederick recognized the dangling man earring that hung from one of his coup. It had belonged to Spada.

The next morning, Freya accompanied Spada to breakfast. He still wore the earring.

I've begun to lose all track of time. The nights seem shorter, unless we're out on a mission, and the days just seem filled with endless carnage. Valhalla must be getting crowded. There never seems to be a lull in the fighting.

What is it all for? The money never really mattered when I was alive, but at least there was a reason to fight. Maybe it wasn't my reason, but at least it was someone's.

Kill an enemy, kill a friend, it doesn't seem to matter.

Each day it gets harder to hold back the vomit.

Frederick's company was dispatched to attack an encampment on a rocky mountainside. The fighting was heavy, and lasted all day.

That night, instead of partaking in the usual festivities, he decided to do a little reconnaissance, and quietly approached the enemy encampment.

Hiding behind a rock, he observed a group of soldiers making idle conversation. He thought he recognized the voices.

Then it dawned on him. This had been his camp,

and the voices were Rico's, Spada's, Butler's, and his own.

He slipped away from the encampment, and ran to tell the others, but ran into Freya along the way.

She cut him in half with a burst from her uzi.

"See you soon, my hero," she said, moistening her lips the way she always did prior to making love.

First I felt cold, and then I felt the pain again.

I thought I heard doctors and nurses talking in the background, but there weren't any in Valhalla.

The last time I felt pain like this I was alive.

"Yes indeed, Mr. Frederick. You are a very lucky man. We thought we lost you a few times out there, but thanks to cryogenics, bionics, and robotics, you're in better shape than you've ever been before," said Dr. Parker in what sounded like a patented infomercial spiel.

"What happened?" Frederick asked, trying to force away the cobwebs from his head.

"As per your contract with Sonyon, your remains were reclaimed after the battle, and frozen until the time came when you could be revived. Good fighting men like yourself are hard to find in today's world, and the corporation always needs soldiers," the doctor said, still smiling that strangely non-reassuring smile.

"How long?" Frederick slurred.

"Have you been out? Oh, only about forty years."

Frederick raised his hand to rub his eyes, and felt the cool sheen of tempered steel.

His entire arm was made of metal.

Dr. Parker intervened. "I was just about to tell you about that. Now don't be alarmed. I'm afraid that we couldn't save your body, but this cybernetic shell is even better, and it never wears out. I have other patients to attend to, but a representative from the corporation will be in to see you shortly."

The doctor left, closing the door behind him.

I looked in the mirror across the room. My entire body was made of metal, a metallic mannequin in search of a store window. Inside this shell I could still feel the pain.

The door opened again. I thought it was the representative from the corporation, but it turned out to be Freya.

"My hero," she cooed. "Isn't it nice to be alive again? You didn't tell me you were under contract. And they've done such a good job of taking care of you. You know it's a funny thing, man has never been able to invent a more efficient killing machine than himself. That's why they put your brain in this robotic shell. The corporation needs soldiers just like you, and with all of the money they've invested, they're not about to let you out of your contract. Just think, now you can't be killed, and the pain you think you feel is just phantom pain. No you have quite a few more years left to kill, and when your battery runs out, I'll be there. There will always be a cot waiting for you in my bivouac in Valhalla."

She kissed the dome that was my face and left.

I tried to cry, but could not form the tears.

I knew what was in store for me in years to come. Years of carnage without cessation.

And then my final reward, Valhalla.

And Valhalla is hell.

SUSPICION

"Freya always was a bitch," Mentor observed absent-mindedly as he dissolved the screen.

"You seem to know a lot about the Norse gods," Tek commented with more than a question to his voice. His sense of urgency was making him testy.

"They are, ah, a special interest of mine," Mentor answered.

There was a long silence. Finally Tek made a suggestion.

"Can we use your screen to see what each of those who were present were doing when I was attacked?" the war god asked.

"It will take time," Mentor warned, brightening visibly. "No reason not to, though."

Tek was fairly sure he had to determine who his enemy was before answering whatever called him. Sun Tsu had warned that intelligence was the heart of any military operation. Tek would not act until his intelligence was complete.

They spent the next hours watching the party from the point of view of each of those who attended. Tek found it a dreary business, but Mentor encouraged him to persevere. As they watched, Tek made a data file containing an alpha list of those whom they observed. When it appeared they had examined everyone, he stood and stretched. With a gesture, the war god caused the teacher's enchanted television to vanish.

"We need to check Vili yet," Mentor protested.

"He was the thirty-first guest we checked," Tek corrected brusquely. No one was unaccounted for. In fact, no one else was even in a position to see the attack, much less guide the monster.

"Perhaps we should check each one again?" Mentor suggested.

The young god was in no mood for another long session of reliving the small talk and petty games that constituted the party. No one there could be guilty. That left only one suspect.

"You have been most helpful." Tek began his next sentence carefully. "But I am wondering about why in all my data banks there is no mention of a 'Mentor' for the gods. Just which of the muses are you?"

"Not one of the better known ones," Mentor explained. "The Greeks were only concerned with words and drama, not learning. Those like me were mostly ignored."

"So you are yourself part of the Greek Pantheon?"

"Only in a way," the teacher answered vaguely. "I prefer to be allied to none of the godly factions."

" 'When the mystery has no probable solution, then we have to look at the improbable,' " Tek quoted from a file on mystery novels he had accessed earlier.

"Which is?" Mentor suddenly began pacing and seemed nervous.

"Whomever we haven't already eliminated," the young god reasoned.

"There was one war god present later," Mentor quickly added. "He at least would have motive."

"Thor," Tek agreed, "but he was drunk when he arrived."

"That's never slowed him down before," Mentor said conjuring back the screen. "Let's see what he was up to."

THE GRAY GOD'S CHALLENGE

by M.Z. Reichert

Saturday, March 20, 1958
Norristown, Pennsylvania

The crumbling mortar of Norristown's museum bounced echoes through the Viking collection. Booted feet clomped across the tiled floor. "Look at this . . . look at this . . . look it . . . lookit . . . lookit!" Childish voices demanded attention, their appeals broken, on occasion, by a parent's admonishment or foiled attempt to read a placard aloud.

Eleven-year-old Jon Skell stared at the pitted, corroded swords in the central case, oblivious to the noise and movement around him. A dozen families entered through the arches from the Celtic display, breezed through the roomful of swords, helmets, and *skeggox* axes, then rushed beneath the mounted, tenth-scale model of the *Gokstad* ship to the dinosaur skeletons beyond.

Yet Jon noticed none of them. The walls around him seemed to melt into a vast battle plain ringed by evergreen forest. The Norristown strangers became a raging horde of faceless enemies in armor of leather and iron slats. Jon felt the reassuring weight of his own belted mail shirt pressing against his underpadding. The grip of his longsword had gone slick with blood, and fatigue pressed him nearly to unconsciousness. He had lost his helmet earlier in the battle. Now, blood and sweat matted his blond hair into clumps that dangled across his forehead and cheeks to tangle with his beard. His shield seemed to weigh a ton, and a huge dent pocked its metal bossing where he had blocked an axe's hammering stroke.

Jon's dream-self staggered, grasping desperately for "the wolf," the guardian that lent him its wild ferocity in battle. For the moment, no enemies pressed him, and he savored the reprieve, searching desperately for his brother. "Erik! Erik Raven!" A quick twist of his head revealed a semicircle of friends turned corpses. Outnumbered hundreds to dozens, the small band of viking Norsemen had finally met an army that outmatched them. "Erik!" Despite huge casualties, Jon never doubted that he would find his brother alive. A natural warrior, Erik had won his first duel at eight. No other had ever managed to match his skill with any weapon. In spar, he bested them two and three at a time, and, in war, he slaughtered them in droves.

"Wolf." A feeble voice cut over the distant chime and bell of swordplay and the moans of the dying. Recognizing his brother's voice, Jon spun. The sudden movement broke the last strands of his shield's grip. The shield slid from Jon's grasp as he took the first step toward Erik. He tripped over the metal edge, sprawling onto an enemy's corpse. Horrified, Jon recoiled. Not bothering to waste the energy to stand, he abandoned his shield, crawling between the bodies of enemies and friends.

"Erik."

"Wolf." The whisper came from closer.

Jon hurried across the plain, grasses scratching his hands and face, knees pounding against the hard ground. "Erik!" Fear clutched at him, and sweat trickled bloody droplets into his eyes. "Raven!" He shoved aside a handful of green-brown weeds to reveal his brother lying on a bed of wild flowers. His splintered shield lay by his left hand, the metal edge torn through and twisted. Scarlet striped his fingers. His right hand clutched at a ragged gash in his thigh. Blood stained the grasses and flowers, more than Jon believed could have come from one man. Yet, no other lay nearby.

"Raven!" Not bothering to search for bandages in his pouch, Jon tore his tunic from over his mail.

"Wolf." A stupid smile spread across Erik's face. His right hand slid from the wound, like a huge red flower. "I'm sorry."

"No!" Jon screamed. "You're not going to die. Do you hear me, damn it!" He entwined the mutilated tunic around the wound. "Don't die on me, you worthless coward!" Tears sprang to Jon's eyes, and he tried to keep them from his voice. "I love you, brother."

Erik's bloody right hand closed over Jon's fingers.

The tears came in a painful torrent, streaking zigzags through the grime of Jon's face. "Fight it, damn you!" He quoted their father, "Bare is the back brotherless. I need you."

Suddenly, a wind sprang up, whipping Jon's hair into a wild dance. Erik's moist, blue eyes rolled to the left, and his grin became more peaceful. "They've come for me."

"What?" Jon jerked up his head. At first, he saw nothing but the weeds riffling in the breeze, alternately exposing and hiding the scattered corpses. In the distance, the evergreens bowed their heads, as if in prayer. Then, a woman took shape before him. Yellow-white hair tumbled about her shoulders, as thick and powerful as a waterfall. A helmet crushed bangs against her forehead, and the depthless, blue eyes that looked out from beneath them held fire, ice, violence, and joy at once. Seamless gold armor encased her, though it hid none of her warrior's muscles and stole nothing from her perfect female curves. An axe girded her waist. She glided toward Erik.

"No!" Jon leapt to his feet, his exhaustion forgotten. He sprang between the woman and his brother.

The apparition laughed. Then, a voice boomed forth, decidedly feminine yet as strong as any commander's. "Step aside, little man. Your time will come. I've come for Erik the Reaver, the one you call Raven."

"No!" Jon said again. He drew his sword, crouched for defense, shielding Erik with his body.

The woman glared. Her expression alone quailed him. "It is my right to take the dead."

"He's not dead."

"He is close enough. Step aside. Don't make me kill you. You'll freeze in Hel."

A chill spiraled through Jon, and all of his fatigue returned. From habit, he delved deep within himself for "the wolf," the war rage and reserves his guardian would bring. "I'll take that chance."

"Then you are foolish as well as brave." She hefted her axe. Even as she moved, a sister appeared on either side. The triplets glowered down at Jon, their stances perfect and coiled for violence.

Jon felt his legs go shaky. He dug into his core.

And the wolf came to him. Its howl shook him, spiraling through his marrow. Its muscled, black form gave him power, and its savage red eyes drove him to a berserk frenzy. "If you want my brother, you'll have to kill me first." Spurred by the guardian, Jon dove on the *Valkyries,* his sword a silver blur that crashed against their axes.

A stranger's voice jarred Jon Skell from his daydream. Startled, he stiffened with an abrupt violence that spiked pain through his limbs. "What? Who?" His hand flew naturally to his chest, and he could feel his heart slugging against his palm.

A boy a few inches taller than Jon watched his antics curiously, a smile of amusement on his features. His dark blond hair ended in a three inch D.A. that curled from the back of his neck. Freckles sprinkled across his cheeks. Eyes as blue as Jon's own riveted on the key chain clipped to a belt loop of Jon's jeans.

"I said I like your sword. I didn't mean to scare you."

Jon's gaze followed the other's naturally. In addition to the keys to his mother's new house and garage, he carried a pewter replica of a Viking longsword on his ring. "Thanks," he said. "And you didn't scare me. You just surprised me a little."

"Oh yeah? Ya jumped about a million feet. When you get scared, you must go supersonic."

Jon scowled.

The boy smiled, softening his teasing. He continued, saving Jon from the need for a clever, face-saving comeback. "I get the same way around this Viking stuff. My dad won't come to this room with me any more. He says he has to fling me over his shoulder and carry me out kicking and screaming."

Jon laughed, his annoyance evaporating as the focus of the joke shifted.

"It's sort of like I belong here. Like one of these swords is mine, and I'm supposed to be out chopping up guys instead of sleeping through math." The boy curled his hands as if around a hilt, making a few brisk, coordinated motions simulating sword strokes that looked real to Jon.

Impressed by the other's agility, Jon warmed to him

instantly. "Yeah! It's just like that. Like I'm really a Viking deep down, and I'm just stuck in this world accidently."

"Yeah!" the stranger said. He made a few more thrusting motions.

A pause followed during which neither boy spoke. Jon ran a hand through his tousled, red-blond hair, wishing his mother would let him wear a D.A., too. "My name's Jon Skell."

"I'm Eric Skulason. What school do you go to?"

"Huh?" Surprised at the name "Eric" so soon after hearing it echo through his imagination, Jon lost the thread of the conversation.

"What school? What grade?" Eric smiled again, in the winning way that diffused his sarcasm. "I know it's a brain teaser, but I think you can get it if you think on it a while."

Jon recovered quickly. "Norristown. Fifth. My mom and I just moved here. I start Monday."

Eric studied Jon from the top of his strawberry blond mop, down the tee shirt and jeans, to the sneakers. He nodded with mild approval. "You can't be any worse than Jerk Sawdrins."

"Jerk? There's a guy in your class named Jerk?"

"Dirk, actually. We call him Jerk. I've had to sit next to him for four years. Now you'll have to. But at least you'll get me on the other side."

"How do you know that?"

"Sawdrins, Skell, Skulason. Think about it."

"Oh." Another prolonged pause. Finding the silence uncomfortable, Jon broke it. "Good." He clarified. "The you part, not the Jerk part."

Eric changed the subject. "Listen. I've got this new tree fort my dad and I just built. It's gonna be a Viking club. Would you like to be the first other member?"

Excitement flashed through Jon. He had expected difficulty finding friends in a new city, a thousand miles from his home. Yet, within days, he had already come upon one who seemed the epitome of cool, a boy his own age who shared his love for all things Viking. It seemed too good to be true. Jon maintained his composure, not wanting to look too eager. "Sure. Okay."

"There's dues."

Jon's hand wandered to the change in his pocket. "How much?"

"One Viking item."

Both boys' gazes fell to the pewter sword on the key chain. Jon's memory kicked in at once, the lazy Sunday afternoons when his father had taken him to his favorite museum, letting him stare for hours at dragon-headed prows, *scramasax* swords, and pre-served wooden shields. Despite a party with all of his friends and his favorite ice cream cake, Jon's fondest memories of his tenth birthday were of the quiet time after the celebration had ended. His father had taken him to the museum gift shop and let Jon choose any item under ten dollars. The pewter sword had not left his side since that day.

Jon remembered, too, his parent's final argument that he had overheard through his bedroom window. His father's voice remained as firm and calm as always, though his tone betrayed a hurt that cut Jon to the heart. "I know why you're leaving. You think that if you move far enough, you can sever the bond between my son and me. But you can't. He knows I'm his father, and he knows I'll always love him. You can lie to him; you can make yourself believe your own lies. You can try to run from your past, but it'll follow you. And no matter what you do, I'll always be my son's father!" Jon felt tears sting his eyes.

"Yoo hoo! Earth to Jon Skell." Eric's voice cut through the heavy burden of memory. "Do you want to join or not?"

"I want to join," Jon said. "But not if costs my sword." He felt the need to explain, but the words came with difficulty. He had never discussed his parent's divorce with anyone. "My dad gave it to me. I'm not going to get to see him much anymore."

"Your folks don't live together?"

The topic made Jon irritable. "Will you take something else for dues or not?"

"Jeez, don't bite my head off." Eric Skulason leaned on the glass case that held the Viking swords. "How 'bout if the sword stays just yours. But we keep it locked in the fort when you're not carrying it. Would that be okay?"

Jon nodded carefully.

"I've got something special to keep there, too. Found it in the farthest corner of the basement last year. I've never shown it to anyone before. It's got Viking writing and everything."

Awe and doubt warred within Jon. "Are you sure it's Viking writing?"

"Positive. Come on. I'll show you."

The Skulason's tree fort perched on a long, flat branch of a twisted oak. It smelled pleasantly of new boards, still pale brown with darker knotholes, and moisture had not yet rusted the nails. Leaves closed around the wooden railings, screening it from the sky as well as from trespassers below.

Jon Skell crouched on the plank floor, fingering the pewter sword on his key chain. He watched in silence as Eric slid a metal box from beneath the continuous bench that circled the wooden boundaries just inside the railings. Eric set his parcel carefully on the bench. Kneeling in front of it, he pulled a key from his pocket and inserted the key into the lock. It clicked open. Eric hefted something from the interior and set it beside the box. His shoulder hid the object from Jon's view.

The Skulason's brown and white corgi, Cerberus, stared up through the branches, watching every movement with his head cocked in question.

Curious, Jon moved to Eric's side. The object was

a book, its leather binding worn to silky smoothness. The front cover had been torn away, revealing a page covered with runic scrawl that looked similar to the silver and bronze ornamental inlay on many of the museum weapons. Jon stared. Eleven years in Chicago had made him wary, and he had prepared himself for scams intended to make a fool of the new boy in school. Yet, he had seen enough ancient, museum writings to believe. The uneven, yellowed page could not have been forged by an eleven year old, and the ink strokes looked fine and old. He reached out to touch it, focussed on an edge of the page.

Eric drew in a sudden, sharp breath.

Cerberus barked.

Jon retreated, annoyed that Eric could touch the manuscript but would not let him do the same. He turned his head to say as much, only to find Eric's eyes riveted on the page.

Confused, Jon followed his companion's gaze. The strange runes remained, yet now their meaning came to him in simple, English rhyme:

> *Speak these words;*
> *Take a life without value.*
> *Skirnir will bring,*
> *That which will bind you.*

A string of Nordic letters followed. And, though Jon could not translate these, he somehow felt certain of their pronunciation. A chill swept through him, but he kept the presence of mind to doubt. "This is a joke, right? How did you do that?"

Eric ignored the accusation. His gaze remained fixed on the page.

Jon leapt to his feet. "Cut it out. It's not funny. You're giving me the creeps."

Eric still made no reply.

"What's it say on the other pages?" Jon tried to turn the upper leaf, but it remained rigidly clumped to the others. Hefting the book, he tried to shake the pages free. They remained adherent to one another and to the back cover.

When the writing disappeared from his sight, Eric finally spoke. "I can read it. I've never been able to read it before." He blinked, but apparently still could not look away to meet Jon's gaze. When Jon replaced the book, Eric's attention refocused on the lettering.

Jon froze. Either Eric was serious, or he was the best actor in the world.

"Can you read it, too?"

"Yes. What's it say to you?"

Eric read, speaking the exact words that Jon saw, down to the pronunciation of the final line. Finally, he managed to tear his gaze from the page and meet Jon's. "What do you think it means?"

"I don't know," Jon said. He considered. "Well, according to the myths, Skirnir's the servant of the god, Frey. I guess he'll bring us something if we say that . . ." He pointed at the final line. ". . . and kill someone worthless."

"Or something," Eric added thoughtfully. "It doesn't say it has to be a person."

Eric's serious consideration spiraled horror through Jon. Still, the idea seemed morbidly fascinating. "I'm not killing anyone."

"My sister has mice."

Jon liked mice. "How about an insect? That's about as worthless as life gets."

"Okay."

The boys scrambled to their feet, searching the oak leaves for an insect. At length, Jon discovered a huge, black ant crawling across a twig. "Got one." Gently, he pinched it between his thumb and forefinger. "I'll squash, you read."

"Okay." Eric cleared his throat. He spoke each syllable cleanly. As he pronounced the final word, Jon smashed the ant between his fingers.

Eric's voice seemed to tumble into an abyss of

silence, and the intensity of the quiet transformed the ripple of wind through the branches into a rattling, whistling gale. Nothing obvious happened. Jon glanced down through the branches. Cerberus lay, waiting for his master at the base of the tree. Jon had heard that dogs could sense the supernatural. If anything had come of their attempt, even the animal had not noticed it.

Jon loosed a nervous laugh, wiping ant guts from his fingers onto his jeans. "I guess it was just words on a page."

Eric frowned, obviously unconvinced. "My family lived in that house for ten years, and we weren't the first. There's a reason why everyone missed that book but me. And there's a reason why the writings got clear today."

"What are you saying? We met because of fate?"

"There's this Viking I've been drawing for years. A guy with hair exactly your color and a real sword just like that little one you got."

Jon held his breath, recalling the brother in his own reverie. "Named Jon?"

"Well, no. Ulf. But I still think it's supposed to be you." Eric studied Jon cautiously, apparently waiting to see if he had gotten too familiar too quickly. "I think Ulf means 'wolf.'"

"Wolf?" Excited and frightened at once, Jon tried to reassure. "In my daydreams my brother's name is Erik. With a 'k.' And my symbol is a wolf."

The boys stared at one another for several moments, uncertain what to say next. Suddenly, Eric whirled. "I'm getting a mouse."

Before Jon could protest, Eric scrambled down the first several wood block foot rests. He jumped the final six feet to the ground, his light easy landing enviable. Eric ran toward his house, Cerberus chasing at an easy lope.

Jon paced, trying to take things all in at once. Yesterday, he had found himself alone in a strange town in Pennsylvania. Now, he had found a friend who, in a matter of hours, had become more like a brother. Accustomed to daydreaming, he had a firm grasp on the differences between imagination and reality, and he knew that the events of the past few hours were real. Again, he stole a glance at the book. The runic letters remained, boldly printed on the page. He could still remember the translation, though it had become harder for him to discern the English words. He wondered if that had more to do with time or with Eric's leaving.

Shortly, Eric returned, clambering up the toeholds one handed. He cradled a coffee can in the crook of his other elbow and clutched a brick in that hand. As he reached the floor of the tree fort, he scooted the brick across the planking, then lowered the coffee can. He scampered into the clubhouse. "Got it."

Cerberus barked once, then again settled at the base of the tree.

Jon took the coffee can, peeling back the lid a crack to expose a white mouse. Its beady red eyes stared at him. He closed the lid. "I don't know if I want to do this."

"You chickening out on me?" Eric did not wait for an answer. "Come on." He picked up the brick and offered it to Jon.

Jon ignored the offering, taking another look at the mouse. Its whiskers twitched. "Won't your sister miss him?"

"I left her favorite."

"Won't she miss this one?"

"So I'll buy her another one." Eric shook the brick. "Here."

Jon removed the lid from the can. Reluctantly, he lay the can on its side on the bench. The mouse looked out cautiously. Jon looked at the brick, and the idea of pulverizing a living thing repulsed. "Do we have to squish it?"

"No. Do it anyway you want. I just thought that'd be easiest."

Jon considered. "Could we poison it?"

"With what?"

"Rat poison?"

Eric threw up his hands. "Do you happen to be carrying rat poison?"

"No." Jon stared at his feet.

"You big chicken."

"You're so damned brave, you do it."

"All right. Fine. I'll do it. You read."

Relieved, Jon stepped aside to stand in front of the book. He spoke each syllable gingerly.

Eric raised the brick, smashing it down on the mouse, pressing it further until a red stain spread across the bench seat. A pink foot poked from beneath one edge.

Jon felt his stomach lurch, and he tasted bile. He turned away, struggling against his heaving gut. A gust of ice-grained wind caught him square in the face, staggering him against the rail. An odor seeped into his nostrils, thick, ancient, and cloying, a sickening combination of mold and honey. Jon gave up the battle. He sagged across the rail, vomiting to the ground below, pain aching through his stomach.

"Oh my god!" Eric whispered. "Oh . . . my . . . god!"

Before Jon could turn, thunder slammed through his ears, cruel agony against the drums. Light flashed, its reflection a blinding fog off the tight umbrella of leaves. Sensation tore through Jon, a cold ugly feeling of fear and wrongness that drove him to vomit again and again until his stomach heaved dry. Only then did he manage to whirl.

Eric sprawled on the clubhouse floor, still. A figure hovered over him, cape flapping and cracking in the gale, a blackened, blood-stained tunic clinging to his muscled form. A huge sword girded his hip.

Jon screamed, the sound muffled in his thunder-deafened ears. As he adjusted his perception of sound, he could now hear the whoosh of the wind, Cerberus' constant, wild barking, and the soft words of the creature before him. ". . . she can save him. The book." The voice emerged as deep and low as a bassoon, and it enhanced the obvious aberration of its presence. More than anything in the world, Jon wanted it to go.

As if in answer to the need, lightning cracked open the sky, thunder booming around it. Whiteness bathed the creature, then winked out in an explosion that stabbed Jon's vision. He closed his eyes instinctively, afterimages of the creature flashing in colored pictures on the insides of his eyelids. The thunder trailed into silence, leaving the ceaseless rattle of rain on the leaves overhead, pierced by the whines and barks of the corgie below.

"Eric?" Jon approached his friend cautiously, blinking to clear the huge white spots obscuring his vision. "Eric? Are you all right?"

Eric did not move. He lay as if in sleep, halfway under the clubhouse bench. Despite otherwise complete relaxation, Eric kept his right hand tightly clenched. Jon shook him. "Wake up, Eric." The head lolled, revealing a scalp cut and a winding trickle of blood.

Jon recoiled, alarmed. "Eric!" Panic suffused him. He knew he had to get help immediately. Yet, he felt shamed by the proceedings, and he knew no one would believe what had happened in the clubhouse. Another thought broke through the savage boil of fear. *What if they think I killed him? What if they send me to the electric chair?* His thoughts shattered, scattering in random directions. *He's not dead. Eric's not dead. He can't be dead.* He seized an arm, poking at the wrist for a pulse, uncertain whether he felt a heart beat or just his own movement. Then, the otherworld thing's advice returned to him. *She can help him. The book?* He spun, staggering across the planks to the book.

The top page had disappeared, revealing another

scrawled with Nordic runes. Jon discovered that he could still understand, though the words had changed:

> *Read the words inscribed here;*
> *Kill a beloved pet.*
> *That will bring Sif's mercy*
> *And save a friend's life yet.*

Horror clutched Jon, and he felt as if his heart had stopped beating. *A beloved pet.* Jon and his mother had no animals. *No pets.* His eyes finished the thought long before his mind found the strength to function. His gaze slid down the tree's trunk to alight on the dog below. Cerberus stood at the base of the tree, tail wagging, head cocked to one side as if to understand.

No. Jon felt the sickness return, though nothing remained in his gut. He glanced at Eric. His new friend lay absolutely still. Jon looked back at the book. The letters on the page remained, but they had gone fuzzy and indistinct. The writing seemed to smear, becoming less legible by the moment. His mind groped for an answer, and it struck him with all the abrupt force of the gale that had arisen with Skirnir's coming. *When Eric went away before, I could no longer read the book.* The conclusion came without the need to ponder. *When these instructions disappear, Eric will be dead.*

Knowing what he had to do, Jon Skell leapt to his feet, snatching up the book. He seized the brick in his other hand. Mouse remains slid from the surface as he raised it, and the gore gave spongily beneath his grasping fingers. Illness rocked him. He stared at the dog. Cerberus watched him with happy curiosity, and desperation engulfed Jon in a muscle-locking convulsion. *So sweet. So trusting.* He gauged the distance to the dog's head, yet he did not throw. For several moments, he knelt on the wooden floor, frozen immobile. Then, the lettering smeared nearly into oblivion, and he concentrated on Eric, knowing that he had to place a human life before that of a dog. Locking his gaze on the book, Jon hurled the brick and read.

A yelp cut through Jon's mental fog. Then, the tree shook, as if in the throes of a giant seizure. Light flared, bright as a thousand spotlights. Then, Jon Skell collapsed to the clubhouse floor, overtaken by oblivion.

Jon Skell awakened to a vigorous shake, with no comprehension of time and place. Gradually, the tree fort took its familiar shape around him. Eric Skulason stood over him, the freckled face split into a joyful grin. The book lay on the floor near Jon's knee. A glance through the hole in the floor leading out of the tree revealed Cerberus' still form on the ground, and memory returned in a painful rush. He twisted to face Eric, hiding the sight from the corgie's owner. "You're all right! Thank god, you're all right."

"*I'm* all right? You're the one k.o.'ed on the floor."

"But you were . . ." Jon trailed off, thinking it better not to continue. Apparently, Eric had no knowledge of his near death. Better he never found out that the new boy had killed his dog. Better he believed that the same event that had floored Jon had killed the dog. Eric looked so normal, Jon feared that he had destroyed Cerberus without need. The thought speared guilt through him. For good or ill, he hated what he had done.

Eric did not wait for Jon to finish his sentence. "Look what he gave me!" He held out his right hand.

"Who?"

"Skirnir. Look what he brought." Eric opened his hand, revealing a pewter sword exactly like the one on Jon's key chain. The resemblance was so striking, that Jon could not help taking a quick glance to make certain that his father's gift still hung in its proper place. Finding it there, he looked at Eric's again.

"Isn't it great? We have a club symbol."

The words seemed incongruous and distant. Assailed by guilt, terror, and the certainty of a friend's death narrowly averted, Jon could find nothing to say. He felt as if he had discovered a third world between Eric's and Skirnir's, and little of sense came from either of the other two. Unable to speak, he turned his attention to the book near his knee. A new page fell beneath his scrutiny, and he read with no conscious attempt or desire to know:

> The words incribed spoken,
> A stranger killed,
> The favor you need
> Shall be fulfilled.

There was no doubt in Jon's mind that, next time, the book would demand a human sacrifice. The thought ached through his belly until just the effort of breathing shot agony through him. "Promise me," he managed. "Promise me we'll never ever *ever* use this book for anything again."

Eric laughed. "Sure, he was kind of awful, but he did give me . . ."

Jon lunged, grasping Eric by the front of his shirt, the need desperate within him. "Promise . . . me!"

Finally, Eric's expression grew appropriately serious. "Hey, I thought it was cool. But if it means that much to you, fine. No more using the book." He twirled the pewter sword between his fingers.

Jon sank back to the floor.

Saturday March 20, 1969
Pleiku, Vietnam

The drab walls of the military hospital seemed to close in on Spec. 4 Jon Skell, but the medicinal odor that eternally permeated the hallways wafted to him like perfume. He walked the bleak hallways in silence, ears only half-tuned to the rush of stretchers and the moans of the injured. Soon enough, a chopper would rush him and several other medics to the hills surrounding

Kontum to tend the wounded there. Soon enough, Jon Skell might find himself as one of the patients on the hospital stretchers.

The thought sent a chill shuddering through Jon. It would not be his first experience with death. Once, in high school, when cars had been the end all and be all of masculine cool, he had skidded off the road during an impromptu race. His memory of lying in the Surgical Intensive Care Unit remained vivid. He had seen the tunnel of light that so many who experience near-death experiences described. He recalled the sensation of utter tranquility, unlike anything he had experienced in life, a feeling he believed he would never find the words to describe. He had embraced death, needing to escape the pain that was all life could promise.

Jon could never forget what had happened next. A woman had come to him then, her figure more perfect than any model. His mind told him that her face had matched the flawless precision of her body, yet he could not recall the features. She had seemed more picture concept than reality, and she had admonished Jon that his time had not come. Still, despite her beauty and gentleness, Jon's mind had rebelled against her. There was an alien impropriety about her that made her seem more a tool of the devil than of God, yet nothing about her seemed servile. For some time, he had hovered, uncertain whether to fight for or to stifle his last breaths. Then, she had taken him by the hand and ripped him back to the world he had known. Alive, against all medical odds.

Jon continued through the hospital corridors, remembering how he had taken a vow to help others near death. From the moment of his awakening, he knew he was destined to become a doctor. And, that ambition had rescued him from a choice. When Eric had enlisted to fight the war in Vietnam after two years of college ROTC, Jon had remained behind to finish his studies. And, until recently, he had never regretted that decision.

Irony lashed through Jon, relentlessly pursuing his thoughts. His medical school acceptance and his draft letter had come on the same day. *A medic. A fucking infantry medic, at the front, if this war could be said to have a front at all.* Outrage dribbled through him, unable to spark to anger. It was no man's fault. *Another few years, and I'd be the one in that operating room sewing the wounded back together, helping the injured return to their loving families intact.* Jon knew he would have put his all into the schooling. And he would have become a good doctor if the effort killed him.

Jon Skell raised a fist to pound the wall, just as a pair of doctors rounded curve into the hallway. He pulled the blow, though they seemed not to notice him. Engaged in conversation, they passed without a glance, and their words wafted clearly to him.

"Well, I don't care what anyone says. There's something funny going on. That's the third guy today with knife wounds, and they're all from the same damned platoon."

"Self-inflicted?"

"No way. That one guy can't wait to get back. Says God's fighting on his lieutenant's side. And there's been too much fire action. Guys don't stab themselves in the middle of a firefight and certainly not in the groin like that medic. In fact, guys don't stab themselves at all when there's perfectly good guns . . ."

Jon listened until the doctors' footfalls obscured their conversation. Fear winched down on him, its source uncertain. He knew that he had only heard a partial conversation, that he had no reason to make assumptions about identifications or facts. Yet, his mind grasped the certainty that the mentioned platoon was the 1st platoon of C company, 2nd battalion, 503rd infantry, the one led by Second Lieutenant Eric Skulason. *There's only one way to find out.* The doctors had mentioned that the medic had come in injured, and Eric's letters to Fort Sam had detailed that man with a description Jon believed he could pick out of a crowd in New York City.

Jon spun, retracing his steps through the corridor, his mind racing. He scarcely noticed the dank, sterile hallways, did not bother to acknowledge the few others he passed in the halls. At length, he found the open ward serviced by the physicians he had passed. Quickly, Jon scanned the ranks of the injured, his gaze drawn to a shirt thrown over a blanket that covered a sleeping soldier. It bore the insignia of the 4th Infantry Division. Jon followed the lines of the sleeping man, discovering a rugged, black face topped by curly, dark hair. A long-healed, zigzagging scar lay, deeply etched, on his left cheek.

Jon resisted the urge to run to Spec. 4 Coby Jackson's side. Instead, he matched his gait to the brisk pace set by the nurses and orderlies. It seemed like an eternity before he stood at the medic's bedside. He knelt at the head. "Jackson," he whispered.

The man did not stir.

Jon hesitated, afraid he had chosen the wrong patient. Final identification would require the medic to open his eyes. *Or I could just look at the name on his chart or tags.* He fingered his own tags through his shirt, feeling the reassuring contour of the long-familiar, pewter sword through the fabric. This time, he used the nickname he knew Eric used for the medic. "Cobra."

The medic's eyes flared open, as huge and blue as Eric had described them. An expression of welcome wilted in confusion. "Who are you?"

"My name's Jon. Jon Skell."

The congenial look returned, then broadened into a smile. "Jon the wolf?" He looked Skell over. "Cool. Feels like I know you already. The Ragin' Raven says you're the best. Says you're a mean man with a sword."

"With a sword?" Jon recalled the days when he and Eric had bought every *Kendo* and fencing book in existence and learned to bat at one another with sticks. In college, they had topped their fencing class, though Eric had always proven the more competent of the two. "Yeah, well whatever ability he attributed to me, double it and stick it back on him. At least he translated that skill to guns, too. If I shot into a herd of cows, I'd be lucky to hit the ground. And what's this Ragin' Raven stuff? Sounds like a college football team."

Coby Jackson rolled to his side to meet Jon's gaze more directly. "He came up with the Raven thing. Said it made him sound like a thinker. The Ragin' just fit."

"Knowing Eric, I don't doubt it." Jon laughed. "Excuse me getting right down to business, but I hear things down your way have been kind of strange. What's going on?"

Jackson's eyes narrowed, and his smile disappeared. "You some kind of shrink?"

"Spec. 4. Medic. Just like you." Jon tapped a shoulder patch, showing the yellow eagle on its olive green background.

Jackson made a wordless noise that indicated mistrust to Jon.

"Look, I'm just worried about Eric. You can understand that. His letters told me you were his best buddy out there."

"Never took your place, though." Jackson warmed slightly to the compliment. "Look, if you're really Raven's Jon, show me the thing."

"What ..." Jon started, then caught himself. Professing ignorance would lose him what little of the medic's trust remained. "Eric and I grew up together. We shared lots of things. Give me a small hint."

Jackson considered. "There's a thing he carries. Says you got one just like it. Says you had yours first. Says you'd carry it on you."

This description clinched the thing's identity in Jon's mind. He thrust his hand into his shirt, pulling free the tags and the pewter sword hanging amid them.

Coby Jackson relaxed visibly.

Jon tucked the tags away. "Now tell me what happened out there. Between you and me."

Jackson lay back, blue eyes scanning the ceiling, as if to find the answer written there. "We were on a night ambush and got hit. Lead and shrapnel spraying everywhere. I saw six guys go down in about a minute, and I knew we were in trouble. I was patching one guy, my back to the gooks, protecting him from fire like I'm taught to. Then, this guy in front of me goes down." Jackson paused, finger tracing angles, apparently considering trajectory.

Jon nodded his encouragement. The idea of walking out into this kind of action chilled him to the marrow. He, too, had been told to shield his patients during his advanced individual training at Fort Sam, yet the logic of the maneuver was lost on him. *What good's it going to do a platoon to have its medic killed guarding one wounded man when there's others who need tending?*

Jackson continued. "Looking later, I can't see how that round didn't pass through me before him. Perfect shot, too. Through the neck. He went down dead, and I didn't bother with him. Then, all a sudden, all the sound went away. I figured I'd gotten hit and went deaf. Then, I noticed the guys all hiding there, so still, looking up. I hadn't heard no choppers, so I looked too. And there's this giant of a guy flying round through the sky, a gleaming sword clutched in his fist. And he's leaping right for them gooks!"

Jackson stopped, studying Jon to read his mood and decide whether he should bother to continue.

Jon imagined he looked as frozen and stupefied as the soldiers Jackson had described. Logic hammered him with the only possible answer, yet loyalty forced him to believe that Eric had kept his promise, that he had not dared to use the "book." Then, another thought drove his mouth and eyes to stinging dryness, and panic charged through him. *Of course Jackson didn't feel the shot that killed his buddy. Because that shot came from behind. That man was Eric's sacrifice.* A deeper part of Jon's conscience rebelled. *No! Impossible! Eric is a commander and a good one. He wouldn't shoot one of his own men.* The evil inherent in such an action went beyond Jon's imagination. *Not Eric, damn it! Not Eric.* The image of the smashed mouse filled his memory and the sequence of events that had allowed Jon, himself, to slaughter a friend's dog. "Oh my god," he said softly.

Assuming Jon's words were a response to his story, Jackson nodded. "That was my first thought. Course, I never pictured God like that. Too young. Too white. He was as blond as you." The medic laughed. "Gunfire and grenades didn't seem to touch him. He hacked through those gooks like nothing, bloody sword weaving, his glowing presence like something out of a horror movie. Except on our side. A bit overzealous though. He cut a couple of ours, though I don't think he actually killed anyone. Caught me a good blow. In a bad place. I'm out for the duration, and I'm almost kind of sorry. Always liked living life on the edge. Liked Raven, too. And I think we could really kick some butt with God on our side."

Terror lashed Jon to a desperate need for action. *What's this war done to Eric? I have to stop him.* He caught one of Jackson's huge hands. "Where's the platoon now? Exactly."

"As of this morning they were on Hill 796, seven klicks southwest of Ben Het in the Ngok Kom Leat Mountains. Why? You're not planning go there."

"Not as far as you know."

Jackson lowered his voice to a bare whisper. "You can get in deep shit."

"Yeah, well let 'em find me. I'll be the first guy in

history to go AWOL *into* combat. They can court martial my corpse." Jon stood, keeping his voice as low as Jackson's. "But you didn't hear it from me. I didn't tell you anything." He turned to go.

Jackson touched Jon's hand. "Wolf?"

Jon glanced back over his shoulder.

"Say 'hi' to Raven for me. Be careful, man, okay?"

Jon nodded. "Yeah, all right. As a favor to my best friend's friend." He strode from the Ward, headed for the orderly room of the aviation unit. He had never heard of DCS bothering to ask for authorization for a liftoff to the front.

Twilight found Jon Skell standing in a field of trampled elephant grass beside two seasoned privates, patched and ready to return to war. Dust kicked up by the rotors covered his fatigues, and he watched the medevac's retreating form, the red crosses glaring through the surrounding camouflage paint. The pitch of the helicopter changed as it rose higher, then disappeared beneath the voices of nearby men. Jon's eyes flit across the ready field of fire to the higher grasses beyond it and the distant horizon of jungle. Finally, he let his gaze settle on the hastily assembled camp. Strands of concertina wire surrounded a myriad of dug and half-dug bunkers. Beyond the wire, men scuttled, finishing the preparations.

"Let's go," said Don Millson, a tall, lanky redhead that Jon had met on the flight.

"This feels wrong," the other private, Ken Kittilano said. He hunched his small, broad form, his discomfort stabbing fear through Jon.

"Let's go," Jon repeated, wishing he could do anything to get his non-bullet-riddled butt back on the medevac. The company's camp did not look strong enough to keep out an old woman on horseback, let alone an army with artillery. *I can't believe I'm doing this.*

The three men headed toward camp quickly, even

as the sun settled below the horizon. At the lead, Millson hailed C Company from a distance. Kittilano's uneasiness pervaded his every movement, and it became infectious. Jon caught himself shivering uncontrollably.

Kittilano whispered, "This area's hot. Something's about to happen."

"Shut up," Millson returned.

The darkness caught them still a hundred yards from the perimeter. As if it were a signal, mortar fire blazed through the darkness behind them, covering a charging wave of NVA troopers. AK fire rattled through the night.

All three men collapsed to the ground. Machine gun fire answered from the camp, and Jon lost control of his bladder. "You all right?" Kittilano whispered.

The words sounded ludicrous and misplaced. "Untouched," Millson answered. "We gotta get inside. Let's move it. Quick."

"Inside," it appeared, was a relative term. Jon felt paralyzed, and it took him several heartbeats longer than the others to make his move. Lights flashed and howled around him, a blaring cacophony he did not dare try to decipher. Placing his life in luck's grip, he hunched and ran for the perimeter, dropping to a crawl as he watched the shadowy forms of Millson and Kittilano skitter for entrance beneath the wire.

A muzzle flash broke the blackness around them, from inside the perimeter. Something warm and liquid splashed Jon's face. Kittilano went still. Millson screamed. "I'm hit! I'm hit!" He flopped and writhed, moaning something about friendly fire. The urge to run seized Jon, and it took all the effort of his being to remain in place. The crossfire whizzed and buzzed above his head, and he had little choice but take his chances. He crawled faster, calling with every movement. "Don't shoot me; I'm with you." He could not hear himself over the pop of gun fire, but he could not stop shouting.

Once through the concertina wire, Jon found himself

staring down the barrel of an M-16. *I'm dead.* "Don't shoot me . . . !" The cycle of his screaming continued as he awaited the final blast.

The barrel dipped. "Jon?" It was Eric's voice.

Jon felt certain he had died. He could not fathom the odds against some man recognizing him before pulling the trigger nor the chances that that man would be Eric Skulason. Yet fate made him certain it could have happened no other way. He looked up into the other's face, past the sweat-spangled cammo paint to his friend's familiar features.

"Eric. Christ, don't shoot me."

"I'm not gonna shoot you. I'm gonna hug you." Despite the sentiment, he drew Jon deeper into the camp before daring to fulfill his promise. Then, he enwrapped Jon into an embrace that crushed the breath from him. Tears soaked through the shoulder of Jon's fatigues, yet he denied them. *Humidity. It has to be humidity. Eric's done this too long to cry.* "Buddy, I don't know what brought you here now, but it was obviously meant to be."

Despite the slamming echo of explosions, Jon heard Eric clearly. Yet the words seemed to make little sense. "I don't know what you're talking about. What brought me here was the book."

A strange expression appeared on Eric's face, one Jon did not recognize. It terrified him. The grease paint only magnified its evil foreignness. "Yes," he said. "The book."

"You *do* have it here."

Eric nodded. His blue eyes fixed on Jon.

"You promised never to use it again."

"That was before your accident."

"What?" The words seemed like a non sequitur. Jon scarcely noticed the rush and noise of the men around him. Radios blasted their messages through the camp, yet Jon heard none of it.

"Your car accident. Remember? I called Sif then.

Without her, you would have died. I couldn't let you die *then*."

Something about the pronunciation of the word "then" sent a chill through Jon. Still, he managed to focus on the more significant parts of Eric's explanation. Now, he understood that Eric had spoken the truth, and that that truth should have seemed obvious from the day a goddess had ripped Jon from the arms of death. Yet denial had allowed him to disbelieve. "You killed someone to save my life?"

"Do you remember the pathetic, old drunkard who walked the railroad tracks?"

"Gray Charlie, of course." Then, truth hammered Jon. He had not seen the old drifter since his accident. "Oh my god."

Eric said nothing. His eyes glittered in a weapon's yellow-white flash. He unslung a pack from his back, then separated out a .45 side arm, the familiar book, and something smaller that he slipped into his hand too quickly for Jon to identify it. He placed the book on the ground, held the pistol, and knelt beside it.

Jon crouched to Eric's level. "You've used it here, haven't you?"

Eric said nothing.

"I spoke with Coby Jackson."

"Did you now?"

"There's no destiny involved. I came because of what he said." Jon fidgeted, forcing himself to raise the important issue. "Did you kill one of your own men?"

Eric looked up. Tears trailed lines through the cammo paint. "Yes." He made the confession without attempt at defense.

"How could you?"

The tears continued to flow, and Eric's head sank again. "It was him or the whole platoon. What choice did I have?"

"How do you know what would have happened?"

"I'm trained to know. I knew."

"You murdered one of your own men."

Eric said nothing.

Deep inside Jon Skell, honor warred with loyalty. "I love you, Eric. You're the only brother I ever had. But I can't sanction murder."

"We're in war, Jon. There is no such thing as murder."

"You killed one of your own men."

"You saw what happened to the men you were with. Was that murder?"

"That was an accident. You knew exactly what you were doing. Exactly who you were killing."

"Yes." Eric said. He raised his head, looking beyond or through Jon, focussed on the ceaseless pops and explosions. Screams cut over the gunfire, most indecipherable. Someone shrieked, "Medic!" repeatedly.

Jon stiffened. Eric's focus back on the war reminded him of his own duties. He had come against orders, yet it made him no less liable for the men in his own mind.

Apparently guessing his friend's intentions, Eric caught his arm. "It's too late for that one." All of the remorse had left his tone. The tears stopped with unnatural suddenness. His fingers pried open Jon's hand, and he stuffed something small and metal against Jon's palm. "Soon enough, it'll be too late for all of us. It's my duty to see that my men survive."

Jon glanced at the object in his fist. It was Eric's pewter sword. A chill swept through him. "What are you doing?"

"I'm sorry," Eric said. Then, his words became incomprehensible.

It took Jon's mind unreasonably long to register what was happening. By the time he thought to read the book's final page, Eric was enunciating the last Nordic rune:

The speaking of words,
A brother's slaying

Will bring the Gray God
On your enemies preying.

The significance slammed Jon like a hammer blow. "Eric, no!" He dove blindly for Eric Skulason. His hands struck his friend's arms, driving them downward, just as the .45's discharge joined the deadly pandemonium around them. Jon collapsed, sobbing at the betrayal. He awaited the pain that never came, and he wondered if he had fallen dead before he felt it, waited for his mind to register the end he already knew. Yet still the oblivion would not come. He opened his eyes.

Suddenly, the earth seemed to fold and shake beneath him. Light cracked open the heavens, obscuring moon and stars in a blinding flash that ached through Jon's eyes and ears. Wind funneled down from the sky, a bucking gale that pounded Jon, nearly knocking him flat to the ground. Pain and pressure made his head feel as if it would explode. An odor nearly overwhelmed him, rancid with the reek of things long dead, the charnel odor that had sent him into spasms of vomiting as a child. Then, a giant stepped through the hole in the heavens. A simple, gray cloak enwrapped the figure, the hood in place. Yet, it could not hide muscles as thick and prominent as a draft horse's. The face lay in shadow, and a single blue eye glared forth like a beacon. Gripped in both weathered hands, he clutched a sword the size of a two by four. His laughter reverberated over the battlefield, reducing the mortar rounds, grenades, and machine guns to the volume of child's toys. He leapt for the NVA.

The pewter sword in Jon's hand twitched. Then, suddenly, it snapped to the size of a real sword. Startled, Jon sprang backward to stare, keeping hold of the haft by luck and habit alone. Only then, the answers came. *This sword is of their world. Eric knew it would become life-sized when he set off that spell, because he's done it before.* Jon took the logic one step further. *And he gave it to me because he never intended to kill me. He intended—* Jon attempted to cut off the thought, but his mind moved faster. *—to kill himself.* Instantly, he translated the idea to action, ignoring the charging god, ignoring the panicked screams that shattered his hearing, ignoring the guns that blattered at a creature not of this world, a god they could not harm.

And Jon turned his attention to Eric. His best friend lay still, eyes closed. Blood pulsed from a ragged hole in his leg, the flow lessening in the instant it took Jon to react. A lake of blood surrounded the wound. "Eric, you stupid, fucking hero." Jon hurled down the sword, hauling a bandage and a stick from his medical pouch. A tourniquet might well lose Eric his leg, but it could save his life. Jon's mind kicked in. He kept the facts, for the moment holding emotion at bay. It was probably already too late, but that did not stop him. He wrapped the bandage, twisted until the flow stopped, then deftly tied the wrap in place. Only then, his fingers slipped to the other femoral artery, near the groin. A pulse fluttered against his touch.

Alive! Joy rushed through Jon. He howled in exaltation, the cry lost beneath the rush of the wind. He caught a glimpse of the gray god, Odin, bullets flying around and through him, RPG-7's exploding against him, then raining shrapnel over the NVA. His sword flung red arcs like dawn light through the night-dark sky, and his laughter rang like thunder. The odor of fresh blood mingled with the dead smells. And Eric's pulse disappeared from beneath Jon's touch.

"No! Don't die, damn you! You can't die now." Springing to Eric's head, he sealed his mouth over his friend's, administering two solid breaths. The chest rose and fell without effort. "Live, you son of a bitch. Live. I need you here!" He performed the chest compressions, then leapt back to handle the airway again. On the second cycle, a weak but steady pulse answered his attempts. "Thank god."

Jon Skell looked up.

A woman stared back at him, her face savagely beautiful and her expression cruel. She wore the seamless, gold armor of the *Valkyries* in his reverie. She clutched a war axe in her fist. "Move aside. He is ours."

Jon picked up the sword, heart pounding. "You can't have him."

"Then I will take him."

Rage turned Jon's vision red. Too much had happened too quickly. He had long ago accepted the presence of these mythical figures summoned by his friend who was more like a brother. He had worked too hard, given too much, to lose the battle how. Without warning, he lunged and thrusted. The point jabbed through metal and flesh. Shock registered on the woman's face. Then, she collapsed, screaming once, and was still. Where the bullets and grenades had failed, the blade from their own world had succeeded.

Again, light snapped and flared. Where one *valkyrie* lay dying, eleven others appeared to take her place. Every one clutched a war axe. Bloody blond hair flowed in waves from beneath their helmets, and their blue eyes gleamed red from the flash of their own entrance. They advanced on Jon.

Jon Skell held his ground, checking his fear. He took a defensive stance he had learned in a book, surprised at how natural the position felt. "Do your worst. You may get me, but I'll take more than one with me! How many *valkyries* can you spare?"

The injured one went still, dead. The others hovered, their pale faces darkening at once. Yet, they did not press forward. Behind him, Jon could feel each of Eric's breaths as if linked. Without knowing how, he accepted that his brother still clung to life. To believe otherwise would undermine the rage that drove him to face certain death.

"Hold!" Odin's voice boomed through the night, raw agony in Jon's ears. He did not give ground, even when the darkness split and the gray god appeared beside his entourage. He towered over Jon, his simplicity and expressionlessness somehow more intimidating than his killer frenzy. His great sword dripped blood. "Jon-Ulf Haakonsson, it is not your time. We came for your brother, Erik the Reaver. He gave himself to us, and it is my right to have him."

"Why!" Jon screamed in frustration, not expecting an answer, though he got one.

"Because he would have been the best warrior in Valhalla. Because with him we could have won the Ragnarok! We could have won! And the gods could have lived forever!"

"It's too late," Jon said.

"No! I've transcended time, and I can take him back."

"No." Jon clutched the sword tighter, trying to hide his pale, shaking fist. Blood from the *valkyrie* trickled, warm, across his fingers. It took an effort of will not to collapse, vomiting, to the ground.

Odin's voice made the earth tremble. "You stole him once, Jon-Ulf. You chased my Choosers away on the battlefield and let The Reaver die of age instead. It will not happen again."

"Go back where you belong."

The *valkyries* shifted uneasily, obviously fighting their own rage and need for vengeance. Odin studied Jon Skell. Then, he lapsed into a crazed fit of laughter. "You can't stop me, but I do admire your courage. This is your choice: You may step aside and let me claim what is rightfully mine, and I will let you and your pitiful soldiers live." He made a gesture of dismissal toward the company. The men fixed bunkers and tended the wounded, uncertain whether to attack, flee, or stare in curiosity. "Or, I can kill you and take what I want! The choice is yours, Jon-Ulf. Make it before I raise my sword, or I will make it for you."

Terror gripped Jon, and the urge to flee became an all-consuming fire. Yet, deep within him, a spark of honor flared. *Bare is the back brotherless. Eric and I live or die together.* "You can't have him." Jon sprang to the battle. His blade swept for the giant's groin.

Odin met the attack with an effortless block. His riposte blazed for Jon's chest. Jon blocked, the massive strength of the blow driving him to his knees. Pain lanced through his arms, stealing control. His sword plummeted to the ground. Still, he managed to keep his fingers clamped to the hilt. His arms throbbed with an agony that stole thought, and it took several seconds for him to realize they were not broken. Odin's sword whipped downward, aimed to split him in half.

Jon ducked and rolled. The great blade nicked his shoulder, tearing open the flak jacket and numbing his arm to the fingers. Before Jon could return the strike, the god's sword rose for another attack. This time, it came in a broad sweep that Jon scarcely dodged. He tried to redirect the blade with his own, but the god's power proved too much. Jon's sword snapped in two, inches from the hilt. "No," he sobbed.

Then, a sound cut through the din of wind and steel, so soft Jon would have missed it had it not been Eric's voice. "Wolf." Though delivered no louder than a whisper, it drove new vitality through Jon. He funneled energy from his core, drawing on the power of his guardian. And, suddenly, the "wolf" was with him. Jon dropped the sword and launched himself at the grim gray father of gods.

Briefly, it occurred to Jon that the mythology named a wolf as Odin's slayer. Then he gave himself fully to the animal, and felt the wolf's form, chaos, and vengeance become his own. Joyful, berserk frenzy seized him, and all else faded to colorless background. He snapped and frothed, his teeth gashing arms, legs, face, never in the same place twice, a whirling flame of killing fury. The taste of blood only crazed him further.

Now, Odin screamed, the sound cutting over all like

a siren. He staggered backward, lost his balance, and crashed to the ground, the wolf's jaws clamped around his head. Lost in the wolf's need, Jon made its attack his own, giving himself over fully to the mythos.

Abruptly, the wind died. The world split open, revealing the hulking shapes of concertina wire, guns, and corpses on one side, and the blue-green meadows of Asgard on the other. The *valkyries* retreated, dragging Odin with them, the wolf's jaws still locked on his head. Jon stepped forward, then back, uncertain of his identity or his home. The frenzy burned him, promising an eternity of power on a world without guns. And loyalty pulled in the opposite direction.

Jon released the wolf, and it snapped away, drawing his strength with it. He felt as if life and soul were being stripped from him, tearing free of his earthly body and leaving him an empty shell. Agony ripped through him. Then, the wolf disappeared forever, along with the opening to the other world. And Jon Skell collapsed into darkness.

Jon Skell awakened beneath a threadbare blanket on a cot. The drab, bleak walls of the army hospital surrounded him. *Eric.* Jon whipped his head to the left, rewarded by his best friend's familiar presence in the bed beside him. Two feet jutted from beneath the covers. His chest rose and fell evenly, and his eyes lay closed in sleep. One arm dangled free of the covers.

Jon reached as far as he could, catching his best friend's fingers. Eric's hand closed about his briefly. "Clothed is the back," he murmured, without bothering to open his eyes.

"Shielded is the back," Jon corrected, then laughed. He fingered the miniature pewter sword, still hanging from his tags, and was seized with a sudden urge to visit his father and to thank him for teaching the values of love and bonds and family.

And to show him his medal.

EPILOGUE

As the image of Jon and Eric faded Tek returned to the problem of discovering the identity of his attacker. Thor had been busy back on the earth, angling to gain more heroes for Ragnarok. He was no longer a suspect.

This left only one person who could have caused and guided the monster. The war god sat for a long moment before accepting the conclusion. Then he stood over his teacher and glowered.

"Why?" Tek demanded. "What can you have gained?"

The god that had been disguised as Mentor seemed almost relieved the charade was over. With a self satisfied smile Loki changed back into his true form.

"Time, my less than astute new godling," he taunted. "Time for those allied with my brothers the Desert Giants to pluck a juicy plum off the coast of their lands."

"What's that got to do with me?" Tek demanded. He could feel his anger rising. The kind of pure, fiery anger that burnt everyone around it.

"Your damned technology can thwart my brother Djinn. They have only the desert and its wind and sand." Loki's voice was different from Mentor's now too, shrill and more sarcastic. "Once the forces of nature were enough to drive the primitive machines away, but today our bravest warrior is just a target fix calculated by your worshippers from the safety of their bunkers. They're as cowardly and unfeeling as you."

Tek smiled. It was not a pleasant smile. Loki didn't care. He had been hiding his dislike for the cold, new god and now was giving it full vent.

"No one called for you. No one needs a war that doesn't need courage."

"Perhaps I am feeling enough to be willing to engage in a bit of revenge," Tek threatened moving toward the half god and half giant.

The look in Loki's eyes changed from hatred to fear. Then he was gone. Tek jumped to his console and caught the image of the fleeing god on his scope, checked it with sonic sensors and confirmed the sighting from a satellite he created just for the purpose. He then knocked the fleeing god out of the sky with a few Surface-to-Air Missiles, and willed himself to the spot where his former teacher fell.

They met on a empty area of the Ethereal Plane far from the mountains or castles of other gods. Loki cringed, but his eyes never left Tek. Tek summoned an M-16, but Loki managed to dodge the 30 rounds he sprayed.

Loki fought back by summoning the Fenris Wolf. The ten-foot-tall monster growled thunderously as it jumped toward Tek. Tek only smiled and countered Loki's wolf with his own panther. But this panther was the kind that fought on the Russian front and the massive wolf's teeth ground uselessly on the steel armor. Two rounds from the dreaded 88mm gun sent Loki skittering for cover, and two hundred rounds from the machinegun mounted in the tank's hull discouraged his ally. Fenris snarled once at Loki and vanished.

Encouraged by his success, Tek changed the tank to the new M1A Main Battle Tank that was capable of travelling cross country at over 60 miles per hour. Through its infared sights he could see the Norse god conjuring frantically. He waited patiently while Loki summoned a swarm of trolls. Determined to not only defeat, but also to embarrass his opponent, Tek reacted by turning them into sludge beneath his treads. By the time he had run down the last of the fleeing creatures, Loki had crept some distance off. The tank's running gears were gummed so Tek abandoned the tank, taking on the appearance of a Chief Petty Officer in the SEALs. In this form he was well armed with an automatic shotgun and his face, covered with camouflage paint, was a frightening visage. The helicopter carried him to a perfect insertion, about fifty feet from Loki. The war god fired a few shotgun rounds and Loki once more retreated, mumbling hard on yet another summoning.

Still, even as he enjoyed the battle, the war god couldn't help feel something was still wrong. He had solved the mystery and was also enjoying himself immensely. So all should be well. Instead he felt even less content than before.

Loki's new champion appeared. This time it was a massive giant, standing nearly a hundred feet tall. The earth shook as he approached threatening the puny god. Tek willed a selection of AT and AP mines to appear where the giant next stepped. Their shaped explosions sent the massive figure dancing with pain. Unable to resist a barking laugh, the modern god of war then summoned his own giant. Even he was impressed with the result.

Rather out of place in the desert, the USS Alabama levelled her computer controlled guns. Astonished, the Loki's giant stared into the gaping barrels at near point blank range, but he rallied and swung his fists toward the battleship. The roar of the eighteen inch guns firing overwhelmed even the giant's battlecry. When the freight car sized shells hit, they tore through the gigantic figure, throwing what remained onto its back several hundred yards further distant. With an accusing look at Loki, the giant faded from view.

The war god turned to face his opponent. To Tek's amazement Loki still smiled. It took a moment of calm reflection to understand why. The god of modern, calculated warfare was embarrassed to realize that he had been caught up in the joy of battle.

"One last lesson," he acknowledged.

"My pleasure," Loki answered in the voice he had used as Mentor and giving the young god a sweeping bow.

"But now I must be gone," replied Tek. He was rewarded by Loki's expression changing from superiority to frustration as Tek willed himself to finally answer the call of his faithful.

In the Persian Gulf, the face of the war changed almost instantly. Where for the first few days the Iraqis had been able to do as they willed, now the entire nature of the battle changed. The jets and missiles sent by the U.S. began to take their toll. Scuds fell to countermissiles and laser guided bombs found their marks with what one officer described as "miraculous precision." It had taken a while, but Tek, the new god of scientific war, had at last arrived.